Thank you, Derek, Noah, and Grace for always
supporting, encouraging, and believing in me.
You three are incredible and irreplaceable.

Mission Mind

Bones Abode

Rachel Elspeth Shanks

ISBN 978-1-63844-731-3 (paperback)
ISBN 978-1-63844-732-0 (digital)

Christian Faith Publishing, Inc.
832 Park Avenue
Meadville, PA 16335
www.christianfaithpublishing.com

Printed in the United States of America

1

Found and Founded

B orn into the dark world of drugs, where evil dwells and runs with vengeance, was young Yedaiah Hallohesh. He lived in more foster care homes than he could count, for the better part of his childhood. Because his parents could not stay clean and sober and they were not responsible enough to care for him, Yedaiah bounced around from loveless location to loveless location. Whenever he asked about his mom and dad, he was informed of their positions in jail or prison. He had no memory of his father due to the fact that he had never met him and only a handful of his mother because he had only lived with her for one year when he was very young.

Home for him was located south of Downtown Seattle. South Park had a crime rate 187 percent higher than the national average, making it the most dangerous neighborhood in Seattle. There were twenty-four daily crimes that occurred in the neighborhood for every one hundred thousand people, and he had a one in twelve chance of being a victim at any given time.

And Yedaiah was the victim more times than he cared to keep track of. He was battered and beaten and held at gunpoint on several occasions. It seemed to him that none of his possessions were his own; everything he ever owned or cared about was stolen from him, right off his person. One time his school gifted him a brand-new backpack which he had for all of three hours before it was stripped from his shoulders and he was given double shiners.

He slept on the streets and ate from trash cans when he was hungry. There wasn't a single adult that cared about him, and the kids he was around were not the type to cling to for friendship. He was often approached by scary predators to join gangs or sling drugs. Any worldly prediction would label him hopeless and doomed to the land of prison, coming from the horrible streets.

He learned at a very early age that his only hope and comfort came from within. For a brief three months, Yedaiah had one foster parent named Ms. Jade, the only one who was ever kind and caring to him, who happened to attend church. Ms. Jade brought him along with her every Wednesday evening and Sunday morning to listen to the "Good Word," she would call it. The very first day he stepped into the house of the Lord, Yedaiah felt the presence of God in an unexplainable way. As if a spirit was filling the whole room with the freshest and lightest air you could imagine. He wanted to float on it like a cloud. He felt big strong arms hugging him so tight, but there was no visible figure touching him. He felt his heart overflowing with the sense of love, but no one was talking to him or telling him they loved him. The sanctuary was the warmest place Yedaiah had ever experienced in his life. Prior to this, Yedaiah had never heard about God the Father, His Son Jesus, and the Holy Spirit. He closed his eyes, thinking he could get used to this. Then the pastor of the church called all children to the kids' ministry wing of the building. Savoring the feeling, he headed down the hall away from the magical encounter.

At the end of class, his new Sunday school teacher explained to him that if he believed that Jesus is the Son of God and that He came to earth to save us from our sins by dying on the cross and rising again, we could spend eternity with Him in heaven, and He would send His helper, the Holy Spirit, to walk with us all the days of our lives on earth. "All you have to do, Yedaiah," she said, "is invite Him to come into your heart, and He will never leave you, no matter what!" Without hesitation, he asked the Lord Jesus into his heart that very first day, and from then on drew all his strength and willingness to overcome his hardships from the Father that lived in him. Little Yedaiah was only eight years old at that time, but even at that young age, he knew that God had big plans for him, and he would not spend the rest of his life in South Park, cast to the misfit world of violence.

Attending school was important to him. Although most of the students at his public grade school were living a similarly desperate life and were often mean and nasty as they were raised to be, Yedaiah was different. He didn't carry around hatred or anger with him. He was Holy Spirit–filled and seemed to radiate light and love everywhere he traveled. The other children were drawn to him; they didn't pick on him at school and often came to him with their sadness and problems. He was somewhat of a child therapist, praying with kids and encouraging them through their pain and hopelessness. He also stood out from the student body because of his perfect report cards, receiving straight As every term. He loved reading, writing, math, and really every subject taught to him. He dreamed of being an educator when he grew up, maybe a teacher or professor.

In the year 1950, when Yedaiah reached the ripe age of sixteen, he was a bleach-blond, six-foot-six-inch, muscularly built teen. Wise beyond his years, he was on his own, caring for himself from a local shelter. It wasn't always easy for him. He often felt alone and downcast, wondering what was going to become of him. He prayed fervently about his future and then did his best to leave his fears in the hands of his faithful God. At the peak of his pleas to the Most High, Yedaiah felt a shift in his relationship with God. Something tangible began happening.

He started hearing whispers. They always came at night, when all the lights were out and everyone bunking at the shelter was on their cots, where the large open common room was filled with darkness and snores were heard in abundance. At first, he toyed with the idea that he had a mental illness. Truly, he wondered who was talking to him and if he should even listen to the voice. It was always a deep and powerful voice whispering, and a breeze entered indoors and swirl around the room every time, but for the first few weeks of hearing it nightly, he couldn't make out what it was saying.

Then, one night about a month after the whispers began, a mighty wind blew the shelter windows wide open and settled like a tornado over Yedaiah's cot. The voice who had been whispering to him all these weeks became a loud command, and he recognized in an instant what it was saying. Lying right there on the gross, stained, roll-out bed, Yedaiah heard the words crystal clear as they were spoken to him. It declared, "Yedaiah Hallohesh, your pain and suffering are not to be wasted. I am God, Jesus, the Holy Spirit, and I am preparing a beautiful path for you. You will go now and start a covert, undisclosed, classified discipleship academy. The mission of this establishment is to guide, teach, and train warriors for Christ to move against our enemy. It will be dangerous at times. There is a real spiritual battle taking place between good and evil. Satan is on the loose, and I am calling an army to take him down at every turn. I am God and will prepare the way for you. I will personally call all those who will attend. Will you willingly be my fearless leader, Yedaiah?"

From the deepest inner parts of Yedaiah's body came an overexaggerated and definite "Yes!"

For the past eight years, he knew something huge was coming his way, and he had been biding his time waiting for what it was. And now, on this night, it all became certain. God Himself was going to use Yedaiah Hallohesh, the ratty, poor kid from the streets, for battle and victory. As the wind died down and the house manager closed all the windows, he drifted off to the most peaceful sleep he had ever known.

The next morning, he opened his eyes and peeked out of the window next to his cot. The sun was the color of gold and was casting shadows of the most beautiful royal color on the whole neighborhood, maybe even the whole world. He felt as if he was in a king's castle instead of the dumpy shelter. As he pulled on his clothes for the day and stuffed all his worldly belonging into his backpack, the manager of the shelter approached him. "Yedaiah, there is a fancy car and a driver here to pick you up!"

Heading out the front doors, for what would be the last time, he spotted a bright gold-colored limo and a fancy-looking gentleman holding the back door open for him.

"Mr. Hallohesh, I am Joshua Zane, your driver for today, and every day that you need me, for that matter," the kind-eyed man stated. "Well, come in and buckle up, because, boy, are you in for the ride of your life."

Cruising out of the slums of Seattle, Yedaiah felt a sense of wonder. Whatever this was, was happening so fast. The window between him and the driver, Joshua, was rolled down, but Yedaiah couldn't think of what to say or ask him. He wasn't quite sure that this wasn't a dream he was about to wake up from, back on the stained cot in South Park. So he sat in complete silence, peering out the window, watching the slums fade away to beautiful buildings, lush trees, and what seemed to be a clearer brighter sunshine pouring down. The fog of the life he knew and had grown accustomed to dissipated, his new bright future shown ahead.

Seeing Joshua pull the long golden car up to the docks in West Seattle, Yedaiah had to break the silence.

He questioned, "Hey, Joshua, what are we doing at the ferry docks? Where are we going? Are you going to fill me in on where exactly you are taking me, or is it all a big mystery?"

Joshua, wanting to put Yedaiah's mind at ease, quickly replied, "It's not a mystery anymore, Mr. Hallohesh. All is being revealed and will be revealed in due time."

And with that, Joshua pulled the luxury car into a stone-and-rock-built garage, closing an extremely large mahogany door behind them.

Saying a quick prayer, asking for safety, wisdom, patience, and peace, Yedaiah grabbed his only bag of belongings and exited the golden limousine.

Without uttering a word verbally but talking up a storm in his own head, he followed Joshua to the back of the stone box they were parked in. The wall was bare to the naked eye, but as they approached, Joshua instinctively pushed on a series of stones, in what seemed an exact science, to reveal two golden handles. One of the handles was carved into an exquisite fierce powerful lion's head, and the other was the shape of a petite adorable helpless lamb's head.

Joshua looked straight into Yedaiah's eyes and said, "Shall we?"

He then grabbed both elegant handles from the middle of the door and slid them upward to the top of the door, opening it immediately. Behind the stone wall at the back of the garage was a waterway, with one beautiful golden ferry floating on top.

"Climb aboard," he heard Joshua say.

As Yedaiah was climbing onto the boat, he noticed a fancy-looking plaque on the outside. Leaning in close to get a better look, he read what it said:

MMA
Methuselah
Established in the Beginning

Yedaiah wondered, but didn't say aloud, what in the world that could mean: "In the Beginning." Stepping both feet on board, he was wishing that Joshua was more of a talker. He had so many questions that he didn't know how to formulate into words, and Joshua wasn't giving up any information of his own will. Yedaiah figured he would have to resign to learning as he went. He also figured that if God called him to something, he didn't have to worry himself about the details. God was always faithful and had never and would never leave him.

So Yedaiah found a seat at the front of the floating vessel and did his best to take in everything surrounding him. It was definitely an exquisite ferry with the most elegant of details. As Joshua started it up, the engine of the boat made a small purring noise, not much louder than an actual cat's purr, and the boat glided forward. As it picked up a bit of speed, Yedaiah noticed a large red heart shape, floating on top of the water, ahead of him. Before he had a chance to realize what was happening, the boat dove right through the heart shape and down below the water. It all happened in the blink of an eye, literally!

The craziest part though was popping up next to a dock the very next second, completely dry and no visual memory of being under the water's surface. Yedaiah tried not to have a surprised look on his face when he set his eyes on Joshua.

"What was that, man?" was all he could muster up.

"That is our ground entrance to O Be Joyful Gardens," Joshua replied matter-of-factly.

"The ground entrance," Yedaiah questioned. "Does that mean there is an air entrance?"

Joshua didn't answer in words, but the one-eyebrow-raised look he gave in return sure said yes.

After the shock of the journey wore down a bit, Yedaiah set his gaze upon the land he was about to step onto. In complete awe, he gazed at what appeared to be every type of butterfly and bird fluttering through the air as if it were a playground for them. Every color of the rainbow flitting about. The sky was a deep and bright shade of blue, with puffy white clouds shaped into all the creatures of the animal kingdom. He could clearly see a turtle, tiger, hippo, and seahorse form from clouds! As the wind blew, the animals moved in perfect unison. It was a vision! The grass on the ground was the most glorious green color and seemed to go on forever. There was also a gold-and-silver pathway that winded its way into the beyond.

Yedaiah wasn't sure that he hadn't died and was looking at heaven.

"You ready to walk on?" Joshua said, bringing Yedaiah back to a sliver of reality.

"Yes, please," he replied. "I am not sure where we are or where we are going, but yes, please!"

"We are headed to Mission Mind Academy, right up this path. It sits on one thousand acres, which are all a part of O Be Joyful Gardens. It is where you live now," Joshua declared.

He was then told by Joshua, "This property belongs to God. He created it in the beginning. The Holy Ghost runs this whole garden."

Mouth hanging wide open, Yedaiah started putting one foot in front of the other on the magical-looking gold-and-silver path. As he walked, he couldn't help but feel how much the world around him was alive. It wasn't just the animals in flight. Squirrels and chipmunks were sprinting around all over, and every kind of tree you could imagine shot up from the soil. From palm to aspen to pine, they were all there, growing in the same garden. Deer were picking snacks from fruit orchards, and rabbits were pulling vegetables out of the ground to nibble on. It was the most glorious sight.

Seeing the wildlife brought Yedaiah such great joy. He loved animals but never had been able to have one of his own, due to the condition of his childhood. This was going to do just fine living among all these creatures, he thought to himself. And as if on cue, a little prairie dog came up to him and seemed to hug his ankle.

"This is the animal God chose specifically for you, Yedaiah," Joshua simply stated.

"A prairie dog!" Yedaiah said, laughing out loud. "He's astounding!"

With that, he picked the little guy up, tucked him into his arm, and continued walking.

The whimsical winding path was almost a mile long from the golden ferry dock to Mission Mind. As Joshua, Yedaiah, and the prairie dog were approaching the academy, the sweet sound of a harp began drifting through the air and into their ears and maybe even their souls. The sweet sound was captivating, and Yedaiah wondered where it was coming from.

Joshua, finally breaking the peaceful silence, explained, "We have speakers everywhere, even underground. They are to fill our hearts and minds with surround sound worship."

He then went on, "I was called to O Be Joyful when I was sixteen years old too, which has been twenty years now. It has been just me, the critters big and small, and the Holy Spirit on campus until today. I have been praying for you and your arrival. God has been preparing me for what is to come. He has vast, out-of-this-world plans in store, there is no doubt."

Yedaiah's heart felt as if it were about to explode as he replied, "I have not had an easy life up to this point. But I have never doubted the full-sized purpose for my life. This is the best day and the first day of the rest of my life. Thank you for welcoming me here, and I sincerely hope we can be friends."

"Are you kidding me, Yedaiah? I have been praying for you for twenty years and here you are in the flesh. You will be the head of this establishment. God makes no mistakes. We already are friends," Joshua stated with a smile.

The little prairie dog started squirming in Yedaiah's arms to be let down. After setting his new buddy gently on the path, he turned his attention toward the incredible building standing before him. It was like a colossal monument with sunbeams streaming upon it from the heavens above.

From what he could see, the entirety of the structure was made of gold. *Gold!* It was a castle made of gold!

It wasn't just a regular school structure, that was for sure. It was an elaborate castle. A golden castle at that. Maybe this would be unbelievable to a common person, but Yedaiah, coming from the worst part of Seattle and spending the last two years in a shelter, this was beyond mind-boggling. He was waiting for someone to pinch him and bring him back to reality. But no one did. This was real.

"Okay, young man. Are you ready for the tour?" Joshua said as they approached the massive double front doors, made from gold of course.

The door handles, Yedaiah noticed, were exactly like the ones at *Methuselah's* boat dock: one a fierce lion and one a frail lamb.

"Why don't you do the honors," Joshua encouraged Yedaiah.

Grabbing both elegant doorknobs, he slid them upward on a smooth track. The doors opened on their own at that point, revealing a large grand entrance, more splendid than anything Yedaiah had ever witnessed with his two eyes.

Joshua and Yedaiah toured Mission Mind Academy for the rest of the day. It revealed several halls of bedrooms, several classrooms for study, a large hall for dining, a ballroom, a restaurant-size kitchen, an enormous library, rooms for lounging, an entertainment room with games and televisions, and a magnificent terrarium filled with fresh produce smack-dab in the middle of the castle. And not unlike the outside, the interior was all made from gold as well.

"This entire building, inside and out, is made of solid gold. How is this possible?" Yedaiah asked with very large eyes.

"As I mentioned, God created this at the beginning of time. No human hand has touched the building of this structure or the grounds around it."

He then went on to explain, "This was all designed way back then but was intended to be used now. Today it is just the Holy Spirit, you, and me here with the animals, but soon there will be much life buzzing around. God will call the rest. The teachers and students will arrive, and the purpose of this place will be fulfilled."

O Be Joyful was joyful indeed. After throwing together a sandwich from the very large kitchen, Yedaiah headed outside to be with the animals. He felt as if he was visiting a zoo with no enclosures. Animals of all kinds roamed free. Taking the path behind Mission Mind, he could see horses galloping in the distance, a giraffe stretching its long neck up to eat from the trees, and even a family of elephants grouped together.

Looking down at his prairie dog friend, he figured the first order of business would be naming the little guy. He remembered seeing the petite woodland creature picking fruit from a fig tree on three different occasions that day and decided upon the name Fig.

"Hey, Fig, ya tiny buddy of mine, do you like that name?"

Fig seemed to accept it because he wrapped his short arms around Yedaiah's leg again in a hug.

"Okay, Fig it is," he spoke down to his new pet. "Let's head on, pal!"

Fig and Yedaiah happily continued on their walk, taking it all in. As they came upon a pond with ducks, geese, fish, and frogs in it, they decided to sit for a bit. All was silent for the first few minutes until a loud rumble filled the air.

Then a deep voice spoke, "Welcome to O Be Joyful, Yedaiah. All that you see is here for you to enjoy. Soon I will deliver the teachers and staff for this establishment. Until then, spend time with me. I am everywhere and want to hear from you and talk with you endlessly. Spend time in the library reading the books of knowledge and wisdom I have provided for you. All will be revealed to you in proper time. Study the Bible every day of your life. I love you, Yedaiah Hallohesh. You will do great things for My kingdom."

"Oh, there you are," Joshua called from the distance. "Let's get you settled into your chamber for the night. A good night's rest will provide new clarity in the morning."

"This is amazing, Joshua! God was just speaking to me. Aloud!" Yedaiah practically yelled.

"Yes, He will do that once in a while around here," Joshua said with a chuckle.

They made their way back to Mission Mind and settled into bed for the night. Before dozing off, Yedaiah stared up at his ceiling, made of gold, of course, but pounded into a beautiful design of constellations. He stared at the Little Dipper, seeming to pour out into the Big Dipper. It was a comforting sight to behold. He felt that God was pouring into him until his cup was overflowing. Saying prayers of thanksgiving, Yedaiah closed his eyes for slumber.

Joshua was right, when he awoke the next morning, he didn't feel like he was in a dream anymore. He was comfortable and confident and ready to seize the day. It was as if he had always been here on campus, which is a far cry from reality, as he had just arrived from the shelter yesterday. He popped right out of bed, with the teenage heart and energy to meet any adventure that was to come his way.

Tromping out of his room and down the spiral staircase, he and Fig were on the lookout for Joshua. As they turned the corner to head into the kitchen to make some breakfast, he heard Joshua talking with someone. It was a soft, velvety, calm-sounding tone of a woman. Without much hesitation, Yedaiah poked his head through the double doors and spotted the lady in a long white dress with a golden-laced apron stirring a pot of oatmeal.

"Well, good morning, sleepyhead," Joshua chimed up. "This is Mrs. Heathers. I picked her up this morning on *Methuselah*. She is our incredible head chef."

"Pleased to meet you," Mrs. Heathers said, reaching her hand out to shake Yedaiah's.

"Nice to meet you as well, Mrs. Heathers. Thank you so much for making breakfast this morning. I am famished."

"Well, grab a seat and I will have this ready for you in a few moments," she replied with a smile.

She was a beautiful woman, with a smile that came directly from her heart. And boy, could she cook! When she presented the plate in front of him, he couldn't believe his eyes—oatmeal, bacon, fresh fruit, homemade croissants and jam, hash browns, juice, and a steaming mug of coffee with sugar in the raw.

"Wow, Mrs. Heathers, this is amazing. I don't believe I have ever had a meal this fine—ever! Thank you!"

"Well, you are most welcome, Mr. Hallohesh. I hope you enjoy it. And don't worry, there is plenty more where that came from," she enthusiastically responded.

After the meal was over, Joshua, Yedaiah, and Fig headed out on the O Be Joyful grounds. They made their way to the horse stable, where Joshua introduced Yedaiah to his chosen pet.

"This is my Clydesdale, Jehoshaphat," he said. "I know, I know, it's quite a mouthful of a name. But doesn't it fit him so well?"

"He is a beautiful very large animal. Do you ride him? Can we go riding?" Yedaiah almost begged.

He had never been on the back of a horse and had always desired to.

"Of course, pick one. They are all so tame and smooth I don't even saddle them. Climb on and let's go to the west end of the property," Joshua said with a smirk.

Yedaiah jumped up on a black beauty, and to his surprise, Fig did too. His pet settled in, right in front of his lap, ready for the action. With that, Yedaiah and Joshua laughed aloud and galloped on.

Along with riding horses, picking fresh food from the gardens and orchards, and spending time with the animals, Yedaiah soaked in the knowledge from the extensive library. The books were ones that he had never seen before, Holy Spirit–inspired and filled. The words of wisdom jumped off the pages as if they were alive and settled smack-dab in the middle of his core being. He spent hour upon hour in the library room, which had a title of "Grow in Wisdom" written on the outside door.

And day after day, a new faculty member arrived at Mission Mind. The first day was the chef, Mrs. Heathers, who made the most delicious food in the universe, if he could say so himself. But after only four short weeks, twenty-eight adults were on staff.

Each new recruit had a different story to tell, about the way they were called and the excitement of taking *Methuselah* through the red heart portal. And as they climbed off the golden floating vessel at O Be Joyful and walked the glorious path, they were all greeted with their chosen pets. No two people had the same breed of animal for companionship.

Friendships were formed between teachers, tutors, instructors, administrators, the physician, cooking staff, and housekeepers. The Holy Spirit spoke audibly, often. God, the encourager, was always with them, preparing them.

Joshua was so full of joy at this point of life. It had only been him for twenty years on campus, and now in the year 1950, there were thirty Mission Mind Academy members. All that God had revealed to him over the last two decades had come to fruition.

Now that the academy was filled with instructors, the waiting game came for the student arrivals.

Mission Mind Academy at O Be Joyful was a bustling place at last. Joshua had accompanied all twenty-nine members with pleasure. Now he was excited and content to let Mr. Yedaiah Hallohesh escort the students one by one to their new lives.

2

The Golden Calling

Grace Hayes was a big-haired, big-hearted outgoing eleven-year-old from the Rocky Mountains of Colorado. She had been homeschooled from the beginning of her education, and she loved it. It gave her time to daydream and flip around her gymnastics bar throughout her days. She was a very bright young lady and loved all animals unconditionally. Her border collie–blue heeler, Roxy Ann, was one of her best friends in the entire world. Because of her compassion and kindness, she thoroughly enjoyed every person she met, from newborns to hundred-year-old grandparents. Life was good and peaceful. She had her faith and seized every day as if it were her last.

On one super sunny day, she was out climbing a boulder at her family's home, located at nine thousand feet, singing her heart out about anything that came to mind. Boy, could she belt loudly at the top of her lungs. At the peak of her volume, she thought she heard a voice. A whisper maybe. Looking around finding no one, she chalked it up as an echo or her full-sized imagination. Maybe she was hearing her own voice? Grace had an imagination like no other. She enjoyed all things concerning drama and acting. She never questioned whether she was meant for the stage. It just seemed to be a part of her from birth. Singing and dancing her way through life was where it was at for her.

Not twenty minutes had passed when she was headed back inside for the day and heard the voice again. What did it say? Was she going nuts?

Then, clear as day, it uttered, "Grace, My daughter, I am calling you. Still your voice and still your mind. Listen to the plans I have for you."

Grace thought of her faith, believing in the higher power of God, believing in His Son, but this was something way bigger than her young brain could comprehend. Sitting down, stilling her questioning mind, she closed her eyes.

Then the voice spoke again, declaring, "I have perfect plans for you, Grace. I am the Holy Spirit, and I am sending you to Mission Mind to train you for your assignment. Go without delay!"

Grace looked upward toward the sky feeling a great wind on her face. She sat there for what seemed an eternity waiting to hear if there was more. But all was silent. What just happened? What should she do?

Slowly standing up, she walked toward her house, Roxy Ann at her side. She bent down and snuggled her pup, shaking with energy and disbelief.

Upon entering her house, she could hear her mom's Glenn Miller Orchestra playing on Pandora and pots and pans clunking around in the kitchen, where her mom was undoubtedly whipping up food for the family to eat. Her mom was her most favorite person. Beautiful, loving, committed, and the best cook in the Rockies. She was also pregnant with Grace's first sibling. Grace always wanted a sibling and could not wait for the little buddle of joy to enter the world.

What was she going to say to her mom about the voice? What and where is Mission Mind? So many confusing thoughts and questions clouded her head. In boldness and determination, she walked right up to her mother and blurted it out. Everything that happened on that boulder, every word she heard spoken to her, she just right out confessed. Wide-eyed, Mrs. Hayes stood speechless. She was processing what her daughter had said.

Then in a calm manner, she replied, "I have always known you were meant for something unique, something huge. Let's pray."

Sharing this revelation with Grace's father, Benjamin Hayes, was something else. He, being the fixer and logic in the family, went into action.

He said, "We need to find out what Mission Mind is and what this means for you."

Grace just wanted to be back out with the voice. It had made her feel calm and at more peace than she knew existed. How could the whisper from an invisible stir her so much inside?

A week passed by and everything was as it had always been. It was summertime, and Grace was busy swimming, hiking, reading, playing with friends, and spending time with her parents. It was as if the experience never happened. She had decided to keep that day to herself. She did not want to freak out her friends or show herself crazy. She didn't think her two besties would understand. They believed in God, but she still didn't think they would accept her encounter as real. I mean, she barely believed it herself, especially because nothing had seemed to change since. Every day she would wake up expecting something different, but nothing was. Her mom was still cooking up deliciousness in the kitchen rocking out to her tunes. Dad was working and planning camping trips like he did every summer. And Roxy Ann was still her faithful friend, hot on her heels wherever she ventured.

On one particular afternoon, she was headed to their community pool to cool off from the hot sun. The pool and clubhouse were about a mile down her mountain road, and she was looking forward to the walk. So much was stirring in her she just wanted to clear it all away. Maybe even forget the voice and call for her life. If nothing was going to come from it, why did it even happen?

Patience was the virtue that Grace always struggled with. She wanted to know all manors of business immediately and had an extremely hard time not having answers. Kicking rocks and throwing a stick for Roxy Ann continually, she reached a breaking point of frustration. Sounds came from her throat, almost in a screech.

"What do you want from me!" Then again, "What do you want!"

Nothing. No answer. Silence. Even more frustrated, she continued, resolved to lose her thoughts in the cool water waiting on her.

Reaching the clear blue swimming pool, she was relieved to discover solitude. She didn't feel like small talk with neighbors she barely knew. Thankful to pull off her overclothes, she dove in without hesitation. After several laps and a few cannonballs, she pulled herself up to the side and sat dangling her feet in.

Just as she was feeling blessed by the peace and quiet, Roxy Ann darted off into the woods. Grace did not think too much about calling her back; that dog was always bolting after squirrels, deer, birds or anything that moved. She always came back after the chase. Such a smart and loyal dog. Grace loved that she could trust her enough to roam free.

Laying her beach towel on a soft upholstered chaise lounge and lathering up with sunblock, she was ready for a warm nap. Just as her eyes were closing and she was dozing off, she heard a rustle in the bushes. Positioning herself in the direction of the sound, she saw Roxy pop her face through the bush. She had found something. It wasn't an animal, but she most definitely had something hanging between her teeth. In the sunlight, it looked like a golden ticket to Willy Wonka's chocolate factory. Grace resolved that it must be a piece of trash that caught her pup's attention and closed her eyes once more for the slumber she so badly craved.

Sometime later, glossy-eyed Grace struggled in the sunlight to focus her eyes on the world. Naps always left her groggy, and she had to really focus to bring herself back from dreamland. Extending her arm down to give Roxy a little love, Grace discovered the piece of trash was still in her mouth. "Release, Roxy Ann," she demanded of her best buddy. In the next moment, a beautiful majestic golden envelope came into view, and it had only one thing written on it, GRACE HAYES. Her name, right in front of her eyes, in big bold black letters!

*****

Noah Wilson had been away on the calling for his life for two years now and was feeling a great loss of passion. He was inspired for change. He knew the inspiration came from none other than his heart. He most definitely felt the Spirit deep within him but often deemed himself unable to attain the use of His mighty power. On a regular basis, he looked up, hands high in the air, and bellowed. He didn't exactly know what he was crying out about, but he was 100 percent sure who it was to.

It seemed like just yesterday he was enjoying his blessed simple life in Knoxville, Tennessee. Back then, at eleven years old, he flourished in his private Christian school, played several sports, and with his free time, he hung out with friends and family. He missed his family on the regular. His mom and dad were so much fun to be around. They always had a surprise up their sleeves, and he relished in the excitement. He even missed his little sister. Elizabeth sure could get on his last nerve, but she was so happy and joyful and animated.

And sports. Oh, how he desperately missed playing sports. Football, soccer, tennis, pickleball, snowboarding, hockey, paintball—you name it, he had played it. Noah was beginning to feel the absence and loss of these things.

If he could just create a game for fun and competition at Mission Mind Academy. He knew they had the numbers in students for teams, and he was fairly positive he wasn't the only one wanting organized physical activity because others had expressed the same desire.

Noah was also sure that the Holy Spirit had laid this burden on his heart. This is the reason why he kept a journal and mechanical pencil with him at all times. He didn't want to miss an ounce of inspiration or ideas. He was meant to create a brand-new organized game. He knew it from the bottom of his heart. He had already jotted down multiple thoughts. He was so desperate for his ideas to come to light he spent most of his free time praying and brainstorming. He had formulated some rules and plays but just couldn't get anything pinned down at this point.

His ideas were leading to a sport mixed with soccer, tennis, hockey, and football. Noah had adapted the motto "Never give up" when he was just five years old, and this embarkment would be no different. He wouldn't stop until there was action.

They had a tennis court, basketball court, and a multiuse field at O Be Joyful Gardens. God had provided the space. Just how could he use it?

Ideas of teams on either side of the tennis net, kicking a soccer-type ball back and forth until someone scored a point in the hockey-sized goal at the back of the court, danced in his head.

With his passions untamed, Noah was bound and determined. There were some days that he felt unmotivated in the planning process. And on those occasions, he simply gave the creative expressions up to God and left them with Him to formulate. He believed that if God called him to it, it would be completed in the perfect time and in the perfect way.

Because MMA, up to this point, was all classes and hanging out, and because sometimes he missed his family so much it hurt, Noah could feel downcast at times.

On a cloudy day, young Mr. Wilson sprawled out on the front lawn outside his room and forced himself to remember back to the reason he left that wonderful world that he used to live in for this one. Doing this helped lift his spirits and encouraged him to keep on the path chosen by God.

Dreams. Vivid dreams. They were the reason for all this.

Every single night for two months he experienced a specific dream that led him here. For sheer entertainment, he would lie in bed at night reading Harry Potter, which was all about wizards and witches, and then pray to the Holy Spirit, God Almighty, for clarity on his own life. Drifting off to dreamland, he would have the same dream nightly. He would envision a beautiful magical place full of miracles and purpose. He would hear an audible voice that said the same thing.

"Noah, you were created for more. Follow My guidance. Train for your mission. Go to Mission Mind without delay!"

Each morning, during this two-month period, would bring confusion and angst for Noah. What did the dreams mean? Did this have something to do with his favorite Harry Potter series he was consuming several nights a week, or was it his prayers being lifting up to God before he nodded off? So many questions. He tried researching Mission Mind and came up completely empty. Out of widespread frustration, he decided to let the matter go. If he was supposed to have the same strange dream every night, so be it. There was no purpose for them. It must be his sister's wild imagination rubbing off on him.

But then something happened. Right after he resigned to let it go and not stress over the purpose of these intense dreams, a touch of magic happened. On his eleventh birthday, May 17, 2016, Noah headed out to collect the mail. He was hoping for a couple birthday cards with cash included so he could complete his Harry Potter movie collection. He wasn't allowed to watch PG-13 movies yet but wanted them on close hand for that special day he could. Opening the mailbox, he only found one lonely single envelope. A bit bummed, Noah snagged it and headed back inside, not taking special notice of what the letter was until comfy in his favorite recliner. Then came the complete shock. The letter was addressed to him, and it was typed in huge bold black letters, NOAH WILSON. But the shocking part was the absence of an address or return address. Also, the envelope was a shiny, eye-catching, magnificent gold color. Opening that delivery was the beginning of the rest of his life.

This life he was living that had him wondering what was next. This life that seemed to lack the adventure and danger and excitement he had imagined it would. He had hoped to be in the middle of battles, whatever they looked like, by now. But all that he had accomplished at Mission Mind so far was lots of classes, training him for missions and coming up against the enemy. But what enemy? Noah believed that the accuser was on the loose, but on campus for the last couple years, everything seemed to be rainbows and Jesus, peace and comfort. How was that combat?

Maybe it was the young boy in him, but Noah wanted war and weapons and confrontation. He was ready to take down the enemy. Where was he?

He guessed that the accuser was scared. And he should be. The Holy Spirit had all power, and nothing could stop Him.

Yep, Mission Mind Academy was feeling, dare he say, boring. He did have a few saving graces on campus, however.

❋❋❋❋❋

The Brown family was a welcome comfort for Noah. He was thankful to find true friendship with real warriors for God. Matthew, Michael, and Malachi were born into royalty at O Be Joyful Gardens, having parent educators at Mission Mind Academy. Being away from home, Noah depended on this family for all manners of things: companionship, comfort, fun, advice, and adventure, just to name a few.

Matthew, the eldest brother of three, was brilliant at all things electronic. Blond hair, fair skinned, and super tall for his age, the kid was a genius. Since birth, it seemed he understood the technical world and was able to tweak anything with a computer brain. Robotics was his specialty. At the ripe age of fourteen, Matthew invented a robot that had the capabilities to fly, walk, talk, and hold philosophical conversations. Matthew, who was better known as Matt, used his gifts wisely, and Noah was drawn to his intellect. He looked up to him and learned a great deal from his smarts.

The youngest of the three brothers was spitfire, passionate, hilarious Malachi. The kid was pure charm and loads of fun to boot. He was blond-haired like his oldest brother with beautiful bright blue eyes. He always knew where to bring his worship and was so brave and daring most were afraid to even try to keep up with him. Scheming adventures, he had a wanderlust that was straight from heaven. Malachi kept his family and friends alike on the top of their game and the tip of their toes. His thrill-seeking and carefree ways captivated everyone. Noah was two years older than Malachi but enjoyed his company immensely.

Michael, the only brunette in the bunch of boys, was Noah's closest of friends. Built like a gymnast, his kind eyes sparkled like the ocean on a sunny day. The two had everything in common; only a few weeks apart in age, they were two peas in a very large pod. They enjoyed and struggled in the same classes. Their pure hearts were filled with compassion, encouragement, and strength. Both boys were wise beyond their years and were friends to all.

However, their greatest desire was for athletics. Always known to have a pick-me-up game of some sport going, they craved competition. Having a longing for organized sports, Noah was thankful to have Michael in his quest for a new sport to play at Mission Mind.

Michael often brainstormed with Noah. Spending late nights in the planning process, they were unwavering on their efforts to create something exuberant.

The three Brown boys were a triple threat. With Noah thrown into the mix, the four young men seemed to have all bases covered. They were all very strongly built, able-bodied young men who faced fear head on. They were kind to others and treated everyone with the upmost respect. Anyone who met any of the four boys could quickly feel the Lord Jesus in them. And having Mr. and Mrs. Brown on the premises was the whipped topping on the cake. Mom and Dad Brown brought the love and discipline to keep things nice and tight.

No one seemed to be called to Mission Mind Academy in a "normal" way, the Brown family included.

Eighteen years earlier, on their wedding day, in the year 2000, Gabriel and Keilah Brown's world was, in no small manner, flipped upside down. Having plans to settle into their little community of Ashland, Oregon, to start and raise a family, they were in for an awakening.

Gabriel Brown, who was Irish with reddish blond hair, was a youth pastor at the local church and tapped all his efforts into the children under his care. A strong man in stature and mind, Gabriel was deeply zealous for reaching all mankind with the Gospel of Christ—his number one aim, you might say. There was nothing he wouldn't do to accomplish this aspiration.

Keilah Brown was strikingly beautiful with flowing long dark hair and a contagious laugh. She tended to be the backbone of the relationship and supported Gabriel in everything he pursued. She helped out in the youth group ministry and worked part-time tutoring middle schoolers having difficulty in their studies. Kind to the bone, she was loved by all.

Both Gabriel and Keilah received master's degrees in teaching and envisioned utilizing their skills one day soon, hoping that after the wedding day came and passed, they would have time to focus on teaching careers.

On their special day, Keilah all dressed in white with a graceful long veil, Gabriel dressed to the nines, received a "present" on the present table they did not register for. Their day was perfect. The weather, food, guests, vows, and dancing all came together in picturesque harmony.

When the ceremony had come to an end and the newlyweds were collecting and loading up their gift blessings in the back of a friend's truck, one smallish envelope caught their attention. They were planning on waiting until they returned home from their honeymoon to open gifts, but this one just pressed them to open it immediately. First off, it was bright gold and sparkled in the sunlight. On the front in big bold letters was written, "MR. GABRIEL AND MRS. KEILAH BROWN." The two newlyweds looked into each other's eyes, and both knew they had to open it on the spot. Sitting in their getaway car, after flower petals had been thrown all over them by family and friends, they broke the seal and pulled out the letter.

Because of that one wedding gift envelope, the couple passed on their honeymoon to Hawaii, sold the house they had just purchased, and threw caution to the wind, embarking on whatever the good Lord had planned.

Their getaway car drove straight from Ashland, Oregon, to the stone garage on the Puget Sound, where they entered *Methuselah* for the most exciting ride of their lives.

3

The Letter

Mission Mind Academy at O Be Joyful Gardens

The Holy Spirit of God has chosen you for the preparation and training He Himself has orchestrated.

There is a spiritual battle at hand. Satan is on the prowl. The accuser is after our bodies, minds, and souls.

God wants you to join in the war against evil.

Should you accept this mission, you will give up the comfortable life as you know it. In return, you will receive all powers of the Holy Spirit. There will be nothing you cannot claim victory over.

Your instruction begins immediately.

Your ride will arrive shortly.

4

Transforming Transportation

Immediately following the reading of the letter, Grace Hayes, who was in complete shock, hightailed it up her mountain-road home to share it with her mom and dad. The words in the letter addressed to her just would not sink in. Where was she going, and when would she be leaving her family? Was she to pack a bunch of her favorite clothes and special thing from her life or only a few? Reaching her front porch, she plopped down, out of breath, to collect any tangible thought she could before entering her house. She called Roxy Ann to her side and loved on the best buddy she had ever known. How would she say goodbye to Roxy? That black-and-white four-legged friend had been through everything with her. She wasn't interested in leaving without her. Grace was having doubts and thought it best to go share this wild golden letter with the ones she loved most.

Mr. and Mrs. Hayes were sitting in their office, researching what looked like RV camping sites. They welcomed her and asked how her swim was.

"Did anything eventful happen at the old pool house this afternoon?" Mom inquired.

"Well," Grace began, "as a matter of fact, yes. I received a letter from Mission Mind!"

Her parents did an about-face, wide-eyed and open-mouthed.

"What do you mean?" Dad finally managed to squeeze out.

Grace proceeded to explain each moment that took place since heading to the swimming pool.

"I don't know how to take this, if I want to go or not. I am excited and super scared all at once. I don't want to leave you, but I only want God's will for my life," she cried to her mom and dad.

They all embraced in a hug, Roxy Ann making sure she was right in the middle of the snuggle. Baby Hayes due in a couple months even seemed to leap for joy in her mom's womb from the bear hug.

Mom, with tears in her eyes, declared, "I feel deep down in my soul that this is the plans for your life. You will follow the guidance of the Holy Spirit and embark on an amazing adventure with Him. Your father and I gave you to the Lord in prayer and deed and will support you in all that you do. We love you. Do not be afraid. You will never be alone."

Grace thanked her mother and father for always supporting her and giving her unconditional love and then headed to her room. Letting her dog in behind her, she closed her door. Her large floral duffel bag was in the back corner of her closet. After pulling it out and tossing it onto her bed, she began searching through her drawers to select some things to pack. Underwear, shorts, leggings, shirts, a tank top, pajamas, a sweatshirt, her toothbrush, a hairbrush, and some socks and shoes all got thrown into the mix. Grace grabbed her favorite stuffy, the one she had been sleeping with for the past several years. Roxy Ann was not the only super special pet in her life. Penelope, her stuffed pink pig, went everywhere with her too. Slumber parties, road trips, weekend camp trips, airplane rides, the lovey brought her comfort and peace. Hurling the fiber-filled animal into her duffel, she couldn't think of anything else to bring.

Just as she was zipping up her bag, Grace heard her mom calling her to the dining room for dinner. Shuffling upstairs, she smelled vegetable lasagna and garlic bread, bringing joy to her rocky and unstable emotions. The table was set with beautiful dishes and cloth napkins, and she could not wait to start digging in. They all sat down, Roxy under her feet hoping for a crumb or two, joined hands, bowed their heads, and closed their eyes.

Her father began, "Dear Heavenly Father, we come to You this evening with full faith and confidence in You. We believe that You have called our wonderful daughter Grace to a new beginning and a special purpose. Her life is Yours. Her mother and I will miss her dearly but surrender her completely to Your loving and capable arms. Thank You for all that You bless us with. We worship Your holy name. Jesus, You are our everything. Thank You for this delicious-smelling food that Mom made for us this evening. In Jesus's name. Amen."

Tucking Grace in for bed brought about a roller coaster of emotions for Mr. and Mrs. Hayes. They had a sense that this might be the last time in a while they would savor the sweet smell of the top of her head, kiss her silky cheeks, and sing her favorite VeggieTales song, the one they had sang almost every night since she was born. Surprisingly, their daughter drifted right off to sleep. They were not as settled, and the two of them stayed up into the wee hours of the morning talking, praying, and cuddling one another. They had not expected to be saying goodbye to their little lady this early on in her life. It was bittersweet, but more sweet than bitter somehow.

Popping out of bed at the first sign of the sun peeking over the horizon, Grace felt sheer joy and excitement. She sang through her shower, danced as she dressed, and skipped the whole way to the kitchen for breakfast. Mom was already up, early as usual, although she was looking a bit red-eyed. Dad strolled into the room in his pajama bottoms and slippers looking red-eyed as well. Making small talk, her parents made their coffee and took a seat next to her at the breakfast bar. They all picked up their spoons to dig into their home-made oatmeal bake when they heard a loud sound outside of their mountain home.

Off their back porch they peered into the sky, only to discover a very large basket with an enormous balloon attached to the top. Headed right for their porch was a hot-air balloon with the huge black letters MMA on one side and a striking emblem on the other. The emblem appeared to have a bright golden cross in the middle of it, with the biblical words of the Armor of God and the Fruit of the Spirit directly to the left. It was a magnificent sight to behold. Roxy Ann was barking her head off from all the excitement, and Grace just stood in shock, not having a clue what to do or think in the circumstance.

The balloon landed not even ten yards from where her family was standing. Grace could see a white-haired man climbing out of the basket big enough for at least ten people. As the man walked toward her, she felt as if she was seeing a close friend or relative. She knew for a fact that she had never met this man before, but he was so familiar to her she shook from within. Approaching them, the man took ahold of each of her parents' hands and smiled warmly. Then he looked Grace straight in the eyes and embraced her in a hug.

"Welcome to Mission Mind, Grace Mary Hayes," he stated. "I am Yedaiah Hallohesh, and I am the dean of Mission Mind Academy. All who attend Mission Mind, teachers and students alike, are called on by the Holy Spirit to attend. I have come here today to meet you, welcome you, and safely transport you to our glorious garden. We are thrilled to begin your instructions and preparations for what the Holy Spirit has planned for you."

With tears in her eyes, Grace gazed over at her parents; they too seemed to be experiencing waterworks.

Shaking Mr. Hallohesh's hand, Grace replied, "It's very nice to meet you. I am nervous and excited all at once. How much time do I have with my parents and Roxy Ann?"

Then, taking her by complete surprise, Mr. Hallohesh replied, "We will leave within the hour. However, you do not have to say your goodbyes to your dog. Roxy Ann will be making the voyage with us and will be your faithful companion at Mission Mind."

Leaping for joy, Grace ran into her parents' embrace. Hugging for a solid five minutes, Grace released hold of her mother and father. She couldn't find words for them, so she gave them her biggest smile and then bounded for her room.

As she walked through her bedroom, Grace gave one last long look around, grabbed her duffel bag and a tote to throw Roxy Ann's belongings in. She filled it with all the things her dog would require and exited her room.

Closing the door, she said a silent prayer to her Father in heaven, "Praise Your holy name, Father!"

Wholeheartedly, Grace headed back upstairs to board the gigantic hot-air balloon to who knows where. She said one last goodbye to her amazing parents, giving her mother's belly, carrying her little sibling, a kiss, and climbed into the wicker box. Mr. Yedaiah Hallohesh set out steps for Roxy to climb aboard, and just like that, they began floating up into the sky. Her house began appearing smaller and smaller as they rose in altitude, and after only a few minutes, she could no longer spot it. She could feel the fresh air on her face as she closed her eyes. Taking deep breaths, one after another, Grace's nerves and anxiety all melted away.

Mr. Hallohesh stayed quiet for a couple hours, giving Grace the opportunity to talk with God and find her peace in Him. As they soared over the Rocky Mountains of Colorado, the presence of the Holy Spirit was without a doubt with them. The morning quickly turned into afternoon and hunger set in. Opening a little wicker basket, Mr. Hallohesh encouraged Grace to enjoy the picnic he had brought, packed with love from Mrs. Heathers. Gobbling up a peanut butter and jelly sandwich, a pickle, and some tortilla chips and guacamole, she cozied up with her dog and drifted to sleep. In her slumber, Grace dreamed of friends she didn't know and a school she wasn't familiar with. She heard whispers of kindness, love, support, and encouragement. She saw the beauty of gardens and flowers. She smelled the fresh scent of sand and water. Butterflies and birds fluttered around her dream. She was so content and happy in her dreamland she never wanted it to end. But as quickly as she dozed off, she found herself wide awake.

A thud sound and jolt to her body brought Grace to the realization that they had landed. Glancing up toward Mr. Yedaiah Hallohesh, the sun directly behind him making its grand exit for the day, she grabbed ahold of the side of the balloon's basket and pulled herself to a standing position. Peering over the edge, she witnessed the most spectacular sight of her entire eleven years. The incredible dream she just awoke from was displayed out in front of her eyes. All of it. It was as if she didn't wake up.

The smells wafting through the air were like sweet perfume. Dragonflies and butterflies flittered around everywhere. It was as if they knew she was coming and wanted to welcome her and check her out, landing all over her. There were huge gardens everywhere—vegetable gardens, rose gardens, colorful flower gardens, and even orchards of every kind of fruit. It reminded Grace of what the garden of Eden must have looked like when God created it. There were trees of every kind, all in the same location. She could see several great ponds glistening in the sun. It was a glorious sight to see.

It was not what she expected. But after seeing with her own eyes the parts of the dream she dreamt in the hot-air balloon come to fruition, Grace was hopeful that the love, kindness, and friendship part would come true too.

Gathering up her belongings, she looked toward Mr. Hallohesh. He gave her a loving, fatherly smile and said, "Shall we, my dear?"

*****

Noah Wilson could see Mission Mind's hot-air balloon come into sight. Someone else has been called by the Holy Spirit, he thought to himself. The vision of the balloon and the excitement of another new student brought him out of his own mind and wonders. It had been almost six months since a new student arrived on their campus. A new brother or sister in Christ always brought joy to the staff and students at Mission Mind. Another vessel for God, another set of unique spiritual gifts to add to the body of their school. Noah began praying for whoever was being transported by the miraculous golden hot-air balloon shuttle. He loved that balloon. It had carried him on an amazing journey across the beautiful country, from Tennessee to the lush forests and waters of Washington State. He remembered the first time he spotted the red heart in the clouds, looking as if someone poured red food dye in the sky. He would never forget flying in the balloon straight through the heart and coming out the other side at O Be Joyful. It was another world entirely. To the earthly eye, Mission Mind Academy was located in Port Orchard, Washington, on the Puget Sound. But with godly vision, it was a hidden paradise only accessible through the ground and air-heart portals. No one outside of the members at MMA and their families, to his knowledge, knew that O Be Joyful or Mission Mind Academy existed or at least where it existed.

Today it was providing transportation for some blessed soul from who knows where. Whoever was on board was special, no doubt about it. Everyone at Mission Mind was. He was anxious to meet the newest member. Noah decided to make his way to the landing pad to greet Mr. Hallohesh and meet the newbie. The last person to climb out of the basket six months ago had become one of Noah and the Brown boys' best buds. The first girl in their close-knit group, Kiera Scott, quickly made her presence known, and her larger-than-life personality was one to grab ahold of anyone.

Noah moseyed over to the bench beside the large black-and-gold X. Plopping down to wait patiently, he actually found himself twiddling his thumbs. His chosen pet was snuggled up in his lap as usual. Turbo, his German shepherd, was as loyal as they come. The large pup thought of himself as tiny and, therefore, a lap dog. Turbo had run up and licked his face the second Noah climbed off the air taxi on his first day at MMA. They have been inseparable for the past two years at this point, and Noah couldn't ask for a better companion.

As the balloon was coming in for landing, he felt butterflies in his stomach. He didn't know why, but he had a strong feeling whoever emerged was going to be a lifelong friend.

✿✿✿✿✿

The Brown's just finished up a card game when the school anthem started loudly playing in the courtyard. There were so many speakers placed around the outside of the school every faculty member and students could hear what came through them. The anthem was a sign that a new school member was arriving, and everyone was to stop what they were doing and pray. Gabriel, Keilah, Matt, Michael, and Malachi formed a circle and clasped their hands together.

Gabriel articulated, "Father, we lift up the dear soul You are delivering to us today. We pray for comfort and peace in their transition from home to our school body. We ask that You provide friendships and joy to this special person. Thank You for another warrior for Your kingdom. We praise Your perfect name and ask that You use us all in a mighty way. Amen."

After the anthem and prayer ended, the three boys bid their parents goodbye and bounded out the door toward the landing pad. Running down the stairs of their on-campus, in the golden castle, apartment, they spotted Kiera on her way as well. Catching up to her, they all gave their classified handshake and eagerly kept on toward their destination. Kiera was stoked when she recognized Noah already sitting on their favorite waiting bench. He must have been close by when the music began, she thought. Reaching the bench, they greeted one another and then proceeded to sit in silence until the balloon hit its mark.

❋❋❋❋❋

Kiera Scott was transported from Missouri to Mission Mind not quite six months ago. She came from a great family. Her mom and dad were no longer together as a couple but, without a doubt, loved the Lord and Kiera. They were completely devoted. Her mom worked hard to provide for her in every way, and her dad sacrificed his life in mission work. Her parents were best friends, and she always felt safe and content with them and in her life. She was a very happy child and enjoyed her life in Missouri immensely.

When she received the call to Mission Mind, she was on a date with her dad. They were at their favorite local ice cream shop enjoying a double scoop when a messenger waltzed through the door. A beautiful woman, wearing a gold-colored dress, came right up to their table and handed her a golden letter. All the events that have taken place since opening the letter are best described as a whirlwind. She was in the beautiful hot-air balloon by the next morning and had made best of friends with Noah, Matthew, Michael, and Malachi since the moment she flung herself over the edge of its basket. The four brother-like buds of hers were sitting on the bench, waiting on her arrival. Now she found herself on that very bench, waiting; she was really yearning for a female companion. Lifting up one last prayer to God for a girl's face to appear, she closed her eyes and waited.

As she sat in anticipation, Kiera couldn't keep her mind from wandering back to the trip she made in the gold-and-black floating taxi. It was nothing short of magic. For starters, Mr. Yedaiah Hallohesh and herself drifted from Missouri to Port Orchard, Washington, all in one day. They set off at a little after 10:00 a.m. in the Ozarks and landed at their destination, five states away, by dusk. While traveling through the sky and clouds, Kiera felt as light as air. The things that held her back in her walk with Christ, like self-doubt, shame, sin, and negative thoughts, vanished completely. She felt like a new person.

Kiera had just celebrated her twelfth birthday the week prior to the ice cream date and letter. It was the beginning of December, and as all kids were, she was looking forward to Christmas. All of the amazing food and sweets her grandmother cooked up at the holidays was her favorite part. Peanut brittle, fudge, cookies decorated in every color of frosting, and pies for days. Lights hung on houses and businesses, beautifully wrapped gifts were under trees, and festive sparkly window displays adorned every corner. It was her absolute favorite time of year. She shared a birthday month with her King Jesus and couldn't wait to honor Him alongside her wonderful family.

But in Mission Mind's hot-air balloon, just two weeks prior to Christmas, she was not feeling loss or longing. It's as if the wisdom of a thousand years landed upon her brain and heart in a matter of moments. She wasn't sad about leaving her family as she surely expected. She was overflowing with the sense of home, even at eighteen thousand feet above the earth, with a gentleman she just met. Mr. Hallohesh exuded more godly attributes than anyone she had ever known. His presence alone brought about unimaginable peace like a river, love like the ocean, and joy like a fountain, just like the song she grew up singing at church.

All fear and stress vanished from Kiera's body, mind, and soul on the memorable ride across the country to her new beginning. She felt like she was in Willy Wonka's fabricated elevator, gliding over the hills and valleys of America. Time didn't exist. The travel was best described as traveling through time in a time machine. It brought her from one location and state of mind to a different location and state of mind—Transforming Transportation. That's it, she resolved!

That's the name for the miraculous hot-air balloon that transports people from one life to the next. And she was in a new life for certain.

The most amazing part of the Transforming Transportation was just before it landed at Mission Mind. As she was looking straight ahead, in the direction they were flying, she saw a giant cloud shaped like a heart. It wasn't white or gray like the other clouds surrounding it, however. It was bright red! And as the balloon approached the red fluff, she realized they were going to soar directly through it.

On the other side of the red heart, Kiera turned around to get another look and was astonished when there was no sign of it left. She stole a glance at Mr. Hallohesh, who didn't look the least bit surprised by the crimson-shaped cloud and its disappearance. She then returned to the front of the basket only to discover that they had already landed. Peeking over the side, she witnessed the most beautiful sight of her life.

They had entered a new world or a new dimension; she wasn't quite sure at that point. It was a land of perfection. Kiera had arrived. She was in some kind of paradise.

Sure, after six months at MMA, Kiera missed band and music classes, she loved and missed spending time with her friends back in Missouri, and she most definitely missed her daily life with her inspiring mother and father, but she was in the right place and at the right time in her life. This adventure, wherever the Holy Spirit was guiding her, was every answer to every prayer she had ever prayed. They were obviously not her exact prayers, she couldn't have dreamed any of this up, but they were undoubtedly for her life. She was thankful for such a big purpose at such a young age.

❋❋❋❋❋

On the trusty oak bench, next to the enchanted landing zone X, five buddies remained. Noble Noah with his dog Turbo, mechanical Matthew with his chipmunk Chunk, multitalented Michael with his rabbit Rambo, marvelous Malachi with his squirrel Scout, and kindhearted Kiera with her sloth Speedy sat together as one Mission Mind family.

5

Beyond Be Joyful

From the moment Grace and Roxy scrambled out of the hot-air balloon basket, they were greeted with the utmost kindness. As she stepped onto the dark green grass, she spotted five smiles beaming at her. One of the smiles, a pretty brunette, ran right over to her and embraced her in a hug.

"Hello, I am Kiera, and boy, am I glad to see you. I was hoping and praying that our new recruit—well, you—would be a girl. As you can see, I am wildly outnumbered by these four bruisers," Kiera said with a laugh and a joking look toward the boys.

Grace, who was having an out-of-body experience, couldn't think of anything witty to say and gave a simple "Nice to meet you too."

Kiera then proceeded to take ahold of her hand and almost pulled her over to the bench to meet four male students and a truckload of animals.

"These are my buds, Noah, Matthew, Michael, and Malachi. And these are our chosen pets hanging with us."

Shaking each hand and giving the animals a little pet, Grace had the gut feeling she was going to love her new life here.

"This is my dog, Roxy Ann. I call her Roxy. She is my best friend. What is a chosen pet?"

Noah chimed in first, "When students arrive at O Be Joyful Gardens, God assigns each person a pet companion, which we call our chosen animal. With the exception of the Brown brothers, they were born on campus and received their pets in their toddler years. The most amazing part is that they will live as long as we do if they don't leave the O Be Joyful property. They pass away to heaven with us! Your dog Roxy is the first animal we have ever seen arrive here with a student. She must be some kind of special pup!"

"Hey, my brothers and sisters in Christ, let's get Grace familiarized and settled in, what do you say?" came Mr. Hallohesh's voice from the landing zone. With that, they all followed their headmaster to Mission Mind Academy castle to show her around.

Upon entering through the massive golden double doors, Grace realized that her dream in the balloon taxi did come completely true. She already had five friends at her side to comfort her. She was so filled with joy she couldn't contain her tongue.

"Praise Jesus! This is much greater than my wildest dreams. I love it here already, and it's only been fifteen minutes!"

Noah and Kiera replied at almost the same time, "We all felt that way upon arrival!"

Hearing the five loud chimes on the speakers, Kiera gave Grace another hug and said, "Noah, Michael, Matthew, and I have to head off to class. I will catch you later in our room. Mrs. Vand, our Mission Mind organizer, informed me a few minutes ago in the hall that we are roomies."

After that she was gone.

Malachi offered to show Grace around, while the others attended their evening Heart of a Missionary class. He could tell that Grace was a cool cat that he would enjoy hanging around. But it was her dog Roxy that really caught his attention. He loved dogs and was quite intrigued that Roxy came from outside of their protective haven.

"Let's head to the west end of the acreage. Since I was born here on campus, I know the grounds like the back of my hand. I can reveal to you a thing or two," Malachi said with a mischievous grin. "I am not sure about your adventurous side as of yet, but I have something to show you, if you're up for it."

"Sounds good. What's at the west end of the acreage?" Grace asked in wonder.

"Don't be impatient. We will be there soon enough. Let's head to the pasture and stable and hop on the back of a horse. We will make better time. It will be dark soon, and we want to be back by the dinner chime. Mrs. Heathers, our chef, doesn't appreciate tardiness. She wants us all to 'get it while it's hot,' she likes to say."

As the two kids headed for the stable and the west end of the acreage, they made lots of small talk. Grace told Malachi about her life in Colorado and how she was about to become a sister for the first time. She couldn't hide her slight disappointment in her tone for being called away before the baby was born.

Malachi mentioned how he feels special and blessed to have been born and raised at O Be Joyful but curious what it would have been like if he was born in the real world like the rest of the world. He told Grace how he felt a little left out.

The two found it easy to talk to each other, and for Malachi, that was a first. He usually was all fun and games, keeping his innermost feelings to himself. But with Grace, maybe because they were the same age and he was usually surrounded by kids a couple years his senior, he was an open book.

Trotting through the orchards on their horses, Grace could smell the fresh scent of oranges wafting up her nose, then the distinct sweet smell of pears. But galloping through the flower garden brought the most aromatic scent of all, the wonderful roses and lilies. Every flower Grace could have imagined was drifting by her as she rode past, smelling like a flower shop. And Roxy was hot on their tails, sprinting through the trees, as happy as ever.

"Good girl, Roxy Ann! You really love it here too, don't you?"

"It's amazing that you brought Roxy here with you. How cool that she got called along with you. That dog must have a huge purpose to fulfill here. She is such a pretty dog and so well-mannered," Malachi mentioned as they came to the end of the property.

"I do feel so blessed to bring her. I don't think I could have left her, to be honest. If you ever want to throw a ball for her, it's her life," Grace said with a giggle.

The two dismounted their horses and walked over to the wooden fence, which had solid golden hardware. Looking down the fence line, Grace was in awe by how the setting sun caught each nut, bolt, hinge, and emblem. They sparkled in the sunset and cast a warm glow over the whole area.

"This is spectacular!" she finally stated.

"Yeah, it's a very magical place. People on the outside wouldn't believe it if we tried to describe it. Not that we talk about this place on the outside. You will learn very quickly that how we live and exist here isn't for the outsiders to know. It's top secret and for good reason. No one has ever stepped foot at O Be Joyful Gardens without being called by God and being transported either by *Methuselah*, our ferry via water heart portal, or Air Share, the hot-air balloon you entered via cloud heart portal."

"Wow, this is all craziness to me. I'm not sure I have a clue why I am here or what is going on." Grace laughed again.

"You will get in the groove before you know it," he said in reassurance, "but I brought you out here to show you something specific. Something not perfect and beautiful. Do you see way out there on the horizon at the top of that peaked hill?"

Grace strained her eyes to focus on what he was pointing at.

"I see an incomplete house, waiting to be finished."

"It is finished. That is the Bones Abode. That is where the accuser dwells. The enemy waits up there for the opportunity to attack. He has his vision set on this place."

"How can he see us here? I thought we were invisible and secret," Grace said as a chill ran through her body.

"He is the reason we are all here. Although God is all-powerful and victory is already ours, there is a real enemy out there with power too, and as long as we are on this side of heaven, he will be lurking and threatening." Malachi went on to explain, "I don't think he has ever been able to enter in, but he will not stop trying. He is why we train for spiritual battle."

Grace looked up at the Bones Abode, taking in the creepy lines of the wooden frame. There were no walls, but it did possess the wooden framing, and at a closer glance, she could see dark shadows blowing through and around the structure. It was literally spooky. It appeared haunted, and for the first time since entering O Be Joyful, she didn't feel joyful.

"That place is scary! I don't understand who the enemy is and what he wants to accomplish. Is he a person? I am confused."

"I am sorry to say that I don't have answers to your questions. We don't know much about him and his plans at this point. But one thing is for sure: God knows and will never leave our sides or let us down. We do not need to live in fear. Let's get back to Mission Mind for dinner. I didn't mean to scare you, Grace. I am sorry if I did. I just wanted you to know what we are up against."

And with that, the two of them hopped on the backs of their horses and headed back to meet the others for dinner.

Grace and Malachi reached the others in the dining hall, and they all grabbed seats for dinner. She realized she must have been carrying a disturbed expression on her face because Noah, Michael, Matthew, and Kiera all glared toward Malachi with annoyance.

Kiera spoke up loud and clear, "Malachi, where did you take Grace this evening? By the ghostly look on her face, you must have shown her the Bones Abode. Why do you always bust that door wide open as soon as a new student arrives? You did that to me too. Couldn't you have waited until one of the professors explained it to her?"

"Sorry, not sorry, Kiera! I believe it is right to expose the purpose of our training before the actual training begins. The staff waits to bring up the Bones Abode until months down the road. I think it's confusing. Anyways, she handled it like a champ. Didn't you, Grace?"

"I don't know about that. I am a bit queasy, and I can't stop thinking about it. How eerie can a place get! I want to know more about this enemy. It's going to haunt my dreams until I find out more. How can we find out more?"

Matthew, always thinking from a logical aspect, mentioned, "We can head down to Grow in Wisdom, our library, to gain some clarity and knowledge if you wish. We are not encouraged to spend our mind power on the enemy, but I believe if we are called to battle him, we need to know about him. I have been wanting to dig into some research on the Bones Abode for years now, but none of these chickens have been interested."

Noah and Michael whispered to each other for a few moments before they both agreed to go there after dinner. Michael had to give a warning to his brothers and friends, however.

"Once, I was so curious that I did open a few books to study up on the Bones, but some strange things started happening in Grow in Wisdom, so I shut the book and shut the door to the research."

Kiera, a bit spooked, asked, "What strange things, Michael?"

"I can't explain them. I just know that I felt the need to hightail it out of there. I am willing to go back, if we all go together. Strength in numbers. With the six of us, we can handle anything."

So the children quickly scarfed down their delicious pot roast and headed to the library for an evening of research. Grow in Wisdom was a large library with thousands upon thousands of books, shelved by interest. There were oversized comfy plush couches and chairs to lounge and read in all over the place. The windows were spectacular stained glass, one for every book of the Bible—sixty-six windows representing God's Holy Word. Grace imagined how beautiful it would be in the daytime with sunlight pouring through the ornate glass. She imagined rainbows of colors dancing on the walls. GIW was such a beautiful room she felt like a queen just standing in it. It took her to a different place in her mind. A place she had never been before. A land of euphoria. She was in such a light and happy place she had completely forgotten why they were there.

Kiera, noticing Grace's distraction, broke her trance, "You okay, Grace? It looks like we lost you. The boys and I are over in the Darkness section and have already pulled a few books to begin. Do you want to come over to our corner and join us?"

"Oh, sure, I'm sorry. This place is captivating. I can't get over the details of beauty. I had forgotten we were here to dig into something dark. I feel like a princess just standing in this room. The windowpanes are amazing!" Grace declared.

"Yeah, they really are. But come help us find out more on the Bones Abode. I, for one, am determined to equip myself with answers."

Joining the boys in the dark corner, the two girls scanned the Darkness section from top to bottom, searching for the best resource. They read covers titled *Demons, Losing Mind Control, Spiritual Attacks, Hades, Good vs. Evil, Drug World, Monsters*, etc., but none that would wise them on the Bones Abode. The boys had found a book called *Satan Lurking* but so far could find no mention on the creepy unfinished house. Malachi, who had some impatience about him, brought up the unthinkable.

"What if we go there ourselves and have a look around?"

Noah, who was not amused, responded, "Malachi, are you out of your ever-loving mind? You know as well as I do that it's off limits and playing with fire."

"Agreed," Michael chimed in. "There is no way you, or any of us for that matter, are stepping foot around that haunted house. *Not a chance, bro!*"

"I just think that we need to know what we are up against. We don't know what we are dealing with. Should we become attacked by what looms there, how will we defend ourselves?" Malachi reasoned.

Matthew, being the eldest brother, was having none of it.

"God will prepare us for whatever comes our way, little brother. There is no sense in taking it upon ourselves to ready ourselves. Now let's stop all this nonsense about going there and find out what we can from the safety of the Mission Mind walls."

"I found something," Kiera almost yelled, interrupting the boys' discussion. She pulled a book off the shelf titled *The Black Spirit of the Abode*. "Maybe this is talking about the Bones Abode!"

As she plopped the huge hard copy on the reading table and pulled the cover open, a small black shadow flew off the pages and into the air around the six of their heads. It swirled around and around, making an eerie wind-blowing sound.

All the children scrambled under the table together in complete shock. The shadow continued swirling around and around in a circular motion, then headed toward the stained-glass windows. It then repeatedly banged itself against the pane of the Genesis window so hard the kids thought it would shatter.

"What is that?" Grace whispered. "It looks like it's trying to escape.

"I wish our animals were here with us so they could chase that thing for us. We should have gone and got them after dinner to bring," Grace added in desperation.

"Let's try to get it locked back up in the book," Kiera recommended.

"No way am I going to try and catch that thing! Maybe we should go get Mr. Hallohesh or dad and mom," Michael suggested.

"They will not approve of us stirring up trouble in the Darkness section. I don't want to bring them into this. Let's pray and ask God what we should do!" Noah said with authority.

They all joined hands under the table, and Noah began, "Holy Spirit, we believe that we unlocked and welcomed something dark and scary tonight into Grow in Wisdom. Please reveal to us what this is and show us what to do from here. We need your power, wisdom, and help. Amen."

They all slowly released hands and opened their eyes. The tiny black shadow had disappeared.

"Where did it go?" Malachi asked.

"Let's climb out from under this table and see," Matthew responded.

Crawling on their knees and keeping as low to the ground as possible, the six frightened students peered around the room. Everything seemed completely back to normal.

Glancing at the table where the book had been, Matthew declared, "The book is no longer here. Where did it go?"

Kiera made her way to the bookshelf and found *The Black Spirit of the Abode* back on the shelf in perfect order.

"It's right here where I first found it!"

The six bemused children were speechless, their eyes as wide as their mouths. As if on cue, they all headed for the door out of Grow in Wisdom. None of them felt like growing in wisdom anymore.

Still speechless, with the faces of people who witnessed a ghost, because they had, the children made their way down the hall back to the dining hall for dessert. Although they had lost their appetites, they wanted to keep up the appearance that all was well. As they sat back down at their table, the Brown boys' parents came by.

"Hello, kids, we just wanted to meet your new friend. Hello, we are Gabriel and Keilah Brown," Gabriel said as he extended his hand toward Grace.

"Hello, I am Grace Hayes. It's nice to meet you two. You have three very kind sons, who have been gracious enough to show me around today."

"I'm happy to hear that. What have you kids been up to this evening? We saw you all duck out of here rather quickly after dinner, and you all look a little green in the face. Are you feeling okay?" Keilah Brown said as she put the back of her hand to Michael's forehead.

"Yes, Mom, we are fine. We were just…um…um…showing Grace the ropes," Michael said in a bit of a shaky voice.

"Okay, rambunctious bunch, but keep out of trouble," Keilah replied with a wink. Then Mr. and Mrs. Brown made their way from the room.

"They know something is up," Matthew said. "Mom is like an undercover detective. That woman is impossible to get anything past. She is a hound dog! We have to be careful or we are going to end up in Discipline Training Hall with Mr. Regulations."

Looking at Grace, he explained, "That is his name, no joke. Mr. Regulations is in charge of training us in discipline. Outside of our parents, of course. But if you are caught doing anything unruly, you have to endure an entire course in correction with him. I do not recommend it!"

"He thoroughly goes over every biblical verse on discipline and makes you write a couple of papers on what you learn. It is wicked boring, and I am not interested in going back," Malachi chimed in.

"I love God and the Bible, but I don't like being called out on my faults."

Malachi, full of ideas, said, "Let's get a couple of binoculars and head out to the west end of the property just before sunup tomorrow and do some surveillance. Maybe we can get a glimpse of something if we spend quality time watching it."

The rest of the five were reluctant, to say the least, but ended up giving in and agreeing to meet the next morning at 4:00 a.m. at the stables to head there together.

"I think it's time for us to all get some rest. Come on, Grace, let's head to our room and get some shut-eye." Kiera took charge. "You have had a very big first day here, haven't you?"

"Yes, I most certainly have," Grace replied. "Good night, Noah, Matthew, Michael, Malachi. Thank you for welcoming me here so kindly today. See you guys in the wee hours of the morning."

The children all headed off to their bedrooms. Noah roomed with the Brown boys in a bunkhouse room next to Mr. and Mrs. Brown's apartment. The four boys often stayed up late chatting about life, but not tonight. They all decided to go right to sleep so they wouldn't oversleep for their 4:00 a.m. plans. They did have a few words about Grace.

"How cool that she brought her dog," Malachi mentioned.

"Roxy is awesome, and Grace seems like the perfect fit here. I am happy for Kiera to have someone other than us to hang out with," Noah said with a chuckle.

"She needed a good girlfriend. I think we can annoy her at times."

Grace and Kiera got themselves brushed and ready for slumber but were not tired when their heads hit the pillow. They had so much excitement that day they couldn't rest their minds.

Taking a deep breath, Grace confessed, "This has been the craziest day. First of all, I arrived here in a hot-air balloon through a heart-shaped portal. Then I met you all. Then the Bones Abode and the dark creepy-looking ghost. Now I am going to bed in a golden castle and waking up tomorrow to chase the dark spirit. I couldn't have guessed this day would happen in my wildest dreams."

"Yeah, we really rang in your arrival day with a bang, didn't we? I hope that you are not overwhelmed by all of this," Kiera said with kindness.

"No, I'm good. It's all very exciting."

Grace was pretty sure she had just fallen asleep when the alarm went off at 3:45 a.m. She was bleary-eyed, but her nerves for their adventure got her heart running at full speed.

They quickly and quietly dressed and then tiptoed down the hall toward Grow in Wisdom. They planned on exiting through the side door in the library so as to not wake or run into anyone. But as they stepped into GIW, they noticed a lamp on in the very far corner of the room. Then they saw Mr. Hallohesh in a reading chair with his Bible on his lap.

He must have felt their presence because before they could exit and find a different door out, he turned and said, "Hello, girls, what are you doing up this early? Getting a head start on your studies?"

A bit nervous to respond and not wanting to lie, Kiera said, "We were actually planning on taking an early morning walk and watching the sun come up."

"Wow, that is brave and ambitious of you ladies. Enjoy!" he responded.

The girls decided to use the library door after all, as to not act suspicious. They really were planning on a walk and to watch the sun rise. But they did fail to mention spying on the Bones Abode.

"I am getting a little nervous," Grace had to admit.

"There is nothing to fear, friend. God is always with us. Never forget that He has your back."

The girls found the golden silvery path lit up by the sparkling crescent moon. As they made their way down it, they spotted the boys just outside of the horse stable.

"You two are late," Matt whispered.

"We ran into Mr. Hallohesh in the library when we were using the exit. He was up reading his Bible," Kiera explained.

"What did he say? Was he suspicious?" Matt said with a bit of concern in his voice.

"No, he thought we were up early to get a head start on our studies," she laughed, "but we explained that we were headed for a walk and to watch the sunrise. He didn't seem to mind."

The six of them followed the Wizard-of-Oz-looking path, toward the west end of the property. No one had much to say. Maybe because it was so early and they were still groggy. Maybe because they wanted to keep quiet and not draw attention to themselves from the animals or other residence. But most likely because they were all a bit frightened by what they were digging into. They were taught to focus their energy on good and leave evil up to God to handle. And here they all were putting their minds, energy, and precious sleep hours toward discovering more about the dark one, the accuser.

The kids all had their pets with them. They didn't go anywhere without them except the dining hall and kitchen, and that was only because they weren't allowed. Also, they weren't allowed into most classes. Roxy had become friends with Noah's pup Turbo since her arrival the day before. And the two were leading the whole pack down the trail. Kiera, on the other hand, was pulling up the back of their train that morning, always carrying Speedy on her back in a special-made pack. Having a sloth didn't exactly lend to promptness if she let it walk. She did love her pet, however, and was thankful for his sweet nature and cuddliness.

Breaking the silence, Grace brought up, "This is a much longer journey via foot. Horses sure speed this trip up. Yesterday it seemed as if we were there and back in a flash. This is a very long walk. Do you think we will make it before the sun pops up? I would hate to miss breakfast. People will question where we are. It's my first full day. Maybe I should have stayed back. I don't have any business opening this door of darkness. What was I thinking?"

"Calm down, girl," Malachi cut in. "It will be fine. We have plenty of time to get back before breakfast. Breakfast doesn't start till 8:00 a.m. Take a deep breath and chill. We are just going to observe, nothing more."

It ended up taking over an hour to reach their destination. If they all hadn't been speed walking, it would have been much longer. When they got to the fence, they perched themselves up onto it to sit and rest. There was a soft glow on the horizon now indicating the arrival of the sunshine. Malachi pulled the several pairs of binoculars he had scrounged up out of his backpack and handed them to the others. Looking through the lenses in the direction of the Bones Abode, they saw the hardware on the open roof, catching the sun's glare. Bright sun on the unfinished rooftop and dancing dark nightmare like shadows below. The ground around the Abode looked as if there was a ghost ball going on. The black shadows moved to and fro, like a celebration was going down. The thick trees around it were blowing back and forth as well. The wind was heavy around it.

"What is that, at the very tip-top of the roofline? Guys, do you see that?" Kiera had spotted something.

The small black ghostly thing that flew out of the book the night before was flying in circles around the structure. Then it would dive down to the ground, disappear for a few moments, and then reappear back on the roof beams. It did this several times.

The kids couldn't stop watching it do its thing.

"What is that creepy thing up to?" Grace wanted to know.

As if the shadow could hear her question, it stopped dead in its tracks for the first time and looked straight in their direction. For several minutes, it didn't budge. It just stared at the fence that they sat upon.

"It's looking at us. Can it see us? It looks as though it wants to fly straight toward us. Can we get out of here?"

Grace was done with this little excursion.

"I can't imagine it can see us. We were told that no one could see this place from the outside," Michael replied.

"That is not a someone though. It's a something. And it sure does look like it can see us. Do you think it remembers us from last night? I am ready to go back," Noah finally added his two cents.

"Yeah, we are out of here. It's still watching us," Matt said as he jumped off the fence and headed back on the path to Mission Mind.

"Come on, guys, we are done for today."

As the pack of friends and their furry companions made their way back down the yellow brick road, which Grace had dubbed the golden path that morning, they all felt shaken and a bit creeped out. Thoughts of the small ghostly shadow staring undoubtedly in their direction gave them all the heebie-jeebies. The worst part of the freaked-out feelings they were experiencing was the fact they couldn't tell an adult soul. Gabriel and Keilah Brown would be disappointed in their carelessness, and Mr. Hallohesh and the other teachers wouldn't understand and would punish their curiosity.

As they were walking up the back steps to Mission Mind Academy, Grace was the first to express her mood.

"Is it just me, or do any of you have the feeling something or someone is watching us still?"

"I have the same sensation," Kiera assured her. "We need to shake this darkness off our bodies and minds. What do you guys say to a dip in the pool after breakfast and before Power of Thoughts class with Mr. Vand?"

They all agreed that was a great idea. They would have a solid forty-five minutes to take a dip and cool off before class started.

What they would do with their nerves after that, who knew! That crazy dark shadowed flying creature was going to stick with them until they figured how to shake him. God had something planned. He always did. But what, no one knew.

6

Thought Authority

Mr. Vand's 9:30 a.m. lecture happened to be a highlight as far as classes, lectures, and study halls went for kids. He was a very brilliant man with lots of education. As a former teacher, chaplain, and Bible scholar, he had loads of experience with children and instructing. Mr. Vand (no student knows his first name) in his late sixties, had raised a family before he and his wife Mrs. Vand (no one knows her first name either) came to Mission Mind to teach. He and his wife, who's gifted in keeping all kids in line with her strict, structured, systematized, and exceptionally kindhearted, compassionate personality, brought lots of thrilling energy to the school.

The two lovebirds kept things fun and lighthearted. They were known to play games in their off time with students, be it cards, board games, or physical sports. They often team-taught and were nicknamed the dynamic duo. Mrs. Vand was the MM organizer, filling in as a mother hen to the students in the absence of their own parents. Students were young and needed a motherly figure to comfort, encourage, and love on them. Raising two children of her own, a boy and girl, who were grown and involved in missionary work in third world countries, she had the experience and the heart.

After their bizarre morning spying on the Bones Abode, the five veteran friends felt the need to reassure Grace about her first class at Mission Mind.

"Mr. Vand is amazing, sister. He will help you with your running mind," Kiera told her confidently.

"Mrs. Vand teaches with him ninety percent of the time, and she will put all your worries to rest. It's her gift. You will love her," Noah added.

As they entered the classroom, which had stadium seating like a theater, they walked to the front row to sit.

Michael commented, "We don't miss a word from Mr. Vand. He has so much wisdom, hence the very front row."

As it was her very first full day at O Be Joyful, Grace's nerves were on overload. She didn't know what to expect or if she could handle the workload or homework. She always did well in school and enjoyed it back in Colorado, but this was nothing like her past life. She was expecting to have the summer off to play and relax, but the golden letter came and then the balloon, and now she was here expected to focus and learn a whole new way of life. Just as she was convincing herself that this was a huge mistake and she needed to get back home to her mom and dad, Mr. and Mrs. Vand appeared at the front of the room.

Both leaders seemed to have their sights focused directly on her. Before they said a word, the two grabbed one another's hands and stepped right up in front of her. Most people would offer an extended hand in greeting, but these two welcomed her in a warm tight embrace. They bent down and wrapped her up in a huge bear hug. "Grace Hayes, you wonderful, beautiful, talented young lady, we couldn't be more pleased to meet your acquaintance. Mr. Yedaiah Hallohesh told us all about you, and it was all we could do to keep from hunting you down at dinner last night to introduce ourselves," Mr. Vand said to her caringly.

"Welcome, sweet daughter of the King of kings!" Mrs. Vand articulated in a matter-of-fact way.

Then the dynamic duo stepped back in front of the class to begin what ended up being the most impactful hour of Grace's life to date.

Without a microphone, but as loud and effective as a preacher with one, Mr. Vand opened with a prayer and a Bible verse.

> For though we walk in flesh, we do not war according to the flesh, for the weapons of our warfare are not of the flesh, but divinely powerful for destruction of fortresses. We are destroying speculations and every lofty thing raised up against the knowledge of God, and we are taking every thought captive to the obedience of Christ. (2 Cor. 10:3–5 NASB)

"I cannot express enough how real and potent the battle for your mind is. Satan is so very real. Do not let anyone fool you into believing that he isn't. He exists! Children of God, as sure as our Heavenly Father is real and alive, the devil is as well. God, Jesus, and the Holy Spirit live in your hearts and dwell in the world, but so does His foe, the fallen one. Our enemy is real and is on a mission to accuse you. Accuse you of what, you might ask? *Everything!* It is a spiritual battle, one that is going on at all times. My job as your professor on thoughts is to help you understand how to squash the beast dead in his tracks! Not only did Jesus create us out of dust, but He also saved us from our sinful selves by dying on the cross and rising from the dead. He lives in us, in our hearts. Therefore, Satan can't touch our hearts. We are safe there. But God, being completely sovereign, has given each of us free will. He didn't make us to be puppets on a string. We are not robots. We are living, breathing beings. He made us to love and to love Him back. So with free will, our minds are open for whatever we decide for it. That is how God Himself created us. With choice, which I am thankful for choice, is wide open spaces. *Wide open spaces!* Spaces to fill as we please. Here is where Satan likes to enter in. We get the privilege to choose what we believe, what we think about life, ourselves, God, and others. He gave us freedom! Kids, listen closely, we choose what we think about. In 2 Corinthians, it says we are taking every thought captive to the obedience of God. Which thoughts? *Every thought!* If a thought crosses your mind that doesn't reflect the heart of God, it is from Satan, and you can choose to disregard it and pick a whole different thought. You have the power. God gave you the power."

With those words, hands went up all over the classroom. One at a time Mr. Vand called on them.

"When my mind runs wild with fear, I sometimes think that is God convicting me. Is that so?" one student asked.

"Not a God of fear is He. His perfect love casts out all fear. The accuser is the one robbing your mind of peace, with fear," Mr. Vand responded.

"Mr. Vand, because of my past failures, I often live with thoughts that I will never overcome and become. I don't know if that makes any sense, but it's how I feel," another student voiced.

"Ms. Clearwater, you precious soul, God breaks every chain and heals every wound. When you put your trust and life in Him, all victory is yours. His will be done. The enemy doesn't stand a chance. The only thing God asks of us is that we always, and I mean always, trust Him and never doubt. Doubt is a double-minded way of thinking. And we are single-minded beings."

More truth nuggets from Mr. Vand.

With a shaky hand, Grace waved it high.

After being called on, she nervously shared her feelings, "I get really scared doing new things. Sometimes it paralyzes me. Like coming here, for example. I am fighting the urge to go home, back to my parents and the comfortable life I lived. I miss my house, family, and friends. If God called me here, why do I battle these feelings? Where is my peace and comfort? Are these feelings coming from God or Satan?"

"Great question, Ms. Hayes, I believe that we have all tossed this one around before. I think that Mrs. Vand and I asked this same question when we were called here to Mission Mind too. The best way to answer this is through scripture. Jeremiah 29:11–14 says, 'For I know the plans I have for you, declares the Lord, plans for welfare and not for evil, to give you a future and a hope. Then you will call upon me and come and pray to me, and I will hear you. You will seek me and find me, when you seek me with all your heart. I will be found by you, declares the Lord, and I will restore your fortunes and gather you from all the nations and all the places where I have driven you, declares the Lord, and I will bring you back to the place from which I sent you into exile.'

"Proverbs 3:5–6 states, 'Trust in the Lord with all your heart, and do not lean on your own understanding. In all your ways acknowledge Him, and He will make straight your paths.'

"Pray and seek the Lord, Grace of Colorado, and I have no doubt in my mind that He will reveal His great and mighty plans and purposes. It's a promise from Him. The negative thoughts you are experiencing are coming from our enemy. God is your peace. Set your mind upon Him," he said in support.

The question-and-answer time continued for the remainder of class time, answered by Mr. or Mrs. Vand, depending on the leading of the Holy Spirit. Every inquiry and response resonated deep within Grace's heart and mind.

When the class period was over and they were all dismissed, Grace was blown away by what she had retained. How could one lecture teach her more than what she had previously learned in her lifetime?

Her five new buddies all had huge smiles on their faces as they walked out of the Vands' double-door classroom.

"We warned you about Power of Thought class. It hits you right between the eyes and sticks with you forever," Noah commented with a chuckle. "We have twenty-five minutes until our next class if you want to grab a snack or a breath of fresh air."

"Yes, if you guys don't mind, I would like to take a few moments alone…well, not alone but with Roxy," Grace said.

"No problem, sister, we will meet you in front of the double front doors a couple minutes before Old Testament Studies," Kiera responded.

"Perfect, I'll catch you guys later," she replied with a toothy grin.

Running up the stairs two at a time, Grace was in a hurry to snag Roxy and get back outside in the fresh air to think. "Come on, girl, do you need to get outside? I have missed you. I need my sweet pup. Come on, Roxy Ann." Her best friend was eager to see her. Leaping into her embrace and licking her face, Roxy always brought peace to Grace.

The two headed back down the stairs and out the door. "We only have twenty-three minutes until my next class, girl. Let's make the most of it." They found an apple tree and snuggled up together underneath it. Grace was thankful to have Roxy at Mission Mind. She so wished she could bring her to all classes with her for comfort and support.

As Grace's mind wandered to all the changes in her life, stress started to rise. The accuser at the Bones Abode was at the top of the list. How had she seen a black ghost? *What in the world am I supposed to do with that, God? I miss my mom and dad. I miss my home. I thought I loved it here, but now I am not so sure. Creepy things flying through the air, scaring us. It's just not normal!* One deep thought after another was bringing Grace into panic mode.

She lay herself down on the ground as she threw a racquetball for Roxy Ann to fetch.

"Go get it, girl," she muttered.

As the dog ran off, she looked up at the sky. The clouds were in their usual animal form. A perfectly shaped mama rabbit with two little bunnies were floating past a large horse cloud, and with the crystal-clear sky behind them, it was as if she was at a planetarium show. Even though she was staring at a spectacular sight, the fear kept rising. Her emotions brought on so much heat tears began trickling down her cheeks.

Just as she had resolved to head to Mr. Hallohesh's office to ask to be taken home immediately, Mr. Vand's words came flooding in: "In all your ways acknowledge Him, and He will make straight your path."

"I have the power to redirect my mind path so that I am acknowledging You, Lord Jesus. Then You will straighten my way!" she proclaimed aloud, with more confidence than she felt.

"Wow!" Grace yelled, although Roxy was the only one close enough to hear.

Her anxieties had completely left her. She claimed the scripture Mr. Vand had told her about over her life and her overwhelming need to go back home went away. All of a sudden, the idea of thoughts being powerful was real. She truly felt stronger and wiser from one class and conversation with God.

This got her thinking about the dreadful Abode again. She wondered if there was a way to overcome the enemy with thought power. This idea was so real to her she felt rushed to get back to the others to open the conversation. Maybe Mr. and Mrs. Vand would be able to help.

She grabbed Roxy's ball, threw it one last time, and then headed back up to her shared room to drop off her black-and-white four-legged friend and meet her five new two-legged friends.

"Love you, Roxy girl," she called to her as she closed her bedroom door and bolted down the stairs two at a time.

She had a new pep in her step and a lead on overcoming the enemy. She was so excited to hear what her buds thought of her mind-power idea.

As she opened the huge golden double doors to head out to the front steps, Grace spotted her new friends sitting there waiting for her. It brought her so much security, already feeling close to other kids. That was what she was most worried about coming to Mission Mind.

"Hey, Grace, fancy meeting you here," Malachi said jokingly. "Ready to head to class number two?"

"Well, I have something I want to talk to you guys about."

Michael chimed in, "We don't have much time. Class starts in two minutes, and it will take us that long to get there."

A bit disappointed that she had to squelch her thoughts and excitement for the whole next class period, she resolved, "It can wait."

With that, they all headed to Old Testament Studies with Mrs. Beck, where Grace was convinced she didn't hear a single word. The class itself wasn't boring, and Mrs. Beck was beautiful, kind, and smart, Grace had no doubt. But the thoughts she was having about thoughts took over her thoughts completely. When class was finally dismissed, Grace let out a breath of fresh air, hoping that her relieved sigh didn't offend anyone. She thanked her new teacher and received a hug from her, promising herself that she would pay strict attention tomorrow in her class. She reasoned that it must be just as impactful of a class as Power of Thought class if it was required at Mission Mind.

Heading back out into the beautiful sunshine, the six friends were happy to have a free period before lunch to chill and spend time together. Noah suggested trying out the new game he and Michael had been creating.

"Get in your sportswear and we can meet at the tennis courts in ten."

Rushing up to their room, the two girls threw their school uniforms onto the floor and changed into shorts, T-shirts, and tennis shoes. They both then tossed their hair up into a ponytail, called their animals to join them, and made their way to the courts. Arriving just as the boys did, they were quite proud of their speed.

"What are the rules of your game, Noah?" Kiera asked with enthusiasm.

"Well, let me lay it down for you," he began.

"Two teams of three, since that is what we are working with, usually five or six players per team. One in the goal with the rest of the team on the court. So this game is a cross between soccer, tennis, hockey, and football."

With a loud laugh, he continued, "Michael and I had to incorporate all of our faves! Anyhow, we use a ball that looks similar to a soccer ball but a little smaller and without the pattern of normal soccer balls. The net is similar to a tennis court net but doesn't cover the whole length of the court, just the center half of it. After one team serves the ball, kind of like tennis but without the racket, kicked right over the center of the net to the other side, the opposing team players, minus the goalie who hangs out in the goal, same size as a hockey goal, go after it. The court players pass the ball and go for a score on the opposite goal. The way football comes into play is the contact. Hence the full-body pads I brought for us all to wear. You can't tackle, but you can use your body to get the other team off of you or the ball. Think of it as blockers in football. The game has two halves, twenty-five minutes each. But we will only have time to warm up and practice. Any questions?"

"This sounds awesome," Matt assured Noah and Michael. "What is this game called?"

"Flanks," Noah responded. "And Mr. Hallohesh made it the official Mission Mind sports program just this morning. Michael and I have been dreaming it up and perfecting it for a year now. There will be actual teams and uniforms. I can picture bringing it to the real world too. But for now, it will just be played at O Be Joyful."

"That's so exciting, and I am honored to be learning it at the beginning," Grace said, almost giddy with anticipation.

Then six friends, with their pets watching from the other side of the fence so not to get in the way and injured, suited up in the body pads and played flanks for as long as they had time. They all had so much fun running around using their bodies for action. They played and laughed and got heated in the competition. It felt good to distract themselves from thoughts and fears and, most of all, the Bones Abode and Satan that dwells there.

As the kids were packing up their pads and chugging water to stay hydrated on the sunny warm day, the thoughts came flooding back in. None of them said so much aloud, but all six of them were quiet and deep in thought.

Giving a quick goodbye, they headed back to their rooms to get back into their school uniforms for lunch and afternoon classes.

Grace had made up her mind to sit with Mr. and Mrs. Vand during lunch. So when she walked into the dining room, she bee-lined her way to where they were eating.

"May I sit with you today?" she asked politely.

"Of course you can, dear," Mrs. Vand responded with her kind eyes twinkling.

Gathering her courage, she said between bites of her veggie wrap, "I have not been able to stop thinking about Thoughts class today. I have been tossing around ideas on how to beat the devil and can't help but shake the idea of mind-controlling him. I don't know if this makes sense. But somehow, I think that Satan can be defeated with our thoughts, not our actions."

"That is powerful, Grace. I believe that you are correct. Satan attacks our minds with dark and negative thoughts, lies even, and we get to choose whether we entertain what he is saying or squash the thoughts. We can choose to listen to the still small voice of God. You are a wise lady," Mr. Vand assured her. "Why do I get the feeling that you are battling something more specific than thoughts?"

Taking a long glance around the dining hall, Grace was beginning to feel uncomfortable with the depths of the conversation.

"Would it be okay if we meet in your classroom to talk about this further?"

Mr. Vand's curiosity was piqued. "Yes, Mrs. Vand and I can meet you there after your last class today, before the dinner song chimes."

"Oh, thank you so much. See you then," she said as she was finishing her last bite of lunch.

Grace couldn't help but hope that Kiera, Michael, Matthew, Malachi, and Noah would join her. She also hoped that they wouldn't be upset with her opening this door of conversation with teachers. They had warned her to leave staff out of their Bones Abode quest.

The afternoon classes dragged on, mostly because Grace's mind was on other things. *So much for controlling my thoughts*, she thought to herself.

"Hey, Grace, what's up with you? You have seemed a bit distracted this afternoon. Is everything all right? Are you enjoying your first full day here?" Noah asked her.

"Yes, I am very much. But I was wondering if I could talk to you for a minute," she said with trepidation.

"Yeah, shoot," he responded.

"Well, I am nervous to ask you this, but I have had Power of Thoughts class on my mind all day and can't help but ponder the significance of it. What I mean is, what if we can defeat whatever is dwelling in the Bones Abode with our thought patterns? If what Mr. Vand says is true, we have mighty power with mind control."

"I haven't thought of it that way. How do you see this playing out?" he asked with curiosity.

"I hope you aren't upset, but I have asked Mr. and Mrs. Vand to meet me, or all of us, if you are willing, after classes and before dinner to talk about it. I know that opening up about our search and determination as far as the Bones goes to adults was not in the plans. However, I really get the sense that the Vands can help. What do you say?"

"Wow! Okay, so you are ambitious about this whole defeat-the-enemy thing, huh," he said in a joking manner.

"Yes, I am, I guess. So do you think the others will be down for meeting together this evening?"

"I am sure they will. Let's go ask them now. We will just pray that the Vands won't be upset with our search and will help us out."

All six of them were open to talking in the Power of Thoughts class, and they headed that way a bit nervously after school. None of them knew quite what they would say or ask or what they were hoping to accomplish. But they did want answers and help, and Mr. and Mrs. Vand seemed like the best adult option as far as staff at Mission Mind went.

Walking through the door one at a time, they spotted their teachers sitting at the front of the room sipping on cups of something hot and steaming. "Hello, kids, welcome back for the second time today," Mrs. Vand greeted them.

"Thanks," they all said in unison. Then they pulled up chairs and positioned them to sit in a rough semicircle.

"What can we help you guys with today? Why do you all have such long faces? Is everything all right?" Mr. Vand questioned.

"Well," Noah opened the conversation, "the six of us have had the Bones Abode on our minds and have been doing a little research on it."

"What kind of research, and what have you found out?" Mr. Vand wanted to know.

Matt answered, "We found a book in the library, and when we opened it up, a smallish black shadow flew right out of it. We were so spooked that we all hid under the table. Then it went for the Genesis window and tried to bang its way out."

He was talking so fast trying not to leave out any wild details at this point. "We prayed, and God answered. When we opened our eyes and climbed out from the table, it was gone, and the book was closed and back on the shelf where we found it."

"Let me guess, *The Black Spirit of the Abode*?" Mr. Vand responded as a matter of fact.

"Yes, exactly!" Kiera said in amazement.

Mrs. Vand had a calm look on her face and a stable voice when she explained to the kids that what they witnessed was an illusion and a scare tactic from the devil himself. "That black shadow is a reminder of why we live our lives for Jesus. He is our protector, and that shadow represents the enemy who is out for us."

Malachi took in what she said and still felt confused and unsatisfied with the answer. "Well, if it is just an illusion that hides out in that book, then why did we see it at the Bones Abode?"

"You were at the Bones Abode?" Mrs. Vand replied with a not-so-peaceful expression.

"No, we didn't go there, but we went early in morning to the west end of O Be Joyful acres and spied on it with binoculars. We saw that creepy thing flying around, among other shadows, and then right before we were about to head back to school for breakfast, it looked right at us and stared."

Malachi's skin was crawling just replaying the situation. "It could see us. It saw right into O Be Joyful. Now tell me that was an illusion."

Both adults looked around the semicircle, into each of the kid's eyes, making sure that they had seen it too, that Malachi wasn't fabricating a story. And sure enough, they were all wide-eyed and spook-faced.

Keeping an assured appearance, Mr. Vand looked toward Grace and asked, "Why did you decide to come to Mrs. Vand and me for help? Why not Mr. Hallohesh? Yedaiah seems like he would have been your go-to person on a matter like this."

"Well, your class was so impactful, and it got my mind thinking, being about Power of Thoughts and all. We don't fully understand what we are witnessing when we see that dark shadow. What I mean is, we know it's our enemy, but we don't know how it's our enemy. What does it want from us? What does it want to do to us? What should we really be afraid of? How do we defeat it? So I was wondering, since our thoughts are so powerful, and we can control our thoughts, can we control them enough, with God as our strength and focus, to defeat the enemy in every situation?"

"Very insightful you are, how very in tune you must be with the Lord," Mrs. Vand said with a big bright sparkling smile.

Mr. Vand, with a serious tone, spoke after what seemed an awfully long silence, "Yes, Grace, I do believe that you can defeat Satan at every turn with the power of God, and since Satan attacks the mind, where God gave us free will, that is exactly where he will be crushed. However, listen carefully now, all of you wise kids, digging deeper and stirring the pot don't exactly bring forth the battles meant for you. We are meant to ready ourselves body, mind, and spirit for when the devil decides to strike at us. We are not called to go start the battle. Focusing yourself on darkness is not controlling your minds for the good, which is God alone. If you put your thoughts on Him only, the ghost that flies around won't even be noticed. Does that make sense?"

The friends all shook their heads in agreement but saw Mr. Vand's response for what it was: a warning. He was telling them to leave well enough alone, to not pursue the Bones Abode and its inhabitance.

The trouble with that was their curiosity was a strong force at this point. They couldn't unsee what they had already seen. The little black shadow was going to stick in their thoughts until they could do something about it.

The kids gave Mr. and Mrs. Vand huge hugs and said their goodbyes. They thanked them and told them they would see them in the dining hall.

All six of them walked out of the Power of Thoughts class with downcast bodies and downcast thoughts.

Grace felt worst of all; she had opened up about her theory on thoughts and ended up with her mind running uncontrollably wild. That chat session only backfired. She felt the need to tell her friends that she was sorry. She kind of felt like she tattled on them. Now Mr. and Mrs. Vand knew their quest and weren't even willing to help them in it.

7

Flanks

A couple of weeks had passed since the Bones Abode chat with Mr. and Mrs. Vand, and not a single word had been spoken about it. The Six-Pack, which was what Kiera had started calling their group of friends, and the Vands were all close-lipped about the dark shadow and the whole research extravaganza.

During free time, most of the students at Mission Mind were out at the courts learning, practicing, and playing flanks. Noah and Michael were having the times of their lives coaching and roughing it up on the court. The two of them had put so much time, effort, and frustration over the years to make the sport a reality, and here it was in action. They had already formed six teams, with six players on each team, five on the court at a time with one substitute.

Mr. Yedaiah Hallohesh had given the boys his blessing to start a practice and game day schedule. Noah convinced Gabriel Brown to be the referee after thoroughly explaining the rules and giving him an official handbook. Mr. Brown was always asking Michael questions about the ins and outs of flanks. Michael enjoyed bonding with his dad. Gabriel was a bit of an athlete himself, playing several sports in his younger years. The two of them would stay up late at night, putting their heads together to come up with new plays and moves for the teams to try.

The season was due to begin in just four weeks, and there was a lot of practice to be had in that small amount of time. Flanks was unique in the way that it had no coaches. Each team of six had to work together to function in their squad.

Noah, Michael, Matthew, Malachi, Kiera, and Grace were on the same team, and they named themselves the Six-Pack—no surprise there. They had use of the courts from the hours of 6:45 a.m. to 7:45 a.m., Monday through Friday. They would also sneak in extra practice when other teams were not scheduled on the courts and they were not in class or at mealtime. With their focused dedication on flanks, schoolwork got a little more challenging. Some nights they were up extremely late, fitting everything in.

The other five teams were also coed and had come up with interesting names as well. There were the Ball Beaters, Jerseys, Hammerheads, Tough Troops, and the Net Rulers. The rest of the school was just as excited as the players. You could find staff and students alike sitting outside at all hours of the day on the bleachers watching practice as they did homework or sipped their cups of coffee. It was the new buzz at O Be Joyful. And that made Noah and Michael oh so happy.

✳✳✳✳✳

The Saturday morning of the first game day was happening at Mission Mind. The whole school was up super early to eat breakfast and prepare. There was a mandatory school-wide prayer meeting in the chapel on campus. Mr. Hallohesh led everyone in the plea to God for health, safety, and blessings on the first day of the new contact sport. The team uniforms with last names, team names, and numbers were put on with great pride and excitement. Protective pads and gear were in place to help with any hard blows. And proper net and ball equipment had been purchased and were ready for use.

There were going to be three games that day, two before lunch and one after. The Six-Pack were due to play the Net Rulers in the afternoon at 2:00 p.m. Noah and Michael had chosen to play last so that they would have the opportunity to watch the sport they created come to life prior. They were the founders and needed to make sure everything went smoothly. They felt completely responsible for whatever was about to go down that day, and to say they were nervous was a huge understatement.

Mr. Gabriel Brown was in a gold-and-white referee striped shirt, with black shorts and a whistle. His main job was to keep the game clean and stay out of the way of the players and the ball, which was not going to be easy because the game moved very quickly by nature. He had a golden whistle that made the chirping sound of a nightingale and a baseball cap to protect his eyes from the glorious sunshine that was out.

The entire school had taken their seats in the stadium and had water and peanuts in hand. The crowd was wild with excitement as Mr. Hallohesh stood on the court to open in prayer. When the prayer ended, he took his place in the front row. He was so proud of Noah and Michael. This was a blessed day indeed. Deep school unity, he believed, would come from this new addition to Mission Mind Academy.

The first two games of the morning went off without a hitch. The Ball Beaters lost 2–4 against the Hammerheads, and Tough Troops pulled out a win 3–2 against the Jerseys.

After the first two matches, the school all filed their way into the dining hall to eat sandwiches, chips, fruit, and vegetables. Mrs. Heathers wanted to make sure to give a well-balanced meal that day and not weigh down the last two teams for their big game that afternoon. She was thankful she got to watch it. A couple other kitchen staff members and she had to miss the morning fun to clean up breakfast and prepare lunch. But she was not going to miss out on the 2:00 p.m. match. She was so proud of their school and the students. Feeding this group of people day in and day out was her biggest joy to date. She took special care to create food to fuel and not bog down their bodies and brains. She knew the importance of food and loved the gardens and orchards she could draw from to create healthy delicious meals.

The wind picked up a bit as the Six-Pack and Net Rulers took their positions for the 2:00 p.m. game. Also, gray clouds rolled in to cover up the sun and darken the scene. Mr. Hallohesh took the court once more for an opening prayer asking the good Lord to hold rain off and keep everyone safe. But as he sat in his front-row seat, an eerie feeling passed through him. Something was amiss, and he dearly hoped it was just his nerves and nothing more.

Mr. Brown blew the chirping whistle to begin play. The Six-Pack won the coin toss for first with ball. After Noah served to their opponents, he quickly attacked on defense to gain possession once more. He passed the ball to Malachi and headed down court for a pass back. Malachi saw the triangle made and passed back to Noah for a score in the first minute of the game. The crowd cheered loudly over the goal. As the teams were repositioning to continue, the wind picked up even more, blowing leaves and dust around everywhere. The sky grew super dark, but the kids ignored the conditions and focused on the game. The Net Rulers were pushing their way down the court to go for a score themselves. They were passing the ball around and around and shoving each other with their shoulder pads to press hard on the goal. As one team member on the Net Rulers squared up to the goal for a chance to tie the game, a black shadow blew past his face in the wind.

Stopping in his tracks because he wasn't sure what he just saw, it flew past his nose again bringing an unidentified sound and smell with it. The Net Rulers team member stood completely still in shock and disbelief. That was when Kiera stole the ball and headed down for a second score for the Six-Pack. The crowd went crazy again, cheering and hooting and hollering. But as the teams reset in their zones, the shadow came down over the net and hovered there. There was a foul smell that entered the air like a dump yard filled with years of trash. The wind blew the stench every which way, causing everyone to cover their noses for protection from the offense. There became a bitter taste in mouths as well. Kids were spitting to try to rid themselves of the horrible taste of sour rotten food. The shadow continued swirling in a sporadic pattern, spreading the fumes like wildfire. An ear-piercing, high-pitched, constant ringing circulated, bringing pain and discomfort to senses like a fire engine siren would a dog.

Students, staff members, and everyone at the courts and on campus were paralyzed by the physical ailments they were experiencing. Every person stood or sat still not having a clue what to do. Mr. Hallohesh had his head bowed in prayer, Grace noticed. And then it hit her—the power of thought. She made her way over to where the other five Six-Pack members stood together.

"This is exactly what I was talking to Mr. and Mrs. Vand about. Focus your minds on God and ignore what is going on around you!" she yelled at them so they could hear her over the wind and high-pitched torture.

The six of them joined hands as they formed a circle. Not saying anything aloud, they all set their minds on the power of God, closing their eyes so they wouldn't be distracted by their surroundings.

The shadow and foulness continued, finally driving everyone away from the courts and back to the Mission Mind building—everyone but the six, who were determined not to lose focus.

Mr. Hallohesh cranked up worship music as loud as possible on all speakers inside and out of O Be Joyful. Students collected in their bedrooms and dining hall praying together and freaking out in sobs and hysterics. The staff, although unaware of what was truly happening, did their best to stay composed so they wouldn't frighten the children further.

The pets that had been behind the flanks fence watching the games and enjoying the fresh air had all found their person and were a source of comfort for them. The animals on campus didn't seem bothered or distracted by the dark shadow; they were concerned only with the discomfort of their humans.

On the court, the black creep continued to swarm and torment like a mosquito, never pausing in one place. It did appear to have its sights set on Grace and her friends, because it didn't follow the others into the building but stayed lingering around their group. The kids continued holding hands, refusing to drift their minds off the One above. They could feel when it buzzed close by, sending shivers down their spines, and the smell was enough to make them lose their lunch, but they stayed focused.

After what felt like an hour but was probably only about twenty minutes, they felt the air calming and the smell drifting away. The ear-piercing pitch diminished, and tranquility returned. They slowly opened one eye to peek around. The shadow was nowhere to be found. It had disappeared.

"I don't know if we did that by our focus or if it just decided it had enough bugging us, but praise God!" Kiera said.

"That was insane. I think it has our number and was there to warn us away from spying on it," Matt chimed in.

The six made their way to the bleachers and sat with their water bottles to recover.

"We didn't get to play our first game," Michael said with a downcast tone.

"There will be plenty of other chances, pal. At least we got two points," Noah reassured him.

"Are you kids all right out here?" It was Mr. Vand checking in on them.

Noah replied, "We are now! Grace urged us to stay focused on God and not the tormenter, so we held hands, kept our minds focused, and ignored it. After a long while, it left or disappeared."

"Do you think the power of our thoughts had something to do with it leaving, Mr. Vand?" Kiera wanted to know.

"Maybe ignoring its existence took away some of its power."

"That was a very brave thing you all decided to do, while everyone else ran away like chickens with their heads cut off." Mr. Vand chuckled. "That shadow did appear to come here to put doubt in our minds and shake everyone up."

"We feel like it was here for us," Noah said boldly. "We were the ones searching it out, and it looked right at us the last time we saw it. I think it knows us and was here to scare us away."

"Fear comes from the devil himself. For it says in 2 Timothy 1:7, 'For God hath not given us a spirit of timidity, but of power, and of love, and of a sound mind.'"

Mr. Vand continued, "It seems as if Satan has indeed entered O Be Joyful. Sneaky bugger."

"What do we do now, Mr. Vand?" All the kids wanted to know.

"I believe you are six very wise children who listen to God. We will trust Him to lead our steps on this matter. Let's begin by setting up a meeting this evening with Mr. Hallohesh to explain all the happenings regarding the Bones Abode, library, and the black shadow. We should keep closed lips to the rest of the students though. We don't want to go spreading a school-wide panic," Mr. Vand said with a kind smile.

"Let's all meet in my Power of Thoughts classroom after dessert tonight at 7:15 p.m. I will make sure Mrs. Vand and Mr. Hallohesh are there."

The children gave Mr. Vand a group hug and thanked him before he headed back toward Mission Mind Academy.

"Wow! This is completely nuts!" Grace finally said. "I feel like we opened Pandora's box. Are we the reason Satan has finally entered O Be Joyful? I sure hope not!"

"Don't forget that God is above everything and has a purpose and a plan. Let's not take responsibility but give the burden up to God. He has this. He will show us what to do." Noah went on, "Maybe he was supposed to enter so he can be defeated. We were all brought here to train for battle against him. For the first time in years, I feel like I am doing exactly what I was brought here to do. I take comfort in that. You should too."

Taking Noah's encouraging words to heart, the Six-Pack decided to play some flanks. They picked up the ball and began to have a practice right then and there. They had wanted to play so badly that day and were feeling ripped off by the devil's distraction. They felt lighter as they passed the ball around, scrimmaging each other back to peaceful minds.

That evening in the dining hall during dinner, the dark shadow was the only topic being spoken about. Students were coming up with outlandish explanations, like it was just a leaf that had fallen from the tree and startled everyone or that it was just a shadow of something outside—nothing to worry about. They explained away the smells and sound by the high winds and cloudy sky. No one mentioned Satan or the devil as a possibility. They didn't believe it could be him, because they were protected as long as they were on O Be Joyful campus. No one wanted to admit that darkness could enter in and threaten them.

But Noah and his friends knew the truth and had a feeling that all the others were experiencing some form of doubt. How could they not be?

When they finished their blueberry cobbler and ice cream, they headed into the Power of Thoughts room as promised. Mr. Hallohesh was already present, as were Mr. and Mrs. Vand. They gave warm smiles and kind greetings to the six kids.

"Thanks for coming, kiddos," Mr. Vand began. "I have not mentioned to Mr. Yedaiah (which is what the staff call Mr. Hallohesh) what this is about. I thought it better if you guys explain in as much detail as possible to him what you told Mrs. Vand and me recently."

Malachi started off by explaining the incident they had in the Grow in Wisdom library. Then Michael went on to describe the happenings when they spied on the Bones Abode. And Noah mentioned how they thought the shadow was there for the six of them during the flanks match that afternoon. The kids were getting pretty heated up over recalling the details when Grace brought up her idea on power of mind control and what they did on the court earlier that day during the dark shadow's torment.

Mr. Hallohesh listened carefully and without interruption until every one of them had a turn to talk and get all that they had experienced off their chests.

Then he said with great clarity, "I am a bit disappointed in the fact that you all sought out darkness. With that said, I am also proud of how you have handled everything that has happened since. I believe that everything under the sun happens with great purpose and is ultimately meant to be. You six have shown great courage and bravery, especially this afternoon. Thank you for coming to leadership for guidance. That was a smart and necessary decision. We will keep this between the nine of us for now, with the exception of Mr. and Mrs. Brown."

Looking straight at Matthew, Michael, and Malachi, Mr. Hallohesh told them, "You will tell your parents everything you have told me today."

"Yes, sir," all three boys replied to him.

"And for now, until we feel the leading of the Holy Spirit, who dwells everywhere here at O Be Joyful, we will not act but pray over the matter. I do not want any of you to dig up books on the darkness or spy on the Bones Abode. Stay away from the end of the west acres! Do I make myself clear?"

"Yes, sir," they all responded, a bit ashamed.

"Let's join together in prayer now, asking God for protection and favor over whatever lies out there scheming against us."

After Mr. Yedaiah Hallohesh closed out his prayer with an amen, the friends exited the classroom and headed off to their rooms for the night. There would be no sneaking around looking for trouble that evening or anytime soon.

Matthew, Michael, and Malachi went to find their mom and dad, not overly excited to share what they had been up to or what they had been stirring up.

8

School-Wide Doubt

After the spine-chilling ordeal during the flanks match, things started changing rapidly at Mission Mind Academy. Everyone on campus, students and staff alike, were shaken up inside. The majestic atmosphere, where everyone was courteous, kind, and uplifting, started changing one action after another. Where patience for self and others used to flow easily, now short tempers and fuses abounded. Where confidence in one's abilities was a given because the knowledge that God was always on their side, now reservations and questions loomed.

Before the dark shadow made its appearance for the whole school to witness, life at O Be Joyful was pure and safe. No real worries or stresses plagued their peaceful community. Everyone knew that the Holy Spirit was among them, and they had no reason to fear anything. It was quite perfect, and no one had a reason to think that was ever going to change. It was almost like the garden of Eden before the sin and fall of Adam and Eve.

Where high fives and hugs were a given when running into others on campus, now making eye contact seemed to be too far of a stretch when passing peers and adults. The vibe at O Be Joyful was growing quite depressing. A big reason for this was the act of keeping the darkness in secret. Something happened on Saturday, five days ago, and no one was talking about it.

Thursdays were usually a day looked forward to by the entire school. Dubbed thankful Thursday years earlier, there were always special happenings going on. In the morning and evening as well as in between classes were fun booths that the staff ran for the students—all the carnival-type games to play and prizes to win. Special treats like cotton candy, licorice ropes, popcorn, and funnel cakes lined the golden path from the Mission Mind building to the horse stables. Everyone brought their beloved pets and enjoyed the snot out of the day.

The Thursday after the sighting was different. Hardly anyone was to be found out enjoying themselves. No one wanted snacks or to play ring toss or cornhole. Kids went right to their rooms between classes to nap or hide out. Friends didn't gather for laughs; they independently read, napped, sulked, or lounged. Most Thursdays the worship music could barely be heard over all the voices and excitement. This downcast Thursday, the music was blaring so loud it sounded like it was yelling at everyone.

Yedaiah was troubled by what he saw, or rather didn't see, down along the golden path—bright tents perfectly positioned, but no one was milling around them. By noon, he was so upset he decided to return to his office for solitude and prayer. Maybe if he prayed hard enough, God would quickly return the harmony that once resided at his school. He knew that he couldn't manipulate God into doing what he wanted, but he could cry out and hope it was God's will.

Bowing his head, Yedaiah besought his heavenly Father for favor at Mission Mind Academy, including all the people who live there.

Aloud he said, "Father, we need You. We are all a bit rattled by that dark figure that swarmed around our heads the other day. Please tell us what it is and what to do about it. I feel as if the souls around here are in complete disarray over it, and I have no idea how to explain it myself. Everyone looks to me for answers, and right now I don't have any. Please, God, please. We need You. I need You!"

An overwhelming answer came with an internal reminder that God's timing is always perfect. Yedaiah didn't have much peace in the thought. He had a sneaky suspicion that things were going to get a lot worse before they were better. An unsettling feeling found its way into him, and helplessness was his new disposition.

It was lunch period, and Noah and his friends ate bean-and-cheese burritos with chips and guacamole in silence. Looking around the room, he decided to break the unhappiness afflicting the place. He stood up on his chair, something he had never done before, cupped his hands around his mouth for volume, and called attention to the room.

"My friends," he began, drawing the faces and attention of everyone present, "I am just going to call it like it is. We saw something creepy and confusing a few days back, and I am worried that by ignoring it, we are making it worse than it actually is."

Then he posed a question, "Who in this room right now is experiencing doubt and fear?"

Simultaneously, every hand raised, some lifting both hands up in double agreement. Faces were already looking less freaked out and more relaxed, just seeing that they were not alone in their uncertainties.

Noah continued, "Okay! Okay! Now that we have established that we are all in the same boat of trepidation, let's talk about what we are going to do about it."

Noah decided that it would be wise to call Mr. Hallohesh into the discussion at this point, being the headmaster and fearless leader of their tribe.

"Mr. Hallohesh, I know I opened this conversation, but I would like to invite you to take over if you might?"

Yedaiah stood up, not on his chair, addressing his staff and students.

"First of all, thank you, Noah, for caring about our uncertainties. You are a fine young man, and I appreciate you and your bravery very much."

Noah blushed a little over the compliment but was more relieved that he was not in hot water for bringing up and talking about the darkness that was looming.

"Thank you, sir," he responded to his superior.

"We all saw, felt, and smelled the black shadow that hovered over the court during the flanks match last Saturday. I have heard much speculation over the incident buzzing around O Be Joyful over the past several days. I would, thanks to Noah's courage, like to address the matter. We believe that, although the Holy Spirit is here with us and always protects us with what we need, Satan has entered our charming property."

As Yedaiah paused, he could see the deer-in-the-headlight looks on everyone's faces: eyes wide and mouths open.

He chose to continue, "I wish that I had all the answers to the questions in your minds, but I am sad to say I don't. What I do know is that God knows why and what to do from here."

One hand raised up, coming from Grace Hayes.

Yedaiah called upon her, "Yes, Ms. Grace?"

With a quivering voice, she said, "I have brought this up a few times since arriving, but I was wondering, should we practice focusing our minds on Christ and not on the enemy to break the power he seems to have over all of us at this time?"

All heads in the dining hall were nodding up and down agreeing that Grace had a point.

She continued, "Mr. Vand's Power of Thought lecture got me thinking. We have all power to control what we set our minds on. We have all been walking around here for days with doubt casting shadows on our lives. We have let the presence of a black flying figure plague us with doubt. Doubt does not come from the good Lord above. Satan has come to accuse us and make us falter in our faith. We need to fight against it, and I believe that war is won in our thoughts, not by a physical battle."

Mr. Hallohesh chimed up, "Grace, I agree with you. This is also a situation that will not be won in solitude. I believe in the power of numbers, and there are a lot of us here and only one enemy."

As if on cue, all the windows blew shut in the dining hall behind the black shadow that flew in. Kids ducked under the tables so fast, and anxiety was at an all-time high. Screams were echoing, and yells were amplified off the walls. Chaos was breaking loose.

Grace thought to herself as she remained in her seat, along with her five brave friends, *What did we just say about the power of thought? Why did everyone hit the deck so easily?*

The shadow swarmed, bringing the familiar foul smell and ear-piercing sound with it. Classmates didn't last under the tables long. Within minutes, kids were running for the doors out of the dining room, the blackness hot on their tails to make sure they were good and spooked. The commotion continued until everyone except for the Six-Pack, Mr. and Mrs. Vand, Mr. Hallohesh, and the dark shadow remained.

That was when the nine Jesus-believing, confident-in-His-power people gathered at one table to stand against it. They stood up on chairs, in a circle, joined hands, and began praying aloud. They were all praying at once, controlling where the paths of their minds went, refusing to succumb to the enemy. Nine brave warriors for Christ standing up against Satan.

The shadow of doubt continued circling their heads, bringing all that it could to disrupt them from their space of godly peace. Round and round it went with smells from the pits of hell. After a half hour of torture, the three adults and six kids were astounded and relieved when it finally gave up, headed out of the dining hall and down the hallway to an open window for departure.

They all made their way to windows in time to see it fly into the distance towards its Bones Abode dwelling place.

Yedaiah proclaimed, "Praise God for His victory here today!"

"Mr. Hallohesh, I can't help but think we need a game plan for defeating this persistent pest," Noah spoke up.

"Noah, I believe you are correct. I am sorry to say that I don't know what that game plan would be, however. Truthfully, I have taken the lead from you and Grace at this point."

"Sir," Grace assured him, "I have taken my lead from you and Mr. and Mrs. Vand's wisdom. I guess we are all in new territory at this point."

Malachi admitted, "I can't help but feel a bit responsible for the shadow's appearance. I pressed the matter of seeking him out and learning about him. I wouldn't let it rest. I am sorry."

"Young Mr. Brown, you are not to blame for Satan's attack. The battle between good and evil has been going on since the beginning of time. All happens just as it should. Take heart, son, God is in control. Not a single thing happens under the sun that God is surprised or threatened by!"

Thankful for Mr. Hallohesh's comment but not convinced, Malachi continued, "Yeah, but I pushed my friends to seek out the Bones Abode. I was even tempted to go there and check it out in person. Now the shadow is here at our amazing campus causing doubt in everyone."

"Yes, it is, but have you thought that maybe we need to be tempted by doubt in order to find complete trust?" Yedaiah wanted to know.

Everyone considered his question, even the Vands. They all pondered the reason and significance of the dark shadow's appearance.

"All right," Mr. Vand spoke up, "I think the first order of business is to get the school-wide doubt epidemic under control. I saw a whole lot of disturbed students and faculty. How do you propose we address this matter, Mr. Hallohesh?"

"If you don't mind, let me take the afternoon to pray over the situation and get back to you, Mr. Vand. Thank you for being a steadfast light in all this. I appreciate you and Mrs. Vand standing by the students and me, more than you know."

Noah, Grace, Kiera, and the Brown boys headed out to the horse stables to regroup. As they made their way outside for fifteen minutes of fresh air before their next class, they heard Mr. Hallohesh on the loud intercom declaring the rest of the day of classes canceled. He said that they would have a school-wide meeting in the auditorium, addressing the happenings on campus, at 4:45 p.m. that afternoon, directly before dinner.

"I am so relieved to avoid all the downcast faces moping around this place. We are called to be joyful. Why is everyone freaking out so bad?" Kiera really wanted to know.

"I hear you," Grace replied. "Doubt is taking over our unity and wreaking havoc. How can we help? What can we do? I think we are the only ones not off our rockers at this point. God help us all."

Matt, always acting the oldest, because he was, said, "It will be okay, Grace. This is precisely what we have been schooling for at Mission Mind. I am blown away that everyone is so surprised. The golden letters we all received, calling us here, let us know we were training for spiritual battle. Well, here it is!"

"Agreed," Michael responded. "I just can't believe it all went down during our opening day of flanks. What do you say we all mount up on horses and ride this afternoon, now that we have unexpected free time?"

"I'm in," Noah agreed, followed by four more yeses.

The Six-Pack picked horses to ride, chosen pets in tow, and rode off into the sun, down the sparkling golden path, wind in their faces, feeling free as could be in their current circumstances.

Just before the group of six friends were about to steer their steeds into the stables, a cloud cover came overhead, and they all looked upward at the dark sky that formed. Roxy began barking uncontrollably at the shadow swirling around her head. Grace and her buddies stopped in their tracks and looked toward it. Right before their eyes, the shadow split into two, doubling the trouble they were facing.

"Quick, into the stable!" Noah called out.

They all jumped off their horses and pulled them into the stalls, calling after their beloved pets to follow them. The stench of trash and sewer filled the air behind them, eerie shrieking filling their ears and minds.

"What do we do?" Malachi yelled above the noise.

Matthew, grabbing a shovel, began swinging at the two flying objects, causing them to rise higher up toward the ceiling of the barn.

"Quick, make sure you have your animals and let's make a run for it back to Mission Mind!" Noah hollered.

The two shadows were hot on their tails as they sprinted toward the school building. As they approached the back door to the Grow in Wisdom library, they tried their best to file through without letting the unwelcomed guests inside. Failing miserably short of their mission, the flying darkness duo successfully entered in, bringing all of the foulness with them.

"What do we do now?" Grace called out in a panic.

Noah yelled to the group, "I think we should try to trap them in here."

"I have a feeling they cannot be trapped anywhere, best buddy," Michael answered back.

"Let's crawl under the same table we were when we first met this tiny beast and pray them away!" Kiera suggested.

"Yes, that is our best bet," Grace agreed.

All six of them, with the two dark shadows buzzing their towers, crawled under the big study table, closed their eyes, and began praying. Several minutes later, when they could no longer hear the hideous sound or smell the rotten stench, they opened their eyes to complete peace and calmness.

"Praise God, He has done it again," Matt said with great relief. "Now let's get to the auditorium stat. We have two minutes before our school-wide meeting about the crazy flying devil, or should I now call them devils?"

Entering a couple minutes late, they had the opportunity to see the anxious faces on everyone. Noah was still feeling blown away by the massive change in demeanor of the whole school over the past few days. Everyone looked as if they had seen a ghost. They did see a ghost, but he couldn't imagine what the student body would be doing if they had encountered all that the Six-Pack had. He thought maybe they would be dead in their graves. He truly wasn't scared. Noah had been complacent and ready for action for quite some time now, and it was looking like this was his go time.

Noah whispered to his five buddies, "The whole front row is open. Let's make our way up there to the front of the room. I think we are a big part of this and need to be able to interact easily."

As they took their seats, the only ones brave enough to sit in the first row, or the first three rows for that matter, they gave big smiles to assure Mr. Hallohesh that they were there for him. The six of them feeling like this whole debacle was because of them and their intrusion.

"Attention, students and faculty. I have called this assembly to order this evening to address what we all saw happen last Saturday afternoon during the flanks match on the courts and in the dining hall earlier today. I know there has been much debate and trepidation over the dark shadow, smells, and sounds you all heard. I wish that I had every answer you are undoubtedly searching for. But I don't. I will begin this discussion in prayer and then open the floor to a question-and-answer forum." Yedaiah took a deep breath and prayed for the Holy Spirit to meet him in this room for support, "Heavenly Father, we know that the enemy is threatening us. We do not know what exactly he is up to, but it is apparent that his plan is to cause fear and doubt to slip into the minds of those that attend Mission Mind Academy. We ask that You stop him at every turn. Bring peace back into the hearts of Your believers and bless O Be Joyful in abundance. We believe that You are all-powerful and have already defeated the enemy. Thank You for loving us in and through our doubts and fears. Amen."

Hands started popping up all over the auditorium as soon as the amen was muttered. A young girl, barely eleven years old, was the first to be called upon.

"I want to go home. I am scared to be here any longer. I want my parents," she cried out.

As she spoke those words, the whole room erupted in shouts and sobs, yelps and blubbers, wanting the same thing. Doubt had definitely crept in.

Noah, being called on next, hollered over the cries, "You all are letting darkness win. If you leave now because of this one incident, he wins. Don't you get it? This is his plan. He wants to place doubt in our minds and hearts and hold us captive to fear. Don't let him win! Our mighty God is all-powerful and has already defeated the enemy on the cross. Just calm down and let's discuss what Christ would have us to do now."

Yedaiah felt the need to step in over the roars of his beloved students. "Quiet down, please," he almost begged. "No one is going anywhere. We will stand united, under God's reign, not succumbing to fear but living with the blessed assurance that God is with us in every trial and tribulation. All we are called to do is be still and know that He is God."

As chaos broke loose, the two dark ghostly shadows entered in. The auditorium doors slammed shut and locked themselves. Wind filled the indoor space, and echoing noises bounced off the walls. The student body silenced and froze.

"Here we go again," Kiera said with irritation to Grace.

"Just don't lose your cool. We have to stay calm," Grace responded with more strength than she knew she had.

That is when a shrieking voice began speaking. The voice was no doubt coming from the shadows, but it was hard to make out what it was saying over the windstorm brewing and blowing.

Straining their ears in determination to hear, they could make out a terrifying warning.

"Run away! Run far away!" it cautioned. "You have no power. I will defeat your efforts. Just run away. Don't come back here. I am taking over Mission Mind. I have a new mission."

It repeated this warning several times before unlocking the doors, flying down the hall and outside toward the Bones Abode.

Again, kids fled, screaming as they did, heading straight for their rooms to cower and sulk. Some had already begun packing their bags.

9

Where Are Our Pets?

Kiera and Grace both hunkered down in their beautifully decorated room. They were afraid but refused to give completely into
their fears. They sat crisscross applesauce at the foot of their beds,
snuggled up to their lovable pets, the ones that always seemed to
bring them comfort and peace. Roxy Ann was lying with her head in
Grace's lap, on her back, with her four paws up to the ceiling, to better expose her belly for a rub. Grace scratched it back and forth, back
and forth, thankful for her furry friend. Kiera had Speedy curled
up in a half-moon shape on her lap. Her sloth was so enchanting
and dependent on her. Wherever they traveled, Speedy was carried
in a front or backpack, in order to keep up with the troops. Her
slow, silky sloth enjoyed having his head gently petted and his arms
stroked in a slow, mild fashion.

The girls had strung twinkling white lights around their room,
had beautifully selected artwork hanging on the walls, and tried to
always have at least one fresh bouquet of flowers in a vase, on a table
by the window—something to brighten the room and give off a fresh
aroma. This was a favorite space for the two friends to spend time
together. They often stayed up late at night having meaningful chats,
and during the day, when time permitted, they enjoyed a card game
or two. They both loved laughing or giggling, depending on who
you asked. Their four best guy friends often teased them over their
loud girly cackling, calling them giggle boxes, when they would get
going and couldn't stop themselves, almost to the point of wetting
their pants.

This evening didn't bring on giggles, due to the creepy shadow, whispering doubts and threats to the entire school, but they were finding solitude in their private sacred space. Grace began a conversation about their pets.

"I am so thankful for the furry friends of ours, Kiera. They are all so wise, understanding things that we could never possibly get. For instance, every animal on O Be Joyful can read our minds, I'm convinced of it. They know how we are feeling and what to do to make our lives easier. I am extremely grateful for them."

"I agree one hundred percent," Kiera replied.

The girls kissed their two beloved creatures good night and climbed under their tightly tucked sheets for a good night's rest. But they couldn't help but to toss and turn, trying to fall asleep. After giving falling asleep a healthy shot, they simultaneously began chatting each other up, recalling everyone's chosen pet on campus, trying their very best to remember everyone's names and who went with each animal. It was great fun, kind of like recalling every Christmas song you can think of around the holidays.

They of course intimately knew and had hilarious stories about the Brown boys and Noah's pal, as if they were their own. They spent so much time with Noah's dog Turbo and loved to cuddle with Chunk the chipmunk, Rambo rabbit, and Malachi's squirrel Scout as often as possible. Animals were simply important to life. Attending Mission Mind Academy, and all the responsibilities that came with it, they knew the fur babies really did make the whole experience worth it. They most definitely took the sting off missing their families back at home. God blessed them with His miraculous creatures, and Grace and Kiera were genuinely grateful. As far as they could tell, everyone on campus felt the same exact way. Kids and staff were always loving on and spending time with their animal best buds.

The two girls talked for so long about the animals at O Be Joyful they both practically dozed completely off midsentence. Not saying good night to each other or purposefully closing their brains down. Enjoying sweet dreams, neither experiencing nightmarish, tainted with dark shadows or scary ghost ones.

*****

Noah, Matthew, Michael, and Malachi all agreed on playing a few rounds of cards, thinking it would be a good distraction from replaying the night's events over and over in their minds. Sitting in a circle around a spherical table that sat directly in the center of their sports-poster-walled, kind-of-messy-with-things room. Having an area that shared a wall with Mr. and Mrs. Brown's apartment, it was the only kid's dorm space with double bunk beds. It was also double the size of all the other student's quarters. But having four bodies instead of two in a single room tended to cause twice the stuff and twice the clutter. Clothing was somewhat strewn about, and sports gear tended to fill in every last square inch of empty space. They functioned well in their environment and got along surprisingly well, for all their diverse and unique personalities cramped together.

Sitting in four blue-painted chairs, a project Michael solely worked on the previous summer, because he wasn't a fan of the brownish color that they adorned prior, the boys cherished the evening. With each of their chosen pets lying dutifully and loyally under their chairs, content on being in the presence of their owners and best friends, life was pretty good. All eight of them as content as could be, considering the scare they encountered just hours before. As they proceeded to flip red or black card after red or black card, Noah brought up a conversation about animal races. "What do you guys think about having a contest with our animals? We could have them compete in different things, a whole bunch of different challenges, so that each animal has an advantage in at least one event. Or we could group them into animal type categories so they could have more specific challenges. What do you think?" Noah, always turning life into sports, was pretty proud of his brilliant idea.

Coming from like-minded Michael, he responded, "That's an awesome idea, buddy. We could even do a relay race. We could train them and run practices. I think we could fit it into our schedules."

Michael was an optimistic kid and was always up for trying new things, especially if Noah suggested it.

This got the conversation flowing easily between the four boys, everyone coming up with creative and super funny ideas. They laughed their heads off at the thought of some of the smaller and flying pets overcoming certain challenges and busted up when they considered a horse using fine motor skills.

The discussion continued for hours, time flying by, until the lights-out signal chimed in. With honest-to-goodness joy in their hearts, they each climbed into their personal bunks, calling their fur buddies up to their feet, in order to deliver them nuzzles, before laying their heads on their pillows and drifting off to a deep slumber.

* * * * *

Grace woke up unwelcomingly early. Having finished two glasses of water before bed, she needed to get to the ladies' room and fast. As she sat up to plop her feet on the floor and paddle down the hall, she glanced at the clock. It was only 4:35 a.m., and she was thankful that she still had the opportunity to sleep for another hour and a half before rising to start her day.

Returning to her bed, grateful to be cozying back down into her still warm sheets, she reached down to give Roxy a little love before getting herself back to sleep. Strangely, when she bent over to feel her soft fur, all that touched the skin of her fingertips was the patterned quilt that lay across her mattress. After doing her best to focus her eyes, she scanned them over the floor of her room, looking everywhere, but no Roxy. Where was that girl? She was usually such a good sleeper, always cuddled into a rather tiny ball for her size, secure at her feet, not moving an inch all night.

She strained her neck to steal a peek at Kiera's bed, thinking maybe Roxy had unusually decided to hunker down with Speedy for the night. But she couldn't even see Speedy anywhere. Where were they?

A panic started to rise in the pit of her stomach, a mix of butterflies and nausea in the belly, threatening to take her down.

"Kiera," she first whispered.

When her friend didn't budge, a loud yell came out of her mouth, "*Kiera!*"

"What?" Kiera sat up in a confused alarm.

"Speedy and Roxy are gone! Where are they? We have to find them!"

The girls threw on their slippers and robes and grabbed flashlights before they sped out into the hall, whisper-yelling for their pets, shining flashlights down long hallways and stepping into closets and bathrooms out of desperation. They even popped their heads and lights into other girls' bedrooms in hopes to find them. Nothing. Nowhere.

"What are we going to do?" Grace was almost crying at this point. This was possibly her worst nightmare.

All Kiera could come up with was "Let's get the boys. They will help us!"

"We are not allowed in their room," Grace reminded her.

"We won't enter completely in. Let's just sneak in the back door at the end of their hall and crack open their door. We can flash our lights on them and call them awake. Then we won't technically be entering into their room."

"Okay, that sounds good. Let's go, quickly!" Grace was beside herself.

They searched deep and wide for Roxy and Speedy during the walk to their best friends' room, coming up empty and even more desperate and discouraged than before by the time they arrived.

Again with the whisper-yelling, the girls called out, "Noah! Noah! Noah!" to no avail.

"Malachi! Michael! Matt!" the girls continued in unison.

Malachi sat up abruptly, groggy.

"Hello?" he called out into the darkness.

"Malachi. It's Grace and Kiera!"

They waited for him to process the information before continuing.

"Speedy and Roxy are missing! We are freaking out! Can you guys help us find them? Please!" Kiera cried to him.

Finally registering what was happening, he jumped into immediate action, waking the other three boys up and switching on the overhead light. As light filled the room, it caused all six of them to squint for quite a while, but when they finally could open their eyes wide, something horrible transcended.

Noah broke the tension, hollering, "Turbo! Rambo! Chunk! Scout! They are all gone!"

The Six-Pack went into full-blown terror mode, all of them dumbfounded and overwhelmed by the situation.

"Let's wake up Mom and Dad," Matt suggested.

With those five words, they all leaped into action, the whole bunch of them storming into Mr. and Mrs. Brown's apartment. And like a herd of buffalo stampeding, barged in their sleeping parents' master suite. They were all talking at once and so fast that no one could understand what anyone else was saying. Gabriel, still with his head happily on his pillow, used his deep, loud, commanding voice to be heard over them.

"Matthew, I only want you to talk. Everyone else needs to keep quiet so that I can understand what this commotion is all about. It's not like you all to come in here so curtly, interrupting your mother's and my sleep."

"Dad, our pets are gone. All of them. We don't know what to do. Help!" he managed to get out over his dreadful thoughts.

Gabriel and Keilah slowly arose, not appreciating the magnitude of the problem quite yet. But as they looked down toward the comfy, cozy beds that their precious pygmy goat, Gruff, and potbellied pig, Stout, usually spent the night in, they noticed them missing too.

Keilah asked the children to give them a few minutes, assured the kids everything was going to be all right and she and Gabriel will meet them in the living room shortly. She pulled on a pair of jeans and a T-shirt, threw on a pair of flip-flops, and looked wide-eyed over at her husband. He was getting himself dressed and riffling through his nightstand drawer for his headlamp and whistle he uses for flanks refereeing.

"Don't worry, Keilah, we will find them," he kindly said, knowing what was running through her mind even when she didn't speak a word.

Approaching the living room where six very frightened-looking children stood, because they were too anxious to sit, Keilah put a forced smile on her face. She knew that people fed off other's energy and wanted to always be a rock for her family, students, and friends.

"Let's rally, gang. Snag whatever lights you have and let's find these animals. But always first and foremost, grab hands and let's pray," Gabriel instructed.

Gabriel asked God for favor in finding their pets quickly and easily and thanked Him for being God. Then the eight of them headed out into the still darkness, lit by the moon. Sunrise was still over an hour away, so they were going to have to work with the dimness.

"Why don't we split up in groups of two so we can spread out and cover more ground," suggested Matt.

"Great idea!" Keilah praised her eldest son.

Scattering in four different directions, to be as productive as possible, they set off. Gabriel and Keilah headed to the north end of the property, where the balloon landing pad sat. Noah and Michael turned toward the east, where they would search the area around *Methuselah*'s dock. Matt and Malachi decided to head west to the end of the property hoping to avoid any visual of the Bones Abode, which left the south, where orchards and gardens covered the ground, for Kiera and Grace to comb through.

Grace and Kiera were holding each other's hands as they gingerly strolled through the apple trees. It was still pretty dark outside, and they were looking forward to the sunrise, to shed some light on their dire situation. They had already made their way through the herb garden, pear orchard, grapevines, cherry tree orchard, and were about to head over to the vegetable garden with the greenhouse in the center of it.

As they exited the last row of honey crisp apples, they plucked two off a low branch. They couldn't help themselves. They were big, round, and plump calling to them to eat. The girls were getting hungry doing all the walking and worrying. They started munching and crunching, which sounded extra loud in the still quietness that was otherwise surrounding them.

As they approached the vegetable garden, a couple of property bunnies hopped out of a lettuce patch and frightened the girls to a scream. Realizing what they had just seen and that there was no reason to fret, they continued scanning the property.

"I don't see anything unusual, and I definitely don't see Roxy or Speedy. Should we head into the greenhouse and have a look around?" Kiera asked her friend.

"Good idea. Let's head in through the front," Grace responded.

When they approached the door and reached out to open it, a wind started wrestling the air around them. The girls both froze, because it quickly went from a simple breeze to a full-on tornado-type wind tunnel, blowing so hard they couldn't get a grasp on the handle.

They were both blown backward toward the garden fence, where they clung for their lives, arms tightly wrapped around the top part of the white iron gate, feet flying behind their bodies as if they were holding on to the side of a pool and kicking their legs with all their might in the water.

Yelling at the top of her lungs, Grace relayed, "We are going to be sucked up into that tornado that is ripping through the cherry orchard and headed right for us. It's relentless, wiping out everything in its path."

"If we can make it back to the greenhouse and get in through that blasted door, we would be okay...I think," Kiera yelled back with equal force.

The girls climbed down to the bottom of the sturdy gate and clawed their way along the soil, grabbing patches of vegetables for traction. It was similar to climbing a ladder, only lying on the ground and with a strong wind current causing resistance.

Getting banged up by their young bodies being thrust up and down on the hard ground below them, they persisted. Making their way, although they didn't know how, once again to the front door of the greenhouse. They grabbed hands and pulled and pushed one another up to a standing position, leaning into the building so they didn't fly away again.

They used all four hands and twisted the doorknob, which did relent, and both girls flew to the ground, directly inside the greenhouse entryway. Using their four feet, they pushed with all the strength that they had left, the large door back into a closed position, causing the wind to die completely down.

This was when they were able to hear the whining, screeching sound echoing off the walls. It was so piercing that using their hands to cover their ears was unavoidable. Then the smell—the awful garbage scent filled the space around them. It was so raunchy it could be tasted.

Both Kiera and Grace were feeling hopeless. They scooted themselves together as close as possible, providing comfort for each other. Tears were pouring down their cheeks, mostly because of the smell and sound. But also because they still hadn't located their furry friends.

Just as they were beginning to give up all hope, the front door blew wide open, revealing the other six searchers. They, too, were looking beat up by the wind.

"I am so happy we found you two!" Gabriel said in a relieved voice.

The wind was beginning to blow away taking the noise and scent with it. As the world settled again, the girls got themselves to their feet and ran over to hug the others.

"That was insanity! Satan at work again. We still haven't even found our pets," Grace said with a frown.

The eight of them walked together through the greenhouse, making sure to look behind every stalk or potted plant, desperate for their animals. As they exited through the back door, unsuccessful, they gazed out in horror. The tornado had whipped and ripped through the whole vegetable garden, uprooting everything in its path. Peering beyond the iron fence, they all gasped. The orchards were demolished; branches, leaves, and fruits were scattered all over the ground.

"Oh no!" Grace cried.

"Don't worry, kids, and don't panic. God is in control, and we still have some animals to locate," Gabriel reminded them.

"Where should we go now, honey?" Keilah said to her husband.

"Well, we have searched every inch of the outdoors of O Be Joyful Gardens so far and have only found the dark shadow and a tornado. Maybe we need to check Mission Mind. It is very large, and the animals could be anywhere inside of the castle. I think it would be a good idea to stick together from this point on. Should the ghost decide to reappear, we will do better as a team."

So with Gabriel's instructions, they made their way through the torn-apart produce and upturned earth. It was a pitiful sight, but the scent of fresh fruit and vegetables made the situation manageable. And they all trucked on, heads held high, with new determination for the mission at hand.

Entering through the doors in Grow in Wisdom, they headed out of the library, down a few hallways, until they approached the locked door that led to the basement. Kids were not allowed in the basement due to spiders and bats and the chance for childhood shenanigans breaking loose. But Mr. and Mrs. Brown both possessed keys, and so this would be the first time the kids would ever experience the undergrounds of Mission Mind.

"How would the animals get all the way down there, with the door being closed and locked?" Grace wanted to know.

"I can't tell you that, but I do know that the things I've seen these past several weeks all seemed impossible until they happened, and I witnessed them with my own eyes," Mr. Brown answered.

Gabriel turned the key to unlock the handle lock and then the deadbolt. It was so dark looking down the stairs into the abyss, even with the flashlights they brought along to guide the way, only a foot or two in front of them was visible. Gabriel leading the pack, they fell into a single file line, held onto the handrail, and slowly put one foot in front of the other, descending into what they hoped would reveal their missing loved ones.

The staircase went on for eternity, winding this way and that, taking them deeper and deeper underground. Shuffling sounds on the ground and walls around them was a sure sign of the small critters that dwelled in the world below. Bat wings fluttered and occasionally brushed against them, bringing about a few shrieks and squeals from the kids.

Finally making it to the last step, they walked on to the solid flat surface of the basement. It was pitch-black, and their first order of business was to scan the walls with their hands to find a light switch.

All eight of them rubbed their hands quickly over every inch, coming up empty.

"Why are there no light switches down here in this dreary place?" Kiera wanted to know.

"I have only been down here one time," Gabriel commented, "but I could swear that there were lights down here, because I had a whole tour of the place when Mrs. Brown and I first arrived on campus. And I could see the whole thing. I should warn you that the basement is extremely large. It covers all the area of Mission Mind above us. It is several rooms and winding halls. It could be a long search."

"Until we can come across another light source, we will have to continue with the flashlights and get to searching. The less time we spend here the better," Mrs. Brown commented.

Keilah wasn't a fan of the dark or the basement. She had opted out of the basement tour upon their arrival at school. Although she was wishing now she hadn't. It would be helpful to have a blueprint mapped in her mind this morning.

"I know we said that we should stick together, but for time's sake, let's separate into two groups and head in opposite directions." Gabriel began, "Noah, Michael, and Kiera are with me. Grace, Matthew, and Malachi, go with Keilah. We can meet back here at the bottom of the stairs in thirty minutes."

After saying a quick prayer, they went into action, jogging to cover as much ground as possible in the half hour they had.

As she focused her personal light on every crevice she passed by, a multitude of thoughts were racing through Grace's head. She missed Roxy and wanted her back so badly. With the absence of her, the longing for her parents was amplified, causing her to question if she even wanted to stay at Mission Mind for all this madness. Home was sounding extremely good right now. Her baby brother or sister was due to be born within the month, and she wanted to be there to watch him or her grow up. Doubt about her purpose at Mission Mind was settling in her mind and thoughts. *Where is God when my dog is missing and my heart is broken?* And just as soon as that thought came to her, she felt shame. She was called to trust Him and love

Him and abide in Him and surrender to Him. Then she felt guilt about feeling shameful for questioning God.

Coming to a screeching halt, washing away the mental battle she was just fighting through, Grace called out to the other three, "Guys!" she said in a whisper. "Quick, come look!"

Coming up behind her, Matt, Malachi, and Mrs. Brown stopped and shined their lights, revealing Gruff, Gabriel's chosen goat. The little guy was lying in the far corner of an empty storage room, sound asleep, looking alone but very peaceful.

Keilah rushed over to Gruff and wrapped her arms around it, giving his head a little nuzzle. The pygmy goat opened his eyes and tilted his head into Keilah to hug her back.

She looked up at the children and said, "He doesn't seem to be in any distress. I wonder where the rest of them are. Let's bring Gruff along and keep going. We have so many more to find."

Gruff happily clopped his hooves behind them on the concrete floor as they made their way back into the dark hallway to scope out the rest of the underground.

Thoroughly searching five more rooms from top to bottom with their little flashlights as their only hope, discouragement again began to creep into their hearts.

"We have been looking for twenty minutes now and have only found Gruff. We have to meet the others in ten minutes. This stinks! Where are they?" Malachi cried out.

His mother calmed him a bit with a hug and then turned to the others and declared, "We will search the last several rooms in this wing of the basement and then head back to the stairs to meet the others. I am hoping and praying that they have located the rest of them. Now come on, we only have a little time left."

As Grace, Matthew, Malachi, Mrs. Brown, and Gruff walked back to the bottom of the entrance stairs to meet the others, their heads hung low. They had only managed to find the one pet. And a couple of their flashlight batteries had run out, leaving them in even darker circumstances. Turning the last corner of the basement wing they were investigating, they saw the other four and a bunch of furry friends at their feet.

Grace yelled out, "Yay! They found them! I'm so happy!"

When she reached them, she gave Mr. Brown a high five and then positioned her light on the floor to find Roxy. One pet after another was looking up at her with thankful tender eyes, but Roxy was not one of them. Where was Roxy Ann?

"Guys! Didn't you find Roxy? Where is she? I see all your animals here. Where is she?" Grace called out to anyone willing to answer her.

Mr. Brown came around to her side and put his hand on her shoulder. "Grace, we didn't find Roxy. I am sorry. She has to be here somewhere. As far as I know, we have all the missing accounted for, except for Roxy. Don't worry, she is around here somewhere. And we will not stop looking until she is back in your arms, covering your face in her wet sloppy kisses."

Grace was not too sure. "What if we can't find her? I will just die. I can't live without her."

Noah had felt like Grace was his sister since she climbed over the basket of the hot-air balloon and was feeling really sad for her. He also loved Roxy and decided to make it his personal mission to find her.

He walked over to her and gave her a big hug. "We will find her if it's the last thing I ever do, Grace. I give you my word"

"We can do one more scan of the basement together and then hurry back upstairs for another thorough search inside and out of O Be Joyful," Mrs. Brown suggested.

"Let's get going," Mr. Brown agreed.

Looking high and low, left and right, and in and out of every inch of the underground basement, they came up empty-handed on finding Roxy. As the eight of them, with a pack of furry friends, made their way up the dark stairway, they heard a noise. It was faint and sounded like a crying newborn baby.

"What is that?" Noah asked. "It sounds like an upset kitten. I think it's under one of the steps."

Sure enough, when Noah reached the top stair first, he pried back a stone tile backsplash and revealed an adorable tiny gray-and-white kitten with a soft pink nose. As soon as he picked up the fur-ball, put it into his arms, and snuggled it to his chest, it started purring in pure joy. The rest of the group crammed together around the top step and oohed and awed over the bundle of fuzz.

"What a cute kitten. I wonder where it came from. Can we keep going though? I feel like part of my heart is outside of my chest right now, with Roxy still missing. Bring that cute cat along and let's move on," Grace said to the rest of them.

Noah opened the door and led the way to the main floor of Mission Mind. By this time, school was buzzing with kids getting dressed and ready for breakfast and their day. Staff was bustling around the halls with coffee cups in their hands, greeting each other and the students. Pets were at the heels of their chosen owners, sticking to them like white on rice. The animals never wanted to miss out on anything. Everyone was in surprisingly chipper moods, considering all the happenings as of late. It was apparent that no one had been outside to see the damage to the property. And obvious that no one else was missing their pet.

Mr. Brown addressed the kids before they continued their Roxy Ann search, "We do not want to alarm the other children at this time. I want you all to keep quiet about what has been going on this morning. Please all head into the dining hall and quickly eat up whatever yumminess I am smelling from Mrs. Heathers. I will go over and talk with Mr. Hallohesh, and we will proceed with our search after. Remember, do not say a word about this to anyone. And, Grace, don't worry, we will find her!"

The kids quickly ran to their rooms to feed and drop off their pets and then sprinted back to breakfast. They sat down, prayed, and devoured their portions within minutes. They didn't talk to anyone or even look in anyone's direction so as not to alarm the others. The six of them were convinced that they couldn't hide the worry and desperation in their faces and voices. Better to just avoid everyone until this whole mess was settled and done.

After bussing plates, silverware, and juice glasses, the Six-Pack set their focus on finding Mr. and Mrs. Brown. Neither Mr. Hallohesh nor the Browns showed up for breakfast in the dining hall.

"Maybe we could check Mr. Hallohesh's office," Matt suggested.

"Good idea!" Noah responded as they all made their way in that direction.

Knocking upon arrival, no response came from the inside. "I guess they are not in there," Grace said, growing more concerned by the minute.

Kiera brought up a good point, "I bet they are outside combing through the damage that occurred. Why don't we go outside and search around the greenhouse? I am a bit scared to go back, but we have to find Roxy."

"Come on!" Grace was already headed for the outside door, feeling like there was no time to waste with idle chatter.

The kids picked up their pace when they got into the open air. Running down the path as fast as their legs could carry them. But when they reached the vegetable garden, they stopped dead in their tracks. They looked to one another in utter confusion.

"How could it be?" Noah said in shock. "I saw the destruction with my own eyes. It's like it never happened!"

The vegetables were all in perfect place, tucked tightly in the soil. Straining eyes into the distance, they noticed the fruit tree orchards were all upright and bearing much fruit. The uprooted trees were no longer uprooted. O Be Joyful didn't appear to have suffered wind or tornado damage. It was all as it should be. The kids were speechless, to say the least, walking around in trances, because they knew what they had experienced just hours before. But where was the aftermath? How did it all get put back in normal order?

Taking a quick peek in the greenhouse, which was also in flawless fashion, the kids wanted to see if Roxy was inside; they moved on when she wasn't.

Not knowing where to look for Roxy or Mr. and Mrs. Brown next, the worn-out troopers strolled down the golden path. The benefit of the path was that it eventually led through all of O Be Joyful, giving many spectacular scenes to gaze upon. Maybe they figured that if they took the path, it would lead to Roxy and normalcy.

"Where could she be?" Grace wanted to know.

"After we walk the whole path, if we still haven't found her, we can head back inside and search Mission Mind again. We didn't thoroughly comb everyone's room yet," Noah reassured her.

"Even after we do find her, which we will, we have an even bigger issue to address. Like how did all the animals go from our rooms and end up in the locked basement? And only Dad and Mom's pets along with ours were missing. Everyone else is completely oblivious to the happenings," Matt said, bringing up a good point.

"Maybe it's because we have been the ones seeking the Bones Abode out and the enemy knows us. That thought just shot a shiver down my spine. The devil knows us," Michael replied with a twitch of an eye.

Grace responded, "Yeah, the enemy might know us, but God created us and lives inside of us and all around us. He knows us better, and remember, He calls us not to live in fear but to trust Him. So let us trust Him and go find Roxy. I am going to say a prayer before we continue. Come join hands."

The Six-Pack stood in a circle, closed their eyes, and prayed over the day and circumstances. As they finished up and opened their eyes, they saw Mr. and Mrs. Brown walking in their direction. Mr. Hallohesh was right behind them, carrying a worried look on his face.

"Kids," Mr. Hallohesh called out, "we need to talk to you. Come have a seat in the shade."

With great apprehension, Noah, Grace, Michael, Matthew, Kiera, and Malachi moseyed over to their headmaster and Mr. and Mrs. Brown, believing the worst about what they were going to say but definitely hoping for the best.

Sitting under the shade of a large weeping willow tree, Mr. Yedaiah Hallohesh began, "My students, I want to applaud you for your brave efforts in bringing your chosen animals back to safety. I don't believe they were ever in real danger, but the mystery in how only your pets ended up in the underground still remains. Mission Mind Academy and O Be Joyful have, without a doubt, been under attack. The enemy is pushing in on us. Remember that we are God's chosen warriors, and Satan wants nothing more than to distract and frighten us."

Then looking directly at Grace, he continued, "My dear Grace, we have yet to locate Roxy Ann."

Before he had time to complete his sentence, the itty-bitty kitten that Noah spotted behind the top stair in the basement, which had been tucked into his shirt ever since, leaped out of his embrace, loudly meowing as it flew through the air. It then ran as fast as its little legs could carry it toward Mission Mind Academy. At this point, all nine of them were hot on its tail trying to see where it was off to or trying to catch it, one or the other.

As the baby feline reached the building, it began climbing the side. Noah made a jump for it but missed, as it shimmied itself at a fast pace up the side of the school.

"Where is it running off to?" Mrs. Brown wondered.

"It's so far up there now! Look at the little thing go! We should go to the rooftop access ladder and meet it at the top. I don't think it's stopping until it reaches the roof," Kiera commented to the others.

Mr. Hallohesh agreed with her, and so the whole group ventured into Mission Mind through the library Grow in Wisdom's entryway, which housed a hidden stairwell located behind a rotating bookshelf. Yedaiah pulled and tugged at this book and that, switched a few books around, and then finally plucked a large golden one out. He plopped it out on the table, opened to a specific page with a beautiful picture of color and design. The kids didn't know what they were looking at, but it was breathtaking.

Then in a loud, clear, bold voice, Yedaiah spoke, "Jeremiah 29:11, "'For I know the plans I have for you," declares the Lord, "plans to prosper you and not to harm you, plans to give you hope and a future.""'"

The moment Yedaiah finished saying the word *future*, the bookcase started a slow spin, making a 180-degree turn. The kids stared in amazement.

"That's awesome!" Malachi commented with great excitement.

"After you all," Mr. Hallohesh said with his hand stretched out showing the way.

Since there were three floors, excluding the basement, with exquisite very tall ceilings, the trek up to the top was a workout.

They climbed the stairs, one after the other, until they all reached the tip-top. Mr. Hallohesh took the lead again by squeezing past the others to get to the front of the line and right beside the door. He then opened up the grand golden book once more, this time to a different page with just as beautiful colors and designs as the previous one.

Next, in the same commanding voice, he declared, "Matthew 5:14, 'You are the light of the world. A town built on a hill cannot be hidden.'"

The dead bolt lock turned and unlocked immediately.

Last he said, "Philippians 4:4, 'Rejoice in the Lord always. I will say it again: rejoice!'"

With those words, the last lock unlocked, and the door swung wide open, revealing the magnificent rooftop.

Stepping onto the flat surface, everyone stopped to take in the glorious sight.

The lushest rooftop garden was full of plants and flowers of every color of the rainbow. Multicolored butterflies were fluttering their delicate wings, flitting in and out of the stalks, leaves, and petals. Grass was growing everywhere, like a new thick, soft recently laid carpet.

He was in awe but broke the attention that was on the garden when he spotted the miniature kitten making a dash over the rooftop ledge and bolt to the far end of the grandiose building they were standing on top of.

Noah yelled out, "Over there!" as he pointed in the direction where the cat was headed. "The kitten just ran that way. Let's go!"

In a single-file line, so they would fit down the narrow path through the garden, they jogged in anticipation. Noah was in the very front of the lineup, leading the mission, and was the first to feel relief when his eyes landed upon the sweet snuggly kitten nuzzled into Roxy Ann's fuzzy belly. The two were a sight for sore eyes. They were like old friends, the ones you have known your entire life.

When Grace saw the moment play out, she rushed over to the two creatures and tightly wrapped her arms around them. "I am so happy to see you, Roxy. How did you get all the way up here, girl? And how do you know this little kitty? I have so many questions! I love you, Roxy."

Mr. Hallohesh was so thrilled that Roxy was found safe and sound. He addressed the children and Mr. and Mrs. Brown, "I know there are many unanswered questions still here today. Ones that we will need to be diligent about praying over. But God has answered our prayers for the safe findings of all the missing beloved chosen pets. He has restored the property that was uprooted and upturned by Satan's attack, and he has brought us a new day with new promises. I am proud to be a child of God, and I am proud to be chosen to lead this academy. Praise God! Now, grab that dog and that cat and let's get off the roof."

10

Seattle

The following day was Saturday and a welcomed free day for the staff and students alike. There wasn't a flanks tournament on the schedule and not a single school-wide, organized activity planned, which was rare. So Gabriel and Keilah Brown decided to load up their boys, with Noah, Kiera, and Grace in tow as well, and head off on a field trip outing for the day.

They had agreed on getting an early start that morning as to maximize their time and efforts. The eight of them set their alarms for 7:00 a.m., got dressed, hugged their pets goodbye, grabbed granola bars and yogurt from the kitchen, and began their walk down the path to *Methuselah*'s dock. The birds were wide awake, chirping beautiful songs for the campus to enjoy. Butterflies flitted through the early morning air, finding warmth in the freshly risen sunshine. The children were feeling the same vibes as the wildlife, because a couple of them were humming, one was whistling, and another was singing softly, harmonizing gorgeously with the rustling leaves in the trees as she passed by.

Upon reaching *Methuselah*, Gabriel and Keilah entered first to get a few things set up, telling the kids to relax on the dock for a short period of time. Plopping themselves down in an almost perfect circle, Noah got the idea to bring back his childhood game of duck, duck, goose.

He stood up without mentioning what he was doing and proceeded to walk around tapped one head at a time. "Duck, duck, duck, duck, duck, goose!" He then ran as fast as his legs could carry him around the circle and back into his seat before Malachi had a chance to tag him.

Out of breath, Noah called, "You're it, Malachi!"

The youngsters played several rounds, laughing their heads off the whole time. Then they heard the call to go from Mr. Brown, grabbed their backpacks, and piled onto glorious golden *Methuselah*. Everyone loved the ferry. Grace was the only first-timer. She arrived via hot-air balloon and hadn't stepped off campus since.

"What an extraordinary ferry *Methuselah* is. She sure is a beauty. I have never seen such an amazing boat in my whole life," she rambled on.

Keilah smiled brightly at her. "Yes, she is a magnificent vessel. God made this ferry at the beginning, when He made O Be Joyful and Mission Mind Academy. It all sat here secretly waiting for us to inhabit it. God created, cared, and provided for it then, as He does now. Just as He created, cares, and provides for us. God loves us so much. He made us, died for us, and lives for us. Gives me the chills just thinking about His sacrificial love."

Looking at the children who were listening intently to her every word, she continued, "I get caught up in His love for us whenever I encounter His beautiful creations. And this boat is no exception."

Gabriel, who was driving the boat that morning, asked everyone to make themselves comfortable and take a seat. The quiet engine was running, and the worship music was playing on the numerous speakers sprinkled throughout the boat. They were all singing along with TobyMac by the time the ship was in motion.

Picking up just the right amount of speed, before they even reached the end of O Be Joyful, a large red heart appeared in the water just ahead of them.

"Hold on to your britches!" Mr. Brown joked.

And with that, the boat approached the heart, dipped down nose first, and made its way smack-dab through the center of it. Before any being could grasp what was happening, *Methuselah* was already docked next to her stone garage. Grace looked down at herself, noticing that her clothes were completely dry.

"What in tarnation?" she exclaimed in a state of confusion.

Matt, remembering his first time on *Methuselah*, commented, "Yeah, Grace, it's magical, isn't it? I can never tire of *Methuselah* and her ways. She takes care of us. She even keeps us dry. The most amazing boat you will ever meet in your life. I can guarantee you that!"

After anchoring the bobbing boat, Gabriel collected his belongings, reminding everyone else to do so also. There was a golden awning adorning the backside of the stone garage, where *Methuselah* was docked. Mr. Brown walked under it and pushed and pulled on a series of stones, which led to two golden handles appearing. The lion and lamb knobs were slipped upward on their tracks, and the wall opened up into the garage.

Again, Grace was the only one experiencing a first; sitting in the stone-walled little square building was a royal golden limo. She had never been inside of a limo and had always dreamed to.

"I think I have died and gone to heaven," she claimed with pure joy.

Matt, once more recalling his first time in the golden bullet, as he and his brothers dubbed it, told her, "This is the best limo you will ever experience. It is right up there with *Methuselah* in its awesomeness."

He gave her a nudge and double-eyebrow raise, letting her know that he was dead serious.

When they were all settled into the limousine, Gabriel climbed into the driver's seat and turned on the ignition. The vehicle purred like a kitten, as Keilah pushed the button on the remote, opening the huge wooden door behind them, revealing the real world of bustling Seattle.

"Where are we adventuring to first?" Michael called up to his dad from the very far back of the limo.

He responded, "We have a busy day planned for you guys today. First, we'll be making our way to the Woodland Park Zoo for a few hours of animal love, then having a picnic lunch at Lake Washington, followed by a tour of the Museum of Flight, Space Needle of course, and finally a spin around the big wheel, before we eat a quick bite and jump on *Methuselah* for the short trip back to Mission Mind.

Kiera was so excited. "That all sounds rad! I have never been to Seattle and have always wanted to go on the Space Needle. I see it in pictures all of the time, and now I will get to be on top of it. This is the best day ever!"

As the golden bullet flew through the streets, the Six-Pack took turns popping their upper bodies out of the sunroof. The breeze felt so good blowing warm wind over their faces. It was a glorious day to behold.

Grace was having the time of her life, so thankful for the warm welcome into this amazing group of people. She loved them all very much and was overcome with gratefulness that God would choose her for this awesome life. She was convinced that nothing could take the peace out of her soul. Not even that creepy, pesky dark shadow, who thoroughly enjoyed disturbing the harmony.

The day continued to flow smoothly. The zoo was a big hit as per usual. Even though O Be Joyful was essentially a zoo with animals from all over the world dwelling there, new habitats and scenery were a win. There was a lot of walking involved, hightailing it all over the place, not wanting to leave out a single animal spotting before exiting the park.

"I am starving, and my legs are throbbing!" Malachi proclaimed on their way out.

His mom responded patiently, "We have a huge picnic basket all filled up with yummy deliciousness from Mrs. Heathers to take to Lake Washington with us next. We are only about twenty minutes away."

"Praise the Lord! I am hungry too," Matt chimed in.

Everyone was in agreement that their tiny breakfasts on the go had been long worked off and refueling was a must.

Lunch was filled with food and joy. Everyone sprawled out on blankets while eating, but legs seemed to recoup quickly because as soon as bellies were full, everyone was on their feet again, exploring the beautiful surroundings.

When Gabriel gave a fifteen-minute, time-to-go warning, sighs were heard throughout the group.

Malachi, vocalizing his opinion once more, said, "Do we have to go? I like it here. We are having fun. Can't we just hang out a little longer?"

His dad, not much for negotiating with his sons, replied, "Nope! We leave in fourteen minutes on the dot, now. We have the whole rest of the day to get to."

Malachi was pleasantly surprised when he arrived at the Museum of Flight. He took in a stunning collection of aircraft, spacecraft, artifacts, galleries, and exhibits. He read facts and stories that embodied the past, present, and future of flight. He was beginning to feel a passion for flight in a way that he hadn't felt for anything. As they were coming to the end of their visit at the museum, Malachi closed his eyes and envisioned himself as a pilot, up in a plane, soaring with the eagles. He got so lost in his daydream that Mrs. Brown had to call his name three times to get his attention.

She told him, "I am glad that you enjoyed the Flight Museum, Malachi. We are headed to grab a quick snack before the Space Needle tour."

Malachi caught up with his brothers and friends, who had managed to already make their way outside and were apparently waiting for him. He was slightly embarrassed about zoning off and losing track of his surroundings, but the seed for flying had been firmly planted in that short visit to the museum. And for the first time in his rather young life, Malachi felt wildly passionate about living. He quickly recognized that he had been praying about a direction for his energy and thanked God in a silent prayer for being so faithful to spark an interest in aerospace.

The limo was all abuzz with anticipation of the Space Needle. The Browns had been there once before when the three boys were very young, but the boys had no recollection of it. Matthew remembered going there, but not a single detail about it. Needless to say, when the golden limousine pulled into a parking space, chatter was at an all-time high with excitement.

Purchasing tickets and riding the elevator to the tippy top of the needle, the kids found it more spectacular than they could have ever imagined. Pictures were being snapped at every angle, with every view of the 360-degree building. Kiera and Grace were taking a lap around together having a little light girl chat when Kiera spotted a hot-air balloon way off in the far distance.

"Look out there, Grace, we are so high up we are eye level with a hot-air balloon. Do you see it? It looks like a tiny marble."

"Yeah, I can see it. How awesome. Do you want to go down a level and check out the see-through floor?" Grace wondered.

"Can we stay up here a while longer? We only just got up here a few minutes ago, and I love it," Kiera pleaded.

"Of course we can! We have plenty of time. Plus, the others are still milling around up here too." Grace was enjoying herself as well.

The two girls sat down on a clear bench and peered out over the city. It was so interesting to see things from a bird's-eye view. So tiny and toy-like. As Grace turned her glare up to the sky, she saw the air balloon coming closer in their direction. It was floating its way toward the Space Needle.

Grace drew Kiera's attention to it. "Kiera, look, that hot-air balloon is heading in our direction. What if it hits the Space Needle? That would be insane. I feel like it is moving at an extremely fast pace."

Straining her eyes to assess the situation closer, Kiera agreed that it was heading their way.

The girls watched for a while longer as the balloon made its approach. It was only a short time later when Grace recognized the writing on the side of the balloon. It was the familiar Mission Mind crest symbol, and it was floating directly toward the girls.

"It's Transforming Transportation!" Grace clued Kiera in.

"What is it doing over here? Who is driving it? Can you tell?" Kiera was so curious.

Mission Mind's air taxi floated its way right up close to the top of the Space Needle. Now the two girls were eye level with Mr. Yedaiah Hallohesh. He was lipping some words, but they couldn't quite figure out what he was trying to tell them. His mouth was moving up and down, forming sentences, and his arms were shifting around, giving off signals.

After a few moments of confusion, Grace started making out what he was saying. He had his arms in a cradle fashion, rocking them back and forth, as if he was holding a baby. Then he pointed directly at Grace.

"That's it! I've got it. He is talking about my baby brother or sister. I wonder if my mom has delivered me a sibling! I have to find out what is going on. Are you coming?" Grace said as she made her way through a crowd of people, locating Mr. and Mrs. Brown.

"Mr. Hallohesh is here in the balloon. He is trying to tell us something. I think it has to do with my baby brother or sister. But I am not sure," she explained to them.

"Well, let's go meet up with him and see what it's all about," Mr. Brown replied.

Collecting the rest of the group, they hurried through a set of double doors and caught the next elevator down to the bottom floor. As the elevator door was closing, before a floor button had been selected, the familiar scent of the dark shadow reached their noses. Then the ear-piercing noise took over their hearing. The dark shadow had smuggled into the elevator with them and was flying in circles around their heads.

"Quick! Hit the button and let's get to the bottom floor stat!" Matthew yelled over the volume.

The eight of them covered their heads, trying to avoid as much of the offenses as possible, closed their eyes, and counted the moments until they could escape the torture. As soon as the elevator door slid open, they piled out, ran through the gift shop—the dark shadow hot on their tails—and found their way out of the front entrance. Mr. Hallohesh was standing beside the hot-air balloon, looking anxious by the time they reached him.

He turned his gaze to the shadow, realizing that it was present. Lifting both hands toward it, he proclaimed, "By the power of God, who lives within me, I order you gone!"

The dark silhouette flew straight upward until it disappeared in the sky. Waiting a few moments to make sure that it wasn't returning, Yedaiah directed his attention to Grace.

"Grace, your mom is in labor, and your baby brother or sister will be born soon. Your father called to let me know. He would like you to come as soon as possible. I am your ride, so climb aboard."

"Can Kiera come with me? I really don't want to be apart from her after all that we have been through together today," Grace begged.

Mr. Hallohesh agreed to let Kiera tag along, so the two girls gave the others goodbye hugs before loading up into the balloon for an even more exciting adventure.

"Who will watch over Roxy and Speedy while we are away?" Grace asked Mr. Hallohesh.

"I brought Roxy Ann along with me. She is waiting for you in the basket. And Mrs. Brown, would you be willing to care for Speedy?" Yedaiah asked Keilah. "He is not to leave O Be Joyful."

"Yes, I would be happy to!" she responded.

The Six-Pack had decided to have shared responsibility for the newfound kitten. One week with Kiera, Grace, Roxy, and Speedy and the next with the four boys and their furry friends. Fiona was the little gray-and-white kitten's name. She was sweet and adorable, adorned with a bubblegum pink triangle nose. It was still unknown where she came from, but her presence was a blessing to the kids and their pets. Roxy especially had taken a liking to the little furball. They often played around with each other, Fiona batting her tiny paws at Roxy's face and Roxy licking her up one side and down the other until the cat was good and soaked.

Grace was excited to be going home to Colorado to see her parents and meet the new baby. But she would miss the academy while she was away. The people and animals had all become so incredibly special to her. Mission Mind had become a second home, and she loved everyone there. As they made the climb farther and farther up into the air, Grace bent herself over the basket to give one last wave to her amazing brave friends and felt thankful that Kiera was able to come along and meet her family.

"I wish that Speedy could come along with us, Kiera. I know chosen pets are not supposed to leave O Be Joyful to preserve their unique lives, but I also know that you will miss him, and my parents would absolutely love him," Grace commented to her friend.

"Thanks. I am just excited to see Colorado and meet your family. This is so fun. Thank you, Jesus! I am blessed."

"Mr. Hallohesh, I don't want to ruin the excitement by bringing it up, but that was so amazing how you ordered the dark shadow away and it left. Do you suppose it will return? I am really praying that it won't ruin our visit."

"Kiera, the Holy Spirit sent the accuser away. He receives all the glory. As for if it returns, only God knows. We will pray that it doesn't and believe that it won't."

Mr. Hallohesh made small talk to pass the time and redirect the girl's minds, asking them about their date in Seattle. Both young ladies were having the best day but were a tad bit disappointed in missing out on the big wheel downtown that evening. However, the others would enjoy it without them, and they would have their own awesome adventure.

The balloon ride was a quick one, much faster than the last time Grace was on board. They managed to reach her mom and dad's mountain home within a couple hours of departing Washington. Her mother had planned on delivering her sibling in the comfort of their family home, and when Mr. Hallohesh landed the balloon, Kiera and Grace could both hear the loud screaming of an infant. It had arrived. Grace was a sister!

"I wonder what we had! I have to go see!" she cried as she threw her body over the side of the balloon basket and landed in a dead run for her front door.

When she opened it, her dad welcomed her with a warm hug and congratulated her on her baby brother, Nathaniel Boaz Hayes.

"I have missed you so much, sweetheart," Benjamin Hayes choked out, as he lifted his daughter up into his bear-hug arms, spinning her around and kissing her cheeks.

Roxy had made her way into the reunion fest, jumping and licking with full excitement.

"Roxy Ann is happy to be home too," he added.

He set his tall gangly-legged daughter back down on her own two feet and turned to introduce himself to the other one in the room.

"Hello, I am Benjamin Hayes. It's a pleasure to meet you," he directed at Kiera.

"Hello, I am Kiera Scott. It's nice to meet you too," she said politely.

"Can we meet Nathaniel?" Grace was anxious to know.

MISSION MIND

"Yes, he and your mother are together in our room, but I know that you won't want to miss a minute of your visit. You two scurry in there and take Roxy with you."

As the girls ran the staircase two at a time, Benjamin turned his attention to the hot-air balloon outside in his front yard. He went back outside and welcomed Yedaiah in for a visit.

"I wish that I could stay and visit for a while, but I have got to get back to the academy. There is some important business for me to tend to. I will be back for the girls at 6:00 a.m. sharp on Monday. I trust that will be sufficient for you?" Yedaiah said to Benjamin as he shook his hand and gave him a hug. "Congratulations on your bundle of joy. Sons are a blessing from the Lord. Praise Him."

"Thank you, Mr. Hallohesh. Safe travels home. God bless you."

*****

Mr. and Mrs. Brown decided to hit up Ivar's Seafood Bar for delicious bowls of clam chowder, chock-full of tiny saltine soup crackers. The boys were happy to devour their large bowls, which were made out of freshly baked sourdough bread, before inquiring about the ice cream shop down the street. They were all having a fantastic day, excluding the brief dark shadow encounter.

Keilah, temporarily shutting the boys down, commented, "We better let the huge bowls of dairy settle for a while before we take a spin around the big wheel. We can grab an ice cream cone after the ride before we hop back on *Methuselah*."

"This is the best day, Mr. and Mrs. Brown. Thank you so much for including me in it. I always have a lot of fun with your family."

Mr. Brown gave Noah a shoulder squeeze, responding, "Buddy, you are the fourth son to Keilah and me. We love you. I am thankful to know you and that our boys have you in their lives."

"Thank you!" Noah was grateful for his life.

"What do you say we take a stroll through Pike Place Market and check out the local goods before we make our way to the big wheel?" Mrs. Brown wanted to know.

"Let's do it, Mama." Mr. Brown signaled as he grabbed ahold of his wife's hand.

The leisurely walk through town was a welcomed one. It had been a long day so far, taking in every corner of the city, it felt like. Arriving at the market was just as exciting as the rest of the day's adventures. Colorful booths were everywhere, lining the walls of a gigantic building. The smell of seafood was in the air, with fresh catches of all kinds. There were purple clams, mussels, Shigoku oysters, jumbo lobster tails, Dungeness crab, Copper River sockeye, and shrimp cocktail. It was a pescatarian's dream. Besides edibles, there were also thousands upon thousands of fresh flowers. The Washington climate could produce an untouchable floral arrangement. Every color of the rainbow was spread out for the eye's enjoyment.

Michael and Noah found themselves at a portrait painting booth. The talented artist had crafted paintings of Arnold Schwarzenegger, Michael Jackson, and President Barack Obama. He hit the nail square on the head with all of his pictures. The boys were feeling inspired and wanted to hang one of themselves on the wall of their room.

"Do you think my brothers would sit for a drawing?" Michael asked Noah.

"I bet they would. We could pool our money together and hang it in our room." Noah started getting excited.

"That's what I was thinking," Michael said as he started scanning the room for Matt and Malachi.

The four boys, with Gabriel and Keilah standing by spectating, sat dutifully still for the picture. After it was finished and dry, it was rolled up, stuffed into plastic, then placed in a protective tube for safe transportation.

With their new artwork in hand, Noah, Michael, Matthew, and Malachi stepped back onto the streets, ready for the promised big wheel ride. It would be a perfect ending, besides the ice cream cone still to come, to their already picturesque day.

It was getting later, and the sun was just starting to begin its journey down and out for the night. The Seattle Great Wheel was only minutes away from Pike Place Market, so Noah and the Brown family made their way, via foot. The wind had picked up a bit down by the water, causing a wave of goose bumps to move through them. Grateful that they had brought along sweatshirts and jackets, they pulled them on and started to jog, in hopes of bringing their heart rates and temperature up.

Standing in line for tickets, the four boys started goofing around, pushing and poking at one another. Matthew and Malachi had been together nonstop that day and were pushing buttons to get under each other's skin by this point of their adventure together. Matthew slipped in teasing comments, sure to rile up his passionate little brother. As the two siblings continued, the situation escalated in volume and, in the digs being thrown, to the point of a physical brawl.

"Get off me!" Matt called out to his heated-up brother.

Malachi had lunged at Matt and taken him to the ground. Sitting on top, straddling his older brother, he was determined to do a little physical harm.

"I'm tired of you always teasing me! I am going to teach you a lesson." Malachi called back with his elbow burrowing into Matt's side. He also dug his knee into Matt's thigh, causing a painful charley horse. This was his opportunity to one-up his irritating oldest bro.

"Ow! That hurts, Malachi. Quit it!" Matt, who was already exhausted from their early morning and long day, used the last of his strength to strong-arm Malachi off him.

Mrs. Brown was used to this sort of thing between her two sons. Michael, excluded from the brother wars, was not one for stirring up physical trouble in their house.

She was not in the mood after the long day they had been in to deal with her sons' immaturity and ended their spout of anger with quick, powerful words.

"You two better get your heinies off the ground right this instant and stop all this nonsense. You have both been incredibly blessed today and are acting spoiled and ungrateful. Look around you. We are in a public place, and you guys are down there as if you were toddlers."

Matthew was embarrassed, now that he had given into tormenting his little brother and causing a scene.

"I'm sorry, Mom. I let him get the better of me."

Malachi, who was still red in the face and shooting dirty daggers at Matt, also apologized to his mother and asked for forgiveness.

Mrs. Brown, feeling worn out in general, replied, "Let's just get ourselves onto this giant wheel and enjoy the last of our outing. We need to get back to *Methuselah* and O Be Joyful before too long. I need to get some rest."

"Good idea, Mama, and here are the tickets. We are next in line," Gabriel said as he came upon the scene.

Gabriel, Keilah, Matthew, Michael, Malachi, and Noah climbed aboard the wheel, glad to get off their feet for a short period of time and take in the magnificent city and waterfront views. The skyline was beautiful, and the clean crisp air was a sure sign of fall's soon-to-be arrival. The boys had settled down and were not on the hunt to bug one another any longer. Things were back to peaceful, and Mr. and Mrs. Brown were thoroughly satisfied with their day trip with the kids.

"It's too bad that Grace and Kiera had to miss this. They would have loved it," Noah commented.

"Yeah, but I would be willing to bet that they are having a great time in Colorado and meeting Grace's new sibling. I kind of wish that we could have all gone with them. I have never been to Colorado," Michael added.

Malachi had other concerns on his mind and wanted to address them.

"I just hope that the dark shadow doesn't follow the girls and give them heck while they are away. It seems to have our numbers and be determined to spook us."

Gabriel wanted to put his children's minds at ease, even if he wasn't so sure himself.

"The shadow is gone. I believe it will leave everyone alone for now. Rest easy, kiddos."

The Great Wheel made its 360-degree turn a couple times before their gondola stopped at the very top. They hung for quite some time, causing questions on what exactly was going on. Michael peered his head over the side to try and get a glimpse of the situation but couldn't see anything out of the ordinary.

As he was telling the others that he couldn't spot anything suspicious, the gondola started moving again. It began slowly and spinning at a snail's pace, but as it continued around, it began to pick up quite a bit of speed. They were all sitting back in their seats, taking it all in, expecting the ride to be over shortly. Almost thankful that the ride was about to end, it was time to grab an ice cream scoop and get back to Mission Mind Academy.

"Does anybody else feel like we are gaining speed? I am starting to get dizzy. How many spins does this thing give you?" Matthew was beginning to feel queasy.

Mr. Brown, who, too, was feeling woozy, said, "I have a hunch that this is not normal for this ride. I wonder if it is experiencing technical difficulty."

"I have to get off this thing. I am not feeling very well," Noah chimed up.

The wheel had picked up so much momentum it was spinning like a race car tire, doing its thing on the track. Everyone inside of the gondolas was holding on for dear life, as the gigantic circle continued rotating at Mach speed.

"What if this wheel dislocates from the frame? I can see it rolling all over Downtown Seattle." Noah was slightly hoping.

"No! I need off, now!" Malachi shouted.

Hair and bodies were flying around and around uncontrollably. Screams and cries of fear were echoing throughout the windowed boxes full of riders. From the ground, the Great Wheel crew stood stunned, unable to figure out what had gone wrong or what to do to make the madness stop.

Having a sneaky suspicion, Gabriel shared it with the others, "I believe that Malachi was right on. The dark shadow has returned to torment us, my dear family. We will get off this thing, but can you all help me be on the lookout for it? As we spin, focus your eyes on the surroundings. If we spot the creep, we can try to outwit it."

Gabriel spoke a fast and loud prayer over the commotion, handing the burden over to God, before the six Jesus-loving people concentrated on catching sight of their enemy.

Sure enough, the tormentor was quickly identified by the group. It was apparent that it had multiplied itself, because even at the fast pace they were spinning, they could clearly see three black threatening forms swarming only their specific gondola. To make matters worse, the wind was picking up, which in turn was causing the wheel to sway as it spun.

The boys were becoming very frightened and were huddled together on the metal floor. It helped block out the wind a smidge, and they were able to put their heads together for comfort and silent prayer.

Just as the dizziness from the circumstances got to the unbearable point for everyone involved, the enormous wheel leaned toward the water in the initial descent of its crash landing. Falling at a fast rate, the Brown family and Noah secured their hands by gripping the legs of the benches. Mr. Brown used a free hand to pop open the window at the top of the collapsing, dangling cart, in hopes of jumping or climbing out upon impact.

There was no time for instruction. With the weight of the wheel loaded with people, the crash came hard and fast. The Seattle Great Wheel was finished in a matter of seconds, falling with a huge tidal wave-sized plunge. Once standing on Pier 57, now lying sideways, sinking in Elliot Bay.

After the crash, Mr. Brown immediately checked in with his members, making sure that there were no signs of major injury. Every one of them suffered a few cuts and bruises, but nothing serious or pressing. Gabriel thanked the good Lord above for His protection and then gave instruction to climb out of the preopened window. The wheel was sinking at a rather alarming rate, and they knew that they had to exit before it was all the way swallowed up. It would be an easy swim to the dock should everyone escape in time. Gabriel and Keilah both knew that as soon as they were all safe on solid ground, the two of them would return to the water to help anyone else in danger.

Soaking wet, out of breath, and in shock, the boys sat on a dock bench, waiting for their parents to return from helping other victims. So grateful that they were all alive, Michael looked heavenward to give thanks to the Most High, and as he did, he caught a glimpse of three black specks, not soaring like birds but swarming like pests, off into the distance.

"Guys, look!" He pointed to the devils he spotted. "It accomplished what it set out to do and now it's out of here. Stupid Satan!"

Noah, who was infuriated by them, voiced his mind, "Those jerks are going to get what's coming to them. They are bullying us, and I know that God won't stand for it. He promises in Exodus 14:14, 'The Lord will fight for you; you need only to be still.'"

"You are so right. He fought for us today. All we did was be still and hold on to the seat in the gondola. The whole wheel came tumbling down, and He kept all of us safe. It's amazing to see God's power play out in such a real tangible way," Matthew piped in.

Mr. and Mrs. Brown approached the boys, exhausted but wearing smiles. "Everyone is going to be all right. No serious injuries," Mrs. Brown reassured the worn-out boys.

"Come on, guys, let's get to *Methuselah* and get back to O Be Joyful. I could use the comfort of familiar surroundings."

It was a unanimous decision to take a rain check on the ice cream stop. All appetites were lost, and home was the only priority. They made their way back to Mission Mind on autopilot. No one had the energy enough to be social or conversate.

The day date in Downtown Seattle turned out to be a wild and crazy event, starting with the fact that they left campus as a group of eight and returned with six when it was all said and done.

Pulling into the dock at O Be Joyful, Gabriel, Keilah, Matthew, Michael, Malachi, and Noah had never been happier to be home. They all climbed out of *Methuselah* and headed straight for their animals for a little bit of TLC.

✳✳✳✳✳

Monday morning when the girls walked into their first study class of the new week, they spotted Noah and the Brown boys in the far corner of the room playing a card game of some sort, waiting for the bell to chime them to their seats. Grace and Kiera had just arrived back on O Be Joyful campus. They had been expecting

Mr. Hallohesh to pick them up earlier that morning in the Rocky Mountains of Colorado, but when the balloon landed a hundred yards from Grace's family home, Mrs. Heathers was the one who emerged from the air transportation.

Mrs. Heathers did not have an explanation to where Mr. Hallohesh was. She simply stated that she was put on the task of their retrieval. She explained that she had placed her kitchen assistant staff in charge of breakfast that morning along with lunch prep so she could be free to pick them up and return them before their first class started. She did a great job of completing her goal, because Kiera had time to reconnect with Speedy before her daily commitments. How could they make several states in only a handful of hours? No one would ever know.

"Hey, friends!" Kiera said to the boys upon their approach.

"Oh, hey! Welcome back," Noah replied, feeling surprisingly glad to see them. After the Saturday evening they experienced, he couldn't wait to fill them in on the Giant Wheel ordeal.

"How is your new sibling? Boy? Girl? What did you have?"

"It's a brother. Nathaniel Boaz. He is absolutely perfect. I get to go see him one weekend a month. I already miss the little bundle," Grace told him with a full heart. She had always wanted a brother or sister, and God had heard her and answered her in the best possible way.

There were congratulations all around and then the "get your tushy in your seat" bell rang, redirecting their attention.

As they were cleaning up their cards, Noah told the two girls that they had major stuff to tell them about Saturday in Seattle, after they left from the Space Needle.

"Utter chaos took place!" he relayed. "We will tell you all about it at lunch today. Want to eat outside? We can picnic. I don't want others hearing about it. It will freak too many people out."

11

Confidential Assembly

Yedaiah Hawthorn Hallohesh was the only headmaster to ever lead Mission Mind Academy in the sixty-six years it had occupied students and staff. He arrived at the young ripe age of sixteen and had fearlessly sacrificed his life for the calling God had bestowed upon him. It was an exceptionally good life that he lived, serving alongside the men and woman of God that reside at O Be Joyful. In his wildest dreams, as a small imaginative child, he could have never pictured the grand purpose and privilege that would be entrusted to him.

He had witnessed several groups of classmates raised up in the Lord, who now were back out in the real world living meaningful lives in a number of ways. Lots of Mission Mind Academy graduates went off to far ends of the world to combat Satan and spread the love of God, while others stayed in the country or even stateside in Washington serving the Lord. One such alumnus was Mieke Everly.

Mieke had departed the academy after graduation in the year 2000 and had not stepped foot back on the property for nearly nineteen years. So when she was working with YWAM (Youth with a Mission) in the city of Seattle and received a golden-colored telegram with the Mission Mind Academy emblem on the envelope, she was nervous and excited at the same time. She missed O Be Joyful and the teachers. She mostly missed Mr. Hallohesh, who was a father figure to her like she had never experienced before. They both had the unfortunate childhood of group homes and foster care. Her parents left her at the hospital the day she was born and never returned for her. Hallohesh was like a dad to everyone that entered into their glorious campus.

The gold telegram that Mieke received came via tandem bike deliverer, by a thirty-something-aged brunette gentleman with kind bright-blue eyes. He pulled up to her place of work and lingered outside for, in her opinion, way too long a time. One of her work friends pointed him out, wondering why he was hanging out on the front porch by himself, standing stone-still, peeking in the windows.

"He has something in his hand, and he looks like a deer caught in the headlights," her coworker said to her.

Mieke agreed that he was acting rather peculiar and decided she would be the one to confront him on his loitering. She closed the lid of her laptop and pushed her wheelie chair away from her desk. Standing up, she made her way to the front door. As she approached, the tall dark man made eye contact with her through the front window and wouldn't let go of her gaze. Distracted by his stare, she managed to open the door and step onto the covered porch.

"Excuse me, sir. Is there something that I can help you with?"

"Yes, thank you. I am in search of a Ms. Mieke Everly. I have a telegram to deliver to her," he told her, still staring at her in a way that made her feel like he could see her soul.

"I am Mieke Everly. What is it that you have there?" she replied, avoiding eye contact.

"I am not sure. It has been a very strange day on the job indeed."

"Well, let me have it and see."

She was anxious to find out what it was but was also ready to get the stranger on his way. He made her nervous the way he continually stared.

Handing her the letter, the delivery guy helped himself to a rest on the love seat lounge, sitting in the shaded corner of the porch.

Mieke broke the seal of the envelope, peering at the unfamiliar person lingering at her place of work. Why didn't he just hand her the letter and then leave? Deliverymen were not supposed to hang around after they made their drop. She would get to him later. For now, she needed to know what Mission Mind was sending her.

Her eyes grew wide as she unsealed the letter and pulled it out. It was folded up into three sections, and when she flipped back each side to hold it open flat, very fairy-like golden dust floated off into the breeze and away down the street, leaving behind the distinct smell of cinnamon, oranges, and star anise.

Doing her best to ignore the ongoing stares from the mysterious carrier, Mieke focused her attention on the reading of the note.

They were requesting her presence!

It read,

Dearest Mieke K. Everly,

Mission Mind Academy has immense respect for the efforts that you put into daily practice at Youth with a Mission. We are so proud of all your hard work and accomplishments since graduating from your training for the Lord at O Be Joyful Gardens. We believe that all Jesus followers grow in Christ until the day He brings us home. However, the strengths that He has displayed in you throughout the past nineteen years have greatly impressed us. We have a brand-new, top-secret job opening that we believe God has prepared for you. If you are willing to accept this mission, after you have spent time with God in prayer and petition, come to Methuselah's *dock at precisely 8:00 p.m. tomorrow.*

WARNING: You must not share this letter or information with anyone! It is important that we keep this between you and the few MMA members that know of the assignment!

If you hear God urging you to pass on this assignment, please destroy this letter immediately and forget about this offer.

We have missed you and look forward to teaming up with your spiritual giftedness.

Gripped by Grace,
YHH

Mieke's heart was pounding so hard and fast in her chest she thought that it would be a wise decision to find a seat and take some deep breaths. Looking up to locate said seat, she spotted the stranger that she had completely forgotten about, still resting on YWAM's shaded porch.

Annoyed by his presence and desperate for his departure, she huffed, "Sir, thank you for delivering me this telegram. Is there something else that I can help you with?"

"I am sorry! I just can't bring myself to leave. I have so many questions. For instance, I am not a delivery man, but I was still approached by a persistent elderly man, clearly over the age of a hundred, to deliver this to you. I explained to him that I was only out for a ride on a borrowed bike to deliver it to my sister, but he didn't seem to care. He just looked me square in the eyes and told me that the Lord, God, Most High had chosen me this day for this task. He then handed me the letter, patted me on the shoulder, and told me that Jesus loved me and died for me. He told me that I should surrender my entire life to the one who made me. Then he turned around and walked off as if it never happened.

"So here I sit on this covered porch, at a Jesus-loving mission. And all of a sudden, I am questioning all the beliefs and choices that I have made in my thirty-seven years of life."

"Wow, that is a big day! What is your name? You already know my name, or I would introduce myself," she replied to him with a softer heart than she had before she knew his reasons for sticking around.

"I apologize for being so intrusive and, dare I say, rude. I am Gideon Jethro, and it's a pleasure to meet your acquaintance," Gideon said with a sigh as he stood up and held out his hand to shake hers.

She took his hand into both of her own and shook it profusely as she stared deep into his eyes. "It's very nice to meet you, Gideon Jethro. You have a very strong Christian name. Did you know that?"

"I can't say that I did," he replied, a tad bit embarrassed.

He was not the self-conscious type on the regular, but someway, somehow, everything about the happenings of the day left him upside down and unrecognizable to himself.

Feeling an overwhelming urge to invite him in, Mieke asked ever so politely, "Would you like to step inside for a few minutes for a glass of water or a cup of coffee?"

"Thank you, I think that I would."

The two of them walked through the front door, and Mieke showed Gideon to the group break room / kitchen, where she poured him a glass of water and a mug of freshly brewed coffee.

"The cream and sugar are over against the wall on the condiment table, if you would like to add to it. I don't care for anything in my coffee. Dark and strong are my only requirements," she mentioned, thinking it was a weird bit of information to share with a perfect stranger.

She realized that she was stalling. God had given her an internal burden to talk to this man about who God is and what He did for him. So she invited the letter deliverer to sit down at YWAM's community table for a conversation.

He began by reiterating what he had mentioned on the porch to her. "Okay, so this very old person, who was he, do you know?"

Mieke wasn't positive, but she had a sneaking suspicion that it was Joshua Zane behind the letter and choosing this specific man to get it to her.

"Yes, I think I might know who he was," she confessed.

"The things he was saying really resonated with me. Now, I don't know what's up and what's down! Somehow, I feel like my life is about to change dramatically. When I woke up this morning, all I had planned, beyond my work, was to deliver this here bike to my little sister so she can take my nephew on a tandem ride tomorrow morning. Now I can't seem to get back on the seat to take it to her. You must think me terribly bizarre!"

"I don't think that you are bizarre. I believe that God brought you here for a reason. Would you like to talk about the things that are going on in your head right now? More appropriately, what is happening in your heart?"

She really didn't want to scare him away by getting too personal, but he definitely appeared to need a friend to talk to.

"Can you tell me about Him?" Gideon sheepishly asked.

"Wow. Well, where do I begin? I guess in the beginning. So in the beginning, God created the heavens and the earth. He made all of the animals and then He created man. God loved Adam and Eve, and they loved Him. One day Eve was in the garden of Eden and was tempted by the devil to sin. With this choice, sin entered the world and hasn't left since. We all sin, unfortunately. Over time the world became so corrupt that God sent His Son Jesus into the world to bear our sins for us. He, being the only blameless one to walk the earth, took our sin upon His back, even to the point of death on the cross. He did not stay dead, however. Three days later He rose and appeared to many. He said that He is the way, the truth, and the life. No one comes to the Father except through Him. That if we believe in Him, He will bring us to the mansion He is preparing for us right now in heaven, where we will live with Him forever in His kingdom. Then He ascended to heaven, promising to leave His helper on earth until He returns, the Holy Spirit. The only decision you have to make is to invite Jesus into your heart with a simple prayer, and He will never leave you or forsake you.

"I recommend reading the Bible. A good place to start would be one of the four Gospel books: Matthew, Mark, Luke, or John. They will give you a foundation of who Jesus is and what incredible gift He has given to you. John 3:16 says, 'For God so loved the world, He gave his only begotten Son, that whoever believes in Him, will not perish but have everlasting life.'"

Looking at Gideon, Mieke was praying that she didn't freak him out with her explanation. She had often shared the good news with others, but this man and situation seemed more significant or God-ordained in some way.

"God really does offer the gift of everlasting life to all that simply choose to accept it. It's so easy yet so deep and powerful and real. When He moves into your heart, you become a new person. He transforms you into the version of you that He intended when He made you."

Gideon was drawn in by what he was hearing. "I have never heard anything like that before. No one has ever explained who God is or how He could be for me in my entire life. I really appreciate you,

Mieke, and it was a pleasure meeting you. I have to go and get this bike to my sister's house. Thank you for the coffee and water."

And with that, he was out the front door.

Pouring herself a warm-up on her coffee, Mieke wondered what would become of Gideon. She lingered in her thoughts and prayers for some time about him, hoping that she made an impact or at least lessening his confusion over who God really is. Then the memory of her letter from Mr. Yedaiah Hallohesh came flooding back like a raging river. This was quite the exciting day she was having, and the thought of focusing her mind back on the paperwork at her desk seemed unattainable. So Mieke decided to pack up her belongings and head back to her apartment for the day. The long walk through the city to her apartment would afford her some quiet time to collect her thoughts. She said goodbye to her work friends and left.

✳✳✳✳✳

Flanks practice had ended for the day, and the Six-Pack were pooped.

"I just want to lie around and veg out until bed. These daily doubles of morning and evening practices are wearing me plum out!" Kiera voiced her opinion. "What say you all about playing some cards tonight after our showers? We could meet in the common room at the end of the hallway. I never see anyone there. We should be able to snag a large table."

"I'm in!" Grace agreed, followed by the four boys, who were always up for cards, board games, or dice, really anything competitive.

"Okay, let's meet back in thirty minutes. Bring your pets to hang out. They have been cooped up for too long today. I am sure they'd love the company," Grace added.

The Brown brothers popped into their parents' private living room to let them know where they were headed for the evening, and then the four boys made their way over to the common room. They found Kiera and Grace already settled in shuffling cards, Speedy and Roxy Ann playing with animal toys under the table.

"Shanghai is the name of the game tonight, boys!" Grace giggled. "And prepare for a beating because I am feeling downright lucky."

Malachi, who was not someone to let anything rest, sparked back, "I am going to mop the floor with your luck tonight, Grace, mark my words!"

She laughed as she began dealing each player eleven cards. Sorting and organizing the cards in their hands, the kids happily relaxed, thankful for a couple hours of free time.

After playing three out of the seven rounds of the game, they called a break. The girls shuffled off to the bathroom and then to refill their water bottles at the fountain. Malachi jogged back to his room to grab a sweatshirt and granola bar. Matthew hung around the common area to keep an eye on the pets, especially the newest member, kitten Fiona, the cutest handful you ever did see. She had a way of getting into everything, like climbing curtains, sampling plant leaves, teasing the other animals by batting at their faces and tails, and finding very sneaky hiding places to discretely snooze in. The kids, who loved having her and sharing her, wound up tying a bell to her collar to simplify the daily hunt.

Noah and Michael stepped out onto the back porch, meant for devotion time, for some fresh air, which looked out over a beautiful flower garden, adorning a path through the center, with white lanterns illuminating the multitude of colors, even in the darkness. The two best buds leaned over the railing to get a good look into the night.

"Did you see that?" Michael wanted to know.

"See what?" Noah obviously didn't.

"I saw someone walk past a lantern down there in the garden by the red roses. There it is again! Who is down there?" he said, pointing in the direction of the movement.

Then voices sounded in a faint whisper causing Noah to tune in to the location from which it was coming from.

"I hear people talking, but I can't make out what they are saying."

Both boys strained their ears and stilled their bodies to eavesdrop on whoever was below them.

"I still can't hear. Come on, Michael, let's go downstairs to the lower porch, off Grow in Wisdom, and see if we can hear any better."

Slipping inside, careful not to make a sound because they didn't want to alert the garden dwellers of their presence, the boys filled Matthew in on their adventure just as the other three were returning for round four of Shanghai. Including them also in the mix, the six overly curious kids, with their chosen pets in tow, trotted to the library.

"Hurry!" Michael urged. "We don't want to miss them."

The library was surprisingly full of studiers for the hour before mandatory room time. Most kids got any and all homework done directly after school so they could be free to enjoy campus and friends before room time and then lights out an hour later. But this was a rarity. Most of the tables were jam-packed with students.

Kiera got a sinking feeling in her stomach. "Are we missing something? Is there a big project due or a huge test coming up soon? Why so many people?"

Noah walked up to one of the tables and asked his friend Jeremy what he was up to. He mentioned an announcement about free extra credit points to anyone who spent their time, between the hours of 6:30 p.m. to 8:30 p.m., digging deeper into their classroom-assigned homework.

"That is bizarre! Did any of you hear about the extra credit assignment? I have never heard of that deal before. It doesn't even make sense." Noah was suspicious.

The five of them had not heard about the library study that night, but they unanimously agreed to find a different location for spying on the garden whisperers. They decided to use the porch off the kitchen, because it was close enough to hopefully hear, and they shouldn't run into any kitchen staff or students, being after-hours and all.

So tiptoeing down the hallway, with their pets still alongside them, they prayed that they wouldn't run into anyone and have to give an explanation of their mission. Finally, arriving at their destination, the kids crouched silently and strained their ears once more. They all sat close-lipped, while they intently listened to a conversation that was clearly not meant for them to hear.

It was Mr. Yedaiah Hallohesh and Mr. Joshua Zane having a very private discussion. The kids' eyes grew wide as they stumbled into a hidden exchange, learning of a secret quest. It was only a few minutes after they had gotten to their spy spot that Hallohesh and Zane ended their dialogue and started walking directly toward the back door of the kitchen. At this point there was no turning back and hiding. Counting the pets, their group totaled thirteen, and there was only a minute before they would be approached.

Noah, thinking on his feet, opened and slammed the kitchen door to draw attention to them. He walked up to meet his two superiors and greeted them. "Good evening, Mr. Hallohesh, Mr. Zane. We were just stepping outside for a second of fresh air and a pet potty break. Fancy running into you two," he said with a bit of quiver from nerves in his voice.

"Hello, Noah. Guys. Girls. Animals. It's about time to wrap it up for the night. Please head back inside after the bathroom break. It will be room time shortly. God bless your evening," Yedaiah answered for both him and Joshua, hoping the kids hadn't overheard anything. The Six-Pack were always looking for adventure and, dare he say, trouble. He would hate for them to catch wind of the new happenings and get themselves into a dangerous situation.

The kids wished Mr. Hallohesh and Mr. Zane good night as they watched their two trusted leaders walk away.

"I can't believe it," Kiera commented when she was sure that her superiors were out of earshot. "Who is Mieke, and why do they hope that she will take on the Bones Abode? I have so many questions!"

"Slow down, Kiera. We weren't exactly supposed to hear that private conversation. Maybe we should just forget about tonight and pretend we don't know anything." Matthew was really hoping his brothers and friends were not going to pursue their own investigation. He had had enough of the Bones house and the shadow. "I say that we just pray fervently over whatever it is that is going on and leave it at that. God is able to protect and save us from anything and everything. I am really hoping you all aren't thinking about starting more trouble."

It was clear that Malachi had already gotten fired up inside. "No way, big bro! We have been a part of this attack from day one. Dare I say that we were the ones that stirred him up? Satan is lurking, and we need to nip him in the butt!"

"Why am I not surprised that you want to go and get in the middle of something that doesn't pertain to you. Just leave it. I am begging you," Matt reiterated.

"It does pertain to me and the rest of you too. We have a right to know exactly what is going on around here. It's our home!" Malachi said, looking into each of the others' eyes for confirmation.

"I agree with Malachi," Kiera proclaimed. "I overheard Mr. Joshua comment to Mr. Hallohesh that he hopes Mieke decides to meet them at *Methuselah*'s dock tomorrow night. We should be there!"

Michael, who was on the fence about the situation, chimed in, "It's risky business sneaking around. Maybe we should disclose to Mr. Hallohesh that we overheard his private conversation."

"I disagree with that. Mr. Hallohesh won't be pleased with our eavesdropping and fibbing about it. And he most definitely won't let us be a part of whatever it is. We need to find a way to get to *Methuselah*'s dock without actually riding on *Methuselah*. Or maybe we could be stowaways below deck." Malachi had begun his scheming and would be hard-pressed to be talked out of the adventure he was already envisioning.

"I just wish that I knew what Hallohesh was hiding," Noah whispered. He was all of a sudden exhausted and desperately wanting to end this crazy evening. "We should all just get to our rooms for the night. We can individually pray over the situation, and I am sure by morning, God will shed light on the matter. We can continue this discussion then, what do you say?"

Grace, for one, was on board with Noah. "I agree one hundred percent! Come on, Roxy, it's time for bed. Good night, boys. Kiera, are you coming?"

"Yes, I am coming." She picked up their pink-nosed kitten in one arm and Speedy in the other as she stepped through the kitchen door.

The girls were thankful to be in some solitude. The threats from the stinky, spooky, shady shadow were going to continue. But they were not going to waste another minute of the night worrying about it. They prayed together before retreating to their beds, hoping for deep slumber and uninterrupted rest.

The Brown brothers and Noah picked up the cards from their hallway hangout spot earlier that evening, before taking themselves and their animals to bed. None of them said a word to each other, all in deep personal thought. The kids all understood that whatever they decided to do with the information they overheard, they would do together, whether they left it alone or started a full-blown investigation of their own. They were a team through and through. They were the best of friends and children of God, and He would guide them in all their steps.

❋❋❋❋❋

By 5:00 p.m., the time when Mieke locked up the office and headed home for the evening, she had made up her mind to meet Mr. Hallohesh and Mr. Zane at *Methuselah's* dock. She had prayed fervently over the matter since finding out about the opportunity, and now every bone in her body told her that she was to accept whatever Hallohesh had for her. Why was she the one he had chosen? All her former classmates from Mission Mind were strong believers and warriors for God. She still had several lifelong friends from her years spent at O Be Joyful. So why, then, her?

Mieke knew that she was the type that couldn't handle the unknown. If she was to forgo tonight's meeting at the dock and remain in the comfort of her recognized world at YWAM, the wonder of what could be would torment her forever. She had to rise to the challenge God was bringing her way.

So caught up in her thoughts, she jumped off her feet, high in the air, with a shriek, when she saw him. Sitting in the same love seat at the far corner of the porch was none other than Gideon Jethro. What was he doing here? Collecting herself from the scare, she strolled over to the bench upon which he sat.

"I am so sorry for startling you, Mieke!" He felt bad and embarrassed now for being there, wishing that maybe he didn't come.

"Oh, it's okay. I was deep in thought and not aware of my surroundings. What are you doing here?"

She was surprisingly happy to see his face again, but she was also in a bit of a hurry. She wanted to get home, get changed, and get some dinner before her dock appointment. Her nerves had picked up over the evening's upcoming events, mostly due to the fact that she had to keep it a secret. She always called her best friend before making big decisions, to have someone pray with her and to encourage or discourage her from certain things.

"I was wondering if you have free time for a cup of coffee with me right now. I have something I was hoping to talk to you about." He sounded desperate.

She had to think about it for a moment. She didn't really feel like she had the time, but maybe he would accept a rain check. That didn't feel right though. God would want her to make time for him. She figured she didn't have to go home and change clothes, and she could grab something to eat wherever they went for coffee. It wouldn't be the first time that she had consumed coffee cake and an almond milk chai for dinner.

"I do have a couple of hours to spare. I have a commitment at 8:00 p.m. though. My favorite coffee shop and café is a couple blocks down. Would you like to go?" She felt good about her decision to make time for her Mission Mind, golden letter, and tandem bike delivery guy.

"Thank you! That would be great. It will be my treat, for your time and kindness. I really appreciate you, Mieke." He wanted to compensate in some small way for acting so weirdly, two days in a row, on her work's front porch.

"I will quickly feed the meter to give me a few more hours of parking and then we can stroll that way," Gideon stated.

Mieke's mind was racing, just thinking about the meeting at *Methuselah's* dock. She hadn't stepped foot in the stone garage for years, and the thought of seeing the golden ferry again was a thing of excitement. How was she going to focus her attention on Gideon for the next couple hours if all she could concentrate on was herself and how her life was about to dramatically change tonight?

"I'm all set with the parking. Are you ready to walk?" Gideon approached her, ripping her from her own thoughts, again.

He was sure good at disrupting her internal conversations with herself. She had only known him for a short twenty-four hours, but in that small amount of time, he had managed to infiltrate her heart. She knew from deep within that God had brought him to her for a reason, and she would obediently step into whatever that reason was. If she had learned anything in life, it was that God always has a purpose and will never leave your side as you walk through that purpose in life, if you invite Him.

Jesus loves me.

Mieke reflected on that truth for a moment, abundantly thankful for Him.

She said a silent prayer as she strolled alongside Gideon, "God, I surrender myself to You, that You may use me in a bold way for Your kingdom. Your works are mighty in power, and I desire Your will for my life. I lift up this time with Gideon. May he see Your face when he looks into mine. I also ask that You remove my fears and doubts regarding the golden letter. I am Yours, and You are mine. Amen."

The two new acquaintances made small talk on the way to the café. It was actually mostly Mieke doing the chatting. She tended to babble on and on when she was nervous about being around new people. By the time they reached the front door of the charming coffee shop, she had explained her entire job description at YWAM. Gideon didn't get a word in the conversation but was thankful to get to know a little about her. He felt drawn to her passion and strong sense of purpose, something he didn't grasp the feeling of.

Gideon was a real estate agent, who did very well for himself financially but lacked real joy in the work that he pursued. He was attached to his phone seven days a week, leaving him feeling like he had no personal life. Now that he was thinking about it, he had no spiritual life either. Just work and sleep. How had his life become so mundane?

Mieke led Gideon to her favorite booth in the middle of a huge window, displaying a view of bustling Seattle foot traffic.

"It's entertaining to sit and sip coffee while people watching. Tinted glass is an added bonus when you are trying to be incognito with your stares." Mieke giggled.

"Yeah, I can see how getting caught by all the passersby would really throw off your eavesdropping game," he replied, smiling from ear to ear.

After their orders were placed and their coffee cups had been filled, they rolled up their sleeves to get down to the reason for the visit. Mieke could sense Gideon's hesitation, so she thought it wise to break the ice.

"So I can see that there is something spinning around in your head. Why don't you just go on and be out with it."

"Okay then...I am having a hard time formulating my thoughts into words, which has never happened to me before. I have always been so sure about myself. But yesterday everything changed. I don't know how or why it changed, but I am different today than I have ever been. I also can't find a reasonable explanation for coming to you about all this, but here I am, opening myself up to you."

She knew what was transpiring. "I fully believe that everything that happens has purpose. So the fact that you are sitting here with me is one hundred percent meant to be. What is it about yourself that has changed since yesterday, if you don't mind me asking?"

"It was after that elderly man—what was his name again?"

"Mr. Joshua Zane."

"Yes! It was when Mr. Zane picked me to deliver this letter to you. He chose me on purpose, and ever since, all I can think about is this God you and he speak of. I was up all night tossing and turning in deep thought. When I would finally doze off, my vivid dreams of someone saving me from a pit of fire would startle me awake. I just don't understand what to do. And you were, strangely enough, the only person that I wanted to talk to about it."

Mieke was overcome with raw emotion over what Gideon shared with her. God must be calling him to Him. How amazing! She took a moment before forming a response to pray and ask God for guidance. Then she looked into Gideon's eyes and gave him a warm reassuring smile.

"God made you, Gideon. He loves you and wants you for His own. He desires a relationship with you. He wants to be your everything. All He asks of you is that you choose Him by asking Him into your heart. He sent His Son to die for your sins, and He wants you to accept his gift of freedom. Sin equals death and separation from God. His work of dying on the cross washes the sin away and restores us to Him. Ask Him into your heart. Claim Him as your Creator and Savior, and you will have eternal life with Him. It's that simple yet so profound. The depths will only be understood when we go home to heaven."

He sat stunned for a brief second, contemplating what he had just heard. He believed everything she had just explained. Why before had he never known of this Savior? Yet today he felt as if he had known Him forever.

"I am not sure why today is the day, but I do believe."

She sipped her coffee, letting all that God was revealing to Gideon sink in. Then their food arrived, reminding her of how hungry she was, having skipped lunch that day due to nerves over the Hallohesh meeting.

She asked her new friend, "Would you mind if I bless our food before we eat?"

"I wouldn't mind at all," he replied as he followed her lead by bowing his head, clasping his hands together, and closing his eyes.

She began, "Father, thank You for my new friend, Gideon Jethro. Thank You for opening his eyes to who You are and calling him to You. You are amazing in every way, and I trust You completely. Bless this food to our bodies. Also, please be with me during my meeting tonight. Amen!"

As they were digging into their café dinners, Gideon decided to ask what he was now wondering. "What kind of meeting do you have tonight, if it's okay to ask?"

"It's with some professors from the school I attended way back when. I am a bit nervous, but it's nothing special enough to talk about."

Why had she prayed aloud over this matter? It had piqued his interest, and it was forbidden to discuss with others.

Not sensing her hint to avoid the conversation, he continued probing. He figured that if he asked questions about her, he could avoid any more talk about himself. Being vulnerable was not Gideon's idea of a good time, especially around a beautiful stranger.

"Your old professors make you nervous? Are they mean?"

"No, they are not mean. I just haven't seen them in a very long time." She was doing her best to be vague.

"What are you meeting them about?" he kept on questioning her.

She wasn't sure how to get out of the conversation about her meeting without being blunt. "If you don't mind, I would rather not talk about the meeting this evening. Why don't we stick to the reason that we came here in the first place?" She couldn't hide her irritation or the uncomfortable tone in her voice.

"I am so sorry, Mieke. I really didn't mean to pry into your life. I just feel more at ease talking about anyone but myself, if I'm being honest."

And he meant it. However, he was now curious about the meeting she was attending after she left the coffee shop. Why wouldn't she just humor him and give him a few details?

"I didn't mean to be rude. I am thankful to have met you yesterday. I hope that we can be friends." She did enjoy his presence.

The two continued talking about spiritual matters for a long while, Mieke only slightly distracted every few minutes by checking the time on her phone. Gideon could feel her tension and urgency over what he could only guess was her professors' meeting. When the time finally did come to leave, he paid the bill as promised, opened the front door for her, and walked her back to YWAM's front porch. They exchanged phone numbers for friendship's purpose and said goodbye for the night.

Gideon walked to his truck, climbed inside, started the engine but didn't pull out onto the road. He just sat there thinking, occasionally stealing a glance at Mieke getting herself ready in her car to leave.

He watched her drive away and, without giving it a second thought, pulled out behind her, a few cars in between them. He wasn't planning on following her, but his steering wheel kept turning in the exact same direction as her white Jeep Wrangler with its black convertible top.

"God, I know that this is the first time I have talked to You, but will You please guide me this evening? I am thankful that You brought me a friend in Mieke, and I don't want to screw it up tonight. Amen."

*****

After the last class period of the day's bell loudly rang to dismiss the students from school, the Six-Pack gathered in the hallway that they had played cards in the previous evening. Pulling the plush oversized golden-colored sitting chairs into a circular shape, the kids cozied up for a little powwow.

The most excited one, Malachi, opened up the conversations. "Okay, so how are we going to get to *Methuselah*'s dock on the Seattle side tonight, you guys? I have a couple of ideas, but I wanted to know what you came up with today."

Matthew chimed in first, "I thought that we should eat dinner then maybe play a practice pickup game of flanks. We could invite one of the other teams for a scrimmage."

"What are you talking about, Matt? You know good and well that we have to be at that secret meeting. This has everything to do with us, and I am semioffended that Mr. Hallohesh left us out of the excitement." Malachi was getting all heated up. "What do the rest of you say? Are you afraid, or are we doing this?"

Looking around the group, Malachi noticed a sparkle of interest in the others' eyes. They wanted to go too. He could tell. He decided that this would be a good time to share with the others what he had formulated in his brain that day during Mr. Vand's lecture.

"The way I see it," he began, "is we could stow away below deck of *Methuselah* a half hour or so before Mr. Hallohesh is set to leave. There are a lot of compartments to hide in, and we could keep extra quiet."

Kiera, poking holes in the plan, exclaimed, "The problem is that we don't know exactly what time he is departing. I never heard an exact time for the meeting, did any of you?"

Everyone shook their heads no.

Malachi continued, "We can try to pry it out of Mr. Hallohesh, maybe by asking him if he wants to play cards with us tonight and see what excuse he gives for saying no. Or we could simply ask him what he is up to tonight in a nonchalant way. We will see him at dinner, and we can just open up the conversation and see where it goes."

Matt, still not convinced, said, "I don't think that you are capable of having a nonchalant chat, Malachi. What if we all look and act guilty while digging for information. I, for one, am not interested in getting into trouble."

Although reluctant, Noah's heart was telling him to go. "I feel like we need to be there. I prayed about it so much, and every time I do, I hear the word *yes* in my heart. I believe that we were meant to overhear Mr. Hallohesh and Mr. Zane's discussion and we should pursue this. Malachi, I think that the only way for us to go is the way you mentioned. Outside of just telling Hallohesh that we know and want to join in, it's our only option."

The group of tight-knitted friends unanimously concluded that they would stow away that evening. While at dinner, the six of them set up shop at the teacher's table. They claimed that they wanted to sit with Mr. and Mrs. Brown, that the three brothers just wanted to dine with their parents. But Mr. Hallohesh was the reason, and he was conveniently seated right next to Gabriel. As the meal continued, the questions arose about everyone's plans that night. Gabriel and Keilah shared with the boys that they would be taking an evening stroll along the golden path of the property "because the weather was magnificent," their mother said.

No one else at the table volunteered their arrangements after supper, so Malachi took it upon himself to start singling teachers out. Mr. and Mrs. Vand told him that they were having a low-key movie night. Several other teachers were getting together for a game of trivial pursuit. Mr. Joshua Zane finally gave up the information that he was attending a meeting in the city. Mr. Hallohesh mentioned that he would be going with Mr. Zane.

The kids scarfed down Mrs. Heathers's pot roast and side salad, bussed their dishes, and scurried off to their rooms to care for their pets before the evening of adventure began. They had all agreed on bringing Roxy Ann along, being the only critter safe to leave O Be Joyful, and always a helpful one, she would provide a bit of protection for them. They had planned on meeting in the pear orchard at 7:15 p.m., hoping that they would have enough time to stow away before their superiors arrived and departed.

Sure enough, the coast was clear to enter the boat, undiscovered, at the time they had planned. Slipping in *Methuselah*, they shimmied downstairs to the lowest deck for quality hiding spots. Securing Roxy in a closet with Grace and Kiera, they had brought treats to bribe the pup quiet.

Footsteps above them clued them in on Hallohesh and Zane's arrival. As still as stones and as quiet as a mouse, they hid, as the engine purred and the boat began to move. Michael had a little peephole in the cupboard housing him. As soon as *Methuselah* lunged forward, he caught a glimpse of his mom and dad running toward it. Their hands were raised and waving, and he could see their mouths yelling something. Did they see the kids enter the boat? He was so nervous that his parents knew, but he couldn't inform the others without risking the professors', who mingled above, attention.

When *Methuselah* landed at her designated dock and the kids could hear Hallohesh and Zane departing it, they quietly climbed out of hiding.

Michael, disturbed by the sighting of his parents, clued the others in.

"You guys, I saw Mom and Dad running to *Methuselah* as we were leaving! Do you think that they know?"

"I bet they were just trying to catch Yedaiah and Joshua before they left. Maybe they had to talk with them about something," Malachi chimed in, in denial of the possibility that his parents knew.

"I bet that they saw us enter and were trying to stop us," Matthew, who was the least excited to come, replied to his little mischievous brother.

Kiera wasn't in the mood to debate whether or not they had been spotted. She just knew that unless they got off the ship ASAP, they would lose their opportunity to find a good hiding spot at the dock.

The kids secretly slipped out of the boat and made their way to the back of the stone dock, stashing themselves in a wall of bushes. Roxy kept up with them, staying completely quiet. She enjoyed the meat treats she was receiving by the minute.

The Six-Pack would just wait and see what this was all about. Inside, they were all thinking that whatever this meeting was better be worth all the trouble they were going through to be a part of it.

*****

Mieke pulled her trusty jeep into a parking spot near *Methuselah's* loading dock. As she walked the sidewalk to the familiar stoned building, she thought of all the fond memories she experienced years and years ago there, loading and unloading it for big-city adventures.

Saying a quick prayer before she arrived at the huge wooden garage door, she took a deep breath and then knocked. Immediately the door rose; she spotted the two familiar faces of Mr. Yedaiah Hallohesh and Mr. Joshua Zane. They looked just as she remembered them but almost twenty years aged. If it was possible, they appeared wiser than ever in their advanced ages.

"Ms. Everly, it is so wonderful to see you. You have grown into a fine young woman. We have missed your antics over the years at Mission Mind," Mr. Hallohesh told her as he wrapped her up into a papa bear hug.

"I have missed you two and Mission Mind also," she responded as she moved over to give Mr. Zane a hug too.

*****

Outside the walls of the stone structure, the kids had seen a woman approach. After they watched her knock and then enter, they began to formulate how they would eavesdrop. During their debate, Grace spotted a man lurking around the garage. He came only a minute or two after the woman but didn't enter as she did. He was pacing the building, keeping a safe distance but also keeping a watchful eye on it.

141

"Guys! What do you think that man is doing here?" Grace asked them with a shaky voice from nerves.

Malachi, who wasn't in the mood for surprises, took it upon himself to go ask.

"Hello, mister. Is there something we can help you with? You look lost."

Feeling embarrassed, Gideon answered. "I...umm...I was just making sure a friend got here safely."

"Well, did they?" Malachi asked with an attitude.

"I am not sure. I saw her enter this garage, but I don't know if she is safe. She doesn't know that I am here. I had dinner with her earlier and got the impression that she was very nervous about some meeting with her former professors tonight. She wouldn't share any details, so I followed her. Who are you?"

Malachi, annoyed by the intrusion of the stranger, warned, "We are here on a secret mission, and if you are outside pacing the building, you will blow the cover for all of us."

"I am very sorry to intrude, but I am not leaving until I know that Mieke is safe. My name is Gideon Jethro. Would you mind if I crouch in the bushes you are hiding in with you?"

Rolling his eyes, he said, "Sure."

Back in the shrubbery, the others were confused over the man Malachi returned with. After a brief explanation, they all agreed that they better find a new location to gain information. They were out of sight but weren't in a good spot for hearing what was going on. Tiptoeing out of the bushes from the back of the garage, they crept to the sidewall for a better angle. This was a smart move because as soon as they quieted themselves from the transfer, they could hear distinct voices coming from inside.

Gideon didn't get to close. His goal was not to stalk her for information; he just wanted to make sure she was all right. The Six-Pack, he now understood, did want in on every detail going on inside. They strained their senses, and when one would hear something of interest, they would step back and discuss it. Gideon started growing fascinated and concerned over some of the conversations the children were having—something about a dark shadow and a secret mission. There was mention of a covert school of some sort, leading Gideon to think about the professors Mieke mentioned from a past school she attended.

None of what was happening made sense and got even weirder when the kids heard a noise from inside the stone building. He watched as they gave him a wave goodbye and ran for a golden ferry that he had failed to notice prior. How could he have missed that incredible ferry? Then the large wooden backdoor of the garage opened up to reveal his existence. He was standing there like a deer in the headlights. He spotted Mieke, a wise-looking older man with a white beard, and then he recognized Joshua Zane from the day before. The three of them stared at him.

"Gideon!" Mieke shrieked. "What in the world are you doing here?"

Feeling vulnerable, yet again, around Mieke, he almost outed the six kids he had just seen prowling around spying but thought the better of it at that moment.

"I was worried about you. You were so distracted and nervous at the diner, and I had to make sure you were okay."

"So you followed me?"

"Yes, I did."

Joshua approached Gideon and, while shaking his hand, mentioned, "It's great to see you again, son. Have you been thinking about what we discussed yesterday?"

"I have, sir. In fact, I came by Mieke's work this afternoon to discuss it with her. She mentioned having to go to a meeting with professors after our date, but I had an uneasy feeling deep down and had to follow her to be sure she was fine."

"That is very honorable of you. Hello, I am Mr. Yedaiah Hallohesh. It's a pleasure to meet your acquaintance," Yedaiah said with an outstretched hand.

"Good to meet you too. I am Gideon Jethro."

Mieke was feeling anxious about the entire situation she was in. She had a lot to think about and really wanted to flee for solitude.

Mr. Hallohesh and Mr. Zane said their goodbyes and climbed aboard the *Methuselah*, praying for Mieke and Gideon as they did.

They both had an inner feeling that Gideon was going to be a huge part of their dear Mieke's life.

As they started up the engine on the boat, Joshua heard voices down below deck. He crept down and opened several cabinet and cupboard doors to reveal the busted Six-Pack, Roxy Ann along with them.

＊＊＊＊＊

"I am completely fried from my insanely eventful day today, Gideon. I don't really know how I feel about you following me, but I guess I should thank you for making sure I am safe. All I want to do is go home and relax for the night."

"May I walk you to your jeep?" he said, hopeful.

"That would be great," she surprisingly replied.

As they walked together, side by side, Gideon told her about the six kids and dog that were lurking and spying on her meeting. He assured her that he didn't listen in on her discussion, but the kids put their heads to the wall, heard everything, and were formulating a plan to involve themselves.

"Who were these kids? I will have to let Yedaiah know. Thank you for telling me."

"Also," he continued, "when the garage door began to open, they hightailed it to that amazing golden ferry and climbed aboard. So they are on there right now with Mr. Zane and Mr. Hallohesh."

She reassured him, "If they are on that boat, they will be found out. Don't you worry about that. Yedaiah or Joshua, they have eyes and spies everywhere." She giggled at the thought.

When the two arrived at Mieke's jeep, Gideon asked her if he could take her out for a cup of coffee the next day. She hesitated because of the already complicated life she was about to step into but then agreed to meet him two days later instead. She needed tomorrow to be between her and God, without distraction. Gideon did intrigue her, however, so she just couldn't resist his offer.

12

Special Task Team

O pening the door for Mieke, Gideon braced himself, taking several deep breaths as he stepped through the door of the same coffee shop café they had met at before. It had been two days since the meeting at the dock. He had to further discuss the children and get to the bottom of the mystery meeting. It was all he had thought about for the past forty-eight hours and just simply could not wait a moment longer.

The two were seated and immediately joined by the server for drink orders. Gideon went with water, not wanting to amp up his nerves any farther with caffeine. Mieke ordered a double shot of espresso, needing the extra boost after a long day at YWAM.

"So, Gideon, how is everything in your world?"

"Things are good. I had something I wanted to talk to you about. It has to do with the dock the other day."

Again, the server returned for food orders. They both relayed what they wanted to eat, Gideon hoping to not lose his nerves. He had to get this off his chest and fast. He was feeling a heart attack coming on, or at least a panic attack. He didn't like holding things in, so the past few days had been sheer torture. He had thought about just calling her and talking about it via phone but decided that in-person conversations were always best.

"I am sure that looked kind of strange seeing me having a meeting in a garage down at *Methuselah's* dock."

"Who is *Methuselah?*"

"It's just the name of a ferry."

"The golden ferry? The one I witnessed the six kids dive into after they finished eavesdropping on your conversation?" He had to just throw it back out there.

"Back to those snooping kids, are we?"

"Well, there were six of them and a dog hiding in bushes when I arrived the other day. They most definitely will be involving themselves in whatever it is you have going on. The strangest part for me was the dog that was with them."

"I wonder who the kids were. Probably students at the academy. That would be my only guess."

"What academy are you talking about? The one with a golden ferry and pets and sneaky conversations? I am all sorts of confused right now."

Mieke was in trouble. Gideon was asking way too many questions. In all her life, she had been able to keep Mission Mind on the down low, but it seemed her new friend's curiosity would not be allowing for that any longer.

She wondered how to explain the school to him. Would he even believe her if she did? What would she say? She giggled aloud, just thinking about it. Yeah, so there is a hidden school that you can only reach via air or water portal, where everyone loves the Lord. A place where miraculous things happen on the normal and everyone on campus has a chosen pet. He would think she was straight delusional. She would have to keep her explanation vague, but even then, what would she say?

Wondering about the kids, Mieke resigned that Mr. Hallohesh had found and confronted them. She would have to remember to ask him about it the next time she spoke with him. And as if on cue, as soon as the thought passed by her mind, a telegram in gold arrived at her table from their server.

She said, "Pardon my interruption, but a deliveryman just handed this to me, telling me to get it to you. Are you Mieke Everly?"

"Yes, ma'am, I am. Thank you," Mieke replied as she received the golden envelope.

She looked up at Gideon to see how he might be responding to the exchange. He was bewildered, that was for sure. This was going to be harder than she thought, having a friendship with someone with such curiosity over her life. Especially the part that she had always kept close to her heart and a secret from others.

"Okay, Mieke. I must say, I am beyond intrigued at this point. What can you tell about all this craziness? I have got to know something. Curiosity killed the cat, is all I am saying, and I am the cat in this scenario."

Mieke closed her eyes for a moment to lift a quick plea for help from God. He would have to guide her words if He wanted her to divulge any information. Opening her eyes, she looked down at her shiny golden letter, really wanting to tear it open and see what it contained.

"Aren't you going to open that letter? It's gold in color, just like the one Joshua Zane asked me to deliver to you. It must be from him again, don't you think?"

Looking down into her own trembling hands, she slowly tore the envelope flap open and pulled the folded letter that was inside, out of its protective covering. She turned her gaze toward Gideon and made eye contact for a long while before unfolding the message.

Gideon, even more interested than her in the note, commented, "Don't be nervous. You don't have to tell me what it says, but don't you think that whoever had that delivered to you knew that I was here with you and distributed it anyways?"

"Yeah, I guess you're right. I am being followed and found all over the place these days." She was only half joking.

As she read, her eyes grew wide, and her mouth unintentionally dropped to an open position. Scanning the page, Mieke let out a gasping for air sound, followed by a deep sigh, and then finally a deep breath in to refill her lungs. She had already been in a bit of denial over the original plan that was laid out to her just two days earlier at the dock, but the new turn of events was just way too much to grasp. They included several other people that she didn't even know. How was she going to complete her mission with all the distractions and opinions that came with working in groups of strangers?

On a more immediate note, what was she going to say to Gideon? He was just sitting there sipping his water, staring her down. This was all becoming a tad messier than she had planned. She thought that she would just take a couple weeks off from YWAM and complete her task. She had already started formulating her tactics and was ready to push forward. Now she would have to start from scratch and adapt to other's ideas. Maybe she had made a terrible mistake in agreeing to this risky business. Was it too late to withdraw? She could just call Mr. Hallohesh right now and let him know that she had changed her mind and wanted out.

"Mieke, are you okay? You look a little pale, and you haven't said anything in a really long while. What is it? How can I help? You can trust me. I know that you don't know that, but you can."

"You are mentioned in this letter, Gideon. So are the kids you spoke about earlier. All six of their names are written right here. I am on a special mission, and it appears that you and those kids are being called along for it too."

"Mission? What mission? I wish I knew what was going on here. How am I a part of it?"

"Great question! It just explains that through much prayer, you have been called too. We are to head over first thing in the morning to Mission Mind Academy at O Be Joyful. I am sorry, but I really have to run." Mieke slapped a twenty-dollar bill onto the table and stood up to leave. Before she did, she turned back to Gideon and told him to meet her at *Methuselah*'s dock at 7:00 a.m. sharp. "I hate to leave you hanging, but I just can't stay and explain this to you. I am not even exactly sure about the situation myself."

Running out the door, Mieke took in a deep long fresh breath of air. She didn't know where she was heading to but had to get out of there stat. Gideon and some random children working with her. Was this a joke, God? She had just met Gideon, and he was barely starting to accept the Lord. How could she depend on him? And six students from the academy? They were babies. What would they know about the works of Satan and how to prepare and defeat him?

Mieke started in the direction of home. This was going to be a long night, followed by an interesting day tomorrow.

"God, have mercy," she cried out loud. The Holy Spirit was with her, even now as she walked the familiar path to her house, her brain swimming in confusion and angst.

✸✸✸✸✸

It was five o'clock in the morning, and Yedaiah was up as usual spending time in the Word and prayer. He enjoyed the early hours of the morning in his devotions with God. He was able to feel the Holy Spirit on a deeper level when the chaos of children and adults alike didn't need his constant attention. This was a unique morning for him, however, and he was focusing his prayers and petitions on the unusual business of gathering with past and present students.

The Six-Pack, who had become rather large influences on campus this year, by showing great courage, bravery, and unshakable trust in the Lord, were the present's participants. When the Holy Spirit made it clear to Yedaiah to call upon them for battle, he was in shock. He didn't feel like they were ready. He had found them stowed away in the underbelly of *Methuselah* for starters. But after praying without ceasing and having a long chat with each one individually, after discovering them in the boat, he finally understood God's important purpose for their involvement.

And Mieke Everly, a former attendee of Mission Mind and close friend of his. He loved her like a daughter, as he did all the children that passed through the golden doors of the academy, but she was extra special because they experienced similar childhoods. God called children to O Be Joyful out of all sorts of different circumstances, but her strength to overcome and endure the hardships at such a young age had led her to a mighty fierce woman of God. He was thankful that God was bringing her back into his daily life.

As for the last piece of the puzzle, Yedaiah still wasn't so sure. Gideon Jethro. He had done an extensive background check research on him, as he always did when dealing with important business, but had no personal relationship to go off. The young man was a mystery. Yedaiah's biggest worry and wonder was his soon-to-be arrival on campus. Every single other person that had ever stepped foot on

O Be Joyful Gardens had been a staff member, student, or parent of a student. Having a stranger coming felt off, but trusting God means trusting every decision He makes.

After he finished pouring out his burdens to the One in control of heaven and earth, Yedaiah picked up his Bible to head out in search of Joshua. Mr. Zane was a godsend. He had been at the Gardens the longest and had much great insight and wisdom on all matters concerning it. Yes, Joshua was a major asset to the battle that they were about to embark on.

✳✳✳✳✳

Grace hopped out from behind the covers of her bed ready for the day. She scratched the top of Roxy's head and behind her ears, before throwing on her slippers for the morning-bathroom routine. Kiera was already up and getting herself put together when Grace invited her out for a little morning pet potty break. Grabbing Speedy, she agreed to go. It was 6:15 a.m., and they had forty-five minutes until they had to head to their big meeting with Mr. Hallohesh, Mr. Zane, their four guy friends, and the other two people selected for the upcoming mission at hand.

"Are you nervous about this morning?" Kiera could feel Grace's tight energy.

"I think that I am a whole lot of emotions wrapped up into one. Excited, nervous, scared, giddy, overwhelmed—you name it, I am feeling it."

"Yeah, I can relate. I have the same things going on inside me too. We just need to keep our focus on the main thing. Our all-powerful God is calling us to a preplanned mission. We have already won the battle. This little black flying Satan needs to know when to back off. He will get what's coming to him very soon."

"Maybe we can leave a little early and meet up with the boys before we head to the west end of the property. I think it's a good idea that we are meeting there so we can get a visual on what we are dealing with. I always get creeped out when I am there though. The Bones

Abode is a place of mystery, and not the good kind. It is like a real haunted house, not just one you walk through at Halloween time."

"I know what you mean. My skin crawls every time I catch a glimpse of it."

Kiera was not someone easily spooked, but the intenseness the dark shadow brings when it was around was enough to send anyone into a panic.

The two girls finished getting ready and then made their way to the Browns' apartment. Keilah and Gabriel were made aware of the situation from Yedaiah but were not called to the mission themselves. Their job in the matter was prayer. Not only would they be praying victory over the battle continually, they would also be holding a mandatory night of prayer during the attack. They were an imperative part of the plan and would carry out their belief in the power of prayer fearlessly.

The four boys were sitting on Mr. and Mrs. Brown's living room furniture chatting it up when they heard the knock. Jumping up to grab the door, Malachi was grateful to see them.

"Oh, good, you brought Roxy Ann and Speedy. I was thinking we should bring the animals. I feel safer when they are around."

On cue, their tiny kitten Fiona popped her head out from under the couch and pounced on Roxy. The two fur friends then proceeded to chase each other all over the apartment, enjoying the companionship. It was a special relationship the dog and cat shared, surprisingly. Roxy mothered Fiona, and Fiona trusted and loved Roxy.

Giggling, Grace exclaimed, "Yes, Fiona, you can come too. There will be a couple new friends that you can meet and win over. That tiny pink nose sucks everyone in every time. I think it's your superpower or something."

Before the six child-aged warriors walked out the door, Keilah approached them with a prayer. She prayed for wisdom and protection and the strength of the Holy Spirit over them. Then she hugged and kissed them all goodbye, wishing them luck in their important business.

Gabriel also spoke a prayer over them and then gave each one of them a high five and knuckles. He was maybe the most nervous. He always felt responsible for their safety and lives. God was asking him to completely trust Him, even with his three children. God could and would protect them better than Gabriel ever could. Knowing that made it easier giving the kids freedom and sending them on their way.

After the hugs were passed out and the pets were collected, the Six-Pack walked the golden path to the end of O Be Joyful Gardens, for what could be the most thrilling experiences of their lives to date.

Still a little ways off in the distance, they spotted Mr. Hallohesh, Mr. Zane, the girl they had seen meeting at *Methuselah's* dock, and much to their surprise, the man they spotted lurking outside of the garage.

"What is he doing here?" Malachi cried.

This was the second time Malachi was annoyed with the guy, and it was only the second time he'd ever seen him.

"Is that the gentleman who was spying the other day at the dock?" Matthew was shocked to see him there too.

Noah confirmed, "That is definitely him! This is a weird turn of events. I wasn't expecting him. I heard Mr. Hallohesh mention a woman and man on the mission, but the Peeping Tom? I don't get it."

Kiera wasn't in the mood. "Ya'll, we don't have to get it. Come on, let's just join them and see what this is all about."

As the kids, with their beloved pets in tow, approached the other four people waiting for them, introductions were made, and then Mr. Hallohesh got right down to business. He asked the group to gather and unify for an opening prayer. He mentioned not wanting to leave God out even a second of what they were about to embark on.

The girls whispered to each other about how tired and worn out Mr. Zane was looking that morning. He was crouching low to the ground and keeping quiet—not a usual trait for him. His normal demeanor was one of chatter, laughter, and joy. Kiera couldn't help but be a little worried about him. She did her best to keep her focus in the discussion and not on random things from the distracted nature of her mind. She would remember to ask how Joshua was doing later when they were not all together with important information to ponder.

"Thank you all for being here this morning. Believe it or not, this is going to be your 'take down Satan' team. God had made it very clear through prayer and fasting who He has called to this mission. We will have daily morning gatherings here with the visual of the Bones Abode for the next seven days to consider and deliberate a game plan for the attack on the dark shadow. He has been tormenting us for quite some time now, and it has got to stop. The staffers and students have all been thoroughly spooked by its appearances on campus," Yedaiah began.

Noah had to ask out of sheer curiosity, "Will you and Mr. Zane be participating in this spiritual battle? That's what we are dealing with, isn't it? A battle between good and evil. Of course, good will always win because Jesus has overcome the world, and we are blessed with the Holy Spirit to guide our steps."

Yedaiah assured him that everyone would have a unique role depending on what spiritual gift God was going to be using for the victory. He also mentioned having the pets in on the action.

"The chosen animals are a huge blessing to us all, that we have no doubt about, but God will use them in a way even beyond our understanding of their abilities. I realize that Gideon has never been a part of Mission Mind Academy and will need to be filled in on the splendor and ways of this campus. He also does not have an animal but will be in charge of Fiona the kitten during his stay here. He will be bunking in the spare room next door to the Browns' apartment until further notice."

Gideon, who was still in a state of shock from the portal ride in *Methuselah*, gave a nod of approval, not knowing what to say.

"I would be happy to show Gideon around and familiarize him," Mieke spoke up.

"That would be wonderful, thank you. And I might add that it's wonderful to have you back at O Be Joyful, Mieke. We have missed you around here and so has your pony, Skipper. You might want to go and reacquaint yourself after we finish up here," Yedaiah suggested.

"I didn't know if Skipper was still around! I was afraid to ask. This makes my whole day! I have missed her so much."

After replaying all the instances where the dark shadow showed up and interrupted their lives, for Gideon and Mieke, they decided to break for the day.

A new gathering time of six thirty the next morning was set, so they all said goodbye and strolled in different directions. All were instructed to pray through every thought and situation that came to them until the next morning, where they would report how God was leading them in the matter.

*****

Seeing the stable in the distance only made Mieke pick up her speed down the golden path. Gideon was completely quiet, not even knowing where to begin in his questioning. He was following close behind her, trying to take in the beauty of what surrounded him. The sky, the animals, and the grounds were all so perfect. He had died and gone to heaven. What was this place?

When Gideon saw Mieke reconnecting with her pony, he stood back at a distance. The two cuddled and snuggled like long-lost best friends. It was a precious reunion. She eventually brought Skipper over to meet him and explained to him how chosen pets worked at O Be Joyful.

"Coming from someone who has always doubted in God and His existence, my mind is completely blown right now. How is all of this possible?"

"In the Bible, Matthew 19:26 says, 'But Jesus beheld, and said unto them, with men this is impossible; but with God all things are possible.' Did you hear that? All things are possible with God."

"I just don't think that I am ready or worthy of all of this. My life has always been about me and what I want to do. All of a sudden, it's about God and what He wants me to do. I think I am in over my head here."

"Scripture also says that 'you can do all things through Christ who strengthens you.' So basically, nothing is impossible, and you can do all things. God also promises to complete the good works He began in you. Right now, this is the works, and you, Gideon, will never regret the journey. I can promise you that."

He was thankful for her faith and confidence in it all and decided not to turn back from what was clearly meant for him. How else would he be here, in a dream that was actually reality?

"Come on. Don't overthink things. I want to show you the academy. It's made of gold and is the most beautiful structure you will ever lay eyes on."

Skipper happily trotted along behind the two. She was glad to have her chosen person back; that was obvious. Gideon and Mieke strolled shoulder to shoulder toward Mission Mind, Mieke filling him in on every last detail she could think of regarding the miraculous campus.

She realized how overjoyed she was to be back. It felt like she had never left. Looking into the eyes of Grace and Kiera had taken her back to that age and the remarkable experience it had been attending the academy. God had spoken to her and grown her and walked right beside her every step of the way. She prayed that God would meet Gideon at the Gardens and draw him in close to a personal relationship. She realized now that was her number one prayer request, even over defeating the enemy.

"God, please make Gideon Jethro one hundred percent Yours. Amen," she cried out in her mind and heart.

Through the golden doors they went to explore the school and get acquainted with the ways. The two were getting lots of suspicious looks as they strolled the property. The kids weren't accustomed to unfamiliar people and were whispering about them as they passed by, wondering if they were new professors or what.

The teaching staff, on the other hand, were thrilled to see Mieke Everly's face after all the years that had passed, striking up conversations and asking all manners of questions about who Gideon is. They thought maybe she had gotten married. She would quickly clear that speculation up, not looking for untrue rumors going around about Gideon and herself.

After the tour ended and Mieke reconnected with all of her old professors, she showed Gideon to the room he would be staying in. Curious about his life outside of Mission Mind, she had to inquire.

"So what did you end up telling your job, family, and friends about where you would be for the next who knows how long?"

"Well, I work for myself, so thankfully I didn't have to call in to anyone. And I asked my sister to watch my dog for a couple weeks, telling her that I had to get away for some fresh air for a while. She is so consumed with being a wife and mother she didn't ask any questions. And my niece and nephew couldn't wait to watch over Cooper, my Alaskan husky. They love him."

"I bet you could have brought Cooper. As you can see, this is a very pet-friendly campus. It's almost a crime to exist here without one," Mieke said, laughing aloud.

"I will keep that in mind. I could always go get him if I miss him way too much. I am getting the impression that animals are a big deal around this place. I can definitely dig that! Besides, you heard Mr. Hallohesh. I am in charge of Fiona the cat for now."

"That's right! Yes, they are a big deal! God uses them in unusual and magical ways at O Be Joyful Gardens all the time. I shouldn't have been surprised that Skipper is still living here. When you arrive on campus, an animal chooses you, or God orchestrates the connection is more like it. Skipper galloped right over to me and nuzzled my side just moments after climbing out of the balloon for the first time. We were inseparable for my whole adventurous season at Mission Mind. I was here for almost seven years. Chosen pets, who are born at the Gardens, will live as long as their chosen person, if they don't step foot off campus. I guess Skipper has been waiting for me to return. I got her name from a Barbie doll I had left back home, when I was twelve years old and had been called here." She laughed out loud at that. "I suppose I would have chosen a different name had I been older."

Gideon was ready for seclusion. He let Mieke know that he was going to head to his room and get some rest before lunch. He had a granola bar for breakfast and should be starving by now, but all the excitement of the morning had kept his stomach at bay. He could probably skip lunch and dinner and be fine. He was actually dreading mealtime with the whole academy. He was not looking forward to all the kids' questioning eyes while he tried to eat in the dining hall.

"Thanks for the tour, Mieke. I will catch you in a couple hours for lunch. Save me a seat. This feels like my first day in a new school, and I don't want to be the outcast dining at a solo table looking all lonely."

"That's awesome! I will save you a seat for sure. Now get some rest and I'll see you soon. If you don't mind my suggestion, I would encourage you to take some time to pray. There has been a lot thrown at you in the past twenty-four hours, and I can bet it's pretty overwhelming. I can still remember the feelings of arriving here. Also make sure you take time to look up at the clouds. You will see all creatures floating around up there. It's most spectacular!"

"Thanks. See you later," Gideon told her with a smile of reassurance.

Deciding to make the most of her time, Mieke called for her pony to follow her into Grow in Wisdom. She would do a little light research on the dark shadow that had been appearing and on the Bones Abode it dwelled in. She was curious what it looked like. Mr. Hallohesh and Mr. Zane had explained all the sightings to her, but she couldn't visualize the creature or situation.

Scanning the dark corner of the library, Mieke spotted a book titled *The Black Spirit of the Abode*. Calmly pulling it down off the shelf, she plopped it with a thud onto a study table. Saying a silent prayer before opening it, that God would open her eyes and mind to what He had planned for her, she flipped the old dusty cover to the first page.

Before she could absorb the first sentence, a tiny tornado-like wind started spinning off the page. She looked around to see if anyone else was catching what was going on, but she was alone in the library. The wind continued to pick up, and that was when she saw it—a little black bat-like creature with a pungent smell and an ear-piercing sound. It swarmed up high, diving in and out of light fixtures, wafting heinous smells as it flew in every which direction.

Mieke, not having the first clue what to do, took cover under the table the book was on. She closed her eyes and prayed. She had been there for what seemed forever before she heard footsteps and voices.

"Ms. Everly, are you all right?" Grace cried out over the noise.

"Yes, I am just hiding under this table from that hideous thing. I wasn't sure what to do after it flew off the pages of that book."

Grace, Kiera, Noah, Matthew, Michael, and Malachi all squished under the table with her.

"We experienced the exact same thing from that exact same book not very long ago. Let's pray," Matthew directed.

Closing their eyes and joining their hands together, they prayed aloud, one at a time, asking for protection and deliverance from the enemy. Within minutes the noise ceased, and the smell dissipated. The seven of them crawled out from under the table, noticing that the shadow was gone, as was the book it had flown out of.

Kiera, remembering all too well, mentioned, "It closed back up in that book or headed back to the Bones. The book is back on the shelf where you found it."

"Well, at least I know who the enemy is now. That creepy little thing can bring on some displeasure, can't it?"

"You can say that again. It completely ruined our flanks match and scared the entire school half to death. We have to take it down to the ground, sending it back to the hell it comes from," Noah said, feeling very passionate.

"Agreed! We need a solid game plan," Grace chimed in.

"We can do all things through Christ, and we will defeat this little pest. I am ready to leave Grow in Wisdom now. Come on, Skipper, let's get outside to the fresh air."

Mieke thanked the kids for coming to her rescue and then made her departure.

She took her pony and began a walk along the golden path. She figured she could make the whole loop around O Be Joyful before the lunch music chimed on the loudspeakers.

The children quickly went in separate directions because they really didn't want to arrive late to their last class before lunch. Showing up late would get you a tardy slip and extra time after class, cleaning up the room. No one wanted to do that, especially the class before lunch. Food was sacred to the growing children at the academy.

*****

Joshua was wearing a sour face when he stepped into Yedaiah's office for a chat. He had witnessed something that led to great concern. In all his years at Mission Mind, he had never experienced such pressure from the devil. God had carried him through his long life without much of a fuss. But from the looks of things, that had changed.

"Good afternoon, Joshua! What brings you by this late morning? You look like you have seen a ghost. Are you all right?"

"I saw something this morning that is causing me much internal trouble. I was out on my midmorning stroll with Jehoshaphat. He was happily trotting along when he started going crazy, neighing and bucking up. It was clear that he smelled or saw something because he has never acted that way before. That's when I saw them. There must have been hundreds of them, flying around in a synchronized fashion, moving in and out with their black bodies and shrill sounds. I hopped up on my horse and begged Jehoshaphat to double out of there."

"Oh my! Did they leave? Are they still swarming around campus? I am afraid that if the students get a glimpse of that madness, we will have an empty school. Besides the six kids we have on the mission, the others are spooked out of their minds. I would hate to have everyone go running."

"Yedaiah, in all my days, I have never seen anything so scary. The evil side seems to be growing in power. I think they flew back to their home base because I went back within the hour and all was peaceful and calm."

"Thank you for telling me, Joshua. I am sorry for the fright you received. I just wish I knew what exactly to do. I will continue to pray that God directs our paths in defeating the dark forces that are pressing in on our beloved campus. I know He is up to something big, which is why we have a special task team assembled."

Yedaiah paused for a long while before continuing, "Don't you think it best if we keep these sightings to ourselves for now? When we meet in the morning with the crew, we can discuss all that has happened."

"That sounds like a plan. I will see you at lunch, my brother in Christ."

"Godspeed, my friend."

After talking with Joshua, Yedaiah knew that he needed to take action. He debated and prayed, debated and prayed before deciding his move. He would have lunch with the entirety of the school as normal, then he would quietly sneak off on his own personal mission. He had to get some background on the devil if he was to know how to conquer him.

He boarded the trusty hot-air balloon and floated his way through the portal in the direction of the Bones Abode. It was the first time he had seen it at eye level. And what he saw was not something pleasant. Joshua had been right; at least a hundred dark shadows spun around and around the roof of the partially finished house.

"God, we need You now. I feel the intense energy of the dark one threatening. Please show us the way. I declare victory over these tiny spooky creatures. I lift up this situation and every situation to You!" Yedaiah was yelling his prayer, hoping that not only God heard him but also the evil one.

From the floating balloon, Yedaiah screamed, repeating his prayer several times. On his fourth time through, with his eyes closed and his hands stretched up high to the heavens, he felt a jolt to the basket in which he stood. He fell backward as the swarm took over the balloon's air path, carrying it through the sky back to their scary compound. They plopped Mission Mind's air transportation directly in the center of the Bones Abode, Yedaiah and all.

Then they picked him up by his shirt and flew him down to an underground storage room below the Abode. Darkness overtook Yedaiah's vision as he heard heavy doors slammed shut.

"Dear Lord, what have I done? Who will find me now? Please save me, Father."

The shock then kicked in because his eyes started feeling impossibly heavy—so heavy in fact that he couldn't keep them open. Within a minute, they drifted closed, and blackness surrounded him.

13

Alternate Realms

It had been unusually windy overnight, and Joshua hadn't had the pleasure of much sleep. He was one of the first up on campus every single morning to pray over all the individuals living there and the property itself. He would stroll past each room, lifting the people inside up to God with his thoughts. Then he would make his way outside to the golden path and proceed to wind his way around campus before breakfast. The animals were always prayed over and loved on as he passed by.

This was going to be a unique morning however, because he was meeting the special task team at the end of the property before breakfast, as planned the day prior. Joshua thought it would be wise to seek out Yedaiah beforehand so that they could have a few minutes alone to share their thoughts and what God had been revealing to them over the last twenty-four hours.

So after his morning routine was finished, he directed his path to Yedaiah's office. Upon arrival, he noticed it was empty, and there appeared to be lots of disorganized papers on his desk, which was odd because Joshua could never remember a time that Yedaiah didn't tidy up his office at the end of a day. He would say that he liked to start clean and fresh every morning. Why the mess then? And why wasn't he in doing his daily devotional as normal?

Joshua thought that he must be in Grow in Wisdom reading or catching up on impending work. Stopping by the kitchen to pour himself a hot cup of coffee, he continued to the library but found it silent, dark, and empty as well. Where was Mr. Hallohesh hiding?

Making one last stop to his apartment, Joshua knocked on the door several times with no answer ever coming from inside. He did happen to hear Fig, Yedaiah's prairie dog, shuffling inside though, which was also odd because he usually followed his chosen owner everywhere he went. He guessed that his longtime friend must have switched up his routine and decided to just meet him at the appointed time at the Bones Abode viewpoint.

He decided to go early and stop by to pick up Jehoshaphat. He was desiring a ride on the back of his favorite four-legged friend and had a good thirty minutes to spare.

After a quick gallop through the orchards, Joshua steered his horse in the direction of the morning meeting. He didn't exactly like coming together in the view of the Abode but understood why Yedaiah had chosen to. It helped keep the main thing the main thing—take down that place and take down the evil that dwells there. Simple enough, right?

First to arrive, he dismounted and pulled out a pair of binoculars from the side saddlebag. Leaning against the fence, tired from the day already because of his advanced age and longevity, he brought the Bones structure into clear view. But what he saw was so frightening he quickly dropped the magnified glasses from his face. He began trembling uncontrollably. He was still in the shocked state when the children arrived, Mieke and Gideon only a few steps behind them.

"What is it, Mr. Zane?" Grace came and put her arm on his shoulder, followed by the rest of the gang.

Hesitating while taking several deep breaths, Joshua began, "The Bones Abode's inhabitance has considerably grown. There must be thousands of them now."

Mieke gently grabbed the binoculars from Joshua's hand and pressed them to her eyes. She was silent for several minutes as she focused on the fullness and details of the Abode. When she did finally turn toward the others, she was filled with fear.

"I see something with bright colors in the middle of the building. It appears to me to be parachute material. It looks exactly like our hot-air balloon."

Noah had a realization. "Where is Mr. Hallohesh? It's six thirty-five. He is never late to anything, ever!"

Joshua explained how he had looked for him all morning but to no avail.

They were all greatly concerned and stood quietly for a few moments collecting their thoughts before communicating with one another.

Mieke felt that this was the time for her leadership skills to kick in. All the children appeared frightened and rightfully so. Mr. Zane looked exhausted and not up for the fight. Glancing at Gideon, she saw that he was overwhelmed and didn't even know where to begin in helping. Yes, this was what God had called upon her for. She was to guide this group into the unknown. To take down the devil and to save Mr. Hallohesh, if he needed saving.

"Let's begin by calling Mr. Hallohesh's name on the loudspeakers, asking him to come to the stables. We will wait for him there for fifteen minutes. If he doesn't show up, we will go with plan B," Mieke told the others.

Noah was curious now. "What is plan B?"

"I will let you know if it comes to it! But in the meantime, Kiera, you run to the front office and page Mr. Hallohesh. The office isn't open, and Mrs. Susan won't be in yet. But the door should be unlocked, and you can present the page over the intercom yourself. We will meet you at the horse stable afterward. Now, quick as a tick!"

Kiera sprinted in the direction of Mission Mind Academy, and the rest of the group found their way to the stable. Waiting was a torturous task. Not knowing where Mr. Hallohesh was, was leading to a stressful morning for everyone, Mr. Zane most of all. His best friend was missing, and he had to get him back.

Making the announcement as she was instructed, Kiera ran to meet the others, praying Mr. Hallohesh would already be there when she arrived.

He wasn't.

The crew waited for twenty-five minutes before Noah brought up plan B.

"Mieke, what is plan B? I believe it's time to execute it at this point. I think he is a definite no-show."

With a heavy heart, she laid out the next plan of action. "At this point, our only option is to leave O Be Joyful and approach the Bones Abode. We have got to get inside to find out if that is our air taxi or not. Did anyone see Mr. Hallohesh in the balloon yesterday?"

Everyone shook their head no.

"Before we go, we need to verify that it is missing. So we will go to the balloon garage, have a peek inside, then go from there."

The garage was indeed empty.

"Okay, let's hop on *Methuselah* and do this!" Mieke said, trying to keep a light tone and attitude.

"Everyone, take your pets home besides Roxy Ann—she will be our guard dog this morning—and come straight back to *Methuselah*. We need to get a move on.

"Mr. Zane, I think it would be a good idea if you stay on campus. Someone has to be in charge while Yedaiah is away in case staff and students need you or he turns up here."

"I was thinking the same thing," Joshua replied with a worn-out voice. "I will also hold a prayer meeting with Gabriel and Keilah Brown and Mr. and Mrs. Vand. They know a little about what is going on with our mission against the Bones Abode and will be a good source of support and strength."

Giving him a big hug, Mieke watched him slowly and painfully walk his advanced aged body down the golden path, back to the building.

Gideon, who hadn't said a word all morning, was sitting on the grass near *Methuselah*. He was scared and not in practice of praying over things yet. So he just sat there, staring into the beyond, wondering what craziness this day was going to hold.

Mieke approached him and asked him if he was all right with everything going on. Then she sat quietly down next to him on the immaculate lawn and waited for his answer.

"I asked Jesus into my heart, and I feel like a brand-new man," he began. "I really do feel washed white as snow, which is completely amazing. It's just that now, all I feel like doing is spending time in

His peace. Peace is not something that I ever possessed prior, and I just want to take some time to enjoy the blessing. I know that it sounds selfish, but being thrown into this insane spiritual battle right after becoming a believer is a tad bit overwhelming. I am also highly unqualified for the task at hand, which makes me feel insecure. I do hate admitting that though."

She sympathized with him. "I can imagine that this is all very big stuff to be walking into. If it makes you feel any better, we are all very unqualified. I must say though that the only qualification you need when stepping into God's kingdom work is to be called. Jesus is the one with all the power. Our only job is to seek and trust Him to fulfill the good works He began. I will admit though that the peace that surpasses all understanding is within you, and you will continue to have it wherever you go, even to the Bones Abode. His peace He gives us, along with the promise to fight for us. We have got this, buddy! Do not fear!"

"Thanks, Mieke. I am glad that I met you. I have never met anyone like you. To be honest, I have always avoided people who are Christian. Admittedly, I focused on the human and their human nature and not the God that lived inside of them. I can clearly see how wrong I was about believers. It's ironic how I have become one myself."

"I am one and so thankful for that. God will do spectacular things through you, Gideon. Starting today, as we take down the enemy and save Mr. Hallohesh."

The Six-Pack were walking swiftly down the path toward them, so Mieke and Gideon pulled themselves up from the ground and climbed onto *Methuselah* to warm up the engine.

As soon as the eight of them were on board and settled in, they made the portal transport, this time not to the Seattle dock but a location on Port Orchard Strait where Mission Mind Academy technically was located. It being in a different realm however, it played by a whole different set of rules, including the boat docks. It was always a bit of shock to the system when leaving the realm where O Be Joyful exists and enter the real world.

The ports often had loiterers and addiction problems strung along them. Humans walking around God's green earth, existing but not living the life that they were created for. It was depressing at times, but that was the point: reach the unreached with the true purpose for their lives. God. The One who made them and loves them wants them.

There were all sorts of looks in their direction. People were not used to seeing an exquisite boat made out of gold parked at the docks there.

Matthew, who was feeling the sketchiness, reminded the others to secure and lock up *Methuselah* before leaving it.

"Unfortunately, we do not have our golden limousine here on this side of the water, so we will have to make our way via foot. I grabbed a box of breakfast bars and apples to eat along the way. I also have several water bottles in my backpack, so let me know if you are thirsty." Mieke had stepped into the mother role fairly quickly. How could she not when six out of the seven others were children.

Along the edge of the water, they swiftly walked, keeping to themselves as they did. No one had a plan for when they arrived at the Abode, and nerves were picking up with each step they took.

The only priority was to locate Mr. Hallohesh, and the biggest thing stopping them at that point was the location of the Bones Abode. It was a mystery to them. They had only seen it from campus. If they had the hot-air balloon, they could get a bird's-eye view of the land and have an easier time. But as it stood, they very possibly could be wandering around all day in search of it.

After a full hour of seeking, Gideon had the idea to get to higher ground. "We need to look for the tallest building we can find on this foggy strait then we will be able to look over the tops of all these houses and trees."

Mieke liked that idea. "Great idea, Gideon! We are currently in a neighborhood. We should walk back down to the little town portion by the water."

"Good idea, but if we head down to the water, we will actually be lower. If we stay up high, we can sneak up to the roof of a large multistory house and look down on much of the town," Gideon suggested.

Roxy liked the idea because she immediately left the group and sprinted to a house a block up the street that was tall indeed. They ran after her, finding her rolling around on the front lawn of a huge micro mansion.

"Good girl, Roxy Ann! Good girl!" Grace praised her pup.

Gideon was already doing a search of the property, making sure that there was no one home to interfere with their plan. Not seeing any movement through the windows and a lack of vehicles in the garage and driveway gave him the green go-ahead light. So he gathered the others at the back of the house where he had found an extremely tall orchard-picking ladder. One at a time, with someone holding to steady it, they climbed the towering ladder. Roxy, playing the lookout role, was still enjoying her rest on the lush green grass.

All were scanning the surroundings in search of that dreary unfinished structure. From the visible eye, it couldn't be located. However, a ways off in the distance, they spotted a thick grove of trees, the only one like it in sight.

"Maybe it is hidden by that thick forest over there!" Michael commented.

Kiera agreed, "I think it's our best bet at this point."

"All right then, we will head to the forest," Mieke directed.

Walking back through town, they tried to keep a low profile. Not many people were out looming around yet, being an earlyish morning still and a weekday.

When they reached the tree line, they took a pause.

"Is it me or does this woodland give off an eerie sense? My skin is crawling, and I don't know if I can continue moving forward into it," Grace told them truthfully.

Malachi was on the same page. "I agree, Grace! It's so dark and thick. I even see mist floating around in there. Are we sure this is the way?"

Mieke reminded him, "No, we are not sure at all that this is the way. But we agreed this is the only possible way it could be. We scanned all of Port Orchard from a semi-bird's-eye view and saw nothing. It has to be hidden in here."

Gideon, quiet up to this point, chimed in, "If O Be Joyful exists in a different realm, a spiritual one, then isn't it possible that the

Bones Abode does as well? After all, it is a spiritual battle we are entering into, isn't it?"

Pondering Gideon's words, Matthew replied, "That is a huge possibility, one I hadn't considered before."

Noah, ready to keep moving, encouraged them, "Well, even if that is the case, we still need to exhaust the woodlands first. We don't have any other options, and we need to find Mr. Hallohesh. I am so ready to end this war for good."

The group of slightly frightened people grasped hands and prayed together, asking the Lord for strength, wisdom, and favor in the coming happenings. After they said amen, they stepped into the dark, foggy forest and slowly ambled deeper and deeper in.

Just about the point of no return, when they couldn't see the opening they entered in from, things started to change. Roxy, who was the lead dog at this point, started getting all worked up over something seeming to be invisible. She was protectively barking and running this way and that, chasing an unknown.

"What does Roxy Ann see?" Grace wanted to know. She was getting a little worried about how her pup was acting. "I have never seen her behave like this before!"

Mieke assured her, "She senses something that we don't. Dogs are like that. I would bet that she smells and maybe even sees something that we don't too. Try not to be fearful. That goes for all of us. We need to remember to not live in fear, even now, but trust in the Lord, His promises, and His goodness. God will fight for us."

Roxy was not letting go of whatever hunt she was on. She was so determined to take down the invisible force that she wouldn't acknowledge or respond to the calls for her. They either had to keep moving and hope she would catch up to them or stop and wait for her chase to be over. They collectively decided to keep pushing ahead on the path; they need to find the Abode and fast. With Mr. Hallohesh gone, extra time to chase invisibles was not an option.

Grace lingered in the back of the bunch, keeping one eye on Roxy, inwardly hoping she would finish whatever it was she was up to and join them again. Roxy was a natural protector, and Grace had no doubt that she was keeping them safe from something they didn't even know was threatening them, but she didn't want to leave her.

The woodland was much larger and more multilayered than they all originally thought when they were staring at it from the roof-top of the micro mansion. It appeared to be a thick patch of trees that could easily be maneuvered through, but now that they were in it, it was huge and complicated. Paths winded in multiple directions, taking them nowhere. They had followed several of them to no avail.

Kiera and Noah had been talking as they strolled and thought that maybe it would be a good idea to split up into two groups so that they could cover more land in less time. When they presented the idea, however, the others were in strong opposition.

"We are staying together! Strength in numbers is what some call it," Mieke declared.

"This is when cell phones would come in very handy," Malachi commented.

Mission Mind Academy had amazing technology, the best of the best for students to be as successful as possible in their studies, interests, and gifts. But cell phones were off limits on campus. There were school phones for members of the academy to call from, even phones in children's rooms so that they could easily be contacted by their families, but no cells. This had always worked beautifully, keeping distraction and temptation down and freeing their minds for more creative ways to stay entertained. But when leaving campus and when Mr. Hallohesh goes missing, a cell phone could be a lifeline.

"I have a cell phone," Gideon simply said.

They all stopped in their tracks to stare at him.

"What? I didn't know that I wasn't allowed to bring my phone with me. It won't do any good though. Mr. Hallohesh doesn't possess one, so I don't have anyone to call anyways."

"Do you have a GPS on that thing? Maybe we can find a map layout of these creepy woods. It could help guide us in the right direction," Mieke said with a fresh dose of hope.

"I already checked. There is no evidence of this woodland. When I searched the map of Port Orchard, there was only a field and large parking lots making up this land."

"How peculiar! So we are searching a piece of land that doesn't exist on the maps?" Kiera was fascinated.

"Roxy! Roxy Ann!" Grace wanted her dog back with her and began calling her name on repeat. "Roxy! Come here, girl. Roxy Ann!"

Everyone chimed in, calling for the precious dog in unison. Over and over they yelled for her to "come, girl," but with no results.

"I feel like I need to turn back. I shouldn't have moved on without her. I can't live without Roxy. Plus, we need her with us to protect us. I am scared something happened to her."

Mieke comforted her, "She is okay, Grace. She will catch up as soon as she has whatever she was after handled."

"She is the smartest dog, fear not!" Noah assured her.

As Malachi rounded a path at the top of a small hill, he spotted an extremely large tree, one that looked like it touched the sky. It was a misfit to be sure. None of the other trees in the entire forest looked anything like it. It had a trunk the size of a house, branches that reached in both directions as far as his eyes could see, and thick leaves bigger than any he had seen before. He had to stop and stare when he saw it.

When the others reached the top of the hill, they, too, halted to digest what they were witnessing.

"That is a monster of a tree!" Noah stated the obvious.

"It most definitely appears to be the odd one out here. It is easily ten times larger than every other one. What kind is it? I have never seen any like it before." Grace was in complete awe, even forgetting that her beloved pet wasn't currently with her.

After a brief discussion, they all agreed that the tree was one not seen before by any of them. It almost didn't look real, but when they approached it, rubbing their hands on the barked trunk and crinkling the monstrous leaves in between their fingers, there was no denying its authenticity.

Michael and Noah walked around the backside of the trunk to get a better visual of it. They began tapping on the trunk and stomping on the ground around it. Then they simultaneously pulled off small pieces of the bark, and just as they did, a hole opened up below their feet, dropping them down below ground before spitting them out several yards from the front of the Bones Abode. The hole that swallowed them closed back up as if it never happened.

When the rest of the crew walked around the backside of the tree, they noticed the absence of the boys.

"Where did Noah and Michael run off to?" Matthew wanted to know.

Gideon and Mieke glanced at each other, hoping that the other had a good explanation for where the boys were at. Neither did though. No one knew where they went.

Gideon stepped up. "I have no idea where they could be. They were literally here just a few minutes ago."

Now they had three names to call for. Their six voices rose to yell out, "Noah, Michael, Roxy! Noah, Michael, Roxy! Where are you guys?"

Silence.

"I smell something fishy going on here. I don't like this at all. Let's pray, guys," Malachi suggested.

Mieke agreed, "Great idea, Malachi! Come over here and join hands. We need to be depending on the Holy Spirit if we want to come out of this mission on top. We are already three people and one dog down."

Grace was feeling distraught as they prayed. Her dog! She needed her dog! She had never been through anything scary in her life without her companion by her side except when Roxy herself was missing.

When they finished praying for God to lead their steps and calm their fears, Malachi leaned up against the ginormous tree, hooking his belt loop on a piece of scratchy peeling off bark. When he pulled away to stand up straight again, his pants ripped the piece of bark clean off the trunk.

Before any of them had a chance to take in what was happening to them, the ground below them opened, swallowing them up whole. They fell hard and fast below the earth until they finally popped back up at the Bones. Landing in a dog pile of people, they opened their eyes to see Noah and Michael standing above them.

"Noah! Michael! I am so happy to see you two turkeys! Why did you ditch us and worry us?" Kiera stood up, giving them both a hug.

Michael laughed. "We didn't ditch you. The ground ate us up without warning."

"Yeah, we just experienced that ourselves a moment ago!" Kiera replied.

"Okay, now that we are all here," Mieke began.

Grace had to remind them, "We are not all here. I need my Roxy Ann."

"God has her, Grace. Don't lose hope or focus. We need you to help us find Mr. Hallohesh now," Mieke pleaded.

Standing at the entrance of the infamous Bones Abode was surreal for the group. They had only ever seen it from the safety of O Be Joyful Gardens, and now there they stood face-to-face with the devil's dwelling place.

"What have you two observed so far?" Gideon was anxious to get going. He didn't want to hang out in this alternate world at Satan's house any longer than absolutely necessary.

"We haven't seen or smelled anything, if you know what I mean. Every time I saw this house from afar, I figured it would smell like rotten trash and skunks," Noah told them.

"No movement whatsoever," Michael added. "We haven't been inside yet though. We have been standing here contemplating what we should do since we landed here. I am so glad you all showed up."

Even though the structure was just a shell with no walls to speak of, they couldn't see into it at the angle they were standing. Overgrown shrubs were growing wild at a record-breaking height directly in front of it, covering the whole viewpoint.

"I guess we should probably take a walk around the place. We can't just stand here staring at it all day. What if Mr. Hallohesh is inside?" Matthew encouraged them.

Mieke set out the plan. "We will split up, half of us walking around the house to the left and the other half to the right. We will meet back behind it. Everyone be extra quiet as to not alert anyone of our presence and so we can listen for any noise or movement from within."

Gideon replied, "Great, let's do this. I will take Grace, Kiera, and Noah with me. The Browns go with Mieke, and we will see you in a minute."

As quiet as a nest of mice, the godly warriors scanned the perimeter. When they reassembled behind the Abode, the two groups both reported that they didn't hear or see anything suspicious.

Noah climbed up a few branches in a tree next to them to unveil Mission Mind Academy's hot-air balloon smack-dab in the middle of the house.

"It's right there, you guys! I can see the balloon lying on the ground inside."

"Mr. Hallohesh has to be close by!" Kiera cried out. "We have to go inside and find him."

Mieke agreed, "Okay, Matthew and Kiera are going to be our lookouts. The rest of us will go in. Do you two know what the buddy system is?"

Kiera and Matthew looked at each other nodding their heads.

"Don't worry, Ms. Everly, I won't let Kiera out of my sight."

"And I will not take my eyes off Matt. I know that he depends on me for protection." She giggled, trying to lighten the intensity of the atmosphere.

"All right, the rest of us are going through the back door opening for a look around. For now, we will stay together as a group. I do not want anyone roaming around alone here today."

After saying goodbye to Matthew and Kiera, the six others crept into the accuser's lodging place. The inside of the unfinished building was crawling with vines and foliage. Digging their way through the overgrowth, they finally found the location of the balloon. It pathetically lay on the center of the dirt-and earth-covered floor in a heaping pile of color.

Still no sign of life, they continued to peruse the inside, desperately hoping to find a hidden space or clue to where Mr. Hallohesh might be.

Gideon and Mieke collectively deemed the house empty and guided the four kids back to the outside of it. Just as they were reconnecting with Matt and Kiera, a wind started instantly blowing. It was like zero to sixty in seconds. The trees furiously blew, threatening to topple over, and the sky grew so dark with clouds and debris vision was hindered. That is when the band of shadows flew overhead. Hundreds, maybe even thousands, of hair-raising black beings swarmed them at alarming speed.

"Quick," Mieke screamed over the commotion, "we have to find cover!"

They ran as fast as their legs could carry them into the Bones Abode, knowing that they were asking for more trouble entering into their house, but not having any other choice in the current situation.

The storm continued to pick up power and speed, opening the sky up to dump sheets of rain down from the heavens. They all huddled together, silently praying for help and relief.

As he waited, hunched over in a bundle of people, Noah spotted something shiny from the corner of his eye. It was the only thing that sparkled in the whole place, which struck him as odd. Whatever it was, was bright and inviting. Noah knew that he had to break away from their protective clump to find out what it is.

He released his arms from around Gideon and Michael, fought with everything in him against the force of the wind, and scrambled several yards to the bright beacon. When he found his footing, holding on to a four-by-four next to him, he ever so slightly touched the object. When he did, a trapdoor in the floor opened up, revealing a long winding staircase leading down into the depths of the earth.

"Guys! Over here. I found a secret door! Come quick!"

The seven of them, half relieved, half spooked out of their minds, released their embraces and fought against the wind to the staircase. The dark flying creeps did not let up once on their objective. No one ever knew exactly what their objective was.

When they were back together as one, they quickly ascended one at a time down, down, down, deeper into the depths. The spiral stairway winding so far below that even after one hundred steps, they hadn't reached anywhere.

"What is this place? I don't think we should keep going! What if it's a trap and we will never get out?" Grace was not so sure of their path.

"We don't have a choice, Grace. If we are going to get Mr. Hallohesh back and end whatever threats the devil keeps attacking us with, we have to keep going," Kiera explained to her friend.

"Grace, don't doubt Jesus now! He holds the world in the palm of His hands. He created everything and is in complete control. We are just meant to trust Him and not fear. Fear means that you doubt His power, goodness, and plans," Matthew explained.

Grace knew everything that Matt had said from the depths of her heart, but her mind was playing tricks on her peace. If Roxy wasn't still absent, she would be a whole lot more confident in their adventure. Who was she kidding? This wasn't an adventure. It was a very important mission. One that would help everyone at Mission Mind. One that she was called to by God Himself. She had this! With God, all things were possible.

Another hundred steps, the exhausted bunch came to a large open room with three doors to the visible eye. The doors were large, black, and locked.

"It would just be way too easy to have an unlocked door," Noah joked.

They could hear the screeching sounds and smell the raunchy odor of the enemy wafting down the stairs from the room they were in, reminding them that they didn't have a lot of time and would have to hurry in their efforts to unlock a door.

"We have to get through one of them! I don't know how long they will swarm around up there. I am surprised they haven't followed us down yet. How are we going to get in?" Kiera was racking her brain.

Gideon was thoughtfully assessing his surroundings. There had to be a key or switch or knob or control somewhere close by. The room was only dimly lit with a needle head of daylight trickling hundreds of feet underneath the earth's surface. Gideon remembered his phone in his pants pocket and retrieved it for the flashlight feature. Turning it on shed more perspective. He followed the length of the wall scanning it for anything helpful.

Noah spoke up through the concentration, "It's ironic that the Bones Abode is a shell of a house to the naked eye, but below it is a fully walled, fully completed creation."

"Agreed, I can't believe all this exists." Grace was in awe.

Gideon went to his hands and knees to thoroughly search the floor. He crawled around everywhere, asking the others to do the same. There were eight of them—that is, sixteen eyeballs. They should be able to figure this out.

Matthew spoke up, "What if the key is not even in this room? We could be looking for it all day to no avail."

"I hear something! Hurry, over here," Malachi shouted.

They all hovered around the door that he stood at.

"Put your ear up to the door and be quiet. I hear someone's distanced voice in there."

Sure enough, a muffled male's voice was somewhere deep behind the walls they were currently stuck at. It was too far away to make out what it was saying, but it didn't have a distressed tone in it.

"What if that's Mr. Hallohesh!"

"If we can hear him, he can hear us!"

"Let's all scream his name in unison at the count of three!"

"One, two, three."

"Mr. Hallohesh! Mr. Hallohesh!" everyone yelled at the top of their lungs.

Then they silently waited to hear if they would get a response.

They did! A faint "Hello, I am here!" came from the belly of the underground lair.

"It is Mr. Hallohesh!"

"We have got to find a way in. Maybe we can bash the doors down!" Malachi was ready.

"We don't even know what door to go through," Grace commented, as she closed her eyes to pray for God's direction.

Mieke was bound and determined to get to Yedaiah. He was so special to everyone on campus, and she was going to bring him home safely. That was when she noticed something that caught her eye. Five steps up from the staircase they had ascended down was an off-colored stair. It was hunter green while every single other stair was black. It only caught her attention because Gideon's light was shining on it.

She asked Gideon to follow her over with his cell phone to further investigate it.

"It most definitely is a different color than all the rest!" Gideon felt a splash of hope.

Mieke crouched down over it and began pulling at the stair, willing it to move. She tugged and pulled with all her might. Then Gideon propped his phone up on a higher step to free his hands to help. They yanked together until the entire face of it ripped off, sending them back into a tumble.

When they regained their footing, they peered at what was uncovered and shouted, "Praise God for His leading. We did it."

Revealed was a single black key lying by itself in a little open box.

As soon as Mieke picked it up, an alarm sounded in the room. Red lights began obnoxiously flashing overhead, and wind bellowed down the stairs forcing them to quicken their steps.

Mieke chose the middle door first. She connected the black key to the hole in the middle of the handle and turned. No luck. She then attempted the door to her left. As she twisted the black key, the door let loose, opening into a sizable hallway filled with damp walls and thick spider webs. Their crew entered in, seeking solace from the storm that was brewing around them.

When Gideon was last through the doorway, he slammed it shut with gusto.

"Keep moving forward, guys. I know that it's beautiful in here, but we don't have spare time to peruse," he joked.

Walking ahead into the darkness, they were all super thankful for Gideon's cell phone flashlight. Unfortunately, it was running low on battery life, so in order to avoid wandering blindly, they would have to hurry.

As they traveled forward down the cold wet passage, they repeatedly yelled for Mr. Hallohesh. They were not getting a response, but that didn't stop them from calling. The hall, much like the stairs, continued on for what seemed like eternity. It just kept going and going. Thankfully the wind stayed behind the door, back in the room they had just left.

Michael was becoming a little worried about the path they were taking. He whispered to Noah, "What if we chose the wrong door and we just wander through the underbelly of this house aimlessly forever?"

"It's okay, buddy. I think we are on the right track. God is leading us, I have no doubt. Look! Right up ahead, way down there is light! Where is it coming from?"

Everyone spotted the glow. It was a beacon of hope, quickening everyone's steps to a fast jog. Wet sticky webs clung to their faces as they passed by, but nobody cared. They just had to get there.

Their voices and footsteps echoed off the walls giving a surround sound effect.

Grace, noticing, began singing her favorite worship song as she scurried, "Jesus, Jesus, You make the darkness tremble. Jesus, Jesus, You silence fear."

One after another filed into the well-lit bare room at the end of the hall. It was a stark contrast to the rest of the Bones Abode. Just as they all stepped foot into the room, the floor began spinning. It started off slowly, turning in a clockwise motion, but began picking up speed with every 360-degree turn it made. Around and around the eight of them went, causing confusion and a bit of nausea.

"What in the world is happening? Can anyone see an off button? I don't know how long I can handle this!" Kiera tended to get queasy on anything that spun.

As they spun round and round, hair and limbs flying in the craze, the ceiling above them slid open to reveal a faux sky, pitch-black with tiny white star-like dots twinkling over their heads. Then the rotating floor began rising up toward the darkness, forcing them all to lie down to avoid tumbling around. Flat on their backs, a few of them holding hands, they rose higher and higher with no end in sight.

Mieke felt an obligation to the others, her mothering instinct still strong. She peeled her eyes away from the beyond above to focus on the other surroundings. They needed to get off the spinning rising floor, out of the Bones Abode, and back on solid ground with every member of Mission Mind Academy.

She glued her eyes to the walls around her, willing herself to locate a way out. Like a hedgehog, she rolled herself up into a tight ball, preparing for transport. Then she rolled herself over to one side of the rising floor, where it met with the wall, and stuck her hand out for a touch. It was almost impossible to use her eyesight for clarification, so she proceeded to use her hands to feel around blindly. Rubbing her hands along the wall as she rose past it, she invited the others to do the same.

Projecting over the chaos, she instructed the others, "Everyone get themselves to the sides of the floor. We need all hands on the wall as we pass by it. I think it will be our ticket out of here."

Not everyone had maneuvered their way over yet when Mieke realized the texture her fingertips were feeling on the wall changed. It went from smooth to patterned, leading her to believe she had found something.

Sure enough, as soon as she pushed in harder on the wall, giving it more force and pressure, it began to crumble. Still rising and still spinning, Mieke called for the others to apply pressure.

All eight of the godly warriors used their hands and feet to break down the walls that were caging them in. With all their might, they kicked and pushed, kicked and pushed, until finally, the unending hedge collapsed below, leaving them wide open to the world around them.

They had joined the outside world. The floor that they had been spinning on for way too long had come to a halt. They sat in a daze, so relieved to be off the hamster wheel they couldn't focus on where they had landed.

When the walls came tumbling down, the floor had shot off and landed on a thicket of trees outside of the Abode about one hundred yards away, leaving them extremely discombobulated and woozy.

After quite a few moments, Gideon stood up, collecting himself before he made his rounds to check on the others. Noah was the greenest but in good spirits. Michael lost his breakfast in a bush but was feeling more like himself directly afterward. One by one they each came to, standing up to regain their balance.

Grace was maybe the most coherent and ready to continue the search. Not only had they not located Mr. Hallohesh yet, even after that whole debacle, but Roxy was still missing as well. She had vowed to herself earlier that day that she would not stop until they were found.

"Come on, you guys! Our mission is definitely not completed yet!" she cried out to the others.

She retied her shoe and began walking right back over to the Bones for round two, not afraid or deterred from the previous experience they had just encountered.

The others reluctantly followed, a bit shaky and less enthused than Grace.

Noah could read Grace and wanted to encourage her. "Grace, I know that we will find Mr. Hallohesh and Roxy Ann at any moment. I am sorry that you miss your pup."

"It was one thing for Mr. Hallohesh to have gone missing, but to lose Roxy in the process of finding him is over the top for me," she said with all honesty.

"Agreed!" Malachi chimed in. "Do we have another plan going back to the Abode? I don't want to repeat what we just went through. I don't think my stomach can handle even one more turn around."

"No," Mieke confessed, "we don't have another plan. We are just winging it at this point. But I do know for a fact that God has a plan and His plans are always perfect."

As they were reapproaching the haunted house, Matthew caught a glimpse of something moving around inside. Peering through the open wall toward the center of the unfinished building, he spotted someone moving around their hot-air balloon.

"Over there! Look! Is that Mr. Hallohesh?" he whisper-shouted to the others, not wanting to alert whoever it was of their presence.

Pausing to see more clearly, the rest of them verified that it was indeed him! And a four-legged animal running around at his feet.

"Roxy!" Grace shouted at the top of her lungs, unable to contain her relief and excitement.

Her pup heard her voice and made a mad dash over to her, knocking her over to have unlimited access to her face for licking.

Grace laughed with sheer joy, praising God for the safe reunion of her favorite friend.

The others ran over to Mr. Hallohesh to envelope him in a hug. He looked exhausted and banged up here and there. He had been through even more than they had, no doubt about it.

Mieke couldn't remember ever being so relieved in her life. She couldn't release her arms from around Yedaiah, so thankful for his safety.

"What happened? How did the accuser get ahold of you?" Mieke had so many questions.

Yedaiah, who was so thankful to be reunited with the group, didn't have words to describe the incident.

"Let's just get back to O Be Joyful. We can discuss the happenings at a different time. I am so tired. I really just want to sleep for the unseen future," he commented with a chuckle.

He still possessed his keen sense of humor, and for that, they were all grateful.

Straightening their trusty hot-air balloon out of its crumpled state of existence, they all piled in to hitch a ride back to the dock, where they loaded up onto *Methuselah*. The Brown boys rode back with Mr. Hallohesh via air transport, while the others went by water. Praise the Lord, no sign of the black shadows lurking about.

"I guess we won the day. We are all back together in one piece," Gideon stated.

His introduction to Mission Mind was a wild ride so far, but he was finding that he felt at home in the crowd of believers. He fit in with them and enjoyed the adventure as well. Yep, after well over thirty years, God had brought him to his place in the world.

When Methuselah was safely docked at Mission Mind Academy, the troops quickly disembarked, overly anxious to see their beloved pets. Mieke advised the children to retreat to their rooms for rest. She vowed that she would have Mrs. Heathers send food to them.

With the promise of a morning briefing, they departed ways—the boys off to reconnect with Mr. and Mrs. Brown, the girls to their cozy room, Mr. Hallohesh to find Joshua and then bed, and Mieke and Gideon to a bench on the property, the two of them desiring comfort from one another. It was a lot of pressure being the adults in intense situations. The sense of responsibility for the others had taken a toll on both of them that day.

As they took a seat in the orchards, they were both thankful that tomorrow would be a fresh start, hopefully with clarity and strength for what was to come next.

They both knew that the devil was still lurking close by. The battle was most definitely not over yet.

14

The Lull before the Smog

The week following the Bones Abode incident was rather ordinary and uneventful. The other students at Mission Mind didn't have a clue what went down the week prior. Classes were carrying out a usual, and there was a gleeful buzz in the air due to the flanks match to be held in just a few short days.

It was Thursday, and O Be Joyful members were out enjoying their golden sidewalk carnival between responsibilities. The sun was shining brightly down upon them, and the delicious scent of popcorn was drifting about.

Mr. and Mrs. Vand, along with their pets, Sticks the beaver and Yodel the duck, were running the dart-throwing booth, which was a brand-new game that week. The line for their activity was so long it was impossible to see the end from the front. Each individual received three darts to aim and toss at a wall of blown-up balloons. If they were successful in their throw, they earned a free homework pass in the Power of Thoughts lecture.

Mr. Vand was not a heavy homework hitter, but the freedom to pass on one of his assignments was a breath of fresh air for his students. His topics of study were usually very deep and personal. When studying or writing required work, brains were known to turn to mush. Digging deeply into one's self was a draining process, which everyone wanted a scored dart to exempt them from.

Mrs. Vand was happily handing out golden slips one by one as students popped the inflated rubber shapes to be had. She offered words of encouragement and a warm hug to each child who waited and walked through their line. Mrs. Vand was a one-of-a-kind woman whom the children loved dearly. She was the person most went to for advice on a weighty topic or comfort during times of struggle.

She loved every minute of it. After years of teaching and raising her own children, kids were her specialty. So when Grace reached the front of the line, eyes puffy and red, about to burst into tears, she felt a clear burden to help.

"Good afternoon, Ms. Grace. How are you today? Are you ready to win a homework pass?"

"Hello, Mrs. Vand. Yes, that would be nice to have in my back pocket," Grace replied with a soft voice and long face.

"Is there anything bothering you today, beautiful lady?" Mrs. Vand pushed.

Grace took hold of her three darts, positioned her feet just right, and tossed her best throws at the balloon board. She was incredibly determined and ended up nailing all three.

"The homework pass limit is only one, but great job!"

Grace wanted to open up to Mrs. Vand but wasn't enthused to do so in front of a huge line of her peers. So she reassured her that she was all good and moped along her way. She wasn't feeling in the mood for games that day. Thankful Thursday was always a favorite of hers, but nothing could draw her out of the sadness she was carrying that particular day.

Due to attend a flanks practice in an hour, she resolved to spend the last of her free time in her room with Roxy Ann. She would read or nap or just lie on her bed and stare at the ceiling. The blues had settled in as soon as she opened her eyes that morning. At first, she didn't know where the despair was coming from. Things had been going so smoothly since the return of Mr. Hallohesh. No sighting of the wicked shadows, which kept everyone's fear at bay and no campus drama whatsoever. She actually hadn't ever experienced campus drama except for the dark shadows' spooky appearances.

Just as Grace had plopped her body onto her nicely made bed, there was a soft knock at her door. Taking a big sigh, she told whoever it was to come in, trying to keep the annoyed tone out of her voice. She wasn't in the mood for company and didn't want to talk to anyone about anything.

The door swung open, exposing the presence of Mrs. Vand. She was alone, besides her little duck waddling behind her, and wore a big bright welcoming smile on her face.

"Hey, Grace. Fancy meeting you here," she lightheartedly opened the conversation.

"Hello, Mrs. Vand. Is there something I can do for you?"

"As a matter of fact, there is. I have a tugging feeling in my old bones that you could use a listening ear. Is anything bothering you?"

She continued as she stepped all the way into the room, leaving the door open to the hallway behind her. No one was out loitering in the halls though; they were all out enjoying the fun, giving them a moment of privacy.

Grace hesitated before she gathered her thoughts enough to share.

"The truth is that I am not exactly sure what is going on with me. I woke up today feeling downright blue, and I don't like it one bit. This is not a feeling that I get often, and it doesn't feel good."

With compassion, Mrs. Vand stepped closer to Grace to speak. "I am sorry that you are feeling this way. Maybe we can sort out what is going on in your life to cause this unsettlement."

"The only thing that comes to mind is the intense amount I miss my family. I love it here, don't get me wrong, but I want my mom and dad. I am missing out on priceless moments with my brother that I have waited my whole life for. I just sometimes want to give up and head back to Colorado. I loved my life there. Even though I always knew God had something incredibly important and unique for my life and could not wait for it, now that I am here, I often want to go back to the way things used to be."

"Change can be excruciatingly challenging, to say the least. I can remember when Mr. Vand and I arrived here at O Be Joyful. Leaving behind all the wonderful things in our old life was so hard. It took me about a full year, maybe more, to understand that we are all on a nonstop journey. We are always moving forward, never staying stagnant, which leads to unending changes. God has a long path for us to walk out while we are dwelling on this side of heaven. Looking back to where we were last year, last month, or last night is only to reflect on those moments, not relive or stay in them."

"I realize that I was brought here for a purpose," Grace voiced, "but I am constantly replaying my former life and can't let go of it. It was easier and safer and carried less pressure, whereas now I feel way in over my head most of the time."

"Yes, I can relate to what you are saying. It is true that growing up can bring about lots of discomfort and uneasiness. As we grow and stretch, we feel the tension in our bodies. But rest assured that is God working things out through us that can only be worked out with His strength, wisdom, and leading. You are feeling unsure, and that is completely understandable, but you don't have to be sure to keep moving forward in the direction you are called to. He will guide our steps and carry us when we are weak and fall."

"Thanks, Mrs. Vand, I appreciate your kindness. I think that I just need a little or a lot of refreshing from God's Word. I have been busying myself so much lately and have neglected my private time in His presence."

Mrs. Vand had an idea. "Why don't we get you out to Colorado for a family visit this weekend?"

"That would be lovely, except that we have a flanks tournament this weekend, and I don't want to let the Six-Pack down. They depend on me, and we have been practicing so hard. I'd really hate to cripple the team with my absence."

"I get that. It was just a thought. Maybe the following weekend, it could be worked out."

"Thanks for checking on me and caring, Mrs. Vand. I am very thankful for you. Will you come to the match this weekend?"

"I wouldn't miss it for anything. Mr. Vand and I couldn't be prouder of Noah and Michael's creativity and all the players' dedication. It is a very welcomed addition to Mission Mind Academy. I hope the sport continues here forever. It has added a level of excitement and joy to everyone."

"I love it. We have so much fun playing together. In fact, that reminds me, I am due at practice shortly. I should head to the kitchen and see if Mrs. Heathers would whip me up a little something healthy to snack on. Plus, Roxy and I love hanging out with her silkie chicken Ernie. He is adorable and so sweet. Still cracks me up that I am friends with a chicken. He runs to me like a dog seeking attention every time he spots me."

"That's hilarious! I like Ernie too. Good idea about the snack. Mind if I join you? My stomach is rumbling, and I could use a bite myself."

"I don't mind at all! Come on, Roxy, let's go, girl. You too, Yodel."

*****

Joshua and Yedaiah were two protective souls on campus that were not getting much internal rest. The burden of the flying threats weighed heavy on their minds. They both knew without a doubt that it was only a matter of time before the enemy returned, bringing about more chaos and havoc.

They were not afraid as much as they were responsible for everyone at Mission Mind. They were the ones that needed to come up with a plan of attack. Leaving the safety of home court at Mission Mind Academy was out of the question. The excitement and intensity of being at the actual Bones Abode dwelling were too much, and if at all possible, they would not be returning.

They would have to come up with a way to defeat them on their own stomping ground. Home court advantage, if you will. They could set up a trap and draw in the beast somehow, maybe. The power the enemy carried over them was threatening but not overcoming. The power of the Holy Spirit would crush the accuser every time. This was the hope and faith that they lived by and would depend on in the battles to come.

Yedaiah had made a few rounds at the fun booths happening outside but then retreated to Grow in Wisdom to glean some much-needed wisdom. He had been sitting in his favorite chair, reading scriptures, when Joshua slowly shuffled in and sat down beside him.

"Good afternoon, Yedaiah. How is your thankful Thursday coming along?"

"Hello, Joshua, great to see you. Honestly, the devil is heavy on my mind, which is why I decided that God's Holy Word was in order."

"I know what you mean. Satan has been spinning around in my mind too. I can't help but feel deep down in my bones that his return is coming soon, and he will come on stronger than ever before."

"Yeah, I am afraid that we stirred the pot by approaching its house. I take full responsibility for that error. I was simply trying to get a view from a distance and pray over the whole matter when the hot-air balloon was taken into their control and their house. If I had just kept my distance and curiosity at bay, we could have avoided that whole scene." Yedaiah's guilt was consuming him.

Joshua wasn't going to stand for it, however. "You did what you felt was right at the moment, and I believe that it was. You are a fine man, Yedaiah, with an amazing relationship with our Lord Jesus Christ. Do not be so hard on yourself. You were sacrificing yourself for the good of others. Going there was an act of bravery. With that said, a buddy system would have been a wise choice. Going anywhere alone is not advisable, especially when it's the devil's house."

"I'll admit that you are very right. I will not be taking any more solo trips to Satan's home, I promise you that. But I do believe that we do need to figure out how to bring him here and on our terms."

"I have come up with a few ideas on the matter. Now don't knock this idea before I finish relaying it to you." Joshua chuckled aloud at the thought of what he was about to say. "I think we should set a booby trap, like the one Kevin rigged on *Home Alone*. We know that the shadows will return, so if we have something waiting for him when he shows, we can one-up him."

"*Home Alone*, huh?" Yedaiah's mind started to spin with ideas. "I think that is a great idea. Let's call a brainstorming meeting with the special task team this evening in the greenhouse. I would still really like to keep things hush-hush around here. Our special task team are such brave humans and can handle this fight, but I know for a fact that there are members of our school that are just too fragile to carry too much information."

"Agreed!" Joshua stood up and shook his longtime friend's hand before exiting the library. He turned around just before he hit the door. "I will call upon the troops for a meeting tonight at eight o'clock. Will that be sufficient?"

"That would be great. Thank you for all that you do. I feel the blessings of your daily prayers, my dear friend. I know your prayers played a huge role in my safe return last week. I don't know what I would do without you."

Joshua slowly walked down the hallway to the front door of the academy. He was now on a mission to rally the Six-Pack, and he was sure to locate them on the flanks court.

Yedaiah refocused his mind on God. He wanted so desperately to capture all his wild thoughts and submit them to his Creator.

❋❋❋❋❋

Michael and Noah grabbed their water bottles, summoned their pets, and tied their shoes on tight before jogging out of their room.

"Let's stop in my parents' house and collect Matt and Malachi. They will want to head to the court early for a warm-up too, I'm sure," Michael mentioned to his best buddy.

"Good idea!"

They went next door looking for and calling for the other half of their male quad but were only met by Mom reading in the living room.

"Hey, handsome boys, what are you two up to?" Keilah asked.

"We are in search of Matt and Malachi. I thought they were over here. Have you seen them?"

"They were here about a half an hour ago. They said that they were heading to the kitchen before practice for a bite."

"Okay, thanks. See ya later, Mom," Michael said as he gave his mom a hug.

"Bye, Mrs. Brown," Noah added.

"Good to see you two. Have fun!" Keilah always enjoyed getting her eyes and hugs on the children.

They decided to skip the kitchen and get set up for the scrimmage they were to have. Scrimmaging was their favorite way to prepare for the tournaments. Recruiting the Tough Troops to play against the Six-Pack, Noah loved the competition.

When they arrived, they saw the girls chatting and stretching at the net, Speedy and Roxy right there with them.

"Hey, lassies!" Malachi called from behind Michael and Noah.

Michael turned around. "Oh, there you are. We went to Mom and Dad's to find you two. Did you snack on something healthy, or are you going to be moving like you are carrying a ton of bricks during our practice match?"

"We split a turkey sandwich, thank you very much. Mind your business, bro," Malachi responded as he walked by Michael, giving him a brotherly shove.

"Your business is my business, bro!" he teased back.

When the opposing team arrived, they were all anxious and ready to roll. With no referee on hand, they decided to play light on the rules to avoid dispute and aggravation. They really just wanted to get out and enjoy the sunshine while doing something physical.

The strangest thing happened, however. Strange at O Be Joyful at least. Not five minutes into the match, Grace felt a cold droplet on her face. Looking upward to the sky, memories of her home in Colorado came flooding into mind.

"Guys! It's snowing!" she shouted out in pure glee.

Kiera was equally as excited. "This is the first time since I've been at Mission Mind. I love the snow. Let's ditch the game and go sledding!"

Matthew looked at her as if she were nuts. "Um, you can't sled unless there is actual snow on the ground, ya goof."

She rolled her eyes at him. "Whatever! Where is your sense of adventure?"

"It's set aside for times when there is really an adventure to be had," he joked.

Noah wasn't having it. "It's barely starting to come down. We can get a game in before the court is too wet and slick, I'm sure."

But they couldn't. Within minutes of the first snowflake, it began dumping on them. So much so that they all grabbed, or called, their fur buddies and ran like the wind back to the castle, spilling into the double front entryway doors just before the blizzard really took off.

For the next several hours, the entire student body snuggled into the walls of their beloved school. It was a winter wonderland, and it wasn't even winter yet. Snow in Washington in the early fall was not a thing, but God poured it down from the heavens anyways.

It was apparent who had experience with snow and who didn't. Some Mission Mind members acted frightened by the white fluff, but most wanted to get out into it.

The storm continued through the night and into the next morning, when the announcement over the intercom declared a snow day. The shrieks of happiness bounced off the walls and echoed through the hallways. Several kiddos dug sleds out of a storage closet and bundled themselves for a morning of adrenaline. They were willing to make the long trek in a couple feet of snow to ride the awesome hill that O Be Joyful boasted.

The Six-Pack were part of the percentage who loved the snow. They were the first to suggest sledding and the first to insulate themselves with layers upon layers of warm clothes. Pulling their saucer sleds behind them by yellow cords, they forged a trail for the others to follow.

The hill was a blast! The group of blizzard-happy people grew to almost seventy-five members. So many staff members were out there either sledding or spectating too.

Hike up. Ride down. Hike up. Ride down. Exercise was in full swing, and everyone's legs were burning. That was when Gabriel Brown had the bright idea to retrieve the couple of four-wheelers from a work shed by the herb garden. He convinced his wife to follow him over so she could transport one of them. It was brilliant. When they showed back up at the sled hill with shuttle transportation, everyone cheered. They all loved to sled down as fast as humanly possible, but the trek up was dreaded.

For hours on end, Mr. and Mrs. Brown taxied. Their dedication to the cause was a major blessing. Without the free rides, the fun would have ended hours before it did.

Noah was having the time of his life. Adrenaline junkie at heart, he found that sledding was just another way for him to get out his worries and focus on something else. Worry had been plaguing him lately with all the Satan encounters they had been experiencing. He often put a lot of pressure on himself to handle everything perfectly and please everyone who had expectations of him. But that approach to life was leaving him anxious and drained. The snow day was exactly what he needed, and he believed with his whole heart that it was a gift from above. God was good, present, and looking out for him. He had a thankful heart.

He had the not-so-crazy-coming-from-Noah idea to have sled races down the slope. So he organized teams as he naturally did in most situations, and they began what would end up being a two-hour, all-out serious competition—one student from each team, chasing the fastest snow-drift against each other, trying to cross the finish line first.

"If we can't have flanks matches today due to extreme weather, we will find another way to compete!" Noah had told the large group of sledding kids.

Grace was all about it. "You know that I am a professional! In Colorado, my friends and I can usually sled for several months out of the year. Snow always arrives in October and is known to last, where I live, until May some years. I can zip past anyone down the hill."

"Then you are on my team!" Noah had been serious. He loved winning, so to have experienced members was important to him.

The day was a total hit. The students and teachers that were not fond of the white cold wetness had indoor games running all over the castle. All fifteen fireplaces were piping hot for warming by, and there was a hot chocolate and marshmallow station set up in the dining hall, thanks to Mrs. Heathers.

Even Joshua and Yedaiah were having a peaceful day. They surrendered their responsibilities for the afternoon to enjoy several games of chess, lounging in Grow in Wisdom by its beautiful golden grand fireplace. The two men were maybe the most thankful for the snow day out of everyone. With the accuser's torments as of late, the peace, stillness, and quietness were much appreciated.

They chatted about everything except the obvious pressure they were feeling regarding the impending mission at hand. The Bones' creepy inhabitance would just have to stay back because no one was in the mood to combat them.

The two men were having such a breath of fresh air and time together they were completely startled when the yelling in the hallway began, jolting them into action. The sound of an adult hollering at the top of her lungs was enough to alert anyone's senses.

Flying to their feet from the cozy chairs they had been reclining in, the fearless leaders went to investigate. As they made the turn into the hallway, they were blinded by a thick gray fog lingering in the air. It was so dense it was impossible to see their own hand, even when they held it up in front of their face. Moist condensation made rain-like weather take over the inside of their school.

The screams were multiplying by the moment by every member of the academy that entered into the haze. People were slipping and sliding all over the place because the floors were so soaked from the mist.

Yedaiah and Joshua kept themselves calm, deciding to retreat to the library for an emergency powwow.

Joshua began, "It appears the enemy is back and in a new form this time."

"It certainly is! What shall we do? Any ideas?"

"We have all those powerful leaf blowers in the yard work shed behind the kitchen entryway. Let's go out the library door and make our way to them."

Yedaiah Hallohesh was not at all thrilled with the unwelcomed visitor and knew they needed back up for the battle at hand.

"We need a few more sets of hands for smog blowing. Let's see if we can collect a couple of people on the way for support."

The two godly men snuck out the back door of Grow in Wisdom and spotted three sledders, all bundled up from head to toe, walking through the deep white powder in their direction. It was unknown who they were with all of the snow gear entirely covering them.

Yedaiah was extremely hopeful that whoever the snow bunnies were would not be overwhelmed by the happenings in the hallway. He needed the backup but knew that some of the students and staffers didn't possess strong enough emotions for the battle with the devil. He pleaded with God for warriors to appear behind the snowy face masks.

And sure enough, God answered his prayers. He heard a "Hello, Mr. Hallohesh. Hi, Mr. Zane. Are you two out here for a ride down the slope?"

There was no mistaking Noah's voice. That meant that the other two bundles were most likely members of the Six-Pack and special force team too.

"No, we need some assistance, Noah. Who do you have with you?" Yedaiah asked in wonder.

"It's us, Mr. Hallohesh," Kiera replied. "Kiera and Grace. What do you need help with?"

"Follow me into the outdoor supply shed to grab the leaf blowers. We have a situation of dense, wet fog in the school."

"The enemy is back?" Noah wanted to be sure.

Joshua didn't want the kids to get themselves worked up before entering in and seeing for themselves. "We are unsure at this point exactly what is going on, but we need those blowers as soon as possible."

The five of them scrambled through the thick snow to retrieve the machines and then trudged back toward the library entrance.

When they entered in through the ornate golden door, they noticed the fog had rolled into their beloved room of books.

"It has spread! We need to act fast. I am sure that the student body is overwhelmed by this point. Let's get this under control," Mr. Hallohesh encouraged his trusty troop.

Joshua suggested that they stand in a large wall, all blowing in the same direction to hopefully clear away the haze. He wasn't sure if it would work, but he trusted that God was with them and a miracle would result from their efforts.

Standing as close as they could to one another, leaving as little space between them as possible without bumping into each other, they turned on the leaf blowers. The sounds of the outdoor machines were loud, especially when all on together, but they ignored it as much as possible, as they proceeded forward one step at a time.

It had turned out to be a brilliant idea. The fog was blowing like a thick moving wall away from the wind, in the direction they intended it to. Within minutes, the fog line was out of Grow in Wisdom, and they made their way into the long wide hallway to combat it. They couldn't see even an inch in front of their faces, but they could hear voices yelling in fear from the fog and now the noise they were producing.

"Calm down!" Joshua did his best to holler over the commotion.

Yedaiah felt a touch on his shoulder, which caused him to jump up off his own two feet in startlement.

"It's just me and Gideon, Mr. Hallohesh!" Mieke cried out. "We came to help!"

"Thank you, Mieke! Please get everyone out of here. Take everyone you can locate on the first floor up to higher ground. I would like the hallway completely cleared out. Can you two see enough to assist people through the thick?"

"Don't worry. Gideon and I have got this!"

They went on their way, holding hands for support. It was like the blind leading the blind. When they heard someone or ran into someone, they carefully escorted them to the second floor. Mieke never ceased praying. She was a bit frightened, even more so than when they were under the Bones Abode. But she felt the comfort, confidence, and presence of the Holy Spirit among them as sure as she felt Gideon's large strong hand in hers. It was going to be okay. It was always going to be okay.

The special force team worked hard, and the magic they were hoping for happened. The fog was being pushed toward the double-door entrance of their beloved building. When they were close enough, Yedaiah instructed Kiera and Grace to turn off their blowers so that they could walk through and open the doors for an out.

The girls were indeed nervous to blindly walk through the smog, but they were going to do it anyways. Closing their eyes because their sense of sight was not important in this task, they focused on their sense of touch. One arm wrapped around each other, they used their free one to feel their way, not wanting to bump into anything. When their hand hit the big doors at the beginning of the hall, they pushed them open, releasing the fog up and out into the fresh crisp cold air.

Yedaiah, Joshua, and Noah strongly held the fog wall with their blowers and finally managed to push it all the way outside. They slammed the double doors closed behind it with satisfaction and then collapsed to the ground in exhaustion.

"We did it!" Noah shouted in joy.

"We sure did, kid!" Joshua nudged his arm and smiled. "Great work! I am proud of you young'uns!"

"We are proud of you oldies but goodies!" Noah teased back.

"Praise the Lord!" Yedaiah called out. "I am not exactly sure what that was all about, but I think that we got it handled."

Kids and staff were trickling into the hallway to make sure all was well again and to regain their sense of security and comfort. Low chatter was bouncing off the walls, bringing positive life back into their golden castle home. Many were coming directly to Mr. Hallohesh for reassurance, who didn't really know how to explain it since he himself was still a bit confused over the whole ordeal.

Gideon was right by Yedaiah and Joshua's sides as the excitement was dying down. It was late afternoon, and the entire school would be convening in the dining hall within the hour. He could sense the pressure and weariness of the older leaders, Mr. Zane and Mr. Hallohesh, and took the chance to tell them what was on his mind.

"Good work, you two! I am thankful for such brave and strong leaders at Mission Mind Academy. You guys handled everything with grace, even the attacks from the enemy. It is quite impressive. I think you have earned the right to a retreat for quietness and rest."

Mr. Zane was not about to argue the request. "Amen, Gideon! I am beat and would love nothing more than some peace and quiet. Thank you for your help today. You are not half bad for a newbie," he joked around.

"Well, thank you very much! And you are not bad for an elderly," Gideon kidded right back at him.

Joshua flashed him a sincere smile and shuffled down the hall, calling after him that he would see everyone at the dinner table. Yedaiah, close behind him, told the others that he would see them then too. He had some thinking to do, and thinking was best done in private.

The rest of the folks that were still in the hallway recovering from the mishap retreated to other parts of the school to soak in their last bit of snow day. The ones still on the sled hill, the Brown boys included, didn't have a clue about the indoor foggy weather that just went down. They were still so immersed in the adrenaline-filled ride down the slope.

Noah, Kiera, and Grace decided to head back out into the white powder to fill them in. They would be having their scheduled special task team meeting later that night and wanted all their members to be informed.

It was time to one-up the accuser. How dare he come into their beautiful home and disrupt their peace. He had to be taken down. Noah, in particular, was revved up and ready to go. He was considering pulling an all-nighter to finish the task once and for all. A scheme had come to him during the fog battle, and he was planning on telling the others all about it that night. He hoped that it would be just what they needed to keep Satan locked out of O Be Joyful for good.

15

Baited Trap

Kiera, acting as the voice of reason, brought up a good point to the others during the covert meeting held in the greenhouse, hidden amongst herbs, plants, flowers, and vegetables.

"I can see that you are all hyped up and ready for war," she began, "but we don't have any proof that the enemy was behind this last incident. It could have just been a fluke. Maybe we shouldn't go stirring the pot yet."

Malachi jumped in before the others had a chance to weigh in, "I wasn't even there to see the last incident, but I will tell you that we need to stir the pot no matter what. That is why we are the special task team. It's exactly what we were called together to do."

Yedaiah spoke up, "Malachi is right. God is with us in this. He has joined the ten of us for something bigger than we could ever imagine. Joshua and I have fervently prayed about our next step long before the indoor fog crept in. We are going to invent and create a baited trap. Then we are going to lure the dark spooks over onto our property, giving us home-court advantage."

Grace, who was an avid Christmas movie fan, giggled, as she cried out, "*Home Alone!*"

Joshua had to smile at the similarity. "Yes, that is exactly what we thought about when we first felt the leading from God."

"But this is going to take some time. It won't happen overnight. We need to formulate something creative enough to take down a flying figure that has evil powers. So with that said, I want us to pair off and come up with one good idea for the booby trap. We will have our next meeting right here in one week exactly. At that point we should have five solid ideas brainstormed. In the meantime, your task is to pray without ceasing over the protection of our academy and for no more sightings this week. All understood?" Yedaiah said with authority.

"Understood!" they all agreed.

"Okay, here are the pairs," he finished up, "Grace and Kiera, Matthew and Malachi, Noah and Michael, Mieke and Gideon, and Joshua and I will close it up. Good night and God bless."

Then he abruptly turned and pushed his way through the foliage to exit.

The others stood for a few moments, taking in the night's events. Joshua gave them all a big smile before saying good night and hobbling out himself.

Gideon told the rest of them that it was probably a good idea to hit the hay. It had been such a long day with the snow fun, fog not so fun, and the late-night meeting; everyone was definitely ready for bed.

He suggested, "Let's all walk together. It is almost time for lights out, and it is dark and cold. Safety in numbers is always best."

Mieke didn't like the sound of that. She had spent so many years at O Be Joyful and never had to worry about safety in numbers or safety at all. It had always been a safe haven. She could stroll at any hour anywhere on the property alone without ever thinking about danger. She could let her mind roam and think and pray undivided. What had happened? *This is it*, she thought to herself. *We will create a trap for the devil and invite him into it.* They had to fight for the peace at Mission Mind Academy. It was a sacred place. How dare Satan to think he can come in and disturb it. No way! She was so pumped up by the time her head hit the pillow, she didn't know if she would ever be able to fall asleep again.

Gideon lay between his sheets with warm little gray-and-white Fiona curled up at his feet, thinking about the night. He prayed to the Father in heaven before dozing off, asking for protection and wisdom. He felt a new responsibility and burden for the special task team. He was the most able-bodied because of his age and physical capabilities in the group but knew that he lacked the long-standing relationship with God that most, if not all, of the others had been blessed with. So he prayed for Jesus to draw him in deep and fast. He wanted to be prepared for the battle at hand to the best of his ability.

As he drifted off into a deep slumber, he dreamed about a trap for Satan, one that would prove most effective when put to the test. God was alive and at work even when he slept.

*****

The special task team was focused on their mission over the weekend. The flanks tournament had been canceled on Saturday due to snow, which gave the Six-Pack time to think and brainstorm their trap ideas.

Malachi invited Gideon to the end of the property where they could have the Bones Abode in view for planning inspiration. He thought coming up with a good plan would be easy, but he quickly realized that duping a spiritual enemy would be much trickier than a flesh-and-bones person.

He liked Gideon and was thankful that the Lord had called him onto campus and into their special team. He thought back to the day at *Methuselah's* dock where they first met. He had thought he was a Peeping Tom and didn't like him at all. Now he looked up to him and wanted to spend time with him. He felt that the whole existence of Gideon at Mission Mind was a testimony of God's power. He called someone who didn't even acknowledge Him and turned him into a warrior for His kingdom overnight. It was incredibly motivating for Malachi.

He had so many questions for him too. Being born and raised at O Be Joyful, the outside world really intrigued him. He wanted to know about his childhood and years in public schools. He had questions about his family and job in the common world. He had about a million questions that he was firing off one after another.

Gideon, who didn't have much prior experience around children, besides his relatives, thought it quite entertaining hanging around Malachi and didn't mind the unending questioning coming from him. There was something magical about connecting with a godly child. Malachi had wisdom at his young age that inspired Gideon. He had never met children who knew God in such a personal way.

Gideon shared with him the dream he had dreamt and the details of the trap God laid out before him, as they sat against a tree with the Bones in view.

Malachi couldn't believe the awesome idea of it. "I can't come up with anything! Everything that comes to mind would only lure and snare a human. This ghostly Satan is a whole different story," he said in almost a whine.

"Don't stress yourself, Malachi. God will give you the perfect idea and plan in His timing. I would say to pray about it every single time you are fretting over it."

"Yeah, I guess I am putting a lot of pressure on myself. I barely got a wink of sleep all night last night. Too much brain noise racing through my thick skull, I guess."

Off into the distance, the two saw someone walking alone down the golden trail toward them. They strained their eyes for a moment to reveal Mieke. She was looking down at the ground as she strolled.

"Hey, Mieke!" Malachi yelled out.

"Hello, you two," she called back.

When she approached them, she plopped herself down on the ground next to them, sporting a very long face.

"What is going on in your world today?" Gideon was a bit concerned by her expression.

"I had to talk to Mr. Hallohesh. When I found him in the library, he had a look of worry on his face. More so than I have ever seen before on him, and he carries a lot of pressure around here."

Malachi jumped in, "What is the matter?"

Mieke took a long deep breath before answering. "It's Mr. Zane. He is ill. Mr. Hallohesh said that Joshua didn't show up for their morning coffee get-together. When he went to his room, he found him still in bed, barely able to keep his eyes open."

"That is not good at all. Where is he now? Still in bed?" Malachi needed more information.

"No. Mr. Hallohesh helped him to the clinic on campus for an evaluation. Mrs. Guffey is seeing him now."

"Who is Mrs. Guffey?" Gideon wanted in on the details.

"She is a doctor and a nurse, believe it or not. She is the best there is. She is also trained on natural healing and can work many wonders on the injured and ill. She has been on campus since before I went here as a child. She is nothing short of remarkable," Mieke reassured.

"I want to go see him!" Malachi stood up to leave.

"Let's wait a while before we go see him, Malachi. We don't want to crowd or overwhelm them by our loud presence while they are trying to figure out what is wrong."

"Okay, but as soon as he is stable enough for visitors, I am there!"

"Sounds like a plan. We can pray for him as we wait," Gideon suggested. He was beginning to see the mighty power in prayer.

They all bowed their heads and closed their eyes to lift up the elderly leader whom they dearly loved and needed.

*****

Joshua was so tired. He slept for the better part of the day. When he woke up in the late afternoon, he felt discombobulated and unsure of what was going on around him.

He forced himself to peel his eyelids open long enough to realize he was in the school's single hospital room. He didn't remember going there, and he didn't have a clue what was wrong with him. He was just so overwhelmingly tired.

Before he closed his eyes shut for more sleep, he noticed that he was alone in the room. Who had brought him there, he wondered. What time was it? He was supposed to meet Yedaiah for coffee, and he didn't want to be late. Worry flooded him before he slipped back into a sound slumber.

The next thing he knew, there was a knock on the door startling him awake.

He cleared his throat and willed his eyes wide open once more. "Come in." His voice cracked and quivered.

"It's me, Mr. Zane," Malachi whispered.

"Hello, kid. Good to see you. You don't happen to know why I am here, do you?"

"Only that you were going to meet Mr. Hallohesh for coffee this morning but didn't show up. So he went to your room and found you in bed barely able to keep your eyes open. He brought you to Mrs. Guffey. You have been asleep for about ten hours today. It's 6:00 p.m." Malachi relayed all the details.

"Thank you for coming to visit me."

"I doubt that I am permitted to be here right now. I was told to wait until you were awake and stable, but I have worried all day long and had to come see that you are okay with my own two eyes."

Joshua was touched. "I am glad that you did, kid."

"So are you okay? What is wrong with you?" Malachi pressed.

"I wish I knew. I am so very tired. In fact, I would love to get back to sleep, if you don't mind." He was already shutting his eyes.

"I don't mind. Rest up. I will be back to check on you later. Mrs. Guffey is right outside your door at her desk. She hasn't budged all day. You are being well taken care of for sure," Malachi said as he walked backward toward the door to leave.

Malachi was not feeling very reassured by his hospital room visit with Mr. Zane. Seeing him lying there in bed in that state aged him decades. He was such a godly, confident, powerful man. His weak body had overtaken that, and Malachi was not okay with it. He needed to help somehow but didn't have the slightest clue where to begin.

Finding his brothers and friends would help. Maybe they would have an idea or plan. Plan. He had completely forgotten about the attack plan he was supposed to be coming up with. Somehow it didn't seem important in light of Mr. Zane's current condition.

As he walked into his parents' living room, he saw his whole family sitting together. It was a welcome sight for him.

"Hi, honey," his mom called out, standing up to give him a hug.

His mom's comforting arms around him melted his front, letting tears stream down his face.

"Mr. Zane isn't well at all," he relayed to the others in a soft, gentle manner.

Keilah squeezed him tighter. "I am sorry to hear that. Did you see him?"

"Yes. I had to go and check on him. He woke up for a few short minutes to softly talk to me but then went right back to sleep. He doesn't look like himself at all."

Gabriel felt for his youngest son. He wanted to have an honest conversation about life and the trials that come along with it.

"Buddy, Mr. Zane has lived a beautiful long life. His body has been keeping up with him for so many years it was bound to need extra rest at some point. He is still the strong man of God that you know and love. Give him some time to get well and regain his strength. You'll see."

"Thanks, Dad. I wonder how Mr. Hallohesh is holding up."

His dad responded once again, "He is also a strong, godly man who I am sure is managing just fine. He has the power of the Holy Spirit to see him through every situation, good or bad."

"Yeah, I guess you're right. I am still going to see him. Would anyone else like to join me?" Malachi asked the group.

His brothers both agreed to join him.

The Brown boys group-hugged their mom and dad before leaving the living room. They would be swinging by their room to add Noah to the mix and possibly pop in and collect Grace and Kiera for the visit. Mr. Hallohesh would be glad to see them, he just knew it.

When the six best friends were all together, they set out in search of their beloved Mission Mind leader. After checking several rooms in the castle, they redirected their quest outside. Walking down the familiar winding golden path for the umpteenth time, they scanned their surroundings for a sign of him.

To no avail, however.

"Where could he be hiding?" Kiera wanted to know.

"He could have left campus," Malachi brought up.

Noah doubted it. "Yeah, he might have. But I seriously doubt it. I don't see him leaving Mr. Zane in his condition."

Matthew disagreed. "I bet he did go. Mr. Zane is being taken good care of by Mr. Guffey. Maybe Hallohesh left for medicine or further medical help."

The kids took a break from their search, plopping down on the ground near *Methuselah*. It was still parked at the dock in all its golden glory, so they knew he hadn't left in it.

Their pets were with them providing entertainment as they sat and waited for an idea to pop into one of their heads.

Grace had something else on her mind. "Have any of you come up with your Kevin McCallister plan yet?"

A whole bunch of nos went around the group.

"Me neither," she continued. "I focused so much energy on it last night that I only got an hour or so of sleep."

Malachi could relate. "I was just telling Gideon the same thing this morning. I think he has his trap planned out. Lucky guy."

Kiera spoke up, "It feels like so much pressure to carry planning Satan's attack. Can anyone else relate?"

A whole bunch of yeses went around the group.

Michael still felt optimistic that the perfect plans would come to mind and formulate into something awesome. God was in control. He reminded everyone that they didn't have to use their own wisdom or knowledge or ideas; God would provide all that at exactly the right moment.

They all believed it to be true and ended the conversation before standing up to restart their search.

Turning back to the path toward their school building, they spotted him. Mr. Hallohesh was apparently looking for them too. His prairie dog Fig ran ahead and reached them before he had a chance to.

"Hey, cute buddy." Grace reached down to pet the little guy.

"Hello, kids," Mr. Hallohesh said with a light twinkle in his eye.

"We have been searching for you," Malachi confessed.

"I have been searching for you too," he replied.

Matthew asked, "We are all worried and wondering about Mr. Zane. Malachi visited him and mentioned that he looks very ill. What is wrong with him? Is he going to be okay?"

Yedaiah plopped himself down on the grass where the snow had melted, patting the ground next to him to invite the children and their animals to do the same.

"As you all know, he is advanced in age. His body is not wanting to keep up with his sharp and active mind as much as it used to. He has been running all over the place trying to keep all our paces, and it has taken a toll on him."

"What can we do to help?" Kiera asked.

"Well, first off, the power of prayer is untouchable and would be a good place to start with our efforts. But I would like to remind you that God is alive and well here at O Be Joyful and alive and well in Joshua's heart. He is ultimately in control of everything on heaven and earth, and His will be done. We are asked in the Bible not to worry about anything but, by prayer and petition, give it to God."

Grace was feeling the sudden urge to get her eyes on Mr. Zane; she was beyond worried, even if she shouldn't be. "Can we go see him now?"

"As Malachi probably mentioned, he is very tired. I have been in the hospital room a couple times today, only to find him sound asleep. I think he just needs some time to recoup and rest. Maybe tomorrow would be a good time for a visit. I don't want to overstimulate him. Plus, I doubt that Mrs. Guffey would approve of it at this point. You know how strict she is when it comes to the care of her beloved patients. So we will pray tonight and leave him in God's loving arms."

Malachi quickly stood up, ready to get his frustrations out. "I know that it's almost room time, but I would like to go for a jog. Would anyone want to join me?"

The rest of the loyal Six-Pack stood up. They were not leaving Malachi alone with his own thoughts. He had such a passionate personality and imagination. No need to let his mind run wild.

Grace spoke for the group, "We will all go with you, my friend. Roxy could get some energy out, and it's too beautiful of a night to waste being closed up indoors."

"Thankfully the snow has melted from the path and some of the ground. Maybe by next weekend we can have the flanks match that was canceled," Kiera added.

"Now you're talking!" Noah laughed. Of course he would be down for that.

*****

The evening quickly flew by as did the weekend and following week. It was the day of the special task team's greenhouse meeting. The one specific meeting where the groups of two were supposed to bring their game plan and ideas to the table for the trap meant to take down the enemy once and for all. At least on Mission Mind's campus. They were not delusional about the fact that Satan would be leaving his mark as long as the world was still in existence or as long as they were walking it.

They were all feeling enormous pressure to deliver perfect blueprints that evening amongst the herb-and-vine-covered walls of the indoor garden. But the stress of the details had their heads spinning.

And to make matters even more of a challenge, Mr. Zane was still lying in a hospital room bed, struggling to stay awake for any length of time, which, in turn, had everyone on campus thrown off their usual game.

The special task team was feeling the loss of his wisdom and presence the most. He brought with him peace that surpassed understanding in every situation. The kids especially didn't want to go through with any of it without him.

Yedaiah had met with Gideon, Mieke, and the children during breakfast that morning to confirm that they were still on for that night.

During lunch, the kids skipped the meal for an emergency brainstorm session in the common area at the end of the hall. The kids usually played cards or board games in this spot, but today it was to be their magical, Holy Spirit-inspired space for creating.

Kiera and Grace rearranged the six plush chairs that were scattered about in the nook area, making a circle out of them. They thought ahead by giving room between each chair for pets to lounge and bring peace like only they could.

Noah and Michael scavenged through the pantry when Mrs. Heathers wasn't looking for snacks and drinks to tie them over.

As they assembled together at the end of the hall, they prayed for a miracle—miracles for Mr. Joshua Zane's complete and quick healing, for perfect plans to be carried out in protecting their sacred space, and for peace of mind as they embark on a battle with the devil himself. It was all so big, bigger than them solo or together as a team.

God was the only way.

The six youngish preteens and teens were positive of it.

God is and always will be on His throne, alive and well. The devil would be stomped out like an ant scrounging a Sunday afternoon picnic blanket. This was the faith and hope the kids would always live by. They had even made a pact with each other over such.

The brainstorming process proved to be a fruitful exercise for them. Kiera and Grace had already formulated their plans for its demise, but the four boys needed a little help in the creative-thinking process. They had collectively decided to team up as a foursome. They figured that with quadruple the mind power, quadruple the results.

Kiera and Grace were a little leery over the boys' decision to join forces. It wasn't the assignment given to them for starters, and having one large plan versus two separate traps was risky, to say the least.

"I like your tag team idea guys. What have you come up with thus far?" Kiera desperately wanted to know.

Matthew wasn't about to open up yet to the girls. "First share what you have schemed."

Kiera gladly piped up with her pictures and description of a very *Home Alone*–themed idea.

"First we lure him in with a bit of light teasing. Maybe send a bright-colored flare over to the Bones Abode to stir the already smoldering pot. When we get him over to O Be Joyful, we will welcome him in slowly, not to startle the beast too early. Then I plan to direct his attention to *Methuselah*'s dock, where we will have a perfect contraption waiting to bait, lock, and sink the punk!" She was so fired up!

"Wow, Kiera!" Malachi exclaimed. "I love the drowning idea. Do you think that you can sink Satan?"

Laughing out loud, she said, "I guess we will see!" Kiera was glad that she was able to amuse the group.

"What about you, Grace? You said that you had a good plan. What is it?" Noah inquired.

"I was on similar wavelengths with Kiera on softly luring him here. From past experiences, I have realized that when we upset him first, the outcome is harsher. So with that said, I had an idea to draw him into the very greenhouse we will be meeting in tonight. When we get the door closed behind him, we will have a ghost-proof clear box to trap him in until he suffocates," she said with confidence.

Matthew stared at her. "Do you really think that Satan can be trapped in a box? Where will you get this ghost-proof box?"

"I don't know, Matt. I just know that Mr. Hallohesh challenged us to come up with a creative way to beat the devil. I came up with the idea. If it's meant to be, the ghost-proof box will work out just as it should." She was slightly defensive.

"What about you?" she continued. "Do you have any ideas at all?"

"Well, not exactly. But this is where we are supposed to pool our outstanding thoughts together for a winning idea."

Noah had been losing sleep over the important task and was ready to share his thoughts. "Girls, good ideas. I am sure that some form of what you have invented will work beautifully. I want to add to them. I have had several sleepless nights dreaming up a ghost-beat-able obstacle course. The problem with traditional courses is that the usual physical challenges that these types of courses bring won't neg-atively affect a spiritual being. So we would have to tweak it in such a way that we could win with mind power."

"Brilliant, buddy. Keep going," Michael encouraged his best friend.

"Okay, so my thoughts are this…" Noah went on and relayed the ideas he had about winning with mind power.

"Grace, your interest in the power of mind really inspired me with this idea. In order to pull this off though, I think it would be wise to consult and bring in Mr. and Mrs. Vand. I have never met any two people with more knowledge and wisdom in mind power."

"I like it!" Grace encouraged.

"Think about it. The power and battle of good and evil exists in our minds. It's really all about perception. Our thoughts control our lives. I believe this wholeheartedly! So as Grace has mentioned more than once, the battle between God and Satan will be won or defeated in and from the mind."

"Yes, Noah! That is what I'm talking about," Kiera supported him. "How do you see this playing out?"

"That is why I wanted to team up. I believe that this is how we will win. I just don't have the creativity to work out the details. I am an idea man, not so skilled at particular details."

Michael added to the conversation, "Noah, I have been seeing visions in my alone time with God. Visions of killing off the enemy with my thoughts. I have an idea to bring your dreaming to life."

Malachi filled them in on his time with Gideon earlier that day, "Gideon told me about his ideas, and they eerily line up with the mind-power theme we have going on."

"That's crazy, Malachi! We most definitely need to bring the Vands in on the special task team. I have thought that for quite some time now!" Grace agreed, remembering how perfectly Mrs. Vand had read her like a book the previous week when she was feeling down and out.

"Should we go find Mr. Hallohesh and ask him about including them? I think I saw him in the dining hall when I snuck by to grab the snacks," Noah commented.

"We can wait until after lunch. I would hate to draw attention to ourselves and make people curious as to why we are not at lunch. I already feel like there are kids catching on to our special task team. I have had a few questions come my way by kids in class. I quickly shut them down, but curiosity is high at this point," Matt shared with the others.

"Okay, we will wait until this afternoon. But I want to talk to him before our meeting tonight so that the Vands can come too," Noah said before he got them back on the trap-planning track.

The kids worked through lunch and right up until their afternoon class began. They were feeling confident in their progress when they had to depart and refocus their minds on other topics.

Grace and Kiera were chosen to represent the Six-Pack's idea to bring Mr. and Mrs. Vand in. The boys were going to go to class ahead of time letting their teacher know that the girls had to stop into Mr. Hallohesh's office before coming in late.

The girls said a quick prayer before knocking on his door.

"Come on in," they heard him say.

"Well, hello, ladies. What is it that I can help you with this afternoon? I noticed the six of you missing from lunch today. Any specific reason for that?" he asked them.

"We were preparing for tonight's meeting. Actually, that is why we are here."

"Okay, how can I help?" he urged them to continue.

"After much discussion, we believe that it would be in all our best interest to bring Mr. and Mrs. Vand in on our special task team," Kiera began.

"Oh, why is that?"

Grace took it from there. "We think that the enemy will be defeated using the power of our thoughts, and who is perfect to assist in such an endeavor but the Power of Thoughts teacher himself? Plus Mrs. Vand also seems to have the gift of reading thought. We just all believe that they would be very beneficial in the battle that is to come."

"I like where you two are heading with this. I think that you might be right. Let me take some time to pray over this subject, and if I feel led, I will invite them to the greenhouse tonight to join in."

"Thank you, Mr. Hallohesh. Now we need to scram to class."

"Thanks, girls. God bless your afternoon. Keep up the good work."

Yedaiah couldn't help being super proud of the youngsters. His heart lit on fire when he witnessed others hot for the Lord and His ways. The Six-Pack, although sometimes too curious and wondrous for their own safety and good, reminded him of himself. He remembered being their age, and even though his life was vastly different from theirs during childhood, he had a similar heart and strength from God. He also was prone to dangerous adventure. After all, it was him who had flown into the Bones Abode alone and unprepared for the trouble that found him.

They were onto something with Mr. and Mrs. Vand. They were a uniquely special couple. He recognized it from the moment he met them.

In that moment, he lifted up his countenance to his all-powerful God and spoke aloud, "Father, I thank You for the wonderful individuals that You have so purposefully placed at O Be Joyful. I lift up Joshua to You this day. Please restore his body back to a healthy state. Give him the energy and strength to get out of bed and resume the things he enjoys in life. He is so wise, and I really depend on him for support on an hourly basis. I also would like to surrender the special task team to You once more. Would You please make it clear to us who is meant to be involved? I pray over Mr. and Mrs. Vand. If they are supposed to join us in the battle against the devil, make it crystal clear. Thank You for being here for me to talk to. Thank You for loving us so perfectly. And finally, thank You for being You and calling us to know You. I love You. Amen."

Yedaiah sat back down in his chair and bowed his head in silence. He sat that way for several minutes. He just wanted to listen. He had spoken to God, petitioning for help, and now was his time to wait and hear what the good Lord said.

Much to his surprise, because he was expecting an answer from within, an audible voice boomed and echoed off the walls of his office.

"Yes, Yedaiah!" resounded the mighty voice.

Just once did those two words be spoken. But that was all it took. Yedaiah recognized the voice and was so thankful for it. It has been such a long time since God had spoken aloud to him. He felt so honored.

"Thank You, Jesus. Thank You!"

He stood up from his seat, opened the door to his office, and strolled down the hall toward Mr. Vand's Power of Thought classroom. He had an invitation to the greenhouse to deliver.

*****

Arriving twenty minutes early to the meeting location, Yedaiah leaned against a workbench among the shrubs and plants, breathing in the fresh smells of life and growth. He loved having fresh vegetation growing all over their campus. It kept the air crisp with hundreds of different smells, depending on the season.

He thought about how thankful he was that the kids were brave enough to ask for the Vands to join the team. He carried so much respect for the godly couple and couldn't wait to see how God was going to use them for His kingdom.

Satan had kept his distance lately, and Yedaiah was not complaining about it. He disliked the flying figures and all that they represented. Grace and Kiera had got his mind spinning when they mentioned defeating the enemy in thought as opposed to deed. It was a noble idea indeed. But what did that even look like in action.

He was getting very anxious for the others to arrive. He wanted to hear the thoughts and plans they had been working on all week.

He had stopped into Joshua's hospital room just before the greenhouse, receiving prayer from him, even though he was the one in great need of prayer. He had not made much improvement at all, which caused Yedaiah and the rest of the school to worry endlessly about him.

Yedaiah had been praying constantly for his good friend and trusted God completely with his life, but seeing him lying in bed so helplessly stirred up several emotions in the head of the school's heart.

Mr. and Mrs. Vand were the next to enter into the shrubbery, giving Yedaiah a few minutes to connect with them before the others showed up. He made sure that they were comfortable with the team and task at hand. He filled them in on all the sightings of the enemy one more time so they were fresh in mind.

Mieke and Gideon strolled in next, bringing laughter with them. Yedaiah couldn't help but notice their fast bond and compatible personalities. He was thankful that God had brought Mieke back to the academy and equally glad that He called Gideon to be her partner during this time of importance. He couldn't imagine if she had to wrangle the kids endlessly without adult interaction. She would have been long gone by now.

Yedaiah chuckled at himself, thinking about the life and craziness the six children brought to Mission Mind and the intimate task group. They were young and unaffected by the years of toil on earth. They were daring and fresh, a perfect mixture for success.

When they arrived with their pets in tow, Yedaiah opened the meeting with a prayer. Then they got down to business.

The Vands listened in the beginning, getting a feel for what this group was all about. But not too far into the discussion, they chimed in. When they did, the kids smiled at each other, all so glad and proud to have invited them. They were going to be a very important key to the success of the mission.

Matthew took the lead for the Six-Pack. "We began last week by individually trying to prepare a minefield to lure the enemy in for payback and victory. But when we decided to have a study group, for lack of better words, we felt strongly on going a different direction. We believe that Satan will never be trapped into a box, which left our booby trap ideas useless."

Mieke and Gideon peered over at each other, intrigued where this was all heading.

Michael took over next. "We think that the enemy is lurking around scaring everyone because of unrepented sin on our campus."

"When we—and I don't even know specifically who we is—let sin dwell in us, we open ourselves up to the devil's work," Kiera added.

"Interesting notion!" Yedaiah didn't see this coming and couldn't believe he hadn't thought about it that way before himself.

Noah continued from there, "So if sin is present among the student body or staff at Mission Mind, we need to locate it. It's our only shot of getting rid of the enemy's terrifying visits."

Grace was next. "We thought that having Mr. and Mrs. Vand on our team would be a huge benefit because sin dwells in our thoughts and minds most of the time. If our sins were in works, they would be easier to spot and take action against. But in the mind, it can stay hidden and suppressed forever if unchecked."

This was where Mr. Vand chimed up and in on the conversation. "You are definitely on the right track here with sin and Satan. In my experience, they go hand in hand. Unrepented sin, even through thoughts, is like a welcome sign hung out for the devil. When we are not meditating on God, living by His Word, and walking down the middle of His perfect path, we are living for the other side. The dark side, that is."

Mieke wanted to know. "How do we detect the sins of others? If it is not the special task team that is carrying around the yoke, how do we stop it?"

Yedaiah had a pretty good idea about the topic at hand. "First of all, I believe that from time to time, even if it is not our intention, we all carry around the *yoke of sin*, as you so eloquently put it, Mieke. But if this is indeed what is welcoming the accuser onto campus, then we will need to include the entire school in the plans for his demise."

Mrs. Vand had been quiet long enough. "I am envisioning a series of courses held and taught for the entire school, specific to cleansing, purifying, and thoroughly checking the condition of one's heart. I imagine that we should get started on this stat. We do not want to give the enemy a foothold on us any longer than we have to."

Yedaiah liked the idea. They all liked the idea.

Mr. Vand started formulating intervention topics and scripture in his mind. He would most likely be the person teaching and intervening on behalf of the group. He was the only professional teacher at the school out of their group and pretty much taught on said subjects daily. But he came to the realization that his current curriculum was not reaching hearts as much as he desperately wanted to.

He told the others, "I will need some time to pray over all of this. I would be happy to be the teacher of these courses, if you will assemble the school body. Give me a few days to create a Holy Spirit-filled heading before we have our first meeting."

Yedaiah was again thankful that the Vands joined forces with them.

"Thank you, Mr. Vand. For now, I think it's best if we leave the details pertaining to the courses vague. I don't see the benefit of everyone knowing why we are holding them. It will just startle our school. Plus, if they know that our goal is the repentance of internal sin to squash the devil, we might be met with rebellion and those who close themselves off from us."

"Yes, the heart and mind are fickle things at times. How often do we do the things we don't want to do even to the point of sinning and ignore the things that we do want to do and know is right?" Mrs. Vand agreed with Yedaiah.

After the next steps were decided, the task team departed ways, retreating to their private quarters to debrief.

Mieke lay in bed staring at her ceiling for hours thinking about the condition of her own heart in light of the night's conversation. She wanted to be good and sure that it wasn't herself inviting Satan's presence. She knew that she was prone to go against the grain. She just wanted to make sure swimming upstream was God's plan for her. When she finally did doze off to sleep, she experienced some wild dreams. Not surprising that they included good and evil, along with the special task team and chosen pets.

Gideon fell into a rich slumber very quickly after such a heavy-topic conversation that evening. He wasn't used to so much spiritual chatter but was becoming quite fond of it. He had no doubt that they were headed on the right track. He had nightly dreams and visions lining up perfectly to the plans unfolding before his eyes. Being a part of the team and such a big purpose gave him life more abundant than he could have ever imagined, prior to Mission Mind and O Be Joyful.

Kiera and Grace snuggled up in their covers and went right to sleep. They were both resting in gratitude for the unveiling plans that were made that night. The new members of the team didn't replace Mr. Zane but added a fresh dynamic to the group. They felt at peace. God was always good and would never leave them. They reminded each other of the fact before they had turned out the light that night.

The Brown boys had spent a little time with their mom and dad before reconnecting with Noah in their shared room. Noah had taken a solo walk around the castle before entering inside. He had to clear his mind of the thoughts that swirled around it. He was thrilled that they had come up with a heading, but unfinished details left him frazzled. He was a thorough individual that liked to know what was coming next. By the time he opened the door to his room, he had surrendered to trust. It all came down to trusting God with the future. He resigned to not having to have it all figured out. *Just trust Me*, Jesus was loudly speaking to his heart.

Mr. and Mrs. Vand sat in their little living room with mugs filled with tea and talked through the evening's events. They most definitely had been thrown a huge curveball. They had known about the special task team prior because of several conversations with Joshua on it. He had shared with them the goal to rid the campus of the dark-shadow appearances. They had prayed fervently together over the matter since hearing about it. But now they were in the middle of it all. It was going to be a shift in thought and prayer for them, but they felt prepared for the task at hand. Mr. and Mrs. Vand knew that they were at Mission Mind for a humongous reason, and after tonight's meeting, they were seeing a glimpse of what that reason was.

Yedaiah stopped into the hospital room housing for one last check on his friend. Joshua was awake, surprisingly. He pushed himself up to a seated position before asking his buddy about how the night unfolded. Yedaiah spent the better part of an hour rehashing the events. They prayed together and hugged each other tight. Yedaiah promised to visit first thing in the morning and then headed to his room for much-needed rest. He worried about his friend but pushed the fears aside, not wanting to be the source of sin through thought.

16

Family Weekend

"Today is the day! Today is the day!" Grace sang through the halls as she scurried down to breakfast.

It was a beautiful sunny Saturday morning, and a joyful buzz was floating throughout the entire academy. It had been a very calm few weeks, but this was going to be a weekend to remember.

In just a matter of hours, Mission Mind Academy students would have the pleasure of showing their families where they lived and learned. Family weekend happened only once a year, and families from all over the country were transported into O Be Joyful for it.

Grace thought that she was the most excited of all. Her tiny brother Nathaniel would be coming along with her mom and dad. Mr. Hallohesh was picking them up himself in the hot-air balloon. Most parents would be flying into Seattle's airport, where they would take an Uber to *Methuselah*'s dock for entry. But Mr. Hallohesh had told Grace that he wanted to accompany her family himself. He was so proud of her for all her hard work and support at their school that he wanted uninterrupted time to relay it to the Hayes.

Mr. Zane was usually the escort on *Methuselah*, but he was still too weak and sick for the task. He had thankfully left the hospital room but was mostly confined to his own room, with Mrs. Guffey checking in several times a day. Mrs. Heathers made it a point to deliver food to Joshua for each meal and even brought her own food along to eat with him and keep him company.

Gabriel and Keilah Brown had volunteered to handle *Methuselah* and the coming parents. Being parents themselves to three students on campus gave them the right touch to welcome the guests. They would be making several trips from the Seattle port to Mission Mind's realm that morning, and they were looking forward to meeting the parents of the kids they had grown to love.

Grace plopped her happy fanny down on a bench in the dining hall next to Noah. He was all smiles as he shoved a forkful of fluffy pancake into his open mouth.

"Good morning, sunshine!" he greeted his friend.

"It sure is!" she replied. "I think I am way too excited to eat."

"I wouldn't miss out if I were you. Mrs. Heathers can make some amazing flapjacks. I am on my third one. And the bacon is browned to perfection," he said, as he shoved another huge bite in.

After she went for a plate of her own food, she sat back down a little less joyful.

"What happened? You were only gone for two minutes and you look worried."

"I realized that it's been a few weeks since we have seen the enemy around campus. I am hoping and praying he stays away while our families are here. Can you imagine what they would think and do? My parents would probably forbid me to stay and take me home with them. I don't want to leave." Grace hung her head.

"Okay. Stop with all that nonsense. Remember it's a battle of the mind, so don't let your mind run away from you. We have to keep positive thoughts. In a few days, we will begin the series of training classes with the whole school, and Mr. Vand will help us all get rid of the accuser," Noah reassured her.

"Yeah, I guess you're right. I think it will be good for the whole school to go through the courses. Whoever has unsettled internal business needs to repent and be free as Jesus calls us to be. I bet we all need to clean the cobwebs out, so to speak."

"You got that right. I still see kids walking around here in fear, and they don't even know half of it. Satan feeds off fear and doubt, and it has to be what is bringing him back to disturb us over and over again."

"Well, he had better just steer clear of our beautiful campus during family weekend, or I am going to have some major beef with him," she threatened the air.

"You are hilarious, Grace. Just eat your food and be joyful. This weekend is going to go off without a hitch. That is my story, and I am sticking to it."

The Brown boys and Kiera plopped down next to them and began shoveling pancakes into their mouths without a word.

Grace giggled. "You are right, Noah, without a hitch!"

Malachi looked around at the rest of them. "Did I miss something?"

"Nope," Noah said, "not a thing," as he gave Grace a wink.

The dining hall was full of excitement; every table was overflowing with talk and laughter. All the children were missing their families by this time of year. They had all been home for a visit at least once by this time, but having fathers and mothers on their stomping ground was an altogether different experience. Many parents had never been to O Be Joyful Gardens before. Stepping onto the campus for the first time was an awe-inspiring event for anyone.

The clouds were in full form that morning too. God seemed to be welcoming the families with a safari in the sky. A large white puffy cloud lion and her cubs floated past the dining hall's window, pausing for a minute before it drifted on. A herd of elephants charged above their heads as a rhino slowly ambled beside them.

"His wondrous ways never cease to amaze me," Kiera commented, looking upward.

The others agreed between bites of breakfast.

The Browns were among the few with parents already on campus, so family weekend only interested them because they liked meeting their friends' moms and dads. Everyone already knew their parents and adopted them as their own during the school year. Gabriel and Keilah were a hit with the student body, bringing love, support, and comfort to everyone equally.

"I think the thing that surprises the new families the most is our chosen pets. I like to sit on one of our benches along the path and watch their faces as they take in the animals here. Some of the expressions you can catch are priceless," Matt told them.

"Sounds like fun times," Noah noted. "Has anyone heard about today's agenda? I am wondering what to do with my parents when they arrive."

We are meeting in Psalm Auditorium for a brief opening ceremony and prayer with Mr. Hallohesh at noon," Grace replied.

Noah stood up, piled his dishes in his arms, and turned toward the trash bin. "See you guys at noon. I am going to take Turbo for a walk while I wait for my parents to come."

"Great idea!" Grace told him. "Don't be surprised if Roxy and I run into you on the path. Roxy is going to be so excited to see my parents and Nathaniel. I really need to get some of her energy out beforehand."

Kiera ate her last bite, chewing it up before she called after Grace, "Mind if I tag along? I know Speedy doesn't exactly have to get energy out, but I sure do. My nerves are on edge." She laughed at herself.

"Bye, Browns!" The girls directed their attention toward their good friends.

"See ya in a few hours, ladies," Malachi responded.

Heading back to their room to pick up their beloved pets, the girls sang as they went. The two were always singing. A worship song, a Christmas jingle, an oldie but a goodie—anything that popped into their mind, really.

Roxy must have heard them coming because as soon as they opened the door, she bounded out into the hall ready for fun. Speedy was awake and lounging on Kiera's bed but was more than happy to snuggle in her owner's arms for a walk, as always.

"Let's go, kids," Kiera said to the furballs.

Roxy picked up her favorite racquetball with her mouth and followed Grace down the hall and out into the open sunshiny day. It appeared that the whole school had the idea to get out and about that morning. The entire breakfast hall had apparently filed outside with their pets too. It looked like a zoo or circus with kids and animals anxiously waiting for their families.

Grace spotted Noah not too far down the golden path near *Methuselah's* dock. She called out to his dog Turbo, who did an about-face and then bolted for Roxy. The two pups were such great friends. It warmed Grace's heart to see her four-legged best friend had another four-legged best friend.

The pups chased each other everywhere, while the girls sank down onto the bench next to Noah.

It wasn't long before the first tour of parents pulled up with Mr. and Mrs. Brown to the dock for unloading. Noah, Kiera, and Grace watched in silence while several unknown faces climbed upon O Be Joyful's dry land. Then they saw kids running, their pets hot on their tails, for their parents, to embrace in long hugs. It was a glorious sight.

As soon as the parents were connected with one of the teachers at the academy, who were standing by to help settle the arrivals in, Gabriel and Keilah hopped back onto *Methuselah* for another round.

The kids sat on the bench long enough to see three rounds of drop-offs; each was a similar sight. It was getting to be too much, waiting for their own parents to get there.

Kiera's were the first to arrive. Her mom and dad were coming from Missouri and appeared bright-eyed and bushy-tailed when their boat pulled in. They jumped off *Methuselah* so fast it literally rocked the boat. They were staring up at the clouds in the sky when Kiera ran to them and wrapped her arms around them.

"Dad! Mom! It's so good to see you!" she cried.

"Honey, it's been way too long. We have missed you so much."

They were still in an embrace when her parents looked down and saw Speedy in a backpack, secured to her.

"So this is the famous sloth Speedy, huh?" her dad commented.

"Yep! This is my favorite wee buddy. We go everywhere on campus together. Two peas in a pod."

Kiera brought her mom and dad over to meet her two best buds who had been taking in their reconnection.

"Mom, Dad, I want to introduce you to Grace and Noah, two members of our Six-Pack team."

"It is an absolute pleasure to meet you two. We have heard so much about you," Kiera's mom said to them.

"So nice to meet you too," Grace and Noah both said with bright smiles.

Kiera saw one of her teachers approaching and knew it was a sign to get her parents acquainted with Mission Mind.

"We will see you guys later. I hope you have great reunions with your parents when they get here," she told her buddies.

"See you at noon!" Grace said to her roommate.

All parents would be staying in rooms in the guest building on campus. It was very hotel-like but also castle-like, in that it was made out of gold, reflecting the Mission Mind Academy structure. Parents would be teamed up with another family for lodging. Two sets of parents per room. Rooms had anywhere from two to six beds inside. There were exceptions too for families like Grace's, who had tiny babies to tend to. They were to get their own rooms for the night.

Noah was off the bench throwing a ball for Turbo and Roxy Ann to chase after when he saw his parents' faces unloading from *Methuselah*. His dog must have remembered them because the German shepherd abandoned the competitive fetch game and bolted to greet them.

Noah jogged to their side to give them a huge hug, following his pup's lead.

"Welcome back, guys!" he told them.

It had been last year's parent weekend since they had stepped foot at Mission Mind.

"It's so great to see you, son. You look amazing. We have missed you very much," his mom squeezed him tighter.

"Is that Grace and Roxy over there watching us," Noah's dad commented.

"Yes, it is. Great eye, Dad. Come meet her. She is waiting for Mr. Hallohesh to return in the hot-air balloon with her family."

"Lead the way, son," his dad responded.

"Grace, I would like you to meet my parents. Mom, Dad, this is Grace Hayes, and this is her dog Roxy Ann, the only pet on campus that came from the real world, for lack of better words. Her dog from home got to come with her to school and is Turbo's best friend."

"It's a great pleasure to meet you, Mr. and Mrs. Wilson." Grace stood up to shake their hands.

"Well, it's about time we put a face to the name we hear so much about. I hope that you enjoy your time with your family this weekend," Mrs. Wilson remarked.

"Thank you. I most definitely will. My newborn baby brother is coming, and I am about to burst waiting for them to get here. I hope you have a wonderful visit at O Be joyful." She smiled at them.

Noah said goodbye to his friend as he walked with his parents down the golden path.

Grace sat back down on the bench, thankful that she spotted the Brown boys in the distance heading her way. She didn't want to sit in solitude. She was so thankful for her group of friends. They were a huge blessing to her from the moment she arrived at school.

"Hi, guys, what's up?" she said when the three reached her.

"Still anxiously waiting?" Malachi asked.

"Yep. I got a chance to meet Kiera and Noah's parents though. They all seem really nice. I would expect nothing else, with the awesome kids they have. What is taking Mr. Hallohesh so long? I just can't wait another second. He needs to get here soon. That's all I've got to say."

"Be patient, lady! They will be here before you know it!" Matt encouraged.

Another boat full of parents arrived, making Grace antsy.

"I have got to get up and move around. What can I do to kill some time?" she asked her friends.

But just then, in the clouds appeared the balloon, coming in hot, with her beloved family on board.

"They're here! They're here! Come on, guys! Come meet my parents!" she yelled to the Browns as she was sprinting for the landing pad.

This is going to be the best day, she thought to herself, as the balloon floated onto the X and her parents' heads poked over the edge of the basket.

"Dad! Mom!" Grace yelled.

"Gracie!" her mom called back as she propped Nathaniel up for viewing.

"Aww, there is my little cutie of a brother."

Yedaiah always felt incredibly joyful watching the reunions of children and parents on family weekends at Mission Mind. Even though he had never experienced parents of his own coming to visit, he had never felt jealous. It was a blessing to see the love in healthy family units.

After he secured the balloon, he helped Grace's wonderful family to solid ground. Roxy couldn't help herself and bounded right for them, jumping on them and licking them silly.

"Roxy girl, we have missed you too!" Mrs. Hayes gave her a little cuddle.

Grace hugged her parents then snatched her tiny brother up into her arms. She breathed in his fresh baby smell and nuzzled her face to his. He was the most precious human in the world as far as she was concerned.

Grace looked up from her brother to see Matt, Michael, and Malachi taking in the scene from a distance. She felt bad forgetting about them and called them over to meet her family.

"These are three of my dearest friends here, Matthew, Michael, and Malachi." She made the introductions.

"It is a pleasure to meet you boys. I have heard nothing but great things about the Brown boys." Her dad extended his strong hand.

"It's really nice to meet you too." They all shook hands.

Yedaiah was ready to get the show on the road if he was going to get the Hayes settled in before the assembly due in an hour.

"Are we ready to head inside?" Yedaiah asked.

"Sure, Mr. Hallohesh, lead the way." Grace was ready.

"What are you boys going to do?" Grace wondered.

Matthew told her, "We are in charge of showing a couple of parents around when they arrive in a few minutes. My parents only have four more boatloads to transport on *Methuselah* before everyone is here and accounted for."

"Awesome. I will catch up with you in Psalm in an hour." She winked at her buddies.

Being their first time at O Be Joyful, the Hayes were extremely taken aback by their surroundings. The cloud formations alone were enough to wow, but the golden path, gardens, animals, and Mission Mind Academy itself in all of its golden glory was sparking like heaven from the late morning sun.

While walking down the large corridors for the brief tour, Grace ran into Noah and his family. She was nervous to introduce her parents to everyone for some reason. She talked about the Six-Pack nonstop when she visited her parents, but it made it slightly embarrassing when they were all together. She wondered if her five friends talked about and cared about her as much as she did.

Noah was taking his mom and dad out on the property for a stroll when they passed them. After they all had a chance to meet, they went in separate directions, promising to save seats next to each other at the assembly.

The morning flew by in a matter of moments, and everyone was sitting in their chairs waiting for Mr. Hallohesh to make his entrance. Kiera, Noah, Grace, and the Browns managed to score a whole row for them and their families, thankful that they had each other for support. Gabriel and Keilah had managed to transport all the families in a safe and timely fashion and were now happy to be sitting with their boys.

When Yedaiah stepped through the backstage curtain out in front of the audience, cheers and applause broke out throughout the whole auditorium. Psalm was one of the most unique rooms at Mission Mind. It was completely soundproof from the outside of it for starters, but the coolest part was the way it was decorated. It looked like Noah's ark. Every last detail on the interior was mimicking the huge boat, with the exception of the smells you can imagine took place, housing two of every type of animals for such a long period of time.

He waited patiently for the clapping to die down before he opened the assembly in prayer. He asked God to bless each family during their stay at O Be Joyful and to bless the family of God as a whole. He asked that the Holy Spirit would protect them from negativity and bring each person peace. He thanked Jesus for His hand in all things and then the whole crowd said amen.

Yedaiah introduced himself and then the entire staff was invited on stage to share who they are and what role they played at Mission Mind. The parents and students sat quietly while they got familiarized with the adults pouring their time and efforts into the kids.

Then he went over the itinerary for the weekend. It would begin with an outdoor garden picnic brunch. Mrs. Heathers and her staff had prepared a feast, complete with massive amounts of tables and chairs set for the occasion.

When the assembly was over, Yedaiah invited everyone to the gardens for food and fellowship. It was a stunning sight to walk up upon. Golden tablecloths covered the round tables, fresh flowers were in elaborate vases, splashing colors everywhere, and large banquet tables were full of the yummiest-looking spread you ever did see.

"This is beautiful. I am starving!" Kiera's mom whispered to her.

"Me too. Let's get in line quickly. It looks like there are a lot of hungry people to contend with!" She giggled while she jogged into line, thankful that they were somewhere in the middle and not at the back. She didn't think she could be patient enough for that.

Before the first plate was filled, Mr. Vand blessed the bounty that they were about to devour. He then went around to the opposite side of the buffet to help serve with his wife. They had volunteered to serve the families, hoping to get a glimpse of their students' parents. It was always very strange to grow super close to children and not having ever met their parents.

Mieke and Gideon had also agreed to be servers during the welcome brunch. Neither of them had children nor were teachers of any of them, so they felt like the natural option is to help.

Gideon was having the time of his life. Being around all the positive energy was a far cry from the world he had just come from. Real estate was a sticky career, and his friends in the outside world, he now realized, didn't bring light to his life. Being around all the believers really forced him to hold up a mirror on his life. He wasn't sure he wanted his old life at all anymore. He did miss his family. His sister was a special person to him, but she even had negative energy about her, constantly complaining about one thing or another.

He looked over at his newest friend, Mieke. Without realizing it, a huge smile grew on his face from one glance in her direction. He couldn't get over how he felt when he was around her. She was confident but not cocky, hardworking but never prideful about it, and sincere and real without ever making things about herself. He was fairly positive he had never met anyone cooler in his entire existence.

His heart skipped a beat when she shot a glance back at him and smiled a huge toothy grin. He felt like he had been caught stalking her every move, even though it was just a quick peek.

They stood side by side—the Vands, Mieke, and Gideon—huge spoons in their gloved hands, scooping pile after pile of deliciousness on each passerby's plate. When the entirety of the line's plates was filled to overflowing, they served themselves and found the last table with four open seats to enjoy the food themselves.

Worship music was playing in the background on the speakers perfectly spread out through the garden, giving the atmosphere a warm feeling. The sunshine gorgeously beat against the golden accents everywhere, but not too warm because of the garden umbrellas scattered about.

The Six-Pack ended up pushing three tables together so that their families would have an opportunity to get to know one another and so the kids could hang out, like they always preferred.

There were chosen pets under tables and mingling around feet, hoping for a spill or crumb to tumble their way.

Yedaiah glanced around at the view and was very pleased. He thought how perfect the day was already flowing. Then a reality hit him square in the face. His best buddy was absent. Joshua was hoping and praying to have enough energy and strength to attend the meal but was unable when it came right down to it.

Yedaiah excused himself from the table he had been dining at and then proceeded back to the food table. He filled up a plate with a little of every single thing offered, filled a golden cup up with lemonade, then made his way to Joshua's room.

Softly knocking on his door, he called out, "Joshua, are you in there? It's Yedaiah bringing food."

"Come in," he heard a faint voice respond.

Yedaiah slowly opened his friend's door with his few free fingers and stepped inside. Surprised to see Joshua sitting up in a corner chair with his Bible opened in his lap, he crossed the room to be closer.

"Are you hungry? Mrs. Heathers has really outdone herself today with the amazing spread she prepared. I thought you would enjoy a plate."

"Thank you very much. I am looking forward to it if it tastes anything close to how it smells. Is that ham I see?"

"It sure is, and it does taste even better than it smells."

"Well then, plop that plate right down here," Joshua said as he pointed to the end table to the right of his chair.

"My pleasure!"

"So how are things going so far on this fine family weekend? I really am bummed that I can't be a part of it. I am getting sick and tired of being sick and tired. I have always been able to keep a positive attitude in life, mostly because the joy of the Lord is my strength, but lately I have been finding it very difficult to maintain. I think it's because I am alone with my thoughts too much with nothing else to do. I just lie around and fret about stupid unimportant things. And don't even get me started on the special task force. I want to be out there fighting off Satan with the rest of our brave group," Joshua shared his true feelings.

"I can understand why you feel that way, my friend. This is a new phase of life for you with a whole new set of trials and tribulations. Never forget that Jesus has his hand upon you and will still use you in a mighty way, no matter where you have to rest yourself."

"Thank you, Yedaiah. I am thankful for you. Now, you better get yourself back down to the party. I am sure that there are at least ten people right now that are looking for you for one reason or another at this very moment."

Yedaiah laughed out loud. He then laid his hand upon Joshua and lifted him up to the Lord.

When he rejoined the party, he indeed did have several people searching for him. He made his rounds and assisted all that he could. When he took a moment to glance down at his watch, he realized it was time for the next activity, which happened to be a flanks match.

There were to be three games that afternoon so that all teams could play for their families. Flanks was still relatively new at Mission Mind Academy, so no parents had witnessed the sport yet.

Noah's parents were so proud. He had told them about it over the phone a few times, but until they entered *Methuselah* and got the lowdown from Gabriel, they hadn't realized what a success it was. They weren't at all surprised; Noah had been generating movement since birth. He rarely stopped stirring since day one of life, which led to lots of creative active play.

The entirety of campus helped clean up brunch before readying themselves for the match. The kids had been practicing but hadn't had time for tournaments in several weeks.

The Six-Pack were playing in the first match against the Hammerheads. Feeling nervous about the large amounts of spectators, the teams did their best to keep focused and undistracted.

Winning the coin toss, the Six-Pack took their positions. As soon as Gabriel blew the whistle, they were off and running.

Yedaiah, from the stands, looked heavenward saying a silent prayer. He asked for fun, peace, and the presence of the enemy to stay clear of their family weekend. He had been experiencing the lingering feeling of dread. What if the accuser made an appearance? How would the parents react? Would they pull their children out of Mission Mind? He pushed the unpleasant thoughts back to the far corner of his mind, not wanting to entertain the ideas.

The matches were a huge success in that everyone enjoyed the entertainment and friendly competition. Parents were hooting and hollering from the stands, and kids were up on their feet jumping around with excitement.

The Six-Pack were undefeated, mostly because of the unending practices Noah and Michael held for them. They also had a huge advantage because not only did they work as a team on the court, but off the court they were the special task team. They knew each other and how each of them ticked, and it showed during the matches. They moved around passing to one another and backing each other up as if it were second nature.

When the Six-Pack's game was finished, they joined their parents and friends in the bleachers. Three hours later, after the third match had been played, everyone was hungry and ready for dinner.

Filing into Mission Mind Academy, in all its radiant golden glory, they made their way to the dining hall to see what was on the menu for the evening.

The wafting smells of pot roast danced up their noses as they took their seats at beautifully set tables.

When all were present, Yedaiah stood for prayer and then an announcement.

"I am so thankful for all the family members who were able to make it here this weekend to support your student and spend time with our Mission Mind family. We have planned a special treat for you all this evening after dinner. We have formed groups of six families together for a little healthy competition. A moonlight scavenger hunt is what's on the agenda."

Cheering and clapping broke out through the dining hall. It was obvious the kids were stoked about the upcoming activity.

Yedaiah waited for the cheering to subside before continuing, "Directly after mealtime, I would like everyone to collect your pets for the fun and then meet in front of the academy, on the lawn in front of the steps. Mr. and Mrs. Vand have graciously planned and prepared the hunt. They are in charge and will give further exact directions on the lawn. So happy eating to you, thanks to Mrs. Heathers and her amazing kitchen staff, and we will see you all out front."

Claps once again echoed off the walls and ceiling as Mr. Hallohesh found his seat to enjoy his meal.

He was sitting with Mr. and Mrs. Vand so that they could fill him in more completely on the scavenger. He was still leery about the enemy making an unwelcomed appearance but didn't want to let the fears ruin his evening of fun. He would be a pathway helper for those who needed it. Mr. Vand informed him that he would walk the golden path for the duration of the hunt, to act as a guide to anyone completely lost or give a clue if teams were stuck. He was handed a copy of the scavenger hunt, filled in with all the locations so he would know how to help.

Mieke and Gideon were the other two chosen to be pathway helpers. They were sitting at dinner with the Vands and Yedaiah and couldn't wait for their role in the game.

"This is going to be so fun. And with the warm breeze outside, it's a perfect night for it," Mieke commented.

Mieke and Gideon were to stay together on the path, because first of all, Gideon wasn't familiar enough yet with all the ins and outs of campus, but secondly, it would be dark, and buddy systems were important. Yedaiah would be the only solo participant in the game. He spent his whole life wandering the grounds of O Be Joyful and felt completely comfortable with it.

He quickly finished up his meal before the others so that he would have time to pop in on Joshua for a short visit before the evening plans. Saying goodbyes around the table, he excused himself.

❈❈❈❈❈

Gideon stopped by his room to pick up Fiona. He knew she would want to pounce around outside during the action. He had told Mieke to swing by the stable for Skipper and then meet him on the front lawn. They wanted to be the first to arrive just in case there were questions from the teams before they began.

Upon arrival, he mentioned to Mieke, "The parents are in for a real treat tonight. It is so magical out here under the brightest stars in the world, and with unexpected warm weather, you could almost be in shorts."

"I hardly think with splotches of snow still on the ground in spots, shorts would be appropriate." She giggled.

"You know what I mean!"

They talked for a while before the rest of the school showed up. Mieke shared with him that she was worried about certain black flying shadows showing up to ruin the evening.

The Six-Pack and their families gathered around the two because apparently some of the kids were worried about the enemy too. They secretly whispered their concerns to Mieke and Gideon without drawing attention to their parents. There was no reason to needlessly trouble them with the notion. But deep down the whole special task team had similar thoughts about him showing up unwelcomed.

Mieke put on a brave face and reassured the children that God was with them and that all would be good.

"It's going to be such a fun night! Don't ruin it with your fears," she said to the kids.

Mr. Hallohesh stood on the top stoop and looked down onto the lawn full of people.

"Good evening, wonderful people of Mission Mind Academy." He waited a few moments to let the chatter die down. When it did, he continued, "I will open us in prayer and then turn the stage over to Mr. and Mrs. Vand for further instruction."

"Dear heavenly Father, I ask You tonight to guide our steps and bless our evening together. I ask that Your Holy Spirit go before us and walk beside us as we step into the night. We trust You and love You. It's in Your name we pray. Amen."

Everyone else followed up, "Amen."

Gideon and Mieke left the instruction huddle first to find a place to stand down the path. Their plan was to slowly walk the golden path one small step at a time to make themselves as available as possible for the others. They started making small talk as they strolled together, Skipper clomping beside them, Fiona pouncing in the grass.

"After this family weekend, we will be getting back to the mission at hand. I don't know if I'm ready for that," Mieke commented to Gideon.

"I know what you mean. It has been peaceful around here lately, but it is the reason that we are here in the first place," he reminded her.

"I get that. It's just that I hadn't realized how much I missed being here. Now that I am back, I hardly want to leave. The devil's presence at O Be Joyful is disturbing enough, but the reality is that as soon as we outwit him, because with Jesus we will, I have to leave again."

"Maybe you don't. Maybe you want to stay and work here," Gideon happily pointed out.

"I would have no idea what I would do here. I am not a teacher, and the staff seems to be filled with capable talented people. I doubt they would need me for anything around here," she continued on.

"I seriously doubt that. But I do know what you mean. I can't, for the life of me, picture myself going back to selling houses for a living, not after coming here and being a part of all of this. It feels so pointless and unfulfilling. Don't get me wrong, I miss a few people like my sister, niece, and nephew. I just don't miss the work I poured myself into my entire adult life. I am not sure that I ever really liked it. I was just good at it, so pride had me striving to be the best."

"Excuse me," a young voice said to the pair, "can you tell me where a garden toolshed is?"

Mieke took the lead. "If you all head behind the greenhouse in the vegetable garden, there will be a little green shed with golden trim door and doorknob. That is what you are looking for."

"Thank you," the young girl replied, as she hurried back to her group.

They continued slowly down the yellow brick road, keeping an eye out for others in need of their direction. Kids and animals were all over the place, a buzz of excitement filling the atmosphere.

Gideon smiled when he saw the Six-Pack with their families in tow. He had grown rather fond of the group of children and admired them to no end. The bravery they displayed at such a young age made him feel inner strength that he didn't know existed.

The night progressed without a hitch. The clues were followed to a tee, and the last hint directed the teams to the end of the property beyond the last row of trees, revealing huge baskets of desserts specially baked by Mrs. Heathers herself. She was sitting there in a lounge chair waiting for everyone to arrive. Excited to share a treat with the school, she clapped her hands when the first team reached her.

The Six-Pack were the big winners, getting there ahead of the rest. It was no surprise to anyone who won. But the other teams were shortly behind and just as excited to join in on the sweets baked to perfection.

They all sat right down on the lawn, some resting up against the trees for support. Music began playing favorite songs from the band Kutless over the loudspeakers while sounds of crickets and owls seemed to sing along. It was a blissful night, and all were enjoying themselves.

When Yedaiah, Gideon, and Mieke arrived last, claps broke out from the happy crowd.

"You all did wonderfully," Yedaiah assured them.

He popped open one of the sweet-filled baskets, offering it to Gideon and Mieke first. Then he picked out a cinnamon roll covered in frosted glaze for his own enjoyment.

As he leaned against a tree to steady himself and distribute his weight, he looked into the distance, spotting a sight which led to great concern.

The Bones Abode came into view, and even though it was dark out with light shining only from the stars, moon, and dimly lit golden path, he could see a glow above the unfinished structure.

What was causing the light, he wondered. He glanced over at Mieke standing next to him, realizing she had spotted it too. Her eyes were wide as she struggled to hide her terrified expression. The last thing she wanted to do was alert the others of the possible threat. Maybe the glow had nothing to do with them. Why open a can of worms unnecessarily?

But when sparks started flying off the roof of the Abode, all attention from the lawn crowd was shifted to it. While the uninformed were excited by the almost-fireworks show, the Six-Pack stood directly to their feet and headed over to Yedaiah.

They knew that it was not a show for the crowd to admire but a huge threat from the devil himself.

"Mr. Hallohesh," Grace squealed, "what is happening?"

He didn't know. He just stared and prayed.

The rest of the special task team slowly made their way to Yedaiah as well, the others completely oblivious.

His first thought was to get everyone away from their current location and back into Mission Mind Academy without hinting of danger.

He cleared his throat, took a deep breath, and announced at the top of his lungs so that all could hear, "It is time for games in the academy. If you would all please make your way down the golden path and settle into Grow in Wisdom, the study lounges, and the dining hall, wherever you can find a comfy spot, we have several hundred games to choose from."

Everyone slowly stood up and walked at a snail's pace back to the school. Why couldn't they hurry, he wondered.

The Six-Pack told their families that they would be right behind them and to get a head start because they wanted to chat with Mr. Hallohesh for a bit. They happily obliged, and the kids were thankful for that.

As soon as everyone was far enough down the path that they were out of sight, the special task team gathered for a quick pow-wow. By this time the sparks were flying in all directions, picking up energy and speed as they did. Satan was up to no good, and they needed to stop him before the others caught on.

Joining hands, they asked the good Lord above for direction and wisdom. They all took deep long breathes preparing themselves for what was to come. And then as the sparks began to shoot over into O Be Joyful, they didn't run; they stood firm, not moving a muscle. They refused to give in to fear, refused to play into the taunting game, refused to run and hide. This was their property, their school, and their mission.

❊❊❊❊❊

Joshua could see the bright white sparks flying from his bedroom window as he was lying in bed reading. He immediately knew that it was not a positive display and was coming from the Bones. He cringed inside knowing that in his frail condition he should stay put, leaving the battle for the more able-bodied, but curiosity and determination pulled himself upright. He was not about to watch from the sidelines. He didn't care whether Mrs. Guffey would scold him; she wasn't around presently, and so he would deal with her later.

Pulling on some tennis shoes, he slowly cracked opened his door. It creaked a little, but he faked a cough to stifle the noise. He peeked out into the hallway making sure that the coast was clear, then shuffled as fast as his worn-out body was able down the corridor and out into the open air.

The sparks were shooting in all directions off into the distance, a good ways down the golden path. He was thankful for that. At least the entirety of the school wouldn't be able to spot them.

Steadying himself for a few moments, he began the truck toward the chaos. It took him longer than he wanted, but as he made some progress, he could see the trusty task team holding hands in a circle. He was proud to witness them standing firm and not fretting over the threatening display. As he got closer, he was noticed by Yedaiah, who immediately broke the prayer chain and ran to his side. He looped his arm through Joshua's and reprimanded him for coming out into the madness in his condition.

"Well, I couldn't just lie around watching all of the fun, now could I?" Joshua teased.

"Yes, you absolutely could have!" Yedaiah was not in the mood to argue with his dearest friend, so he continued helping over to the prayer circle.

The others were glad to see Joshua in the midst of flashes and flickers.

Upon Joshua's arrival, another less friendly presence made itself known. Flying in and out and all around the sparks were three black shadows, bringing their pungent odor and high-pitched shriek with them. The black creeps buzzed around their heads and into their circle, trying their best to bring fear.

The noise had become so loud Yedaiah had to yell over them to communicate.

"This is the time to put on the full armor of God," he shouted. "We will stand firm with the belt of truth buckled around our waist, the breastplate of righteousness in place, and our feet fitted with the readiness that comes from the gospel of peace. Take up the shield of faith, which you can extinguish all the flaming arrows of the evil one. Take the helmet of salvation and the sword of the Spirit, which is the Word of God. We pray in your mighty name, Lord Jesus, to come into this situation and take control. Amen."

With those words, the black shadows went straight up into the air out of sight and then came hurtling down, all three of them directly toward Joshua, nailing him, one on the head and the other two on his shoulders, knocking him flat out on the ground with a loud thud. Then they vanished into thin air, as did the taunting sparks. Everything went silent, like nothing had even happened to begin with.

*****

Mr. and Mrs. Hayes were beginning to worry about Grace and her friends. They were in Grow in Wisdom sitting at one of the tables with Nathaniel on their lap, waiting for longer than seemed reasonable.

As soon as they commented to each other how long it was taking for her, Roxy, who had been lying under their feet, shot up at full speed and ran to the window barking her head off.

"What is wrong, Roxy?" Benjamin asked the pup, who just continued on loudly.

The Hayes began to worry when they couldn't get her to calm down. They finally decided to open the door for her, and as they did, she shot out like a rocket down the golden path.

By this time, the Vands were at their side, wondering how they could help. The four of them, with Nathaniel snuggled in his mother's arms, walked out onto the path to see where she ran off to, but she was too far gone to spot.

Mrs. Hayes asked, "Where could she have sprinted off to?"

The Vands led them back down the same yellow brick road they had walked for the scavenger hunt. They walked on and on until they had almost reached the same area they had left the kids in earlier. Sure enough, they were still there, but it appeared that everyone was crouching down on the ground. Roxy was there too.

Upon arrival, the Vands and Hayes realized there was trouble. They saw Mr. Zane lying on the ground with his eyes closed, appearing to be unconscious.

Mr. Vand inquired, "What happened here, Mr. Hallohesh?"

He regretfully replied, "We had a situation with the Bones Abode, and it did not end well."

Grace's parents didn't know what the Bones Abode was but remained silent, holding their many questions for a different time. Grace did notice the concern in their eyes, however, and was not looking forward to explaining anything to them.

"We have got to get him to the hospital room for Mrs. Guffey to evaluate as soon as safely possible," Yedaiah told the others.

Gideon volunteered to go for the golf cart to transport him, and Mieke offered to locate Mrs. Guffey. The two of them jogged off into separate directions while the others knelt around Joshua in silent prayer.

Not too much later, Gideon returned with the cart, and they carefully lifted the oldest member of Mission Mind Academy onto it. He appeared lifeless, but he still had a pulse and heartbeat, and they were all thankful for those positive signs.

Yedaiah drove the cart with his best buddy in it straight to the hospital room where Mieke and Mrs. Guffey were already waiting for him. After transferring him to the bed, the doctor asked everyone to exit so that she could look over him thoroughly. She had a nursing student on call, who was new to O Be Joyful, that would assist her in the evaluation.

The others moseyed into their golden castle and plopped down by a fireplace in Grow in Wisdom. The fear on their faces couldn't be hidden. Other members of the school and their families began coming by to ask what the matter was.

Not wanting to bring up the Bones Abode or the devil, they simply responded by telling them that Mr. Zane wasn't feeling well.

It seemed to satisfy the curiosity floating around the room, but the ones who knew the truth were shaken to the core.

Yedaiah excused himself from the fire. He wanted to wait outside of Joshua's room, just in case he needed to fill Mrs. Guffey in on what actually happened. He was seriously dreading it. He had come to the grim realization that the attacks on them from Satan were not going to be easy to hide anymore.

He was all of a sudden ready to end family weekend and get on with the school-wide training. The special task team was not going to be enough to take down the enemy. The whole school would have to be on board.

Back in GIW, Grace's parents had started grilling her on what the Bones Abode was and what had happened to Mr. Zane. She told them that the Abode was too complicated to explain and that she didn't really know what happened to him, which was not a lie. After racking her brain on the evening events, she couldn't come up with an explanation.

They stopped pressing her, which she was thankful for, but she was overly ready to turn in for the night. She just wanted to get back to her room with Kiera so that they could process the situation without inquisitive eyes on them.

She said good night to her parents, as did Kiera to hers, and then gave Noah, Michael, Matt, and Malachi a hug before calling Roxy to follow her.

She let out a huge breath of fresh air when she walked into her room. It was a private quiet place, and she had never been so thankful for it.

✳✳✳✳✳

Joshua could hear everyone and everything around him. The commotion that surrounded his being struck down had all his loved ones in a fit of fear. The panic in their voices as he lay on the ground broke his heart. The rush in a golf cart to the hospital room, Mrs. Guffey doing her best to figure out what exactly happened—he could hear it all.

Willing himself to open his eyes and communicate with them was a whole different story. He would focus his clear mind on the task of popping an eyelid open but to no avail. He would pour every ounce of his mental energy into parting his lips to speak a word, but not a peep would make it into the world.

He was frustrated. He wanted to assure everyone that he was all right, that Satan tried his hardest but did not win. Why couldn't he find a way to correspond?

He knew that the blow that came upon him from the devil was a purpose-filled attack. He was an easy target, advanced in his age and already battling extreme weakness and frailty. Satan had been trying to get into his peace of mind for some time now, whispering lies as he would lie in bed day after day, telling him he should just give up and give in, that he was worthless and a burden on his loved ones.

Joshua meditated on God's Word to combat the mental harassment. And God had proved Himself every single time to be faithful and be with Him. He never felt alone, and for that he was unendingly thankful.

This last assault was something else altogether though. He knew Yedaiah was outside of his room by the door praying for him. He could strongly feel his presence. He wished so badly that he could assure him and ease his worries.

When he heard Mrs. Guffey telling the new nurse, who had just joined them days before, that Joshua might just be too weak to ever awaken again, he knew he needed to find a way to get through to them.

He asked God for something that he had never asked Him before. He begged from the depths of his soul for God Himself to tell Yedaiah that he was still with them and in sound mind. And then he believed with everything in him that God would do it and see them through.

After the prayer, Joshua heard banging on his door. Yedaiah was yelling desperately for Mrs. Guffey to open up.

"Joshua's okay. He can even hear you right now!" Yedaiah managed to get out in his excitement.

Mrs. Guffey, looking puzzled, asked, "How do you know that?"

Yedaiah told her as a matter of fact, "God just told me."

She wasn't exactly sure what to believe and glanced over at the nurse to see what she thought about the claim.

"Really, Mrs. Guffey. I was standing on the other side of the door, just fretting and praying, when I heard a whisper as clear as day say, 'Joshua is with you. He can hear you. He wants you to know.'"

Hearing this gave Joshua the chills, causing goose bumps to rise up on his arms and neck.

Mrs. Guffey, standing directly beside them, saw the bumps rise, triggering Joshua's hairs to stand at attention.

"Look at this!" she called the other two over. "He has chill bumps, and his hair is standing on end!"

The three of them all clapped joyfully as if they had just seen the most remarkable thing of their lives.

The new nurse, Ann, had tears in her eyes.

"Does this sort of thing happen a lot around O Be Joyful?"

Yedaiah smiled and replied, "You never know how God is going to reveal His might and power around this place. He never ceases to amaze us."

"Yedaiah, now that we have a little bit of hope and peace, would you mind explaining to me in specific detail what happened to Joshua and why he was up and out of bed in the first place?"

Yedaiah wasn't thrilled about the idea of revealing right then and there what had really happened. First of all, now that he knew Joshua could hear his every word, he had to be choosier about what came out of his mouth. Secondly, he didn't want to alarm Mrs. Guffey or Nurse Ann, especially because she was brand new to the academy.

"I would share with you the details, but at this time I feel it's important to find the ones who saw him go down and give them assurance on the situation. I am betting they are all pretty rattled right now."

He gave her a warm handshake, squeezed Joshua's hand, and then exited the room, grateful to buy some time before he had to divulge the truth behind the matter. Bringing up Satan at a Christian school, during family weekend no doubt, was the lowest on his list.

Yedaiah first stopped by the boys' room. They were all sprawled out on their bunk beds with their favorite animals, lounging with them. He explained to them what God had enlightened him on, that

Joshua hadn't opened his eyes as of yet or spoken but that he could hear and was very present.

The boys were so happy and thankful for the update.

After informing all that were involved, he tiredly shuffled off to bed.

"What a night!" he said out loud to no one but himself. "Thank You, Jesus for seeing us through. I ask that You restore Joshua Zane to wholeness and be with him as he struggles through this trial. Thank You for Your mighty power and for not leaving us. Amen."

Closing his eyes, he drifted off into a fitful night's rest, plagued by images of the Bones Abode and the devil who resided there.

✳✳✳✳✳

The sun rose the next morning, bringing with it a clear blue sky filled with white puffy clouds. No animals floated by, but they were a beautiful display and ending to family weekend.

As excited as the Six-Pack were to spend time with their parents, they were desperate to send them home. The fear of Satan's attacks was at an all-time high, and they were all sure that they would be pulled out of Mission Mind if their parents caught a glimpse of him.

Hugs and kisses took place all over O Be Joyful, as *Methuselah* filled up over and over again for transport. Even Grace's family was taking the ferry home. Yedaiah was not going to leave campus if at all possible until he knew for sure that his friend was stable.

When *Methuselah* returned and docked after its final drop-off, the entirety of the school congregated in the dining hall for a feast from Mrs. Heathers.

While they were dining, Mr. Vand stood at the front of the room and called for everyone's attention. After everyone's voices quieted, he began. "What a blessed weekend meeting all your families. I am feeling thankful for the time we got to spend together."

The kids all broke out in hoots and hollers, clapping their hands and stomping their feet.

"But," he continued, "we have some pretty important things to discuss and step into, now that they are all headed home."

Eyes were wide on him, some with fear, some with excitement.

"As you all know, we have had some unusual things happen on campus as of late. I am referring to the event that took place during the flanks match. But there have been several other similar scares that some of you are not aware of. I am not going to go into detail right now, but I want to tell you something real. Satan does not like that we love Jesus, and he wants nothing more than to destroy the relationship we have with Him.

"So this week, we are all beginning a series of special training. We will meet every day at 9:00 a.m. in Psalm auditorium. We will be equipping ourselves with the power of the Lord God so that when the devil dares to make his assaults, we will be prepared and ready for him.

"I do not want any of you to fear. Remember who you belong to and who will see you through every situation, good or bad, in your life. This is our time to take back our power and school. That is all for now. I look forward to seeing you all after breakfast tomorrow."

17

This Means War

On the first day of Mission Mind Academy's preparation train-ing, the buzz in the room was undeniable. Before Mr. Vand had uttered a word, the auditorium was filled with laughter, determina-tion, lightheartedness, and joy. From the outside of the situation, one would have no clue that there was a threat coming onto campus to wreak havoc. It could have been a pep rally.

The Six-Pack made sure to arrive early for front-row seating. They couldn't help but feel closer to the problem than the rest of their peers. They were beginning to become annoyed with the other students' nonchalant attitudes.

Matthew whispered to his brothers and best friends, "I don't think anyone recognizes the severity of the situation. It seems like everyone is just thankful to be getting out of their first two periods of normal classes."

"Yeah," Grace replied, "they are all just hooting and hollering. I don't get it. Didn't they hear Mr. Vand say that we are in training to take down Satan? Why all the joyful excitement?"

"Well, in all fairness, they don't have a clue about all that we have been through with the Bones Abode. They saw one, maybe two attacks. We have seen everyone, and sometimes they are directly aimed at us," Noah reminded them.

"And don't forget that the assault on Mr. Zane is still unknown to all these kids and the teachers. They just don't have all the infor-mation like we do," Kiera mentioned.

"I still think that if we don't take this seriously, it won't work. We might have to have a little chat with the rest of the student body. I would hate for this to be taken lightly, as if it were a joke. It has to work! I am sick of wondering when he will attack and in what way," Matthew told them.

Malachi opened up, "If they knew about Mr. Zane, they would take it seriously. Everyone loves him. If people continue to take this lightly, I am not afraid to tell them what happened to him. I wish he was here with us right now. I can't stand not being able to talk with him. He always has the best advice and kindest words."

"Yeah, I miss him too," Grace agreed.

"Good morning, Mission Mind Academy." Mr. Hallohesh took the stage.

"Good morning," the crowd replied.

"I am going to open us in prayer and then turn the stage over to Mr. Vand for the remainder of the morning. I just wanted to say thank you all for being here. We have a huge mission at hand. I want you all to remember what we are dealing with here. Satan is not to be taken flippantly. He is alive and real. With that said, our God is alive and real as well, and this is a battle between good and evil in the heavenly realm. I would like each of you to search your heart and souls during our training exercises and see that you are focusing on the truth of the matter," Yedaiah articulated.

After his prayer, he stepped down off stage and took a seat directly in the front row next to Michael. He gave him a wink before turning his head toward Mr. Vand in complete attention.

He realized that most of the students at O Be Joyful were not prepared for the knowledge that was going to be imparted on them like a storm. Mr. Vand and he discussed at length what details to share with the entire school, and they agreed that if they wanted results, they would have to have the strength of everyone as the body of Christ.

Mr. Vand would be giving an account, in detail, of every sighting and trial that had taken place to date that morning. He would even share about the Bones Abode and Joshua.

He didn't know what some would do after receiving the information. He could think of a few kids and adults that might bolt out the back door, never to return. He thought of the worst possible situation, which would be word getting out to the families and the general public.

He didn't let his mind wonder long on the notion, however. He knew that it wouldn't help matters if he walked and thought out of fear. Trusting God, His goodness and power, was the calling for his life. These were the moments he needed to remember that fact more than ever.

*****

Sure enough, eyes grew wide, whispers and frightened chatter began throughout Psalm, and a few fearful souls headed for the exit doors.

Mrs. Vand took it upon herself to follow the ones that left. She had expected a few to do that and wanted to make sure they had someone safe to talk to about what they had just learned. It was not a normal thing for a mind to conceive, Satan's attacks, that is.

She tailed three thirteen-year-old girls, who were the best of friends on campus, and the new nurse Ann out the side exit. They all left at the same time and were heading in the same direction outside, toward *Methuselah*.

Mrs. Vand wondered if they planned to hop right onto the ferry without any of their belongings or someone to drive the boat. But when they settled on the lawn together, on the bank of the water, she plopped down next to them.

She knew all the girls from the years they had spent there and felt comfortable enough to pull the fears out of their minds.

Nurse Ann looked as if she saw a ghost or the black shadows in this case.

"So the older gentlemen I have been assisting with in the hospital room was attacked by Satan?"

Mrs. Vand responded as gingerly as possible, "Mr. Joshua Zane. Yes, he was. He has known about the harassing from the beginning, and I guess the devil targeted him. It was the first time serious physical harm was done in an attack."

One of the teens opened up, "I am sure it won't be the last. I don't want to be a part of any of this craziness! Can I go home? My parents were just here yesterday. I could have left with them."

Mrs. Vand continued to keep her tone light. "Sarah, I can understand your fears and that you want to run, but this is why we were called to Mission Mind Academy in the first place, to train for missions such as this. We are here for the Lord Jesus Christ, and whatever He brings us to, He will see us through. Don't forget that there is always a spiritual battle going on around us in the heavenly realm. Living on earth means we will be in the middle of it most of the time. We do have a choice though. We can choose to believe that God is almighty and all-powerful and will at no time leave us to defend ourselves. He has us in the palm of His sovereign hands and will fight for us."

Sarah's two best friends put their arms around her shoulders and gave her a squeeze.

"We can't leave, Sarah. We have to be brave and see this through."

The girls had been on campus for over two years and knew that, ultimately, they would stay and see the situation through. They were loyal and devoted to God. Nurse Ann, on the other hand, had just arrived and was not feeling the obligation to O Be Joyful.

"I don't think I want any part in fighting off the devil," she informed them.

Mrs. Vand looked her in the eye when she responded, "No one will blame or judge you for not sticking around. But I must tell you that it is by no accident that God brought you to us just days before the truth was revealed. You have a safe home here, and we would be honored if you would see your calling through."

"I will have to think and pray over it before I make a final decision. I am going to go check on Mr. Zane and then retreat to my room for a while," Ann informed the others before heading to the hospital room's direction.

When dinner rolled around that evening and there was no Nurse Ann, Mrs. Vand went to search for her. Finding her room empty, not only of Ann but also of her belongings, Mrs. Vand had a feeling she fled. She didn't blame her; it was a scary sort of thing, preparing for battle against the devil.

Her suspicions were confirmed when she noticed *Methuselah* missing from its dock. She imagined Ann was smart enough to figure out how to drive it. But now she would have to hassle Yedaiah for a balloon ride to retrieve it.

When she walked back into the dining hall, she scanned the room for the three friends who had walked out of the auditorium earlier that day. They were all there and accounted for, sitting and laughing with one another. Mrs. Vand thanked the Lord for giving them strength to fight through their fears, and then she took a seat next to Mr. Hallohesh to explain about Ann.

*****

The first training session, after the description of every run-in with the enemy, was focused on knowing truth.

Mr. Vand was giving simple yet impactful knowledge on keeping minds fixed on the truth and not letting it run away with lies from the devil.

He challenged each student to an exercise that evening. Everyone was to spend time alone with God in prayer, asking Him to reveal specific fears each person was struggling with. Then they were to write each fear down in detail on paper. The fears were to be specific and not limited to the Bones Abode scandal. Every single fear that was running through their minds was to be written down and clarified.

Students and staff were then supposed to bring the paper with them the next morning to training for further instruction.

When the morning bell rang, informing them they had five minutes to find their seats in Psalm Auditorium, everyone scrambled to be on time.

Mr. Vand was already on stage sitting in a tall director's chair. His goal and prayer that day was to reveal how to take fear and give it completely to God.

"Our fears are crippling us. When we carry fear of any kind, large or small, we give Satan a hand up in our hearts and souls. So today I am going to give you some practical ways to hand them over to God. This is step one in defeating our enemy. As long as we are carrying around worry, we are carrying around a piece of Satan's evil plan."

The crowd was silent, mind blown by what they were hearing.

One student spoke up, "Are you saying that fear is sin?"

Choosing his words carefully, Mr. Vand responded, "I am saying that fear of any kind highlights mistrust in God. Although life is unpredictable, God remains the same—always on the throne and always in control. Worrying about anything is the same as questioning God and His sovereignty."

He let his words sink in before continuing.

"If we have fear eating away at us, it's kind of like we have a welcome mat out for the enemy. He is the accuser and wants nothing more than our hearts and minds in distress. It's how he strives to keep us from a wonderful relationship with the Lord. He tries to hide his wretchedness too. How many of you here today were a bit surprised by the worries and fears you wrote down last night?"

Almost everyone raised their hands.

"How many of you tend to ignore fears by pushing them into the back of your minds so you can focus on other things on a regular basis? Like, if you don't acknowledge them, they don't exist?"

Hands raised up all over.

"I am here to tell you that pushing our anxieties to the farthest parts of our minds doesn't make them disappear. It actually makes them stronger, carrying negative power in us but in a way that we ignore them. It makes us an easy target, which is why we have been attacked lately."

A staff member raised her hand in the crowd. When called on, she asked, "So what is the plan of action? Are you saying that we are being targeted and attacked by the enemy because of our fears and doubts and unresolved issues?"

Mr. Vand trod carefully. "Life is not black and white, cut and dry all the time. But yes, I am saying that whatever we are harboring collectively is drawing him to us and our school. We will be going through a series of scriptures specific to breaking us free and will trust the Lord to deliver our academy for good."

After taking a sip of water, Mr. Vand was ready to dive into the plans for the day.

"We are going to be taking this training session outside into the sunshine, where we can draw peace from our beautiful surroundings. We will take a short break of fifteen minutes to use the restroom, collect your pets, and grab some water and snacks if needed. I will see you all on the lawn outside of our glorious golden front doors."

Mieke and Gideon had been quiet up to this point but were asked by Mr. Vand earlier that day if they would share a testimony during a time in their life that they were carrying around hurt, pain, fear, and baggage that was meant to be given to the Lord. They were to share how they felt inside lugging around burdens and how they felt after they acknowledged the worry, prayed about it, and then trusted God with it.

This exercise was to give everyone a solid example of what it is like to be free the way Jesus wants us to be.

Mieke was nervous about opening herself up in front of every-one but knew that she was meant to. She had been praying about the path God had her on and had been asking Him to use her in a huge way. This was just the beginning, and being transparent was a part of it.

Gideon felt unqualified to share, if he was being completely honest. He was a new believer and didn't have the lifetime with God as Mieke did. But he knew one thing for absolute sure: he had been carrying about pain, uncertainty, and discontentment for the entirety of his life, which all ended when he accepted Jesus into his heart. Now he felt whole and alive and certain that God was using Him in an amazing way. That was a fact, and if sharing his story would help even a little bit, he would do it.

The Six-Pack were all anxious for the outside session and hurried to collect their animal, being the first group to the front of Mission Mind, setting up on the immaculate lawn.

"This has got to work, guys," Kiera voiced to her best friends.

Grace patted her shoulder. "Don't worry, sister, it's going to work like a charm. I know that Satan has been secretly tormenting our minds and hearts. His visual appearances have nothing on the damage inner turmoil causes. If we can be set free and we are meant to be, he won't have a place here on campus anymore. God has got this."

When the rest of the student body settled down on the lush green grass, Mieke took her spot right up front, standing on the porch's top step, with the sunshine reflecting off the golden doors behind her. The warm glow cast on her set the mood perfectly for the discussion at hand.

She shared her testimony with the entire school and then pulled a paper out from her pocket. The crowd was all drawn in, hanging on her every word. It was obvious that the Holy Spirit was with them that day, guiding Mieke's tongue and opening the ears of her listeners. He was gifting them with great human connection.

She paused a few moments to look over what she had written down on her slip of paper. She said a silent prayer asking for strength and faith to share what was on it. She had never been so brave or bold in her lifetime. It was a day for the books. She was ready to be set free.

So she began, "I have right here on this note all the things God has brought to my mind through prayer and reading of the Bible. Specifically, the pains, fears, doubts, questions, and hurts that I have been currently harboring. I am going to read them to you so that they may lose the powerful grip they have been holding me in, then I am going to surrender them to the One who can carry them for me. I am going to fully believe that God will take these from me, leaving me with a deeper faith and trust in Him. Here goes nothing!"

Mieke took a deep breath before revealing her innermost secrets. She could do this.

"I am afraid that I have been wasting my life in a job that does good but that I am not called to do. I am worried that I will not find a place in the world that fits me and my spiritual gifts will be wasted. I am afraid that God doesn't have a godly man for me to fall in love with, marry, and start a family with. A sin that I can't get a grip on is comparing myself and what I have accomplished with others. I constantly compare, and I pray in Jesus's name that ends right now, today. I wake up often feeling nauseous with worry over things I can't put a finger on. I am sorry, Jesus, for my lack of joy. You have blessed me so much."

Mieke looked out into the sea of beautiful faces, held her white paper high above her head, and yelled at the top of her lungs, "In the name of the Lord, I release everything written down on this page to You, God. I believe You are in complete control, and I surrender whatever self-power I was holding on to. Today I am one hundred percent free! Praise God!"

Everyone stood to their feet, roaring and cheering, hooting and hollering. Several students and teachers walked up the steps to give her a huge group hug. Gideon had tears in his eyes when he looked into hers. He hugged her the tightest before backing off.

He was so proud of her. He was so inspired by her. He was due to share his testimony the following day and needed to retreat and pray. He wanted to be free as well to walk in the fullness of God. He realized that he would need to surrender everything, embarrassing or not, out and up to the One with the power, mercy, and love. Tough act to follow, he chuckled at himself. Looking back over his shoulder, he made eye contact with Mieke, giving her a wink and a smile.

When Mieke broke free of the hugs, she quieted everyone to finish what she had on her mind.

"Mission Mind Academy members, I have a similar challenge for you. Before we continue on with our special training, I believe that you all need to lose the grip fear, sin, and secrets have on you. We will be breaking up into groups of two so you will have a one-on-one experience. When you have your partner, head out to a private location on the property, pray together, and then share what you wrote down last night on your papers you brought with you. After you have revealed the things holding you back, release them up to God. Ask Him to take the weight off your shoulders and cast it as far as the east is from the west. Claim the power that He has for you. Remember that you are His temples, housing the Holy Spirit inside of you. Be free!"

For the next forty-five minutes, chains were broken, and healing came. The celebration heard all over O Be Joyful was joyful indeed.

*****

The next morning after a full breakfast of lemon pancakes and blueberry syrup, bacon, and hash browns cooked to crispy perfection, the whole school reconvened out on the front lawn once again.

Gideon was to share what God was doing in his life, right after Yedaiah opened up with prayer and announcements for the day.

Yedaiah was planning on spending the better part of the day with his buddy Joshua. He had opened his eyes and could communicate through blinking and nodding but was still unable to speak. It had only been a few days since the attack on his body, but Yedaiah was really hoping he would have regained his speech by now. He was looking forward to sitting with him for the afternoon and early evening.

After praying with and over Mission Mind Academy and all of its members, Yedaiah stepped down to the lawn, eyeing Gideon to take his place on the porch.

Gideon was feeling nervous but brave after hearing Mieke speak the day prior. His testimony was so different from hers. He just found out who Christ is a short time ago and had so much to learn about Him. He chose to share about getting saved and how the journey to O Be Joyful has affected his life.

He went on and on about his life without God as his Savior and Redeemer, shocking even himself at times with the dull and pointless life he led. But then the light inside of him shone forth onto the crowd. Gideon felt filled by the Holy Spirit and empowered by Him. He was on a faith-high that could not be squelched.

"I was a dead man walking. I didn't have a clue how to change the path I was on, so I just kept going in the same direction that I knew. It wasn't pretty. It was a waste of time and energy, and I felt sluggish and sad most of my days. Then I met Mr. Joshua Zane, and my life has not been the same since.

"He asked me to hand-deliver a letter to Mieke Everly, whom I had never met. I was confused because I was not a delivery dude. I was a realtor who sold houses for a living. But I said yes. Mr. Zane told me the good news of how Christ created me and then died for me and my sins so that I could spend eternity with Him in heaven. He said that if I turn from my sin and believe in the Lord Jesus Christ, I will be saved. He boldly told me that Jesus loved me and was calling me to Him. He told me the Holy Spirit wanted to help me through this life on earth. By the time I got to Mieke's work to give her the letter, I knew that my life was never going to be the same again.

"The second time I met Mieke, just after the initial letter drop-off, I followed her to a meeting about the Bones Abode and Satan's threats. The next thing I know, I am on *Methuselah* heading for Mission Mind Academy. It has all been a whirlwind.

"I chose to share this today because I wanted you all to see that even in Satan's schemes and attacks, God has a beautiful purpose. I was saved in the process, and I will forever be thankful. So I am here to clean out the closet of my mind, renewing it on the Lord, and I am ready to stand with Him as He clears our campus from the accuser. Who is with me?" Gideon shouted out.

Everyone stood to their feet, with hands lifted high and voices raised to the heavens. Everyone was ready for battle. It was a beautiful sight. Fear had seemed to lift and leave the faces of God's children. Strength, determination, and trust showed in each pair of eyes staring back at him.

"You did this, God! Thank You!" Gideon yelled up and out to the Lord.

*****

Knocking on Joshua's door before entering, Yedaiah was thankful to see his friend awake, his eyes sparkling blue. He pulled up a chair and plopped down right next to the bed, shifting his friend around to prop him up into a sitting position.

He received a wink from Joshua, bringing him great joy.

"Hi, old buddy, old pal!" he said, smiling cheek to cheek, wishing that Joshua could respond.

He had so much to say to him. He wanted to talk about the training and the testimonies of Mieke and Gideon. But he knew his friend couldn't respond to him, and it made him question what to say and share. It was a one-sided conversation, although he knew Joshua could hear and understand it all.

He trod carefully, not wanting to get too hyped up, exhausting Joshua in his feeble position.

"It was an amazing morning listening to Gideon share about his life and what the Father has done for him. He is on fire, and the kids and staff feel the energy pouring out of him. I am thankful God had you choose him for Mieke's letter delivery. Those two have become as thick as thieves this past month or so. It's a joy to watch, and I hope they stick around O Be Joyful for a long time, even after the Bones task is complete."

Joshua smiled and nodded slowly, raising one hand up to heaven as an act of worship.

Mrs. Guffey popped her head in the door. "Everything all right in here? Do you need anything, Mr. Hallohesh?"

"Good day, Mrs. Guffey. No, thank you, I believe we are doing just fine." He had to ask, "How are you getting along without Nurse Ann? I heard that she didn't make the cut and took off as fast as possible from campus."

"Yes, she did. I wasn't sure about her in the first place. She never spoke, and when she did, it was all complaints. I don't think that is the kind of energy we need around our precious ill patients anyway. I am doing just fine on my own, as I was before she arrived. If God calls another nurse here, I will be open to them, but I am not going to go out looking. That is not how people arrive here, and I am thankful for that. God calls them, and we trust Him. It's a great interview process if you ask me." She smiled at Yedaiah before turning on her heels and leaving the doorjamb.

Yedaiah turned his attention back to Joshua, who was looking longingly at him. Yedaiah wished he knew what his friend was thinking about. He felt helpless, and it hurt. Then Yedaiah got an idea.

Standing up, he pulled a wheelchair over next to the bed, bent down to bear-hug Joshua, and then lifted him into the chair. He pulled a sweatshirt over his shoulders before wheeling him outside for fresh air.

"I hope that this is okay. I thought you needed the breeze and the warm sunshine on your face. Plus, the whole school is outside, and they all heard about the attack on you, so it will do everyone some good seeing you look so light and chipper today.

A smile and grunting sound came from Joshua's lips.

"Wow, look at you, talking again. Better quiet down or you'll scare the birds," he teased, getting another smile and grunt.

Yedaiah's pet, Fig, jumped onto Joshua's lap, snuggling up into a ball for a nap, making Yedaiah eternally grateful for the gift of animals. They always knew what to do and how to act around the sick and ill.

Students ran over group by group giving Mr. Zane hugs and low fives. He loved every minute of it, grinning ear to ear so they knew how much he appreciated every one of them.

It was a glorious day, which gave Yedaiah an idea. Leaving Joshua with Mr. and Mrs. Vand, he ran into the office where the microphone for the school-wide loudspeakers was housed.

After clearing his throat, he began, "Attention, all staff and students of Mission Mind Academy. It is decided that we will rearrange the rest of our day's events. There will be no more classes or training today. We will be holding a flanks tournament."

Cheers broke out all over the property, exciting all the animals that were bounding about everywhere.

Yedaiah waited for the noise of joyfulness he could hear from the inside office to quiet before continuing.

"Get yourselves ready and meet at the courts in thirty-five minutes for the fun to begin. The first teams up to play are the Hammerheads and the Tough Troops. Let's have some fun!" Yedaiah shouted, shutting off the mic.

When he returned back to his buddy in his wheelchair, he asked him if he would want to watch the matches for a while or head back for a rest in the room.

Joshua pointed his hand with all five fingers spread apart toward the court bleachers.

"You want to watch?"

Joshua shook his head up and down.

"Great! Let's go and see Mrs. Guffey beforehand and see if she has any instructions for you. You must be starving too. We can get you a bite to eat. I must say it is so good having you around. I have missed you."

Joshua grabbed and squeezed Yedaiah's arm.

When the entirety of the school was either seated for the first match or warming up for it, Gabriel, standing middle court, blew his whistle to begin play.

It was a nice surprise to have the afternoon off for some entertainment and fun. The Six-Pack were due to play in the second game and were stretching in the grass on the other side of the fence, as to not get nailed with a flying ball.

Grace commented to her best buds, "We are going to dominate our game. I have a feeling in my bones."

"Yes, we are, Grace, and Mr. Zane is sitting over there watching. Did you see him?" Kiera responded.

"It makes me so happy seeing him up and about. It hasn't felt right around here with him in bed lately," Malachi added.

Noah agreed with them before sharing what was running through his head. "Let's just hope it's an accuser-free day. I am not feeling up for any sort of extra battles today."

Michael agreed. "Amen, brother."

The first match was chock-full of excitement and fun. The teams were all improving and becoming really good at the game.

Noah took notice. "Flanks has become such a hit on campus. When do you think the ordinary world will be ready for it?"

"I think it's ready now. It is better than any sports they play. Football is so barbaric, and soccer is way too much running. Is it just me or is regular tennis and golf, for that matter, wicked boring?" Kiera teased around.

"I would say the only thing that rivals its awesomeness is gymnastics." Grace laughed at herself.

Michael had to strongly disagree. "Gym doesn't hold a candle to flanks, and when it reaches Washington and beyond, we will be famous for inventing it."

Before long, the Brown boys' dad's whistle blew, indicating the first match complete. There would be a twenty-minute break before their match was to begin against the Net Rulers.

Grace noticed Mr. Zane being pushed away from the courts by Mieke Everly and wondered if he would be returning to watch them play. She prayed he would.

Everyone had either stood up to stretch from the bleachers or left the scene altogether, probably grabbing a snack or taking a restroom break. Several popped into Mission Mind castle for one reason or another.

The Six-Pack took the court and began warming up when they heard screams coming from the school building. Dropping what they were doing, they all made a run for it, along with the rest of the folks still lingering around the court.

The yells continued and grew louder as they approached the golden double front doors. The doors flew open before they had reached the front porch, and kids barreled outside as fast as their feet could carry them. The Six-Pack, along with Gideon, were the only ones running toward the problem.

Entering the Mission Mind Academy as quietly and swiftly as possible, they already assumed what they were looking for. The Bones Abode's inhabitants had entered O Be Joyful once again. What was it up to now?

Matthew was annoyed that everyone had gone hollering and running.

"Do they not remember to keep calm and not fear? Did they learn anything from our trainings? We are supposed to stand firm and still and let God handle, not go running like a bunch of screaming banshees."

"Lighten up on them, Matt," Michael scolded him. "Not everyone can be as brave as you are."

"Very funny, Michael. It's just that I am ready to be done with this, and when they go sprinting off in fear, he wins and returns. I wonder why he is here today. So much for our flanks fun."

Creeping down the hall, with Gideon leading the way, the six kids quieted to listen for him. It was faint, but they could hear the distinct shrieking sound coming from quite a distance off.

"Where do you think it is?" Grace wanted to know. "I can hear it, but it's so muffled."

Malachi thought he could pinpoint the location. He stopped in his tracks, closed his eyes, and cuffed his ears with his hands. The rest of the group saw him and followed suit.

"I think it's on one of the top-level floors or possibly in the attic!" Gideon articulated to the kids.

As they were all heading toward the stairs, not wanting to take the elevator for safety purposes, they spotted Mieke, who had wheeled Joshua to his room and was back to help.

"Okay," Mieke said, "now is the time to put into practice all that we have learned from training."

Malachi was confused and needed clarification. "I thought that if we all cleaned out our closets, so to speak, he wouldn't return to torment us. But here he is!"

Mieke, wanting to encourage them, replied, "There will be a final battle, even if we are all living in the Lord's light. He isn't going out without a fight. We will have to come to head with him. Keep in mind that you are not alone. God has every detail already handled. We just need to keep trusting and show up for the plan."

Gideon could hear sounds reaching new heights of pitch level. "We should continue this party upstairs. So do we have a game plan?"

"Yes, we will all walk into the scene with our heads held high, godly confidence tacked on, and peace within our hearts. We have nothing to be afraid of, but we do want to act fast and get him out of here. I just hate having our amazing campus and school tainted by the devil. It's just not right."

Mieke started walking forward, naturally urging the others to follow suit. It was eerie with the shrieking echoing off the walls of the almost-vacant castle.

Grace wished that Roxy was with them and almost considered stopping by her room to retrieve her. Their pets were dropped off for afternoon naps in their rooms before the flanks matches began.

As they were ascending the stairs, Kiera noticed something out of the corner of her eye. After doing a double take, she realized that it was only Gabriel and Keilah Brown coming to join them.

"Mom! Dad!" Michael shouted. "What are you two doing here?"

Gabriel reached for his son and wrapped him up in a big hug. "We have come to investigate and help in any way that we can."

Keilah included herself in the hug, grabbing for the rest of the children to smoosh together in their arms. "We can't let you kids have all the fun," she commented, giving them a wink to let them know she was teasing.

"I wonder if we will see Mr. Hallohesh at some point," Noah questioned.

Gabriel had seen him on his way in struggling to keep everyone at peace outside near the stables.

"He is caring for the entirety of the student body and staff at this moment. I am not sure he will be able to break way anytime soon."

"Is everyone all right, Dad?" Matt wanted to make sure.

"Oh, yeah, just a little bit of panic and worry ringing through the crowd. Mr. Vand is with Mr. Hallohesh. They will be able to help get everyone through it. Now, don't worry about them, we have a job of our own to handle."

Mieke continued up the stairs urging the others to hurry along. She did not want to let the devil linger in the academy any longer than it already had been. It was time to take it down for good.

The sound did increase the higher and closer they rose to it, and the stench kicked in when they reached the top floor.

"We are definitely close," Grace said as she covered her nose with the top of her flanks jersey.

After performing a thorough search of the top floor of the castle, they realized they would be needing to go up another level to the attic to locate it. There was some dread bouncing around between them. The attic was extremely dark for one thing, only having one single bulb light to illuminate the whole humongous floor. It was also filthy with dust and dead bugs. It was a known fact that bats enjoyed living up there too.

At the doorway entrance, they all halted, not overly thrilled about entering in.

"Okay, this is it," articulated Gideon. "Do we have a game plan?"

Gabriel and Keilah were in the back of the pack, not quite sure what to expect.

"Yes, we say a prayer, trust God, and walk in like we own the place!" Mieke was ready.

Gabriel volunteered to pray for the group. After a short and honest plea to God, they opened the door.

The sound doubled in volume, which meant that they would have to yell to communicate with each other, and the rest of their group followed Grace in covering their noses with whatever they had on them to squelch the rancid odor. Nothing new for them though; this was always what it was like dealing with the devil.

When they turned the single overhead light on, a very dull glow cast flying shadows all over the walls and ceiling.

"Is that him or are those bats?" Kiera yelled at the top of her lungs.

"It might be both!" Noah shouted back.

When Keilah was through the door last, it slammed shut on its own, causing her to jump back and scream.

"This is so spooky!" she yelled to her husband.

"It will be okay, Mama!" he assured her.

They walked together in a tight cluster under the flying dark shadows above.

As the sound increased their ability to communicate was almost impossible, leaving them all a bit confused as to what to do, they stayed huddled, fighting the fear that they were feeling with the truth they knew to be true. God was in control, and although they didn't know how it would happen, Jesus would defeat the enemy for them.

*****

Yedaiah wished that he was with the original special task team at that very moment helping in whatever way he could. It felt wrong being outside on the lawn when he knew his people were inside dealing with the devil.

He did, however, have a handle on the remainder of the school attendees. All that were initially inside when the incident began were now calmed down.

Yedaiah had given them a job which was proving a great distraction as well as helping the situation. He had commissioned them to pray together in prayer circles of four to five people. He explained that the power of prayer, even from a safe distance, was as effective as being in the dead center of the battle itself.

Everyone agreed and quickly gathered in clusters, spread out as far as his eyes could see into the distance. It was a rather beautiful sight.

Also, on his mind was Joshua, who was safe in bed but most likely wishing he was in the mix in the castle as well. He was thankful for Mrs. Guffey who was staying by Joshua's side. He needed to remember to thank her in person as soon as he could pull away.

Looking back at the beautiful Mission Mind castle, he spotted a smoke-like fume leaking out around the attic windows. It was wafting up into the sky. Gray and pungent he could now smell. The fumes were permeating the air, and he knew that it was only a matter of moments before it reached the others' noses. He sincerely hoped that it wouldn't spark any chaos.

The vibe outside was a gift from God, peace reigning over O Be Joyful. *This is what is going to defeat Satan*, he thought. *The fact that we can't be shaken even when the enemy comes will be the ticket to success.* God is so good and faithful. He is the Prince of peace, and that fact was evident in his children's actions.

He was proud of his school. They had overcome a lot in just a few short days of surrender and honesty. Bringing to light all that was dark inside them, holding them captive to fear, had made them a better, bolder, newer version of themselves. He felt it within himself too—unshakable faith.

"God, Your love is all that I need. Thank You!" Yedaiah shouted out.

"We love You, God!" he heard a voice; one of the students yelled out loud behind him.

*****

Lying in his hospital bed, Joshua couldn't control his wandering mind. What was going on with the battle against the accuser? He seriously contemplated getting himself back into the wheelchair he had been confined to when traveling as of late and wheeling himself with the power of will out to see how he could help.

He knew good and well that his will was never going to get him that far, but he couldn't help but visualizing himself doing just that. Mrs. Guffey was in the room, so maybe he had a chance of talking her into being his assistant by pushing him wherever he needed to go. It would be a very long shot talking her into something so risky, as he thought she would see it.

He mumbled a quick prayer, pleading for a yes. "How are you doing, Mrs. Guffey?" he began, shocked that he was actually able to speak.

"Well, besides that fact that we are under another attack from the devil himself, I am doing all right. How about you, Mr. Zane, how are you? You can talk!" she politely but suspiciously responded.

"To be honest, I would be a whole lot better if I could be out with the rest of the folks making a difference and being in the loop." He grinned at her and then winked.

"With all due respect, Mr. Zane, if you think I am going to intentionally go and throw myself in the middle of a war between good and evil, you are crazy!" She was dead serious. She was not budging; no way, no how.

She is going to be tougher than I originally thought, he told himself.

"I would kindly ask you to reconsider, and here is the reason why." He gave her a small explanation on the importance of his presence currently on the battlefield then immediately regretted calling it a battlefield.

"I will not march myself out with the spook," she protested again. "I trust God with my life. That is why I thank Him and trust Him for directing me into this nice safe room with you. You should be thanking your lucky stars that He planned for you to be here too!"

"I hear what you are saying, Mrs. Guffey. It's just that I feel in my bones—and you know that my bones are old and wise—that we are meant to be more directly involved."

She shut her eyes and leaned back in the comfortable recliner that sat in the corner of Joshua's room. She was not going to acknowledge his plea.

He temporarily gave up the pressure but was planning on starting back in on her as soon as he closed his own eyes and rested for a quick minute. All the excitement of the day had worn him out more than he thought.

The two of them both dozed off for only a few minutes before a loud sound coming from outside startled them awake.

"What is that?" Mrs. Guffey asked.

"I think it's just the wind. It can be very loud when it blows through all the trees on the property," he told her, hoping that it was the truth. He wasn't so sure though, knowing what he knew about the shadows.

For minutes they sat there frozen, waiting for it to blow on through and past them. But the intensity only amplified, rattling the windows and causing the building structure to sway ever so slightly.

Seeping through the caulking around the windows was a colorless odor that filled the room like it was a dump site for dirty diapers.

Not having to say a word to one another about it, Joshua and Mrs. Guffey both knew without a doubt that what they were dealing with was not the wind.

They would indeed be active in the battle between good and evil. They would need to get a game plan and fast. Joshua did not want to be confined to the bed when they were infiltrated upon.

*****

While waiting on the lawn, Mr. and Mrs. Vand held hands. The pair of them had been praying fervently for the Lord to deliver them from Satan's attack. Neither of them was particularly scared over the threat but didn't like the disturbance one little bit.

Mrs. Vand looked out over the lawn of O Be Joyful with a smile on her face. She couldn't help but think that if the devil wasn't attacking, the students and teachers wouldn't be praying. Seeing the prayer powwows was such a beautiful sight. It was so like God to turn a questionable situation into a thing of complete splendor.

She loved the campus they were blessed enough to be called to and was thankful to have her partner in crime, Mr. Vand, to share the experience with. Since her children were grown and living their lives to the fullest, she couldn't think of a more perfect spot for her and her beloved. She cared about the children at Mission Mind as if they were her own and was fully committed to them.

As she raised her face to the sky, looking up to the heavens, something unwelcome reached her nose. It was a very unpleasant odor, smelling like rotten trash and spoiled food.

"Do you smell that, honey?" she whispered to Mr. Vand.

"I sure do. It smells like we have company."

The others out on the turf caught a whiff too, disrupting their prayer time. Everyone was up on their feet, covering their faces. The peace had been interrupted, and cries of complaint rung through the air.

Mr. and Mrs. Vand located Yedaiah in the mob of grossed-out people. They locked eyes and exchanged looks, knowing full well that they were about to enter into a dispute with the devil. Yedaiah was regretting his internal thoughts about being in the middle of the war with the special task team. He should have been thankful to be at a safe distance, but as it was, he needed to prepare the school for battle.

18

Worship in War

The devil was strongly pressing in on every being at O Be Joyful Gardens. The smell alone was enough to take them under with it. It was a deadly combination of sewer and rotten eggs, blowing through the air in an invisible manner. But even more obnoxious was the hundreds, maybe thousands, of black bat-like shadows swirling around overhead.

They flew around and around, sending off signals with high-pitched tones to one another and to Mission Mind members. The sounds reached new levels of timbre, causing everyone's ears to ache and throb.

The devil was there to give his all in spooking God's children. Even the air around them grew cold, damp, and foggy, sending off an eerie vibe.

Chosen pets that were outside in the elements were seen huddled together in furry groups, feeling the brunt of the sounds most intensely with the extra muscles they possessed in their ears. The pets that were blessed enough to be in their rooms crouched under beds and covers to comfort themselves from Lucifer the villain.

The clouds that had earlier floated up in the sky, shaped like the creatures of the earth, had blown away leaving a dismal bleak gray blanket. The beautiful array of birds that enjoyably took flight, tweeting and chirping as they soared through the air, had hidden themselves in houses made of sticks and mud up in the trees, hoping to avoid a run-in with the dark shadows.

The wind picked up, whirling and swirling through the property at an alarming speed, wreaking havoc on the peace that once rang through O Be Joyful.

The student body, along with their trusty leaders, were at a standstill, unsure how anything they could possibly come up with would help dull the attack in the slightest.

It was full-blown war.

Satan meant business.

Yedaiah wondered when and how God would show up. He knew without a doubt that He would. It just seemed like an impossible situation, one that couldn't possibly end in beauty and victory.

By every earthly standard, they were doomed. The oppression should eventually be to their demise.

Being Mr. Hallohesh and the leader of the academy, he knew that he needed to take lead on the plan. He mustered up the loudest voice he could find within himself and roared over the piercing screeches from the shadows.

"I need everyone to gather together in one large group. Please stay calm and do your best to ignore what is happening around you. We need to bind ourselves into a unified force to be reckoned with." He continued when he had all attention, "Satan has nothing on us. We have God living in us, and the Holy Spirit is all around us. Come together without fear!"

Slowly, still covering their faces and ears, the members of Mission Mind joined hip to hip, saying their silent prayers, trusting that in the end, good would win.

Yedaiah couldn't help but wonder how the special task team was and also Joshua and Mrs. Guffey. Had the presence of darkness divided and attack everyone, or had it left them to come out to the larger crowd? He imagined they were still in the throws; otherwise they would be out on the lawn too.

He decided to part from the majority of the school to check in on Joshua. Being confined to his bed without enough assistance would make it tricky to navigate the threats coming his way.

After yelling to the others to hold firm, to not run but to stand still and let Jesus fight for them, he departed to Joshua's room. When he was close by, he could see commotion swirling through the window. He needed to retrieve his friend and the good doctor. They needed to be a part of the group out on the lawn, not tucked away fighting alone.

Yedaiah went to the door and carefully opened it just a sliver of a crack. He didn't want to be noticed quite yet, thinking that he could sneak in and get Joshua wheeled out before the accuser realized the escape route.

Mrs. Guffey was in the middle of maneuvering Joshua out of bed and into the wheelchair, but she was struggling against the surrounding elements offending her senses. Yedaiah realized she was in need of assistance and was quickly at her side, not caring about avoiding the shadows.

"I am so thankful to see you!" she hollered to Yedaiah.

He gave her a small smile. "Let's get you two out of here!"

Joshua wasn't the slightest bit fazed by the whole fiasco. He had a peace about him that could only come from the Lord Himself. Yedaiah knew that bringing him out to join the rest of the school was going to be beneficial to all.

As soon as he safely planted Mrs. Guffey and Mr. Zane on the lawn, he had plans to seek out the special task team. They would have to be unified as a whole to overcome the enemy. He would bring them out of the school and out into the open air where they would have the advantage of space and the open sky.

The three managed to get out of the room door unscathed, but the wind picked up to an unbearable speed outside. Joshua was pinned to the back of the chair, Mrs. Guffey fell to the ground to keep from blowing into the building, and Yedaiah took cover behind Joshua's wheelchair. They were at a standstill and wondering what to do next. The black shadows were swarming and diving in on them.

Mrs. Guffey closed her eyes to block out the madness and prayed for God to show her what to do next. She couldn't see how she would ever escape the shadows, and she knew they wouldn't be leaving on their own accord. After she said amen, she opened one eye halfway to have a peek. In the distance running in their direction against the strong wind was Mr. and Mrs. Vand, holding hands as they traveled.

"Praise the Lord!" she shouted. "It's the Vands coming for us."

When they reached them, Mr. Vand picked Joshua up into his arms and told the others to follow directly behind them. Yedaiah was thankful for his strength because the wheelchair was not going to budge against the powerful force fighting against them.

Mrs. Vand held Mrs. Guffey's hand, and one foot after another, they slowly worked their way to the masses of school members huddled in a crouched position, heads bowed and eyes closed.

Yedaiah mentioned to Mr. Vand that he was planning on heading into the castle to locate the others.

"I am coming with you," he insisted. "Traveling alone in these conditions is an invitation for disaster."

Yedaiah hated leaving the others, but with Joshua's peaceful presence perched on a lounge chair and the rest of the brave staff there to comfort those who needed it, he knew it would be okay.

As he walked against the tornado-like weather, he looked back to take in the sight. There were hundreds, maybe thousands, of black creeps circling around their beloved campus. He knew that this was it, that the outcome of the attack would change O Be Joyful one way or another. It was time to rid the place of the infestation and restore tranquility.

*****

Noah had his arms wrapped around their huddle. He was feeling protective of his friends. He fervently pleaded with God for the answer to defeat the enemy. He considered what they had been training on: mind control; releasing sin and asking for forgiveness; living in the peace of the Lord Jesus Christ by not carrying worry, stress, or fear; and sharing life with other believers to lift each other up. These were all beautiful things, but how would it help today during the worst of the storm?

Kiera, Grace, Noah, Michael, Mathew, Malachi, Mr. and Mrs. Brown, Mieke, and Gideon had been in the same position, holding fast to God's promises without knowing what the outcome was going to be. They were out of ideas and just living in the moment as extreme as it was to every sense they possessed.

It was loud, dark, and smelly and the worst of circumstances, but they would not give in to the fear that tried its very best to bubble up within them.

They had been there for far too long and teetering on the brink of giving in, all silently praying for the next step, for the move they needed to make, when the door of the attic swung wide open, drawing their attention in the direction of it, revealing Mr. Hallohesh and Mr. Vand.

"Praise the Lord!" Mieke cried out.

Grace released her grip on their protective circle they had created and ran with all her might into Yedaiah's chest. He enveloped her in a tight hug as the rest of the huddle joined them, the shadows not letting up for a second on their closeness and threat.

"Let's get out of here!" Yedaiah yelled.

"But we have to deal with this. We can't give up and leave, or we will never win!" Malachi yelled back at him.

Yedaiah realized they didn't know what was going on all over campus. "They are everywhere, bullying the entire campus. We need to all be together. Strength in numbers. Let's go!"

Shuffling down the stairs, down the hallway, and out the golden double front doors, the special task team spotted the tumultuous scene at O Be Joyful Gardens. They bolted as fast as their legs could carry them in the strong wind until they reached the rest of the Mission Mind's inhabitance.

The clouds grew a whole new deep dark shade of grayish black, and the heavens opened up a downpour of water onto the earth. Lightning bolted overhead continually, and thunder clapped with loud banging without rest. The atmosphere was in a war between good and evil.

No one knew what to do but remain and stay strong in heart. This was not a battle for them; it was for God alone. But they were in the middle of it, and their trust in the One who made them was at stake.

The dark shadows of the enemy were closing in on each member of God's family, orbiting around each individual, pressing in with the unpleasant maliciousness of their presence. Students, teachers, and staff alike endured the assault, praying for it to end swiftly.

Joshua sat on the bench, head positioned to the sky above, rain washing over his face. He had been on the receiving end of Satan's plan. He had been singled out and struck down, but Joshua never felt stronger, mentally that was. His old frail body was wearing down by the day, and he knew that it was only a matter of short time until he would graduate to glory with his Father in heaven.

He didn't wonder how God would handle that day. He just knew without a shadow of doubt that He would. And it would be good, and they would have victory. He felt exhausted but powerful beyond measure because of the Holy Spirit who lived within him.

Yedaiah had taken a seat next to his longtime friend who was the closest thing to a brother he had experienced on earth. He could see his friend's body giving out on him, and it was hard to watch from the sidelines.

The rain kept coming, the storm still brewing in epic proportion, and the enemy seemed to be enjoying its wordless tirade. Yedaiah looked out over the members of Mission Mind with joy and admiration. No one was running away, no one was flipping out, and no one appeared frightened. All sat, heads bowed down, hands lifted up.

Peering over toward their magnificent golden castle, which was a blurry form through the hurricane O Be Joyful was being hit with, he saw an unimaginable sight. It can't be, he thought. He rubbed his eyes and strained to get a clearer view. He turned to scan the rest of the area around them. It was real. They were all coming.

Chosen pets from every direction ran toward their people as fast as they could move. Out of the Mission Mind castle's front doors, out of Grow in Wisdom's side door—out every door. Pouring out of the stable, the pond of frogs hopping toward them. The wild animals on campus came to surround them.

Others noticed, bringing about an echo of joy and happiness, dissipating the sting of the accuser's attack.

The Six-Pack, who were nestled together under a tree to the right of the chairs Joshua and Yedaiah rested on, couldn't have been more delighted. They snuggled with their furry companions, praising God for the comfort.

Grace and Kiera were so overjoyed they broke out in song, right there in the middle of the drenched, smelly, obnoxiously loud, irritating scene.

At the top of their lungs, hands lifted high, they sang one of their favorite worship songs from Mikeschair, "There's a raging sea right in front of me, wants to pull me in, bring me to my knees. So let the waters rise, if you want them to. I will follow You. I will follow You."

Noah heard them and joined in, as did Matthew, Michael, and Malachi, "Don't know where to begin. It's like my world's caving in and I try, but I can't control my fear. Where do I go from here?"

That is when, in unison, the entire school united in worship. "Sometimes it's so hard to pray, when You feel so far away, but I am willing to go where You want me to. God, I trust You."

Standing to their feet, despite the horrendous conditions they were in, they lifted their arms high, animals by their sides, and worshipped as one body of believers, praising the Lord through the storm, believing He would fight for them, thanking Him for loving them.

"There's a raging sea right in front of me, wants to pull me in, bring me to my knees. So let the waters rise if You want them to. We will follow You. We will follow You."

They continued on, singing over and over to the Lord Most High, and it reached His ears. The rain died down, the thunder stopped banging, and the lightning ceased.

The multitude of dark black creepy shadows of the devil started spinning in a gigantic circle above their heads, gaining height with every spin around. Their stench lost its grip, and their shrieking sound lost its voice.

The worship continued, getting louder and louder as confidence in Christ grew within each soul.

God's animals were standing upright, gazing their faces upon the heavens, having unbounded faith in the One that created them.

Satan's scheme continued to circle into the atmosphere until a moment-long explosion sounded, and they were blown into millions of minuscule pieces, blowing as far as the east is from the west.

Cheers rang through O Be Joyful like never before. The sky cleared, shining a crisp crystal blue color, casting the gray gloomy clouds and the rain off into the distance. Puffy white clouds shaped like the animals of the earth floated in bringing with it the bright warm sunshine. The fresh smells of trees and flowers took the place of the rancid odor, and birds flew overhead bringing with them the song of chirping and tweeting.

Joshua was maybe the most jubilant of all, looking out over the campus that he himself used to dwell alone on, dreaming of it being filled with the worship that could only come from an army of Jesus-loving believers.

He was exhausted though. His body had been through more than it wanted to take on that day and several months prior. He looked over at his best friend, Yedaiah, who seemed to read his mind.

"Mrs. Guffey," Yedaiah said to the good doctor they were fortunate enough to have at Mission Mind Academy, "would you mind taking Mr. Zane back to his room and get him settled for some much-needed rest? I will have Mrs. Heathers bring in some sustenance as soon as possible for him and yourself."

"Sure thing, Mr. Hallohesh!" she said to him with a peace that flowed like the ocean in her speech and body language.

Yedaiah watched his longtime friend, the one who had brought him to O Be Joyful all those years ago, the one who had been an earthly father to him when he needed it most in life. He couldn't help but wonder how much longer they would have the pleasure of Joshua's presence this side of heaven.

Pushing the thoughts from his mind, he looked out over the members of Mission Mind. It was pure serenity to see the faces of his beloved students and staff. He couldn't help but feel responsible for every one of them. He thanked God for the miracle He had bestowed upon them that day and then made his way over to Mrs. Heathers, knowing that not only Joshua but everyone would be starving after the turmoil they had all endured.

After all were fed, bellies happy, Mr. Hallohesh declared a game and celebration night. He was planning on spending an early part of the evening with the special task team; they had been an instrumental part of the battle they had received victory over.

Noah, Grace, Kiera, and the Brown brothers had proven themselves the bravest of anyone Yedaiah had met in his entire life. He was proud and thankful for their sacrifice of peace in the long drawn-out process. He was pleased to see Mieke and Gideon sitting in chairs next to the Six-Pack, as they were now known throughout campus.

Seeing Mieke again after the years she had schooled at Mission Mind was full circle for Yedaiah. He often wondered about the godly training that was provided for students. He didn't always have the pleasure of seeing where God led them after graduation. Mieke was a gem and gift from above. He hoped that she would continue on at Mission Mind Academy. He couldn't imagine losing her back to Seattle and her prior work.

Gideon was equally special to him. Knowing that Joshua had felt the prompting of the Lord to call him to the family of believers and then seeing his faith play out in such a short period of time was a miracle in itself. He greatly prayed that he would remain on campus too.

"I am so proud of the group of you," Yedaiah voiced to his special team.

"We are proud of you too, Mr. Hallohesh," Mieke reassured him.

Gideon chimed in, "You are a fearless leader, and I am honored to have met you and experienced a period of time under your guiding. I have never met a more influential man in my life."

Yedaiah blushed a little, thinking that was exactly how he felt about Joshua Zane. "Thank you, Gideon. I can't tell you how much that means to me."

After a few hugs and words of praise to the God Most High, Yedaiah excused himself to head off in the direction of Joshua's room. It was all he wanted to do: spend time with the beginner and leader of the academy. The man who stopped by to pick him up in the golden limo so long ago. The man who always had faith in him. The man whose faith in God had never faltered in the decades of years he'd known him. His best friend, his hero in every sense.

19

New Beginnings

The following day Grace awoke with the distinct feeling of relief. Being her first year at Mission Mind Academy, she had been hit fast and hard by the reality when she was asked to be a part of an actual mission. It was no hidden secret when she had been called by the golden letter that the purpose God had was to train her up to be a warrior for His kingdom. And although she had not envisioned actual graphic attacks from the accuser, she had become the fighter she was meant to be through them.

She looked down at Roxy Ann and was overcome with thankfulness to have her presence. She was convinced that without her loyal pup by her side every step of the way, she wouldn't have endured. Of course, she knew that her strength, endurance, and the ultimate victory over Satan, dweller of the Bones Abode, was the power of God within her and her classmates, but the gift of Roxy was worth praise.

Popping up to begin a fresh new day, she peered over at her best friend, Kiera. Her biggest fear in coming to O Be Joyful was that she would be lonely and miss her family back at home, but from the moment of plopping herself out of the hot-air balloon, she realized that was not going to happen. The boys and Kiera had been tried-and-true friends from the first second on campus.

Kiera stirred in her bed, causing Speedy to poke his head up and look around.

"Hey, cute buddy," Grace whispered to him.

"Good morning, Grace." Kiera came to. "Let's get this day started."

"Good idea. I am so excited to see everyone down at breakfast. It's a brand-new day, and I have full faith that the presence of the enemy is far from our glorious campus."

"Boy, are you chipper today! It is nice to see you so full of life. And I agree with getting downstairs. I have my mind set on more important things—blueberry pancakes! Mrs. Heathers mentioned yesterday that they were on the menu, and I think I must have dreamed about them all night because my stomach is grumbling, and they are all I can think about," Kiera said, completely serious.

"Well, what are we waiting for? I could definitely go for a stack myself! I will take Roxy out for a bathroom break and then we can hit the road."

A lighthearted buzz was echoing off the walls in the dining hall. The volume was turned with laughter and playful banter, kids shoveling forkfuls of pancakes and bacon into their joyful faces.

The Brown brothers and Noah were already on second helpings when the girls pulled up seats next to them.

Noah, eager to see them, mentioned, "We were thinking that we need a rematch today after school. The last flanks match ended disastrously, and there is no need to keep our favorite sport tainted for too long."

"I think that is a great idea!" Kiera beamed.

"Do we want to just scrimmage each other, or are you thinking about recruiting another team to play against?" Grace wondered.

"We most definitely need an opponent. I will ask the Hammerheads if they are down for a match."

Michael was looking forward to it. "I am so thankful. After all that we have been through, withstanding the devil's attacks, it will be nice to have a clean game with no interruptions."

Everyone agreed.

"Okay, so after our last class today, let's bring our pets out for some fresh air and get this party started!" Noah was so glad to have the campus back to normal.

*****

Mieke sat in a window seat nook in Grow in Wisdom. She had set up shop in the library to catch up on some reading, which was one of her favorite pastimes, but ended up staring out the window pondering important decisions in life instead. She wondered what to do with her life now that she had tasted O Be Joyful Gardens again. She couldn't imagine leaving campus and going back to her old life but wasn't sure what a life would look like staying at Mission Mind Academy. Reconnecting with Mr. Zane and Mr. Hallohesh after all her years away had been more special to her than she could have imagined. They were the only family she trusted and needed them more than she wanted to admit. Her rocky background of absent parents and foster care lent to mistrust in most people and an extreme case of closed-heartedness.

Gideon was also a source of contemplation. He had popped up in her life in an instant and hadn't left her side since. He was unexpected and had become her favorite person to spend time with. What would he do know that the special task mission was over? And on the note of it being over, she had the realization that at some point Satan would return. Because as long as they were on this side of heaven, the battle between good and evil would continue. Maybe not in the form of flying shadows, but somewhere, sometime, somehow, it would make another attempt on their lives; it was a guarantee.

What then? Would Mission Mind and O Be Joyful be targeted again? She had no doubt it was just a matter of time. But where would she be when it happened?

Gideon must have heard her thoughts, because he strolled into Grow in Wisdom as she thought about his next move.

"Hey, Mieke, what are you up to? I have been looking for you," he said as he plopped down on the oversized chair directly across from her.

"Nothing much. Just contemplating the deeper things in life," she answered, a little bit embarrassed about it.

"Oh yeah, what did you come up with?" He had a light joking tone about him.

"No, really. I was wondering what I am going to do now. What are you going to do?"

"I am heading to watch a flanks match here shortly. Would you like to join me?" He hoped she would come.

"I would like that. But I didn't mean what we would do now. I meant that it's time for us to leave campus. The mission is over. But I don't want to go back to the way things were. I am praying over my next steps."

"I knew what you meant. I am in the same boat as you. In fact, I was up most of the night considering the same thing."

She was relieved that he hadn't simply decided to go back to his old life. It didn't seem fitting for him anymore. With his fresh new faith in Christ, his possibilities were endless. Then it hit her that her possibilities were endless too. She was free to follow the Spirit anywhere, and she didn't need to worry or stress about the next step. God would guide her.

"Let's get to that match. I don't want to miss kickoff." She was done stirring a pot of the unknown. She trusted God, and He would lead her way.

"Great! I was hoping you would say that." He was thankful to be done with the topic of what's next in life; it had been weighing heavy on his mind without any clear answer as a result.

As they joined the others in the stands, the whistle blew to begin the game. Michael had negotiated with his dad to referee, which just meant Michael and his brothers would have to help out with the chores Mr. Brown had on his list to do that afternoon. Not a problem for them though; they loved spending time with their dad even if it was work.

The match was hot and heavy right out of the gate. It seemed that the kids had a lot of built-up steam to blow off. And with the threat of the enemy gone for now, they could put their undivided energy and attention into it.

Yedaiah moseyed over and sat down next to Gideon and Mieke, who right away noticed that something was bothering him. He was downcast, not normal for him. He usually had such an infectious joy about him that others couldn't help but be drawn in. But he was carrying a worry that Mieke was curious about.

She dared to ask him about it. "Is everything all right, Mr. Hallohesh?"

It was a loud atmosphere from the fans yelling and cheering on their classmates, and Mieke could hardly hear herself speak.

"We can talk about it later, dear. Let's enjoy this exciting flanks match." He was not about to get into anything serious right then and there.

She gave him a small smile and then directed her attention back to the game. She would have to track him down later to see if there was anything she could do to help.

As it was, she was planning on moving back home over the weekend in a few days. The thought of it wrecked her. She knew that she didn't want to leave; she just wasn't sure that it was God's will for her to stay. She wouldn't even know what to do there.

She prayed for God to reveal his master plan. What was it He wanted for her life? The unknown was torture, but she knew patience would lead to character and perseverance, all things that she wanted to possess.

Yedaiah hung around, supporting his students until about half-time, and then he told Mieke and Gideon that he was going to Mr. Zane's room to keep him company for a while. He would see them for dinner that evening.

Mieke watched him walk off into the distance, hunched over and downcast. What was bothering him?

She mentioned to Gideon, "There is something troubling Mr. Hallohesh. I am going to seek him out this evening. Would you want to come with me? I think he could use some listening ears. I would think that he would be elated and refreshed after the victory yesterday."

He considered what she said for a moment before responding, "Unfortunately, the creeps from the Bones Abode are not the only stressors for him. He does carry a lot of responsibility here. I know that he feels like a father to the entirety of the school. That can't be a light load to walk around with."

"I wish that I could help shoulder the burden. With Mr. Zane so fragile, I know it has all fallen on him." Mieke's mind ran away with half thoughts and ideas, but nothing felt right.

Gideon could tell that his friend was struggling and really wanted to say something to support her. "Remember that it doesn't all fall on Mr. Hallohesh. It all falls on God's shoulders, and they are strong enough. I will be praying for the decisions you have to make."

"Thanks, Gideon, I really appreciate that. I will be doing the same for you."

The flanks match ended, and everyone in the bleachers filed out onto the property. It was too beautiful of a day to be cooped up indoors.

Gideon watched students laughing and thoroughly enjoying time together on the volleyball and tennis courts. He saw a few groups tossing bean bags at cornholes and horseshoes at metal posts. He took in the group of girls on the backs of horses galloping through the pear orchard. Then he spotted the Six-Pack, whom he had grown exceedingly fond of, walking down the golden path toward the far end of the property. He assumed they were just taking their pets for a stroll after the victory they just locked down, but something inside him said to follow behind their steps.

He looked over at Mr. and Mrs. Vand, making eye contact with them.

"Would you two like to take a walk with me down the most inviting path I have ever laid eyes on?"

Mrs. Vand looked up at her husband before answering for the both of them, "That sounds lovely."

Mr. Vand was fond of Gideon and found it easy to chat with him. So as they strolled, he proceeded to ask a number of questions.

"Gideon, it has been a blessing to have you around campus. Have you given much thought to what you will do now that things have calmed down around here?"

This was a popular topic on the mind, he was realizing. "Yes, I have thought quite a bit about it actually. I was just discussing the same subject with Mieke."

"I was wondering about her too," Mrs. Vand chimed in. "We are hoping that she sticks around for a long time to come."

"I would bet she will," Gideon followed up. "She does love it here and talks fondly of her childhood at O Be Joyful. Mission Mind is an extraordinary place, unlike anything in this world. It is almost like God gifting us with a sliver of heaven here on earth. I don't want to leave. I am just not sure what skills I have to add to it in a positive way. The only vocation that I have mastered is real estate, and I can't see how that would benefit anyone or anything at Mission Mind." He surprised himself by the honest answer he shared with them. He was becoming less closed off by the day.

"Trust us when we tell you that none of us feel qualified to be called by God. I know from personal experience that He does not call the qualified but qualifies the called. He will make His path known to you, and He will work out every last detail precisely how He sees fit," Mr. Vand assured Gideon.

Pink-nosed Fiona was running along the grass beside them as they strolled, keeping up without missing a beat.

"I sure would miss that little furball." He pointed at the kitten that had won his heart over. "I can't imagine leaving her now. I always thought I was only a dog person, but that is now not the case. The chosen pets here are all so special. Everything here is special."

Just as he expected, the Six-Pack were spotted at the far end of the property. Gideon and the Vands proceeded to their sides. They weren't noticed at first because the kids were propped against the fence staring in the Bones Abode's direction.

"Just making sure all is secure?" Gideon teased them.

Noah flipped his head around. "Just look how calm and peaceful it looks with the sunrays shining through the open walls."

Mrs. Vand found it stunning. "And the blue sky and white puffy clouds sure do take the scariness out of it. If I didn't know the history of it, I would dream about taking a picnic there."

"I don't know if I would go as far as a picnic, but it does look like a whole new place. Do you think it will ever be occupied again?" Grace asked the group.

Kiera blurted out, "I sure hope not! I will be praying that it stays vacant for the rest of our lives."

The party next to the fence at the end of O Be Joyful was growing. Malachi noticed his parents striding down the yellow brick road. It felt amazing to have the ones he cared about there celebrating victory. He reflected on Grace's first days at Mission Mind, when he was so desperate for answers about the Bones and brought her to this exact location to share with her the scares of the devil. She had been spooked immediately but proved her God-given strength by not backing down when in the throes of chaos.

Now they could all enjoy the sight of the Bones Abode as if it were a glorious painting displayed for their viewing pleasure.

"It is a mystery to me how the good Lord can take the sting out of the stingiest things. Not even a full day ago this unfinished house embodied Satan. Now it's just an unfinished house." Malachi had maybe been the most passionate about the mystery in the first place, and he had definitely lost precious sleep over it these last few months.

"God heard our cries and answered our prayers, son." Keilah reached for him and rested her hand on his shoulder.

"Hi, Mom." Malachi wrapped her up in a hug.

Gabriel hated to break up the celebration that was going on, but Mrs. Heathers mentioned to him that dinner would be ready in a half an hour.

"Why don't we mosey our way back toward the school and tend to our pets before the dinner tunes begin. We don't have much time," he told the happy crowd.

Matthew made the first move on the pathway and reminded them that they could come back whenever they wanted for the view.

"It sure is nice to not have a shadow staring you down when looking at it," he said in a joking tone but was dead serious.

The Vands, Browns, Gideon, Noah, Grace, Kiera, and their furry buddies walked shoulder to shoulder back up the golden path to their school, all starving and all ready to grub out on dinner.

*****

Pulling himself away from Joshua's bedside, Yedaiah knew that he should let him sleep and head to the dining hall for dinner. He didn't want anyone to be waiting on him for opening prayer. Preteens, teens, and teachers were a hungry bunch who needed nourishment frequently. He felt endlessly blessed to have Mrs. Heathers leading the kitchen crew through three meals a day.

When he was leaving Joshua's room, he asked Mrs. Guffey to join him, telling her that Joshua was most likely going to sleep the rest of the evening away. He didn't expect to see his eyes open until the following day, after all the excitement that had ensured.

She thought about how nice it would be to dine and fellowship with the others and agreed to come along. "Mr. Zane is snoozing peacefully. I would love to dine in the hall tonight. I have that one important thing to discuss with Mieke Everly, and it would be a perfect opportunity."

"Wonderful. Let's go. I am sure it is smelling mighty good, and I don't want to miss out on even a single bite," he joked with her.

"I am with you on that. I am quite hungry myself." She winked at him.

In the dining hall, chatter was bouncing off the walls. It seemed everyone was hungry and excited to see Mr. Hallohesh, because cheers broke out when he entered through the double stained-glass doors.

He took it as a sign to open the feast with a prayer. He gave thanks for the delicious food they were about to partake in and thanked God once again for the victory and peace He had restored to Mission Mind Academy. He prayed for Mr. Zane and the students and staff at O Be Joyful. He closed by telling God how much they loved Him and then said amen, causing the full hall of people to yell, "Amen!"

Mrs. Guffey took a seat next to Mieke and proceeded to make small talk. "How are you liking it back here at the academy?"

"It was awesome when I was a kid, and not much has changed in that regard. I love it here. I had no idea how much I missed it over the years. I can't imagine leaving again," she told her.

"There has been something I have been praying about and thought tonight was as good as any to bring it up," Mrs. Guffey began.

"Oh yeah? What's that?"

"I am in need of an assistant. Well, to be honest, more of a partner running the health-care program here, and every time I bring the need to the Lord, your image pops in my mind. Would you ever consider staying here and joining the staff?" she asked hopefully.

"Wow! I actually have been thinking about staying on campus but didn't know what skills I possess that would be helpful. What kind of qualifications would be needed for the job?" She was curious if she could really be of assistance to Mrs. Guffey.

"All that you need is people skills, which you definitely have, and a willingness to learn the ins and outs. We have a large school, and I am having trouble tending to everyone all by my lonesome. Routine checks as well as assistance with injuries and sickness would be the main duties I am looking for help in. I have already spoken to Mr. Hallohesh, who immediately thought you would be a perfect fit."

"Thank you for thinking of me and asking me. If you don't mind, I will take a day or two to think it through and pray about it before I give you an answer."

"That sounds lovely, dear. I shall look forward to your response." Mrs. Guffey forked a bite into her mouth, feeling excited for the possibility of Ms. Everly's partnership after having her last assistant sneak out the back door.

Gideon had heard the whole conversation between the two women. He was sitting on the other side of Mieke and felt so excited for her. He knew she wanted to stay at O Be Joyful and had just been given the opportunity to do just that. *God is good,* he thought to himself. He reached over and placed his hand on top of Mieke's arm to give it a little squeeze. She turned to him with a huge smile on her face. Yep, she would be staying, and he couldn't be more thrilled for her. She had become one of his best friends, and he wanted all her dreams to come true.

Now if he could just get clarity on his own life, all would be good.

"Maybe we could get the Six-Pack together for a ping-pong tournament tonight. What do you say, you down?" Gideon asked Mieke.

Mieke thought about it for a minute. She really just wanted to hang out alone in her room to worry about the decisions to be made even though she knew that it would be pointless. God already had plans for her. She should just go have some fun.

"Sure. Let's see who we can wrangle up," she ended up saying.

Noah was in the middle of a joke when their table was approached with the ping-pong invitation. He stopped midsentence to respond, his competitive nature always winning priority in life.

Michael responded in similar fashion, followed shortly by the other four. They bussed the table and promised to be in the game hall after feeding and tending to their pets.

"Bring your pets along with you!" Gideon called after them. He had grown so fond of Fiona he didn't appreciate going anywhere without her, and he knew the others felt the same way about their animals.

It wasn't long before the ping-pong ball was making its distinct bouncing off the paddle onto the table sound, and the ones playing were laughing through their serious game faces.

The lightness of spirit on campus was undeniable. It was as if everyone could take a deep breath finally. Songs of praise and thanksgiving had replaced the inner fear that had plagued O Be Joyful for too many months.

The game room was full of people, not just the ping-pong players, but cards and dice and a pickup game of charades were gaining speed in the far corner. It was a beautiful and energetic sight. Mieke took it all in, thanking God for a way to stay at Mission Mind. She didn't want to leave, and with every minute that ticked on, she knew in her heart that she wouldn't. She belonged here with God's chosen children. She smiled at Gideon, thankful for the friendship they had formed, hoping that he would be called to stay too.

❆❆❆❆❆

Mrs. Guffey sat next to Mr. Hallohesh in Mr. Zane's room while he slept the evening away. He had been beyond tired after the hype of the week and couldn't keep his eyes open once he laid his body down in bed and rested his head on the pillow.

After he dozed off, yet again, Mrs. Guffey shared the news of inviting Mieke Everly to stay on at Mission Mind as her assistant. Yedaiah couldn't be more thrilled and said a silent prayer that she would indeed stay. It had been so nice to have her back and such an honor to see her all grown up and living in faith. The impact that former students had on current students was unparalleled. The instant connection couldn't be duplicated any other way.

Yedaiah was thankful that Mieke had found the family and home that she had always hoped for at Mission Mind. He had found the same thing there. Joshua, specifically, was the brother and father he had always hoped for, always there to lovingly guide him throughout the years; a companion to laugh, cry, and pray with—all around his favorite relationship in life. It was hard to see him so advanced in years, struggling with the day to day. He wondered what was next for Joshua and how he would survive without him this side of heaven when the good Lord called him home.

Pushing thoughts of death from his mind, Yedaiah stood up and stretched his arms to the ceiling to get his circulation flowing, before telling Mrs. Guffey that he was going to take an evening stroll around the property.

"Enjoy yourself and don't worry about hurrying back. I have a feeling that we won't see Mr. Zane awake before tomorrow. He looks so peaceful in his deep slumber. I will look after him," she assured him.

"Thank you, Mrs. Guffey, you are one in a million. I am thankful to have you here caring for all of us. I know that Joshua is thankful for you as well, he has told me so himself, more than once!" He patted her on the shoulder before heading out the door into the dark night sparkling with stars and a full moon.

*****

Bright and early the following morning, Yedaiah stopped by Joshua's room after his morning devotions and before a stroll around the golden path. He wanted to see if his friend had awoken and how he was feeling after a long and much-needed rest. After knocking on his door was met with silence, he turned the door handle to crack open the door. Peering in, he could see Joshua still asleep. He figured he would come back after breakfast time for another check-in. Hopefully he would be awake by then and they could have a morning together.

It had struck Yedaiah hard, the thought of his best friend so close to heaven's gate. He wanted to get in as much quality time as possible with him.

Closing his door as quietly as possible, Yedaiah made his way out to the walking path. He had plans to walk the entire thing before ending in the dining hall for one of Mrs. Heathers' breakfast burritos, a favorite of his.

The sun was just starting to rise on the horizon, sending off a fantastic glow on the golden trail. It sparkled and shined, beckoning Yedaiah to take step after step through the beauty of O Be Joyful.

He was keeping a fast pace, trying to keep his heart rate up for health purposes, when he came to a screeching halt at the end of the property. There it was, the Bones Abode. Yedaiah couldn't help but remember the traumatic experience he had there. It had been dark, dreary, and frightening. But in the morning light, it appeared to be a peaceful vibrant unfinished structure, almost inviting.

He reflected on the journey Mission Mind Academy had gone through and overcome over the past months. It wasn't pretty at times, but the unity and strength and willingness of the staff and children were the hidden blessing in the matter. God had seen them through every attack from the accuser and blessed them in so many ways he couldn't begin to list them all.

Looking out on the hill housing the Bones, he lifted his hands in praise and surrender.

He raised his voice as well. "God, thank You for meeting our every need. You protected us from the ugliness of the enemy. He never stood a chance against Your mighty power. You carried us through the storm and set our feet upon a solid rock. I worship You and thank You for being King of our lives. You stripped the power away from the devil and bestowed it upon the weak. You are Yahweh, and I love You."

He bowed down low, feeling the impact of release of all he had been carrying around inside. He hadn't realized how much he had held it together until now, when it all needed to be released.

Standing up, he looked once more at the Bones Abode. It looked glorious and welcoming. He was thankful that it had lost its sting and could be a source of positivity in their lives now. It had held too much negative pressure and weight, but now it was free to shine in the sun, a building without outside walls, the bones.

Strolling along once more, Yedaiah had a new pep in his step. He continued praying as he made his way along the long golden path toward the dining hall. It would be a great day, come what may.

He walked into joyful noise in the dining hall. The kids were all up, ready, eating, and talkative. He soaked in the glorious noise of God's children, grabbed a plate of delicious-smelling grub, and took it beside Mr. and Mrs. Vand.

He looked at the couple with thanksgiving. "I just wanted to thank you two again for your dedication and calm spirits through this last trial. You are priceless, and I am blessed to know you."

"It is our pleasure to be a part of the works God is doing at Mission Mind. Thank you for your peaceful leadership and confidence in God and us," Mr. Vand spoke for both of them.

Mrs. Vand brought up something on her mind. "Mr. Vand and I have been talking a lot about the possibility of Gideon Jethro staying on staff permanently. He has an amazing gift with the children, and he is definitely a natural leader."

"I couldn't agree with you more," Yedaiah responded. "I have been praying about it myself."

"We will continue to do the same." Mrs. Vand smiled.

After breakfast, Yedaiah had another married couple he wanted to have a quick word with. He sought out Gabriel and Keilah Brown as they were bussing their dishes to the kitchen.

He cleared his throat to draw their attention. "Good morning, Browns. I wanted to have a quick word with you before you begin your day."

They looked at each other, hoping that they were not being reprimanded for anything.

"Of course you can. What is on your mind, Mr. Hallohesh?" Gabriel asked.

"I just wanted to give you a special thank-you for the work that you do here at O Be Joyful. You both are wonderful godly parents who not only disciple your own three amazing boys but every student on campus. I know that the kids feel safe and loved by you, and I am so grateful. Also, I know that it has been somewhat of a sacrifice to referee the flanks matches, and I appreciate your willingness, Gabriel."

"It is my absolute pleasure to support the kids' sports. I wouldn't trade any of it for the entire world. But thank you for your kind words. I shall carry them with me today." Gabriel gave Yedaiah a hug.

"You have a blessed day, Mr. Hallohesh," Keilah called after him.

"You too!" he hollered back over his shoulder, on his way back to Joshua's room.

✵✵✵✵✵

Grace invited her best friends, along with their pets, outside in the fresh air. They didn't have anything in particular to do but perched up on the bench and grass next to the hot-air balloon landing zone. The dogs were running around chasing each other, and the smaller animals were climbing trees and digging in the dirt. The Six-Pack made small talk as they soaked up the sunshine.

Noah was thinking about what they had recently been through together. "Remember at the beginning of the sightings we started our research in Grow in Wisdom? That first night when we were all under the table afraid and praying our heads off. That seemed like a lifetime ago."

Michael responded, "But all that took place after that first night is quite the whirlwind—the meetings in the greenhouse, the storms, and the attacks at the flanks matches."

"The Bones Abode's underbelly, looking for Mr. Hallohesh! That was the most insane if you ask me!" Kiera chimed in.

"Oh, the missing pet morning. That was horrible!" Malachi added.

Michael was thankful to be past the whole ordeal, at least for the time being. "We did come through so much together. I am thankful for the guidance of the Vands. They were lifesavers. The gift of mind control and the power to capture all thoughts and give them to Jesus is priceless. Our entire school is better for the trial and training."

"That is why we are here, trial and training," Noah agreed with him.

Grace took a slow long look around at each of her friends. "I am so grateful that God has blessed me with such amazing friends. Thank you for accepting me when I arrived. I am very much looking forward to the next adventure. I hope that it doesn't involve dark, stinky, creepy, high-pitched flying shadows, but if it does, I say bring it on!"

Kiera shot her a look. "Okay, ghostbuster, don't get ahead of yourself. We definitely don't want anyone to take that as a challenge and return full force."

Mieke and Gideon spied the kids as they were walking the yellow brick road and decided to join them.

"Good afternoon, young gentlemen and ladies." Gideon gave them a wink.

"Hi, Mr. Jethro, Ms. Everly," the kids all called out.

"May we lounge here with you this fine day?" Mieke asked them.

Grace was glad to see them. "Of course!"

They had only been there a few minutes when they spotted Mr. Hallohesh coming down the golden path in their direction. He didn't look up at them, rather down at his feet as if he were thinking longingly about something troubling him. When he finally approached the perfect spot they were resting in, he slowly pulled his eyes to meet theirs.

"A whole bunch of my favorite people all in one place," he began. "It is actually a huge blessing that you are all together right now. I have something that I would like to talk to you about."

He paused for a whole minute, willing the tears threatening to leak down his face to subside. A look of concern crossed the eager eight faces waiting for him to continue what he was going to say.

"I spent the last forty-five minutes to an hour with Mr. Joshua Zane. It was a blessed time. He talked to me a lot and with the clearest mind. He knew." Yedaiah stopped.

Gideon felt concerned and wanted to encourage him. "He knew what, Mr. Hallohesh?"

"He knew that it was the end. He relayed to me that his Maker, who had prepared a place for him, was calling him home. He said that God's timing is always perfect, and today was his perfect day. He said that he loved everyone at Mission Mind Academy of O Be Joyful Gardens and would forever treasure his gift of life here. He mentioned how proud he was of every soul here, especially you eight. He was highly impressed by your bravery and leadership skills throughout the trials from the accuser. He said that Satan didn't stand a chance with God's children. He mentioned his love for me and even placed a hand on mine to pray for me. He had apparently been praying over his own departure because God had revealed to him that Gideon Jethro would be the one to assume the role that he had played since the beginning of life here at the academy."

Looking over at Gideon, Yedaiah dropped the hard news. "He then squeezed my hand, closed his eyes, and passed away. He graduated to heaven to be with the Lord for eternity." Yedaiah finally let the tears roll down at any rate they pleased. He was heartbroken and needed to let it out. He then added, "His beloved Clydesdale Jehoshaphat went to glory with him."

Mieke, crying too, put her arms around Yedaiah. "I am so sorry, Mr. Hallohesh!"

Then Michael, Matthew, Malachi, Noah, Grace, and Gideon wrapped their arms around them in a tight group hug.

It was a sad and joyful day.

The memorial for Joshua Zane was held by the entire academy outside in the orchards. Everyone told memorable stories; some that made people laugh and some brought tears. But they all knew that he was in a beautiful place and, for that abundant delight, filled their hearts.

One day they would be together again. Until then, they would keep the faith and fight the good fight. God would be their strength, their fortress, their comforter, and their Father. They would never have to fear.

The training at Mission Mind would continue. They would be ready for the next call to action, come what may.

About the Author

Rachel Elspeth Shanks is a Jesus-loving child of the Most High. After spending over three decades in Oregon, she now resides in the gorgeous Rocky Mountains of Colorado with her best friend and husband, Derek, and her two beautiful middle and high school-aged children, Noah and Grace. She has simultaneously been both challenged by and relished in the opportunity of homeschooling over the past nine years, reclaiming her own education along the way. Rachel absolutely loves traveling with her family in the United States and out of country, dog and cat included. Hiking several days per week around her home located at nine thousand feet amongst the aspens, cooking as a personal chef to her people, crafting anything to get her creativity out, and reading are a few of her favorite hobbies. Writing and journaling have been a new blessing in her life, and she hopes to continue the literary journey for many years to come.

CPSIA information can be obtained
at www.ICGtesting.com
Printed in the USA
BVHW081400051121
620849BV00001B/49